By Deborah Crombie

IN A DARK HOUSE
NOW MAY YOU WEEP
A SHARE IN DEATH
ALL SHALL BE WELL
LEAVE THE GRAVE GREEN
MOURN NOT YOUR DEAD
DREAMING OF THE BONES
KISSED A SAD GOODBYE
A FINER END
AND JUSTICE THERE IS NONE

DEBORAH CROMBIE

NOW MAY YOU WEEP

AVON BOOKS

An Imprint of HarperCollinsPublishers

This is a work of fiction. Names, characters, places, and incidents are products of the author's imagination or are used fictitiously and are not to be construed as real. Any resemblance to actual events, locales, organizations, or persons, living or dead, is entirely coincidental.

AVON BOOKS
An Imprint of HarperCollins*Publishers*
10 East 53rd Street
New York, New York 10022-5299

First Avon Books paperback printing: October 2004
First William Morrow hardcover printing: October 2003

Avon Trademark Reg. U.S. Pat. Off. and in Other Countries, Marca Registrada, Hecho en U.S.A.
HarperCollins® is a trademark of HarperCollins Publishers Inc.

Printed in the U.S.A.

10 9 8 7 6 5 4 3 2 1

To my uncle, A. C. Greene, 1923–2002,
man of letters and storyteller extraordinaire

Let torrents pour then, let the great winds rally.
Snow-silence fall or lightning blast the pine;
That light of Home shines warmly in the valley,
And, exiled son of Scotland, it is thine.
Far have you, wandered over seas of longing,
And now you drowse, and now you well may weep,
When all the recollections come a-throwing,
Of this rude country where your fathers sleep.
—NEIL MUNRO, "TO EXILES"

Acknowledgments

Thanks are due to all the good people at William Morrow for their support and enthusiasm, and especially to my editor, Carrie Feron. Nancy Yost has once again proved herself an agent beyond compare, and Laura Hartman Maestro has provided the charming map.

To those who have read the manuscript, Steve Copling, Dale Denton, Jim Evans, Diane Sullivan Hale, Gigi Sherrell Norwood, and Viqui Litman, I'm sure I couldn't have done it without you. A final thanks to Jan Hull for being a great friend in a pinch, and to my family for putting up with me in the throes of a book.

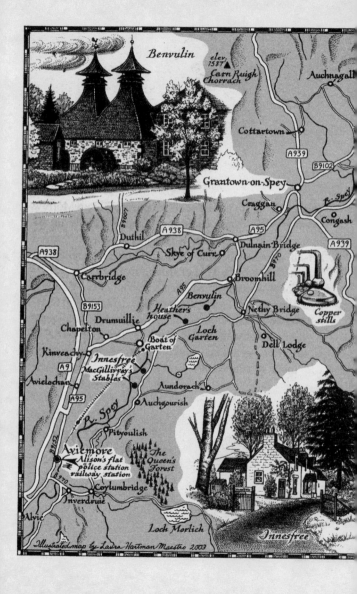

at MacGillivray's
Stables
Murphy

1799'
rn na
Loine

SPEY

Ballindalloch

Advie

Lettoch
llisfure
R. Spey
Duiar

Mains of Dalvey

A95

romdale

Minmore

Shenval

B9008

B9009

Streath Avon

Ballcorach

B9136

Tomnavoulin

Livet

Knockandhu

Carnmore

B9009

Braes of Glenlivet

Fodderletter

Chapeltown

Bridge of Brown

Bridge of Avon

Ladder
Hills

A939

Tomintoul

Milton of Auchriachan

N

elev. 2692'
ical Charn

elev. 2600'
Carn Ealasaid

A939

Maturation
Casks

Cock Bridge

Delnadamph Lodge

NOW MAY YOU WEEP

HOW MAY YOU WEEP

1

If there's a sword-like sang
That can cut Scotland clear
O a' the warld beside
Rax me the hilt o't here.
—HUGH MACDIARMID,
"To Circumjack Cencrastus"

Carnmore, November 1898

WRAPPED IN HER warmest cloak and shawl, Livvy
Urquhart paced the worn kitchen flags. The red-walled
room looked a cozy sanctuary with its warm stove and
open shelves filled with crockery, but outside the wind
whipped and moaned round the house and distillery with
an eerily human voice, and the chill penetrated even the
thick stone walls of the old house.

It was worry for her husband, Charles, that had kept
Livvy up into the wee hours of the night. He would have
been traveling back from Edinburgh when the blizzard
struck, unexpectedly early in the season, unexpectedly
fierce for late autumn.

And the road from Cock Bridge to Tomintoul, the route

Charles must take to reach Carnmore, was always the first in Scotland to be completely blocked by snow. Had his carriage run off the track, both horse and driver blinded by the stinging wall of white fury that met them as they came up the pass? Was her husband even now lying in a ditch, or a snowbank, slowly succumbing to the numbing cold?

Her fear kept her pacing, long after she'd sent her son, sixteen-year-old Will, to bed, and as the hours wore on, the knowledge of her situation brought her near desperation. Trapped in the snug, white-harled house, she was as help-less as poor Charles, and useless to him. Soon she would not even be able to reach the distillery outbuildings, much less the track that led to the tiny village of Chapeltown.

Livvy sank into the rocker by the stove, fighting back tears she refused to acknowledge. She was a Grant by birth, after all, and Grants were no strangers to danger and harsh circumstances. They had not only survived in this land for generations but had also flourished, and if she had grown up in the relative comfort of the town, she had now lived long enough in the Braes to take hardship and isolation for granted.

And Charles . . . Charles was a sensible man—too sensible, she had thought often enough in the seventeen years of their marriage. He would have taken shelter at the first signs of the storm in some roadside inn or croft. He was safe, of course he was safe, and so she would hold him in her mind, as if her very concentration could protect him.

She stood again and went to the window. Wiping at the thick pane of glass with the hem of her cloak, she saw nothing but a swirl of white. What would she tell Will in the morning, if there was no sign of his father? A new fear clutched at her. Although a quiet boy, Will had a

stubborn and impulsive streak. It would be like him to de-
cide to strike off into the snow in search of Charles.

Hurriedly, she lit a candle and left the kitchen for the
dark chill of the house, her heart racing. But when she
reached her son's first-floor bedroom, she found him
sleeping soundly, one arm free of his quilts, his much-
read copy of Kidnapped open on his chest. Easing the
book from his grasp, she rearranged the covers, then
stood looking down at him. From his father he had in-
herited the neat features and the fine, straight, light
brown hair, and from his father had come the love of
books and the streak of romanticism. To Will, Davie Bal-
four and the Jacobite Alan Breck were as real as his
friends at the distillery; but lately, his fascination with
the Rebellion of '45 seemed to have faded, and he'd
begun to talk more of safety bicycles and blowlamps, and
the new steam-powered wagons George Smith was using
to transport whisky over at Drumin. All natural for a boy
his age, Livvy knew, especially with the new century now
little more than a year away, but still it pained her to see
him slipping out of the warm, safe confines of farm, village, and distillery.

More slowly, Livvy went downstairs, shivering a little
even in her cloak, and settled again in her chair. She fixed
her mind on Charles, but when an uneasy slumber at last
overtook her, it was not Charles of whom she dreamed.

She saw a woman's heart-shaped face. Familiar dark
eyes, so similar to her own, gazed back at her, but Livvy
knew with the irrefutable certainty of dreams that it was
not her own reflection she beheld. The woman's hair was
dark and curling, like her own, but it had been cropped
short, as if the woman had suffered an illness. The dream-
figure wore odd clothing as well, a sleeveless shift remi-
niscent of a nightdress or an undergarment. Her exposed

skin was brown as a laborer's, but when she raised a hand to brush at her cheek, Livvy saw that her hands were smooth and unmarked.

The woman seemed to be sitting in a railway carriage—Livvy recognized the swaying motion of the train—but the blurred landscape sped by outside the windows at a speed impossible except in dreams.

Livvy, trying to speak, struggled against the cotton wool that seemed to envelop her. "What— Who—" she began, but the image was fading. It flared suddenly and dimmed, as if someone had blown out a lamp, but Livvy could have sworn that in the last instant she had seen a glimpse of startled recognition in the woman's eyes.

She gasped awake, her heart pounding, but she knew at once it was not the dream that had awakened her. There had been a sound, a movement, at the kitchen door. Livvy stood, her hand to her throat, paralyzed by sudden hope. "Charles?"

The world slipped by backwards, a misty patchwork of sheep-dotted fields and pale yellow swaths of rape that seemed to glow from within. Occasionally, the rolling hills dipped into deep, leafy-banked ravines that harbored slow rivers, mossy and mysterious. The bloom of late spring lay across the land with a richness that made Gemma James's blood rise in response. As the train swayed hypnotically, she fancied that time might encapsulate the speeding train and its occupants in a perpetual loop of rhythmic motion and flashing hillsides.

Giving herself a small shake, she looked across the aisle at her friend Hazel Cavendish. "It's lovely"— Gemma gestured out the window—"wherever it is."

Hazel laughed. "Northumberland, I think. We've a long way to go."

Farther down the car, a mother tried to calm an increasingly fractious child, and Gemma felt a guilty surge of relief that it was not she having to cope. As much as she loved her four-year-old son, Toby, it was not often she had a break from child care that didn't include work. Nor, she realized, had she and Hazel spent much time together away from their children. Until the previous Christmas, Gemma had lived for almost two years in the garage flat belonging to Hazel and her husband, Tim Cavendish. As Hazel and Tim's daughter, Holly, was the same age as Gemma's son, Hazel had cared for both children while Gemma was at work.

"I'm glad you asked me," Gemma said impulsively, smiling at Hazel across the narrow tabletop that separated them.

"If anyone deserves a break, it's you," Hazel replied with her customary warmth.

The previous autumn, Gemma had been promoted to detective inspector with the Metropolitan Police, assigned to Notting Hill Police Station. The promotion, although a goal long set, had not come without cost. Not only had it brought long hours and increased responsibility, but it had also meant leaving Scotland Yard, ending her working partnership with Superintendent Duncan Kincaid, her lover—and, since Christmas, her housemate.

"Tell me again about the place we're going," Gemma prompted. A week ago, Hazel had rung and, quite unexpectedly, asked Gemma to accompany her on a cookery weekend in the Scottish Highlands.

"I know it's short notice," Hazel had said, "but it's only for four days. We'll go up on the Friday and come back on Monday. Could you get away from work, do you think? You haven't had a holiday in ages."

Gemma understood the unspoken subtext. A therapist as well as a friend, Hazel was concerned that Gemma had not fully recovered from her miscarriage in January.

It *had* been a hard winter. The fact that the pregnancy was unplanned and had been difficult for Gemma to accept had made the loss of the child even more devastating; nor had she recovered physically as quickly as she might have hoped. But with spring had come a lifting of her spirits and a renewal of energy, and if she still woke in the night with an aching sadness, she didn't speak of it.

"It's a small place called Innesfree," Hazel told her. "A pun on the owners' name, which is Innes."

"Nice sentiment, wrong country."

Hazel smiled. "It's near the River Spey, at the foot of the Cairngorm Mountains. According to the brochure, John Innes is making quite a name for himself as a chef. We were lucky to get a place in one of his cooking courses."

"You know I'm not up to your standards," Gemma protested, thinking of some of her recent kitchen disasters in the house she and Duncan had taken in Notting Hill. She had yet to master the oil-fired cooker, in spite of Hazel's helpful advice.

"The course is supposed to be very personalized," Hazel assured her. "And I'm sure there will be other things to do. Walks by the river, drinks by the fire . . ."

"How very romantic."

Much to Gemma's surprise, Hazel colored and looked away. "I suppose it is," she murmured, leaning back into her seat and closing her eyes.

Gazing at her companion, Gemma noticed the smudges beneath the fan of dark lashes, the new hollows beneath the well-defined cheekbones. For a moment

Gemma wondered if Hazel could be ill, but she dismissed the thought as quickly as it had come. Hazel—therapist, perfect wife, mother, and gourmet vegetarian cook—was the most healthy, balanced person Gemma had ever known. Surely it was merely a slight fatigue, and the weekend's rest would be just the restorative she needed.

Donald Brodie lifted one section of the wort vat's heavy wooden cover and breathed in the heady aroma of hot water and barley. He had been fascinated by this part of the distilling process even as a child, when his father had had to lift him up so that he could peer down into the frothy depths of the vat. It still amazed him that the liquid produced by combining ground, dried barley with hot water could produce a final product as elegant as a malt whisky—but perhaps that was why he had never lost his fierce love of the business.

Even today, when he had so much else at stake, he had gone round the premises after work finished, as was his habit. He closed the vat and crossed the steel mesh flooring to the stairs, his footsteps echoing in the building's cavernous space. Once outside, he locked the door and stepped out into the yard, stopping a moment to survey his domain.

It had been mild for mid-May in the Highlands, and the late afternoon air still held the sun's warmth. Before him, the lawn sloped down to the house his great-great-grandfather had built, a monument to Victorian Romanticism in dressed stone. He turned, looking back at the building he had left. To the left stood the warehouse, once the home of the vast floor maltings, with the distinctive twin-pagoda roofs that had ventilated the kiln; to the right, the still-house and the now-defunct mill. Although the mill had not been used to grind barley to grist since the

early 1960s, his father had restored the wheel to operation, and water tumbled merrily from its blades. The
building now served as the distillery's Visitors Centre.

The mill was powered by the burn that ran down
from the foothills of the Cairngorms to meet the nearby
River Spey, but the water that went into the whisky
came from the spring that bubbled up from the gently
rolling grounds. In the making of whisky, the quality of
the water was all-important, a Highland distillery's
greatest asset.

The Brodie who had named the place Benvulin had
shown a wayward imagination—*ben* being a corruption
of the Gaelic word *beinn,* or hill, but *vulin,* the phonetic
spelling of the Gaelic *mhoulin*, or mill, was a bit more
accurate.

Tomorrow he would entice Hazel into coming here—a
not-so-subtle reminder of her heritage and of what he had
to offer—but then, he had grown tired of subtlety. The
phone calls, the notes, the casual lunches in discreet London restaurants, spent skating around what they were
feeling; all those things had served their purpose, but now
it was time for Hazel to face the truth. His friends, John
and Louise Innes, had done their part in getting Hazel
here by arranging the cookery weekend; now he must do
his—and soon, he thought, his pulse quickening as he
looked at his watch.

The mobile phone on his belt vibrated. Slipping it
from its holder, he glanced at the caller ID. Alison.
Damn and blast! He hesitated, then let the call ring
through to voice mail. If there was one complication he
didn't need this weekend, it was dealing with Alison.
He'd told her he had a business meeting—true enough,
with Heather, the distillery's manager, who'd insisted on
bringing Pascal Benoit, the Frenchman whose conglom-

erate was salivating over Benvulin. Not that he could put off Alison indefinitely, mind, but a few more days couldn't hurt, and then he would find some way of dealing with her for good.

With that thought, he went to wash and change for the evening, whistling all the while.

Sitting down at his wife's desk, Tim Cavendish began to work his way through the drawers. He was a methodical man, and his time was limited, because Holly, who at age four protested naps with great indignation, would not sleep long. He told himself this was a job, a project, to be approached like any other; he could, in fact, pretend he was looking for something, a lost note, or a receipt. Perhaps that would quiet the ingrained revulsion he felt at invading another therapist's privacy. But Hazel, he told himself, had forfeited all rights to such consideration.

Pencils, elastic bands, paper clips—all the innocent paraphernalia of work. Hazel's appointment book lay open on her desktop; her case files were stored in a separate cabinet. Disappointed, he sat back and idly lifted the corner of the blotter.

The dog-eared photo was near the edge, as if it had been examined often. From its fading surface Hazel gazed back at him, smiling. She wore shorts, her tanned legs seeming to go on forever, and her face, younger and softer, was more like Holly's than he remembered. Beside her sat a large man in jeans, his arm thrown casually, possessively, around her shoulders. His face was strong, blunt, his thick hair a bit longer than was now fashionable. Behind them, the purple haze of a heather-covered moor. Scotland, in summer.

His first impulse was to destroy the photo; but no, let

her keep it. She would have little enough when he had finished with her.

A corner of white protruded from beneath one side of the snap. He nudged the photo out of the way with the tip of his finger, as if touching it would contaminate him.

A business card. Good God. The man had given her a business card, like a commercial traveler come calling. Unlike the photo, it was new, still pristinely white, and it told him what he wanted to know. *Donald Brodie, Benvulin Distillery, Nethy Bridge, Inverness-shire.*

Tim felt an icy calm settle over him. He pocketed the card, returning the photo to its hiding place. Seconds seemed to stretch into minutes, and in the silence he heard the pumping of his own heart.

He knew now what he had to do.

"What if they don't eat meat?" Louise Innes stood at the kitchen sink, filling vases for the evening's flower arrangements. Although her back was turned to her husband, John knew her forehead would be puckered in the small frown that had begun to leave a permanent crease. "Did you not think to ask?"

"I assumed someone would have said, if there was a problem," John answered, keeping his voice even but whisking a little harder at the batter for the herb and mushroom crepes that would serve as that night's starter. Although the kitchen was his province, the house Louise's, she didn't mind questioning his menu choices.

"And venison, especially—"

"Och, it's a Highland specialty, Louise. And Hazel Cavendish is your old school friend—I should think ye'd know if she didna eat meat."

"This weekend was a bad idea from start to finish," Louise said pettishly. Her English accent always grew more precise in proportion to her degree of irritation, as if to repudiate his Scottishness. "I haven't seen Hazel since the summer after university, and I don't approve of the whole business. She's married, for heaven's sake, with a child. You've always let Donald Brodie talk you into things you shouldn't." His wife pulled half a dozen roses from the pail of flowers John had brought from Inverness that morning, laid them across a cutting board, and sliced off the bottom inch of the stems with a sharp knife. The ruthlessness in the quick chop made him think of small creatures beheaded.

Louise had taken a flower-arranging course the previous year, attacking the project with the efficiency that marked all her endeavors. Although she could now produce picture-perfect bouquets that drew raves from the guests, he found that the arrangements lacked that certain creative touch—a last blossom out of place, perhaps— that would have made them truly lovely.

"If that's the case, perhaps ye should take some responsibility," he snapped at her. "It was you introduced me to Donald, ye ken." He knew he was being defensive, because he'd allowed Donald to wheedle him into taking Hazel and her friend without charge, and this meant they'd turned away paying guests on a weekend at the beginning of their busiest season. But then, he had his reasons for keeping on Donald Brodie's good side, and the less Louise knew about that, the better.

Louise's only answer to his sally was the eloquent line of her back. With a sigh, John finished his batter and began brushing mushrooms with a damp tea towel. It was no use him criticizing Louise. The very qualities that aggravated him had also made this venture possible.

Two years ago, he'd given up his Edinburgh job in commercial real estate and bought the old farmhouse at the edge of the Abernathy forest, between Coylumbridge and Nethy Bridge. The house and barn had been in appalling condition, but the recent property boom in Edinburgh had provided him with the cash to finance the necessary refurbishments.

Louise, at first unhappy over the loss of her job and circle of friends, had in time thrown herself into the project with her customary zeal. While he did the shopping and the cooking, she took reservations and did the guests' rooms, as they could not as yet afford to hire help.

Resting the heel of his hand on his knife, he quartered the mushrooms before chopping them finely. A glance told him Louise still had her back to him, her head bent over her flowers. He felt his temper ease as he watched her. She might not have approved of the arrangements for the weekend, but she would do her best to make sure everything went smoothly.

"You'll be glad to see Hazel again, will ye not?" he asked, in an attempt to placate.

Louise's shoulders relaxed and she tilted her head, her neat blond hair falling to one side like a lifted bird's wing. "It's been a long time," she answered. "I'm not sure I'll know what to say."

"I'm sure Donald will fill in the gaps," he said lightly, then cursed himself for a fool. Louise would never be able to resist such an opening.

"That's the problem, isn't it?" She turned towards him, a spray of sweet peas in her hand. "Donald always fills in the gaps, and never mind the consequences. He's as feckless as his father, if not more so. Heather's livid, and we have to get on with her once this weekend is over."

"I don't see why it should make any difference to Heather," he said stubbornly. "Hazel's her cousin, after all. Ye'd think she'd be glad to—"

"You don't see anything!" Spots of color appeared high on Louise's cheekbones. "How can you be so dense, John? You know how precarious things are at the distillery just now—"

"I still don't see what that has to do with your friend Hazel coming for a weekend." He added a clove of garlic to his board and chopped it with unnecessary force.

Louise turned her back to him again just as the sun dipped low enough in the southwest to catch the window above the sink. She stood, backlit, the light forming an aureole around her fair hair, as if she were a medieval saint.

"Why are you suddenly so determined to defend a woman you've never met?" Her voice was cold and tight, a warning he'd come to recognize. If he didn't put an end to the argument now, it would spill over into the evening, and that he couldn't afford.

"Listen, darlin'—"

"Unless there's something you haven't told me." She stood very still, her hands cupped round the finished vase of flowers.

"Don't be absurd, Louise. Why wouldna I have told you, if I'd met the bluidy woman?"

"I can think of a number of reasons."

Scraping the mushrooms and garlic into the melted butter waiting in a saucepan, he considered his reply. He'd never learned how to deal with her in this mood, having tried teasing, sarcasm, angry denial—all with the same lack of success. But the longer he delayed, the more likely she would take his silence for an admission of guilt. "Louise—"

She turned, and he saw from her expression that it was too late to salvage the argument, or the evening. "What's got into you, John?" she spat at him. "How could you possibly have thought I'd approve of your conspiring to sabotage another woman's marriage?"

As the train sped north, the fields of Northumberland and the rolling hills of the Scottish Borders yielded to granite cliffs and forests, and, at last, to the high, heather-clad moors. Gemma gazed out the glass, entranced by the patterns of dark and light on the moor side, as if someone had laid out a child's crude map of the world across the hills.

"They burn the heather," Hazel explained when Gemma asked the cause of the odd effect. "The new growth after the burning provides food for the grouse."

"And the yellow patches?"

"The deep gold-yellow is gorse. Lovely to look at but prickly to fall into. And the paler yellow"—Hazel pointed at the blooms lining the railway cutting—"is broom."

"All this you remember from your childhood?" Gemma asked. Hazel had told her she'd lived near here as a small child, before her parents moved to Newcastle.

"Oh." Hazel looked disconcerted. "I worked here for a bit after university."

Before Gemma could elicit particulars, they were interrupted by the arrival of the tea trolley, and shortly thereafter they drew into the doll's house of Aviemore station.

Gemma eyed the Bavarian fantasy of gingerbread and painted trim with astonishment as Hazel laughed at her expression. "It's by far the prettiest building in Aviemore," Hazel said as they gathered their luggage from the overhead racks. "The station raises great expectations, but Aviemore's a ski and hiking center, and there's not much else to recommend it."

They picked up the keys for their hired car from the Europcar office in the railway station, then emerged into the evening light. At first glance, Gemma found Hazel's assessment to be accurate. The High Street was lined with mountain shops, restaurants, and a new supermarket complex; to the left the stone block of the Hilton Hotel rose from a green slope; to the right, beyond the car park, lay the Aviemore Police Station. But to the east, behind the railway station, rose mist-enshrouded mountain peaks, gilded by the sun.

"Is that where we're going?" Gemma gestured at the hills as they chucked their bags into the boot of the red Honda awaiting them in the car park.

"The guest house is in the valley that runs along the River Spey. But you're never out of sight of the mountains here," Hazel added, and Gemma thought she heard a note of wistfulness in her voice.

Ever more curious, Gemma asked, "You know the way?" as they belted themselves in and Hazel shoved the car hire map into the glove box.

"I know the road," Hazel said, pulling into the street, "but not the house itself."

In a few short blocks, they'd left Aviemore behind and turned into a B road that crossed the Spey and dipped into evergreen woods. "We're running along the very edge of the Rothiemurchus Estate," Hazel explained. "That's owned by the Rothiemurchus Grants—they're quite a force in this part of the world."

"Grants?" Gemma repeated blankly.

"A famous Highland family. I'm— Never mind. It's complicated."

"Related to them?"

"Very remotely. But then most people in the Highlands are related. It's very incestuous country."

"Do you still have family here, then?" Gemma asked, intrigued.

"An aunt and uncle. A cousin."

Gemma thought back over all the hours they'd spent chatting in Hazel's cozy Islington kitchen. Had Hazel never mentioned them? Or had Gemma never thought to ask?

In the time Gemma had lived in Hazel's garage flat, they had become close friends. But on reflection, Gemma realized that their conversations had centered on their children, food, Gemma's job, and—Gemma admitted to herself rather shamefacedly—Gemma's problems. Gemma had thought that Hazel's easy way of turning the conversation from her own life was a therapist's habit, when she had thought of it at all. But what did she really know about Hazel?

"When you came back after university . . . ," she said slowly. "What did you do?"

"Cooked," Hazel answered grimly. "I catered meals for shooting parties, at estates and lodges."

"Shooting? As in the queen always goes to Balmoral in August for the grouse?"

Hazel smiled. "We're not far from Balmoral, by the way. And yes, it was grouse, as well as pheasant and deer and anything else you could shoot with a bloody gun. I had enough of carcasses to last a lifetime." Slowing the car, Hazel added, "We should be getting close. Keep watch on the left."

Gemma had been absently gazing at the sparkle of the river as it played hide-and-seek through pasture and wooded copse, trying to imagine a childhood spent in such surroundings. "What exactly am I looking for?"

"A white house, set back from the road. I'm sure there will be a sign." Hazel slowed still further, her knuckles showing pale where she gripped the wheel. Odd, thought Gemma, that Hazel should be so anxious about missing a turning.

They traveled another mile in silence, then rounding a curve, Gemma saw a flash of white through the trees. "There!" A small sign on a gatepost read INNESFREE, BED & BREAKFAST INN.

Hazel braked and pulled the car into the drive. The house sat side-on to the road, facing north. Its foursquare plainness bespoke its origins as a farmhouse, but it looked comfortable and welcoming. To the right of the house they could see another building and beyond it, the glint of the river.

The sight of smoke curling from the chimney was a welcome addition, for, as Gemma discovered when she stepped out of the car, the temperature had dropped considerably just since they'd left Aviemore. Hazel shivered in her sleeveless dress, hugging her arms across her chest.

"I'll just get your cardigan, shall I?" asked Gemma, going to the boot, but Hazel shook her head.

"No. I'll be all right. Let's leave the bags for now." She marched towards the front door, and Gemma followed, looking round with interest.

The door swung open and a man came out to greet them, his arms held out in welcome. "You'll be Hazel, then? I'm John, Louise's husband." He took Hazel's hand and gave it a squeeze before turning to Gemma. "And this is your friend—"

"Gemma. Gemma James." Gemma shook his hand, taking the opportunity to study him. He had thinning dark hair, worn a little longer than fashion dictated, wire-rimmed spectacles, a comfortable face, and the incipient paunch of a good cook.

"We've put you in the barn conversion—our best room," John told them. "Why don't you come in and have a wee chat with Louise, then I'll take your bags round." He shepherded them into a flagstoned hall filled with shooting and fishing prints and sporting paraphernalia; oiled jackets hung from hooks on the walls, and a wooden bin held croquet mallets, badminton racquets, and fishing rods. In contrast to the worn jumble, a table held a perfect arrangement of spring flowers.

A woman came towards them from a door at the end of the hall. Small and blond, with a birdlike neatness, she wore her hair in the sort of smooth, swingy bob that Gemma, with her tangle of coppery curls, always envied.

"Hullo, Hazel," the woman said as she reached them, pecking the air near Hazel's cheek. "It's wonderful to see you. I'm Louise," she added, turning to Gemma. "Why don't you come into the parlor for a drink before dinner? The others have walked down to the river to work up an appetite, but they should be back soon."

She led them into a sitting room on the right. A coal fire glowed in the simple hearth, the furniture was upholstered in an unlikely but pleasant mixture of mauve tartans, a vase of purple tulips drooped gracefully before the window, and to Gemma's delight, an old upright piano stood against the wall.

As soon as Gemma and Hazel were seated, John Innes brought over a tray holding several cut glass tumblers and a bottle of whisky. "It's Benvulin, of course," he said as he splashed a half inch of liquid amber into each glass. "Eighteen-year-old. I could hardly do less," he added, with a knowing glance at Hazel.

"Benvulin?" repeated Gemma.

After a moment's pause, Hazel answered. "It's a distillery near here. Quite famous." She held her glass under her nose for a moment before taking a sip. "In fact, the whole of Speyside is famous for its single malt whiskies. *Some* say it provides the perfect combination of water, peat, and barley." She drank again, and Gemma saw the color heighten in her cheeks.

"But you don't agree?" Following Hazel's example, Gemma took a generous sip. Fire bit at the back of her throat and she coughed until tears came to her eyes. "Sorry," she managed to gasp.

"Takes a bit of getting used to," John said. "Unless you're like Hazel, here, who probably tasted whisky in her cradle."

"I wouldn't go as far as that." Hazel's tight smile indicated more irritation than amusement.

"Is that a Highland custom, giving whisky to babies?" asked Gemma, wondering what undercurrent she was missing.

"Helps with the teething," Hazel replied before John or Louise could speak. "And a host of other things. Old-timers swear a wee dram with their parritch every morning keeps them fit." Finishing her drink in a swallow, Hazel stood. "But just now I'd like to freshen up before dinner, and I'm sure Gemma—"

Turning, Gemma saw a man standing in the doorway, surveying them. Tall and broad-shouldered, he had thick auburn hair and a neatly trimmed ruddy beard. And he was gazing at Hazel, who stood as if turned to stone.

He came towards her, hand outstretched. "Hazel!"

"Donald." Hazel made his name not a greeting but a statement. When she made no move to take his hand, he dropped it, and they stood in awkward silence.

Watching the tableau, Gemma became aware of two things. The first was that Hazel, standing with her lips parted and her eyes bright, was truly lovely, and that she had never realized it.

The second was the fact that this large man in the red-and-black tartan kilt knew Hazel very well indeed.

2

It was like the worst of the Scottish Highlands, only worse; cold, naked, and ignoble, scant of wood, scant of heather, scant of life.

—ROBERT LOUIS STEVENSON,
"Travels with a Donkey"

Carnmore, November 1898

BRACING HER SHOULDER *against the thrust of the wind hammering at the kitchen door, Livvy eased up the latch. But her slight body was no match for the gale, her preparation futile. The howling wind seized the door and flung it back, taking her with it like a rag doll.*

She lay in a heap on the stone flags, the frigid air piercing her lungs. Levering herself up on hands and knees, she edged round the door's flimsy shelter. The snow flew at her, stinging her eyes and blurring her vision, but she crawled forward, her head down, her gaze fixed upon the dark huddle beyond the stoop. "Charles?" she called out, her voice a croak snatched by the wind, but there was no answer.

The humped form resolved itself as she drew nearer:

man-sized, man-shaped, the darkness a coat, rime-crusted. She dug her way through the heaped snow that had drifted against the sill, frantic now.

He lay against the step, curled in a fetal ball, his head hidden by his arms. "Charles!" Livvy tugged at him, pulling him half onto his back so that she could see his face, and pushed back his wet, cold hair. His skin was blue, his lashes frozen with tiny ice crystals, but she thought she saw his lips move.

"Inside. We've got to get ye in the house," she shouted, trying to lift him. But he was limp, a deadweight, and with the wind buffeting her she couldn't get enough leverage to haul him over the stoop. Pushing and tugging, she exhorted him, but she grew clumsier as she began to lose the sensation in her hands and feet.

At last she sat back. "Charles, oh, Charles," she sobbed, wiping at the tears turning to ice on her cheeks. Then she swallowed hard, her resolve hardening. He had made it home, God knew how, with the last of his strength, and now it was up to her.

But she must get help or he would freeze, and she with him.

Gemma eased her thigh away from its damp contact with the knee of the young man sitting next to her, giving him a bland smile. Not that he was flirting with her—at least she hoped he wasn't flirting with her. But in honor of the weekend's cookery class, the small, square tables that would normally have seated the guests from each bedroom in the B&B separately had been joined, leaving the six people assembled for dinner closer together than Gemma found comfortable. The room was overwarm, as well, and although the coal fire blazing in the dining room's hearth added a convivial note, the ring of faces round the table all sported a faint sheen of perspiration.

No doubt a good bit of that glow could be attributed to the amount of whisky drunk before dinner, and the liberal consumption of wine with the meal. Considering that they hadn't reached the pudding stage yet, Gemma groaned inwardly. Paper-thin crepes with wild mushrooms had preceded tenderloin of venison in a red currant glaze, surrounded by heaps of perfectly roasted potatoes and crisp *haricots verts*. Now Gemma eyed the remaining slice of venison on her plate with something akin to despair. It was too good to leave, but she'd burst if she took another bite. With a sigh, she pushed her plate away and looked round the room. Hazel, she noticed, had artfully rearranged the meat on her plate without actually eating any of it.

Following the sporting theme evidenced in the entry hall, delicately colored paintings of fish swam round the circumference of the white-paneled dining room walls. At first Gemma thought the fish were painted on the paneling itself, but as she studied them she realized they were paper cutouts. The sizes varied, as did the quality of the artwork, but all were game fish of some sort, trout or perhaps salmon. Having never seen either except on a dinner plate, Gemma could only guess.

"They're all hand painted, you know," said the young man beside her, following her gaze. He had been introduced to her as Martin Gilmore, John Innes's much younger brother. "It was a household tradition before John bought the place. Anyone who catches a fish weighing more than eight pounds has to trace it exactly, then paint it."

"Is one of these yours, then?" Gemma asked, nodding at the wall. Martin had the look of an artist, with his thin, ascetic face and cropped hair that emphasized the bony prominence of his nose. In one nostril Gemma saw a puncture, telltale evidence of an absent nose stud. Perhaps Martin had been afraid John would disapprove.

"Not on your life," Martin answered, grimacing. "I'm a city boy, brought up in Dundee. I'll pass on the shootin' and fishin', thank you verra much." His accent, at first more clipped than his brother's, had begun to slur as the level in his glass dropped.

"Oh," said Gemma, confused. "I had the impression John was from this area, but I must have been mistaken—"

"No, you had it right," confirmed Martin. "We're half brothers. Our mother remarried, and I was the child of her dotage."

Not quite sure how to respond to the latter part of his comment, Gemma concentrated on the former. "But you're close, you and John?"

"First time I've seen him since I left school." Martin glanced round the room, as if assuring himself of his brother's absence, and leaned nearer Gemma's ear. "To tell the truth, I thought I'd never wangle an invitation to this place. Couldn't believe my luck when he rang up and said I could come along this weekend for the cookery class."

Gemma edged away from his warm breath. "You're interested in cooking?"

Martin's reply was forestalled by Louise's entrance with an empty tray. "The ice queen herself," he muttered, then busied himself finishing his venison.

"Did everyone enjoy their meals?" Louise asked, smiling brightly at them.

A hearty chorus of assents rang round the table. Louise spoke quietly to each guest as she removed his or her plate, giving Gemma an opportunity to study her table-mates.

Across from her sat Heather Urquhart, who had also greeted Hazel as if they were well acquainted. The woman was in her thirties, tall and thin, her face lightly pockmarked with the scars of old acne, but her most striking feature was the rippling curtain of black hair that fell below her waist. She had kept up an animated con-versation all through dinner with the man on her right, a Frenchman named Pascal Benoit.

Benoit seemed to have some connection with the whisky business, but Gemma had yet to work out exactly what he did. He was short, balding, and slightly tubby, but his dark eyes were flat and cold as stones.

That left Hazel, seated next to Heather, and at the table's far end, the man in the red kilt, who had been in-troduced to Gemma as Donald Brodie. The awkwardness of his entrance into the sitting room had been quickly smoothed over by the arrival of the other guests, but be-fore Gemma could draw Hazel aside with a question, Louise had called them in to dinner.

Now, as she watched Brodie lean over and speak softly in Hazel's ear, Gemma was more curious than ever. Hazel seemed flushed, animated, and riveted on her companion. Clearly, she knew Donald Brodie. And just as clearly, she had not been surprised to find him at Innesfree. What *was* Hazel playing at?

Was Brodie an old flame, and Hazel trying to make the best of an embarrassing reunion for the sake of the cook-ery weekend? Or—Gemma frowned at the thought—was there more to it than that?

Surely not, thought Gemma. Hazel and Tim were hap-pily married, a wonderful couple. Then, uncomfortably, Gemma began to recall how little she'd seen of Tim the past few months—in fact, even before Gemma had moved out of the garage flat, Tim had been absent in the evenings more often than not. And Hazel's distress over Gemma's move *had* seemed odd in one usually so serene, as had the plea in her voice when she'd invited Gemma to accompany her for the weekend.

Gemma gave herself a mental shake. Rubbish. It was all rubbish. The very idea of Hazel having an affair was absurd. That's what police work did for you—gave you a suspicious nature. She found herself suddenly missing Kincaid's presence and his unruffled outlook. He would, she was sure, tell her she was making a mountain out of a molehill.

Determined to put Hazel's behavior from her mind, as well as the small ache of homesickness brought on by the thought of Duncan, Gemma handed Louise her plate. "That was absolutely super," she told her. "A few more days of this and I won't be able to do up my buttons."

"Wait until you see the pudding," Louise answered. "It's a chocolate mousse with raspberry coulis—John's specialty. Would you like coffee with it?"

Gemma murmured her assent, but her mind had gone back to Hazel. Why, if she *were* carrying on with Donald Brodie, had she wanted Gemma to come with her?

As if sensing her interest, Brodie broke off his conversation with Hazel and turned to her. "Gemma, I understand you're not much of a whisky drinker. We'll have to remedy that while you're here." His voice was Scots, but well educated, and pleasantly deep.

"Is that a necessary part of the Highland experience, Mr. Brodie?"

"It's Donald, please," he corrected her. "And from my point of view, it's a necessary part of everyone's experience. I own a distillery."

Gemma thought back to the predinner drinks, and John Innes's rather sly comment about the whisky he'd served. "Benvulin, is it?"

Brodie looked pleased. "Hazel will have told you, then. It's a family enterprise, started by one of my Brodie forebears. You might say it's in Hazel's family, too," he added, with a quick glance at Hazel, "in more ways than one. Heather's now my manager."

"Heather?" Gemma asked, lost.

"Heather and I are cousins," Hazel put in, with an embarrassed duck of her head towards the other woman. "Our fathers are brothers. I'm sure I must have told you . . ."

Gemma couldn't recall Hazel ever mentioning her maiden name. She glanced at Heather Urquhart, saw no wedding ring on her long, thin hand. *Urquhart*, she was sure, she would have remembered. Thinking of Hazel's daughter, she said, "Hazel, Heather, Holly—"

"A family penchant for female botanical names." Heather Urquhart's voice matched her looks, sharp and thin, and her tone was challenging. "I'm surprised Hazel hasn't regaled you with tales of her eccentric Scottish relations."

"Give it a break, Heather," Hazel said sharply, and Heather gave a cat-in-the-cream smile at having drawn a retort.

Gemma gaped at her friend in astonishment. She had seen Hazel occasionally get a bit cross with the children when they tried her patience too far, but never had she heard her snap at another adult.

"You have been a number of years in the south, I think," Pascal Benoit said diplomatically to Hazel in his faintly accented English. A twinkle of malice livened his black eyes.

Hazel turned to him with obvious relief. "Yes, London. My husband and I live in London, with our four-year-old daughter."

Turning his attention to Gemma, Benoit asked, "And you, Miss James? You are also from London?"

"It's not *miss*, actually," Gemma answered, feeling suddenly contrary. "*James* is my ex-husband's name."

Benoit smiled, appearing not at all discomfited. "Ah, one of the more difficult questions of manners in modern society. How *does* one refer to the divorced woman, without using the abominable *Ms.*? In French it is easier. *Madame* implies a woman mature, past her girlhood, but not necessarily married."

"And I take it that in France, to refer to a woman as 'mature' is not an insult?" Gemma was beginning to enjoy herself. Benoit was proving a much more challenging verbal partner than Martin Gilmore, who sat silently beside her, hunched over his drink.

"*Mais oui.*" Benoit smiled, showing small, even, white teeth. "We French appreciate women at all stages in life, not just the boyish ingénue. Unlike the British, who have no more refined taste in women than in food."

Gilmore flushed and straightened up, as if to protest, but was forestalled by a chuckle from Donald Brodie.

"Ouch," said Brodie. "I might be inclined to take that personally, Pascal, if I didn't know how fond the French are of generalizing about the British. But if I were you, I'd be careful of repeating those opinions to our host, when you've just enjoyed his cooking."

This time it was Benoit who colored. "There are always exceptions, are there not? Perhaps Mr. Innes is a Frenchman at heart."

"That might be taking things a wee bit too far," said John Innes, who had come in silently, a tray on his arm.

The rich smell of chocolate filled the room. "Although the French and the Scots have a long and mostly harmonious association, you'll not find a Highlander gives up his identity so easily." He smiled cheerfully at them and nodded towards the hall. "If you'd care to have your dessert in the parlor, Louise and I will join you. I thought we might discuss a few things before tomorrow's class."

Gemma rose as the murmur of assent went round the table, glad enough to quit the dining room's claustrophobic atmosphere. She caught up to Hazel at the door, meaning to whisper a private word in her ear, but found Donald Brodie's large form suddenly insinuated between them. He smelled faintly of cologne, wine, and warm wool; and just for an instant as they moved into the hall, Gemma saw him place his hand on Hazel's shoulder.

Duncan Kincaid squeezed himself through the crowd coming off the train at Notting Hill tube station and ran lightly up the stairs. Reaching the shop level, he came to an automatic halt in front of the flower stall, eyeing the multicolored masses of tulips. Often on a Friday, he stopped on the way home to buy Gemma flowers, and these were her favorites.

But Gemma was away for the entire weekend, he reminded himself, going on. He and the boys would have the house to themselves—a good opportunity for male bonding, Gemma had told him teasingly. And he meant to make the most of it; a video with Kit that evening, football in the park tomorrow, and on Sunday, Toby's favorite outing, a trip to the zoo. The weather promised to be fine, and he had left his paperwork at the office with his sergeant, Doug Cullen.

All in all, not a bad prospect, he thought as he exited the tube station into the street, but that didn't stop him from feeling a pang as he passed the Calzone's at the junction of Pembridge and Kensington Park Roads. It was Gemma's favorite place in the neighborhood for a relaxed dinner, on the few occasions they managed to get out without the children.

He walked along Ladbroke Road, enjoying the soft May evening, and the sense of suppressed excitement that always seemed to hum in the London air before the weekend. The trees were in full leaf, the pale emerald of spring now deepening to the richer green of early summer, but a few late tulips still graced flower boxes and tiny front gardens.

As he passed Notting Hill Police Station, where Gemma was now posted, he thought about how difficult it had been to adjust to working without her. Of course, the change had allowed them to live together, which had deepened their relationship in many ways, but he'd also found that cohabitation did not provide quite the same sense of challenge and unity as working a case together.

Well, he told himself, life was full of change and compensations, and given a choice, he wouldn't trade the present state of affairs for the former. Shaking off the small shadow of discontent, he turned into St. John's Gardens and quickened his pace towards home.

The evening sun lit the house, picking out the contrast of white trim against dark brick, illuminating the welcoming cherry red of the door. He retrieved the post from the letter box and let himself in, stopping for a moment in the hall to identify the unusual odors wafting from the kitchen. Caribbean spices—Wesley was still there, and cooking, by the smell of it.

The case Kincaid and Gemma had worked the previous winter had brought them personal loss, but it had also introduced Wesley Howard into their lives. The young man, a university student with a passion for photography, supplemented his income by working at a neighborhood café, and in the past few months he had also become an unconventional and unofficial part-time nanny to the children.

The click of toenails on tile flooring heralded the arrival of Geordie, their cocker spaniel—or rather, Kincaid amended to himself, Gemma's cocker spaniel. Although the dog had been Gemma's Christmas gift to Kincaid and the boys, it was Gemma whom Geordie adored.

"Hullo, boy," Kincaid said, stooping to stroke Geordie's silky, blue-gray head. The dog's stump of a tail was wagging enthusiastically, but his dark eyes seemed to hold a look of reproach. "Missing your mum, already, are you?" Giving Geordie a last pat, he straightened and went into the kitchen.

Wesley stood at the cooker, a tea towel wrapped round his waist as a makeshift apron, his dark skin glistening from the heat of the pan. "You're early, mon," he greeted Kincaid. "Thought they'd keep you at the nick on a Friday night."

Kincaid stopped to tousle Toby's fine, fair hair. The small boy sat at the kitchen table, drawing with crayons, his feet wrapped round the chair legs and the tip of his tongue protruding as he concentrated. "Skived off," Kincaid said to Wesley with a smile. "That smells brilliant. Chicken, is it?" As if he had understood him, Sid, the cat, got up from his basket with a languid feline stretch and came to rub against his ankles.

"Jerk chicken, with some herbed rice." Wesley gave Sid a warning look. "Would've had cat steak, if *he'd* got any further with the chicken wrapper."

"Jerky chicken." Toby giggled. "Look," he added, pointing to his paper. "I'm drawing Mummy on the train."

Absently, Kincaid deposited the mail on the table as he studied Toby's artwork. The cars were black oblongs with round wheels and large, square windows; from one of the windows a stick figure with red, curling hair waved out at him. "I see Mummy," he agreed, "but where's Auntie Hazel? She'll be cross with you if you don't put her in."

As Toby bent to his page again, Kincaid went to the cooker and peered over Wesley's shoulder at the sizzling strips of chicken, sniffing appreciatively, then the kitchen clock caught his eye. "Shouldn't you be at Otto's?" he asked. "I didn't mean to keep you this late. And where's Kit?" His son was usually to be found beside Wes in the kitchen, a hand in everything.

"I gave Otto a ring; he be fine without me. Café's slow tonight. And Kit, he came home and went straight up to his room. Not like him." Wesley's dreadlocks bounced as he shook his head. "I didn't like to leave. Thought maybe he missin' Gemma already."

"I'll go have a word," Kincaid said easily, but he felt the stab of concern that dogged him now whenever he thought something might be wrong with one of the children.

Glancing in the dining and sitting rooms as he passed, he thought they looked unnaturally neat; books and toys put away in baskets, sofa cushions fluffed, the keys of Gemma's piano covered. All a result of Gemma's tidying that morning, he supposed, as if she were going away for a month instead of a few days.

He climbed the wide staircase, one hand brushing the banister, and knocked at the half-open door of the boys' bedroom. Across the hall, the room they'd meant to use as a nursery stood empty, but Kit had declined the offer of it, insisting he preferred to keep sharing with Toby.

His son lay curled on his narrow bed, a book in his hand, his small dog, Tess, nestled against him. As Kincaid entered, Kit sat up and let the book fall closed. The terrier lifted her head expectantly off her paws.

"What are you reading?" Kincaid asked, sitting down beside them. Experience had taught him to avoid the usual parental gambit—*How was school today?* did not elicit voluble replies, especially from Kit, who tended towards reticence at the best of times.

Had Kit always been that way, or was his quiet and slightly wary approach to the world a direct response to the trauma of his mother's death? Kincaid found it difficult to reconcile himself to the idea that he would probably never learn the answer. He'd come too late into his son's life, and the fact that he hadn't known Kit was his son until after his ex-wife's death did nothing to absolve him of his guilt.

"Kidnapped," Kit answered. "We have to read it for class, but it's bloody good."

"Don't say *bloody,*" Kincaid reminded him. "Unless you mean it literally. But I'm glad you like the book." Smothering a smile, he reached out to scratch Tess, whose small, pink tongue was lolling in a pant. "Is that why you're not down helping Wes?"

Looking away, Kit seemed to draw into himself. "I don't need minding, you know," he muttered after a moment. "I'm not a child."

"Did someone say you were?" Kincaid asked, making an effort to conceal his surprise. Kit and Wesley were the best of mates, and Kit usually nagged Wesley to stay longer.

Kit gave a grudging shrug. "Wes and Toby were waiting for me when school let out. Some of the kids said I had a *baby-sitter.*" He uttered the term with loathing.

Kincaid hesitated a moment, wondering how best to navigate the dangerous waters of a twelve-year-old's humiliation at the hands of his peers. "Kit, I'm sure Wes and Toby went to meet you after school because Toby was anxious to see you, especially with Gemma gone for the weekend. We can ask Wesley to bring Toby straight home, if you'd rather." He smiled ruefully. "I suppose having an adoring four-year-old brother doesn't exactly give you street cred, does it?"

Kit had the grace to blush but still protested. "Why does Wes have to stay, anyway? I can look after Toby—I've done it lots of times. Don't you trust me?"

"You do a great job with Toby," Kincaid assured him. "And we appreciate your looking after him as much as you do. But we also don't think it's fair that minding Toby should be your job. What if you needed to stay late for a project at school, or do something with your mates?"

When Kit didn't answer, it occurred to Kincaid that perhaps it was the other way round, and responsibility for Toby gave Kit a defense against a *lack* of after-school invitations. While he was still trying to work out how to address the issue, Toby came thundering up the stairs to announce that dinner was ready.

"We'll talk about this later," Kincaid said, giving Kit a pat on the shoulder as he stood. "But in the meantime, you might want to compliment Wesley on his chicken."

He followed the boys downstairs slowly, musing on the conversation. They'd known, when they'd moved Kit to London last Christmas, that it might be a difficult adjustment for him. Since his mother's death the previous spring, Kit had been living near Cambridge with his stepfather, Ian McClellan, and spending weekends in London with Duncan and Gemma.

Although Ian had been separated from Vic when she died, he was still Kit's legal guardian. Kincaid had allowed the arrangement to stand because he'd been unwilling to disrupt his son's life any more than necessary, and he and Ian had gradually come to amicable terms. But all that had changed when Ian had decided to take up a teaching post in Canada at the New Year. Kincaid had wanted Kit with him, and Ian had been willing to let him stay. Ian had put the cottage in Grantchester, where Kit had spent his childhood, up for sale, and Kit had come to live with Duncan, Gemma, and Toby.

All very well, but had he fooled himself into thinking Kit had made the transition easily, just because he hadn't complained? He would do better, Kincaid resolved; spend more time with the boy, find out what was going on at school.

But when Wesley had left for the café, and Toby had been put to bed with a story, Kit refused the much-anticipated action video, saying he wanted to finish his book. Kincaid found himself alone in the kitchen, his good intentions thwarted, and suddenly at a loose end.

Of course, he had novels to read, projects to finish . . . there was the telly to watch—something of his own choosing, for a change. But without the comfort of Gemma's presence somewhere in the house, all prospects seemed to pall.

Kincaid snorted at the irony of it: he, who had always been so self-sufficient, reduced to mooning about like a lovesick schoolboy. He'd have to get a grip on himself.

Idly, he picked up the post from the kitchen table and leafed through it. There were bills and credit card applications, the usual circulars, and at the bottom of the stack, a thick, cream-colored envelope. Opening it curiously, he unfolded a sheaf of legal-looking papers. He read the document once, then again, the words sinking in.

The letter came from a firm of solicitors representing his former mother-in-law, Eugenia Potts. Kit's grandmother was suing for custody.

3

The hue of Highland rivers
Careering full and cool,
From sable onto golden,
From rapid on to pool.
— ROBERT LOUIS STEVENSON,
"To You, Let Snow and Roses"

Carnmore, November 1898

LIVVY ROUSED HER *son with a touch on his shoulder.*
He came instantly awake, sitting up and groping for his
trousers. "What—"

"It's your father, Will. Come and help me." *Her teeth*
chattered so hard she could barely speak, and her sodden
clothes dripped upon the bed, but Will asked no more
questions. Quickly, he pulled on his boots and coat and
followed her down the stairs.

The snow had half-buried Charles in the few mo-
ments Livvy had been gone, but together she and Will
managed to pull him into the kitchen and close the
door.

"Blankets," *Livvy gasped.* "We'll need blankets. And

make up the fire in the parlor, Will. That's the warmest room in the house."

When Will had gone she knelt over her husband and began trying to remove his wet clothing. Charles roused a bit, pushing himself up and fumbling at the buttons of his overcoat. She stilled his hand, pressing it to her breast to warm it. Relief flooded through her. *"Oh, Charles, you're all right. I thought—"*

"Livvy . . ." His voice was a thread. *"The storm came on so quickly. I was past Tomintoul. I'd no choice . . . The carriage . . . I had to leave it—"*

"Hush. It's all right, love. Don't try to talk." She eased him out of his coat. *"We'll get something warm into ye, as soon as you're dry."*

Letting his head fall back against her arm, he whispered, *"I can't feel my feet."*

"Hush, now," she said again, knowing sensation would return soon enough, and that when it did the pain would be intense. *"We'll just get these boots off."*

Will came back into the kitchen, carrying a pile of blankets. Together they stripped Charles of the remainder of his clothing and wrapped him in heavy wool, then they half-carried him into the parlor and installed him on the settee. The peats were blazing in the hearth, and the room had already lost some of its chill.

"What about Elijah, Father?" asked Will. *"Should I—"*

"In the barn," Charles murmured, blinking. *"He'll be all right. Don't go out until the storm breaks, Will. Too dangerous . . ."* His eyes closed.

They covered him warmly, and when the kettle boiled, Livvy fed him hot tea laced with whisky while Will supported his shoulders. Charles struggled to push himself upright, a faint color flushing his thin cheeks. *"Livvy, I found a buyer in Edinburgh,"* he said urgently. *"A firm of* blenders. Not Pattison's. Whatever happens, you mustn't sell to Pattison's."

It had been a bad year for whisky. The industry had overproduced and overexpanded in the boom of the early 1890s, and now supply had inevitably begun to exceed demand. Rumors had been flying that Pattison's, one of the biggest blenders in all of Scotland, was on the brink of financial collapse, and Charles had journeyed to Edinburgh in hopes of finding another market for the distillery's stock.

Livvy felt the jolt of fear in her breast, saw the panic flare in Will's eyes. "Of course not, love," she murmured soothingly, easing him down again among the blankets. "Ye can tell us all about it tomorrow, when you've had a wee bit rest."

But Charles tossed his head from side to side, more agitated, shivering. "Tomorrow—the men won't be able to get here. You'll have to manage, you and Will. The distilling—we can't afford . . ."

"Ye'll be back on your feet by then," she told him, stroking his forehead. "No need to worry, now."

Her words seemed to calm him, and after a few moments she felt the tension leave his body as he lapsed into a chill-wracked sleep.

"He'll be all right, won't he?" croaked Will, meeting her eyes as she smoothed the blankets.

"Aye, of course he will," Livvy said sharply, knowing it was herself she sought to reassure as much as her son. "It's no but a chill." She thought of her physician father, snug in his bed in Grantown, and wished desperately for his advice.

But in this weather, Grantown-on-Spey, only fourteen miles away, was an impossible journey. Nor would the doctor be able to come from Tomintoul. The Braes of

Glenlivet in a snowstorm were as isolated and godfor-saken as the moon. There would be no help until the storm broke—even then it might take days to clear the roads.

But she had some skill, and more determination, and she was damned if she'd let this bloody place defeat her. Blinking against the sting of tears, she smiled at her son.

"Och, your father's made it home, Will, when many a man wouldn't. That's enough to be thankful for, till the morning."

"I've always said you were a wee bit daft in the heid, Callum MacGillivray, and now I know it's so." Callum's aunt Janet stood in the door of the stable, her hands on her hips, glaring at him. She was a formidable sight at the best of times, a square, blunt-featured woman, with her graying hair cut short and a face permanently scoured by the Highland winds. Angry, she looked even fiercer, and Callum found himself struggling for a coherent reply.

He was never very good at expressing himself aloud, although he did well enough in his own head, and with the murmured singsong understood by the horses and dogs. Touch, however, was another matter altogether. The lightest grip on the reins told him what a horse was think-ing, let him communicate his wishes to the beast; the del-icate quivers on a rod and line translated to him the language of fish, the deep, slow rhythm of the salmon, the quicksilver music of the trout.

"It canna be helped, Auntie Jan," he said now, knowing he sounded surly, and that it would aggravate her even further. "I've something else to do." He reached down au-tomatically to stroke Murphy, his black Labrador.

"Something more important than keeping this stable on its feet? You know we've had this weekend's riding party booked for months—and how did you think I would manage without your help?"

"Ye can take the party yourself," Callum offered. "Let Dad drive the van."

Janet greeted this with the snort of contempt it deserved. "That would be a fine thing, your father in the jail for drink driving and all the tourists' baggage along with him."

The MacGillivray stables were a family concern, but Callum's father, Tom, had for years been more a liability than an asset. Tom MacGillivray drank, and not even decent whisky but gin, a cheap habit learned during his days in the army. This meant he could be counted on for helping with the morning round of chores, but by midday he was uselessly maudlin and had to be kept out of sight of the customers. By suppertime they had to pry him out of his chair in order to feed him, after which, somewhat revived, he would meander down the road to the pub until closing time.

The stable visitors who did encounter Tom were apt to find him quaint, with his worn tweeds and flat cap, unless they got close enough to smell him.

"Aye." Callum agreed with his aunt reluctantly. "That's true enough. But I still canna take out the riding party."

Tomorrow morning they were expecting a group of six for an easy ride along the Spey valley, with an overnight stop near Ballindalloch. Although the stables still taught the occasional riding class for novices, most of their business had come to depend on the trekking trade. Guided by Callum, a dozen sturdy hill ponies carried riders on jaunts that varied from overnight to a full week, taking in local scenery as well as historic sights. Janet had ongoing arrangements with a number of bed-and-breakfasts that provided accommodation for the guests as well as stabling facilities for the horses, while she ferried the baggage from place to place in the stables' large, green van.

It was a division of duties that she and Callum had perfected, and for a number of years they had worked together as a smoothly oiled unit, a partnership. She stared at him now in consternation, squinting a little against the evening sun. In the merciless light, he could make out new lines around her eyes, and the smears of stable muck on her old jacket.

"Callum, lad," she said more gently, "are ye no feeling well? Is there something wrong with ye?"

He felt ashamed at her concern, but there was no way he could possibly confide in her. "No, Auntie, I'm well enough. It's just that I have some . . . personal . . . things to see to."

Janet's stubby hands balled into fists again. "If by personal, ye mean that blond trollop in Aviemore—"

"It's naught to do with Alison, and she's no a trollop," he snapped back at her, his own temper rising. "And I'll thank ye to keep your opinions of my friends to yourself."

They glared at each other in a standoff until he sighed and gave a dismissive wave of his hand. "Och, I don't blame ye for being angry with me. I've put ye in a difficult position. How would it be if you took the party out, and I drove the van?" That at least he could manage, without abandoning his own plans. "It'd do you good to get a wee bit fresh air," he added, daring her to smile.

Janet snorted and shook her head at him. "You're incorrigible, lad," she said, with exasperated affection. "You'll drive some woman mad, you mark my words. All right, I'll take the ride tomorrow, but you can finish up the evening rounds on your own."

"I don't mind," Callum said honestly. "Thank ye, Auntie Janet."

He watched her fondly as she stumped off towards the house, then he went into the barn to finish giving the horses their evening feed. Murphy settled in the straw with a groan of contentment, and the horses rustled in their stalls, watching him expectantly. Dust motes sparkled like glitter in the slanting sunlight; the air smelled of warm horse and fresh hay, with a faint note of dung and the syrupy ripeness of feed. To Callum, the combination of scents was heaven and had been as long as he could remember.

When he had finished the chores, he went out into the stable yard and stood, gazing at the copper ball of the sun as it dropped beyond the river. Smoke rose lazily from the farmhouse chimney and a light glowed in the kitchen window. Beyond the barn, the ancient cow byre he'd converted into a cottage cast a long, low shadow, and farther still, the pasture sloped gently to a row of birches that shimmered at the water's edge. As he watched, a heron took flight from the reeds.

It was a small world, and for twenty-nine years he had thought it perfect and complete. He'd felt no lack of companionship; he had listened to the guests he guided chatter of children and spouses and lovers with an amused detachment, and he'd taken the wee cuddle when it came his way with nary a thought of commitment. More fool he, he thought now, his lips curving in a wry smile.

He'd drive a woman mad, his auntie had said. How could he tell her it wasna a woman he wanted?

Late again. Alison Grant slammed the door of Tartan Gifts and locked it behind her. *Tartan Tat,* she called the shop when she was feeling uncharitable, which was most of the time. Mrs. Witherspoon, the witch, had made her stay to take inventory on a Friday night, of all times, her excuse being that they needed to get things sorted before the Saturday rush.

Except that there was no Saturday rush—Tartan Gifts not being the sort of shop that ever had customers trampling down the door. The truth of the matter was that Mrs. Witherspoon, with her violet, permed hair and mustached upper lip, thought being shop manager made her God, and that she had it in for Alison in a big way.

Having spent the last two hours on her knees in the shop's back room, among dusty boxes filled with thistle-enameled thimbles, tartan teacups, and refrigerator magnets bearing the simpering likeness of Bonnie Prince Charlie, Alison was very tempted to tell Mrs. Witherspoon to stuff it.

She could have a Saturday morning lie-in for a change, watch the telly, maybe do a bit of shopping herself. Alison lit a cigarette and indulged the fantasy for a moment as she took a deep drag, but by the time she exhaled, reality had reared its ugly head. First of all, she had nothing to go shopping *with*. And she had rent to pay. And then, of course, there was Chrissy.

Alison tugged up her tights where they'd bagged at the knees, eased the strap of her shoulder bag, and started down the hill towards her flat as the lights of Aviemore winked on in the dusk. The road was quiet, except for the traffic in and out of the supermarket. Most shops had closed for the day, but it was still too early for what nightlife the town boasted.

When she reached the forecourt of the flat, she stopped to finish her cigarette before grinding it into the pavement with her heel. She had no place to smoke these days; Chrissy complained if she smoked in the flat, Mrs. Witherspoon would have a coronary if she even thought about smoking in the shop, and Donald . . . The thought of Donald made her grimace.

Around Donald, she washed her hands to get rid of the smoke smell, and sprayed her hair with perfume. He said tobacco kept you from distinguishing the finer points of a whisky, though personally she couldn't tell one of the bloody things from the other, cigarettes or no. Not that she'd tell him that, mind—she'd learned to smile and mumble about "sherried oak" and "herbal bouquets" with the best of them.

She had met Donald Brodie at a party three months ago. He wasn't part of her usual set—but that night he had come with a friend of a friend, slumming, she supposed he'd been, and rattling on to the uneducated about the merits of different whiskies. But he was different, and bonnie enough, and to her surprise she'd found she rather liked listening to him. When he'd noticed her, she had let him pick her up. He'd taken her home to his house by the distillery, and that evening Alison's life had changed forever.

Benvulin House, it was called, after the distillery. It had been built by Donald's great-great-grandfather, he told her, in the Scots baronial style. Oh, it was grand, all stone and warm wood, blazing fires and rich carpets and fabrics. This was how people ought to live, Alison had thought, and in that instant's revelation she had known that it was how *she* wanted to live.

Not like this, she thought now, gazing up at the damp-discolored concrete that made up the square blocks of her building. With a sigh, she went in and began the climb to her third-floor flat. The stairwell always smelled of urine, and as often as not, the lights were out. It worried her, especially on the short winter days when Chrissy came home alone from school in the dark, but it was the best she could afford on her pay.

Nor was there anyone else to help out. Chrissy's dad had buggered off when he learned Alison was pregnant, after claiming the baby wasn't his, and not even Social Services had been able to track him down since. Alison's mum lived on her pension in a two-room flat in Carr-bridge, her dad having died of lung cancer before Chrissy was born.

And any hope Alison had had that Donald might change things was rapidly fading. He called less these days, and when he did he often made excuses for not being able to see her. Like this weekend—he'd told her he had a business meeting, a three-day conference with some European bigwig. "Right," she said aloud, and her voice echoed cavernously in the stairwell. If it were true, which she very much doubted, why hadn't he asked her along? She could have made coffee and been decorative in the corner; she knew when to keep quiet.

But then she'd have had Chrissy with her, and Alison supposed Donald didn't want a nine-year-old running around interrupting his meetings. Not that Chrissy was ever any trouble, but that odious Heather Urquhart, the distillery manager, would complain.

Alison reached the top landing and unlocked the door to the flat, calling out, "Hi, baby, it's me." She sniffed as she hung up her jacket and bag in the tiny entry. Chips and fish sticks again, Chrissy's favorite.

"I've saved you something for tea, Mama," said Chrissy as Alison came into the sitting room and bent down to kiss her daughter.

"Thanks, baby. I could eat a horse."

"Mama!" Chrissy protested, but she giggled, the smile lighting her rosy, heart-shaped face. She sat on the floor in front of the hideous flowered settee—a 1970s hand-me-down from Alison's mum—and she still wore her jumper and tartan uniform skirt. With her feet tucked beneath her you couldn't tell that one leg was twisted and shorter than the other. Chrissy had been born that way, a congenital defect, the doctors had told Alison, but it never seemed to occur to the girl that she couldn't do anything the other children did.

Tonight she had the telly on as usual without the sound. She liked it for "company," she said, when Alison teased her. Open on the floor beside her was one of her inevitable horse books, and lined up beside the cushions she'd placed in a square was a row of her plastic replica horses.

"Who've we got today, then?" asked Alison, kicking off her heels and squatting beside Chrissy as she massaged her aching toes.

"Man o' War. And this one's the Godolphin Arabian." Chrissy indicated a slightly smaller pony. "And this one's Eclipse."

"Are they going to have a race?"

Chrissy rolled her eyes. " 'Course not. They're at stud. That's the mares' barn over there." She pointed at another cushion.

"Oh, sorry." It was Alison's turn to roll her eyes. What business did a child her age have knowing all about mares and studs and breeding procedures? And where had it come from, this passion for horses? "Equimania," Donald called it. He found it amusing, and in one of his more benevolent moods he'd promised the girl a pony.

"Bastard," Alison whispered, standing. Had he known what that promise would mean to Chrissy? And to Alison, who'd thought perhaps he meant to move them into Benvulin House, for how else could they stable and feed a horse? But every day it became clearer that it had been a promise he hadn't meant to keep, and Alison could happily have killed him.

"Did anyone ring?" she asked, although she knew Chrissy would have told her straightaway if Donald had returned her call.

"Callum," answered Chrissy. "He said Max had a sore hoof. The blacksmith had to come today."

Alison frowned but didn't say anything. She'd have a word with Callum MacGillivray—she didn't like him ringing up when Chrissy was home alone.

That had been a mistake on Alison's part, going out with Callum, although he'd seemed harmless enough when she'd met him through the shop. His aunt Janet had a standing order for the small horse-shaped pins that she gave to the stables' trekkers as souvenirs, and Callum had come in a few times to collect the shipment. A looker, she'd thought him, with his lean, muscular body, his sandy hair drawn back in a ponytail, his Hollywood stubble. And when he hadn't said much, she'd thought him mysterious. It was only when they'd gone out a few times that she'd discovered the man was incapable of having a conversation that didn't include horses, fishing, or Highland history. If you wanted to know where the Wolf of Badenoch had made his last stand, or where Cluny McPherson had hidden from the duke of Cumberland's men, Callum could tell you, in nauseating detail. Otherwise, he was useless.

And worse, although MacGillivray's Stables were just up the road from Benvulin, Callum lived in a hovel of a cottage that made Alison's flat look palatial. Chrissy, of course, found the place fascinating and seemed equally taken with Callum, but Alison had been glad of an excuse to cut off the relationship when Donald came into her life.

Except that she hadn't counted on Callum being unable to grasp the fact that nothing was going to happen between them. She'd told him flat out, finally, that he just wasn't her type, but still he hadn't given up. He rang every few days, and if she wasn't at home he talked to Chrissy. Not that Chrissy minded a chat about horse lineaments and trout flies, but it made Alison uneasy that he would use the child to get to her. His latest ploy had been an offer of free riding lessons for Chrissy. Against her better judgment, Alison had accepted, hoping that the lessons might make up a bit for Donald's failure to produce the pony.

Damn Donald, she thought as she went into the kitchen and pulled the plate of soggy fish and chips from the microwave. Where was he this weekend, and why in bloody hell hadn't he rung?

"You must see Loch Garten," said Donald Brodie. "The ospreys are nesting. We'll organize a wee jaunt on Sunday— if John will let us, that is," he added, with a mischievous glance at his friend.

They were all still gathered in the Inneses' sitting room, replete with coffee, whisky, and John Innes's chocolate mousse. Lilting bagpipes played in the background, the fire crackled, and if not for her worry about Hazel and the faint nag of homesickness, Gemma would have been quite content. She'd been sure to claim a seat on one of the two sofas, between Hazel and the arm, leaving a discomfited Martin Gilmore to take a chair on the opposite side of the fire. Hazel sat on the edge of her seat, twisting her whisky glass round and round in her hands. When Gemma had touched her arm in mute query, Hazel had merely shaken her head and looked away.

"Osprey?" Gemma asked now, breaking off her chat

with Louise Innes about the Chelsea Flower Show. "I thought they were extinct."

"They vanished from the Highlands for more than fifty years," John told her. "But in 1959 a pair established a nest site at Loch Garten, and now there are over a hundred pairs. They're protected by the RSPB, of course, but eggs are still stolen occasionally."

"Crime pays, unfortunately," agreed Donald. "And collectors, whether of rare whiskies or birds' eggs, are not always quite sane."

Louise frowned. "The police should do more. I'm sure if they only—"

"I'm sure the police are overworked and understaffed," Gemma blurted, her irritation with the woman's critical tone overcoming her manners. "Without chasing after egg thieves. I mean . . ." She trailed off, embarrassed, as she realized everyone was staring at her. Shrugging, she said apologetically, "Sorry. A bit of defensiveness goes with the job, I suppose."

When the faces around her remained blank, she cursed herself for an idiot. She'd blown her own cover—not that she'd seriously intended to keep her job a secret. "Hazel didn't tell you, then?"

"Tell us what?" asked Louise.

Well, there was no help for it now. "I'm a police officer. CID." Seeing their blank expressions, she added, "Criminal Investigation."

Martin gaped at her. "You're a detective?"

"An inspector," Gemma admitted, beginning to enjoy herself. "Metropolitan Police."

Pascal Benoit gave a delighted chuckle. "Brains as well as beauty, I see. You will give Heather some competition this weekend."

Had everyone conveniently forgotten that Hazel was

a psychologist, and a licensed therapist? wondered Gemma, incensed on her friend's behalf. And Louise—Louise's job must take considerable skill and business acumen. But before she could protest, Heather Urquhart stretched languidly and smiled her little triangular smile, saying, "Well, it's a good thing Donald's family stopped smuggling whisky a few years back." The woman suddenly reminded Gemma of Sid, their black cat at home. There was something feline about the way she sat curled in her chair, with her feet tucked up beneath her short, black skirt, running her fingers through the ends of her hair as if grooming herself.

"Och, Heather will have her wee joke," said Donald, with a wink at Gemma. "The truth is, Benvulin was one of the first distilleries to be licensed. That was in 1823," he explained, apparently for Gemma's benefit, "when the duke of Gordon managed to convince the government to legalize the distilling of whisky. Now, as to what the Brodies did before that, I *canna* answer.

"But what I can tell ye," he continued, lifting his glass and settling back in his chair, "is that making whisky was women's work. It was the wives managed the stills while the husbands were out tending their sheep, or raiding cattle. So our Heather's no setting a precedent." He switched his gaze to Hazel. "And wasn't it your great-grandmother, Hazel, who took on the family business when her husband died?"

"I-I've no idea." Hazel shifted uncomfortably. "That was a long time ago."

"But that's where you're wrong," Donald said softly. "That's your Londoner's viewpoint. To a Highlander, a hundred years is nothing at all."

* * *

"You'll go for a walk with me, Hazel?" asked Donald Brodie, when the party began to break up. "Just so you remember what a fine thing a Highland night can be." Beneath the jocular tone, there was a note almost of pleading.

Hazel had stood for a moment, speechless, gazing up at him, then she'd clasped Gemma's arm. "I— We'd better turn in. We've a big day tomorrow."

"You'll need a good night's sleep to tackle John's porridge in the morning," agreed Louise, with such deadpan delivery that Gemma wasn't sure she'd meant it as a joke.

Gemma took the opportunity to bid everyone good night, then steered Hazel firmly out the door, determined to get her friend on her own. Their feet crunched on the gravel as they crossed from the house to the barn. The crisp air smelled of pine and juniper, and the mist rolling in from the river held the earthy dampness of marsh.

Hazel halted just outside the door to their room and tilted her head back. "Donald was right," she said softly. "The sky's like black velvet. I'd forgotten . . ." She shivered convulsively.

"Come on, before you catch your death." Gemma pulled Hazel into the room and shut the door. "We can stargaze some other time. Right now you're going to tell me exactly what the hell is going on between you and Donald Brodie."

"It was the summer after I left university," said Hazel. She'd stalled, pacing, until Gemma had thrust a mug of hot Horlicks into her hands and pointed at the armchair. "I needed a break," Hazel went on slowly. "And I wanted to see the Highlands again. Cooking was the one thing I could do, so I got a job catering for shooting and fishing

parties." Making a rueful face, she blew across the top of her drink.

"Go on," urged Gemma, settling herself at the head of one of the beds. Their room was small but pleasant, with dark beams in a whitewashed ceiling, and snowy puffs of duvets on the beds. "Was it hard?"

"I'd no idea how primitive some places still were, the shooting lodges. There were days I had to use the floor for a chopping block. It gave me confidence, though— after that I knew I could cook anything, anywhere."

"And Donald?"

"Donald was a guest at a lodge near Braemar, where I was cooking. One day he stayed in from the moor to help me, when I had more guests than planned and not enough food to go round. After that we were—he was—" Hazel shook her head. "I never believed in love at first sight until that day. We were giddy from then on, consumed by it. I stayed months longer than I'd intended, missing the start of the Christmas term for my second degree. We were so sure that we were meant for each other," she added, her voice wistful.

"And then when Donald found out who I was, who my family were, that clinched it. It was to be a dynastic union; I was the ideal queen of his little empire."

"I don't understand," said Gemma. "What had your family to do with it?"

"Whisky," Hazel said shortly, sipping at her Horlicks. "Everything comes back to whisky, in case you hadn't noticed. My family had owned a distillery, almost as long as Donald's had owned Benvulin, and Donald knew he would take over Benvulin when his father retired. He saw us as the merger of two great names, two traditions."

"That doesn't sound such a bad thing."

"Oh, but that's when it got complicated." Hazel's laugh held no humor. "It turns out our families were the Scottish version of the Montagues and the Capulets. Donald had some idea—only he hadn't bothered to tell me—but I hadn't a clue. I had wondered why he seemed so reluctant to introduce me to his father."

"His father didn't approve?"

"You could say that." Hazel's lips formed a tight line, and she resumed her pacing.

"But surely you could have worked something out, given time—"

"No. The distillery meant too much to Donald. And my family . . . When I told my father, he was appalled. But he wouldn't explain why there was such bad blood between the Brodies and the Urquharts, and he died not long afterwards."

"Oh, Hazel, I'm so sorry," said Gemma, feeling an ache of sympathy.

Hazel sighed and sat lightly on the edge of her bed. "We left Carnmore when I was fourteen. My father sold off the stock and equipment and took a job managing a brewery in Newcastle. I never knew him all that well, really. They sent me away to school, in Hampshire—that's where I met Louise—and they cut themselves off from everything Scots, including family here."

"And your cousin, Heather?" asked Gemma, thinking of the woman's obvious antipathy towards Hazel.

"Heather's father was my dad's younger brother; he works for a whisky distributor in Inverness. Heather was just a year younger than I am, both of us only daughters. She loved Carnmore with a passion, and she idolized me. I don't think she ever forgave me for leaving, or Dad for letting Carnmore go."

"If Donald's father disapproved of the Urquharts so strongly, how did Heather end up working at Benvulin?"

"Having your only son marry an Urquhart was a far cry from hiring an Urquhart as menial office help, which is how Heather started there. I even suspect it gave Bruce Brodie a sense of satisfaction to have an Urquhart in his employ."

"What did you do—after you and Donald—"

"I came back to London, took my second degree. I met Tim, and after a bit we got married. We were . . . comfortable . . . together, and I told myself that was the basis for a good marriage, that what I'd had with Donald wouldn't have lasted. By the time I started to doubt my judgment, Holly had come along, and I—well, you make the best of things, don't you?"

Gemma gazed at her friend in astonishment. "Why did you never tell me any of this? I thought we were close, and I never dreamed you were unhappy!"

"I'm sorry," Hazel told her, coloring. "I suppose it was partly therapist's habit—you get used to listening, not confiding—and partly that I couldn't stop paddling. If I stopped making my life *true,* every day, I was afraid I would drown."

"But— How could you— You have everything, the ideal life—"

"Everything but someone to talk to. Tim didn't—Tim doesn't want to hear about my childhood, my life before I met him. I felt as if I'd lost a part of myself, the piece that held all the links together."

"And then Donald came back into your life?"

Hazel nodded. "I bumped into him one day, literally, at the organic market in Camden Passage. It only seemed natural that we should go to lunch, catch up on our lives. Just for old times' sake. And after that—"

Gemma realized that in spite of her suspicions at dinner, she hadn't *really* believed it until that moment. "All this time, you've been having an affair—"

"No!" Hazel stood, hugging herself as if her chest ached. "I haven't slept with him! We just—he'd ring me and we'd talk. It made me feel alive again, truly alive, for the first time in years. We'd meet for a coffee or lunch whenever Donald came to London on business . . . It wasn't— We never talked about— This weekend is the first time—"

"You were going to see what you were missing? And use me as a safety net in case you decided you didn't want to go through with it? Or as an alibi if you did?" Gemma was surprised by the strength of her own anger. She felt used, betrayed.

"Oh, Gemma, I'm so sorry." Hazel's dark eyes filled with tears. "I should never have come. And I should never have asked you, hoping you'd protect me from myself. I've made a dreadful mistake. Tomorrow, I'll tell Donald it's no good. We can get the train back—"

"No." Gemma felt suddenly, enormously, weary. "You had better be sure of what you want, really sure. There's no point in going back divided—you've too much at stake to live it halfway."

Hazel looked back at her, then nodded. She scrubbed a tear from her cheek with the back of her hand. "You're disappointed in me, aren't you, Gemma?"

Gemma thought about it. "No . . . at least . . . not you, exactly. It's just that, after my marriage to Rob turned out to be such a disaster, I based my idea of what made a family work on you and Tim—that's what gave me the courage to move in with Duncan—and now I find it was all a sham. It makes me feel—odd." She rose and slipped back into her jacket. "You go on to bed. I'm going out for

a bit of air." Giving Hazel a shaky smile, she let herself
out into the darkened drive.

She stood, gazing up at the stars, now mist-obscured,
and listening to the faint creaking of the night. What she
wanted, she realized with a shiver, was not air, but to
ring Duncan and assure herself that her world was still
intact.

4

O what lies younder north of Tweed?
Monsters and hillmen, hairy kneed
And music that wad wauk the deid!
To venture there were risky O!

The fearsome haggis haunts the snaw
The kelpy waits—your banes to gnaw
There's nocht to eat but oatmeal—raw
BUT I'M STILL TOLD THERE'S WHISKY O!
                        —ANONYMOUS SCOTTISH POET

Carnmore, November 1898

BY MORNING, THE wind had died, and the world
outside the farmhouse lay encased in a rippling
blanket of white. This Will knew only from peering
out the front windows, as the back of the house was
completely blocked by drifts.

He had spent the remainder of the night dozing in the
parlor armchair, waking periodically to stoke the fire,
watching his mother minister to his increasingly restless
and delirious father. By daybreak, Charles had begun

muttering and clutching at his throat, as if it pained him, and seemed soothed only by spoons of hot water with whisky and honey.

As the cold morning light crept into the room, Will saw that his mother's face was gray with exhaustion. Her thick, dark hair had escaped from its knot in wayward tendrils, and he noticed, for the first time, a single thread of silver.

"He's burning with fever," she said softly, resting the backs of her fingers fleetingly against his father's forehead.

"Mam," Will whispered, "let me look after him. You get some rest now."

She shook her head. "No, Will. I'll bide here. There's porridge in the kitchen for you, and then you'd best see if you can get to the beasts."

With a last glance at his father's flushed face, Will left the parlor. The kitchen was bitterly cold, in spite of the stove, and he shivered as he ate his breakfast. Then he wrapped up as well as he could and, taking the shovel they kept handy in the porch, ventured out the front door.

His boots sank into the powdery snow—a bad sign. Once an ice crust formed over the top it would be easier walking, but for now he'd have to wade or shovel his way through the drifts to the barn and distillery buildings. Beyond the near field Carn More, the hill from which the distillery took its name, rose steeply, its rugged granite face softened by the white icing of snow.

As he watched, the sun rose, gilding the march of the Ladder Hills with a glistening rose as delicate as his mother's best satin gown. The air was so still it felt charged with silence, as if the world were waiting for something to happen.

Will held his breath for a moment, listening, then picked up the spade and dug in.

It took him almost an hour to reach the barn. Wiping a hand across his sweating brow, he stretched his shoulders and contemplated the drifts that reached all the way to the eaves. He could hear the animals moving restively about inside, and he felt a moment's stab of despair at the enormity of the task before him.

Not that it was the first time Carnmore had been snowed in, but always before, he and his father had managed together. He pushed away the unbidden thought of his wee sister, Charlotte, taken from them by a fever at less than a year old. But his father was older and stronger—surely he would be all right.

Will began digging with renewed energy, trying to blot out his fear with the thunk of the spade. Once he'd cleared the snow from the barn door, he was glad to slip into the relative warmth of the stone building. He moved among the shuffling beasts—his father's prize dairy cows, his father's horse, and the pack ponies that carried Carnmore whisky down to the coast—filling troughs and lining the stalls with fresh hay.

Although some of the Speyside distilleries now had their own railway lines, ponies remained the only reliable way to get whisky out of the Braes, even in good weather. The paths the smugglers had used to move whisky down through the Ladder Hills now carried a legitimate product. As for supplies, they warehoused enough barley to last the season, water flowed freely year-round from the Carn More spring, and the peats came from their own moss.

When he'd finished in the barn, Will cleared a path to the distillery easily enough, as the buildings themselves had blocked the worst of the snow. But once inside the main production house, he stood for a moment, trying to decide what to do. Distilling was a continuous process, made up of many interrelated steps. Barley lay soaking in the steeps, waiting for the maltster to determine when it had absorbed just the right amount of moisture; then the barley was spread on the mesh floor of the malt barn to germinate, after which it would dry in the peat fires of the kiln.

Once dried, the malt was ground into grist in the mill, and from there it was funneled into the enormous wooden mash tuns, where hot water would release the sugar from the grains. From the mash tuns the sugary liquid, called wort, ran into the great fermenting vessels. This was the brewer's domain: it was he who added the yeast, he who decided when the wash was ready for distilling. Then the stillman would take over, running the wash into the wash charger, and from it into the first of the great copper stills.

Carnmore used three stills rather than the traditional two, one wash still and two spirit stills. His father claimed that it was this further distillation that gave Carnmore whisky its smooth, light taste, and it was a superstitious practice among most distillers that nothing which gave a whisky its distinct character should be changed—not a cobweb swept away nor a dent repaired in the copper stills.

From the final still, the whisky ran through the glass cabinet of the still safe, where it was carefully monitored by both the stillman and the distillery's excise officer. This was raw, colorless stuff, not yet deserving of the name Scotch whisky. It would take at least five years of aging in oak casks in the earthen-floored warehouse before it would be bottled under the distillery's name, or sold to blenders, and some was kept to age longer. It gave

Will pause to think that he would be near his father's age before some of the whisky now being casked was ready to drink.

Each of these processes had its own time schedule, and each required several men as well as a skilled supervisor. How, Will wondered, was he to manage on his own?

He could make a start, at least, by lighting the office fire. Going in, he lit the oil lamp on his father's desk, then quickly arranged peats and sticks in the fireplace. As the flames caught, he sat for a moment, warming himself and taking comfort from the familiar objects. The great leather-bound ledger lay open on the desk, his father's reading spectacles resting atop it. Along one wall, oak shelves held ranks of bottles covered with a fine layer of dust. The carriage clock ticked loudly in the silence.

Since he had left the Chapeltown school at fourteen, Will had chafed at the limited life of the distillery, dreaming of going to Edinburgh to study medicine like his Grant grandfather. But his father had believed him too young to go so far from home; nor had Charles been willing to give up his own dream of Will continuing in the family business.

Now, as Will recalled the helplessness he'd felt that morning when faced with his father's illness, he wondered if he really was suited for the pursuit of medicine. Then he thought of his father's whispered entreaty to take care of the distillery, and he stood, leaving the old office chair rocking. He could at least turn the germinating malt on his own, and ready the peat fires for the kiln and the stills.

Stepping out into the alleyway between the production house and the malt barn, he stopped, listening, and relief flooded through him. He heard voices, carrying clearly in the still air. Will waded to the rise above the track that led *down to the village and shaded his eyes with his hand. A dozen dark specks moved against the whiteness; it was a good half of the distillery crew, shoveling their way up the track.*

Will shouted and waved, a voice shouted something unintelligible back, and Will began digging his way to meet them.

The men made good progress and soon met Will, with much slapping of arms and thumping of shoulders. It was all the men from Chapeltown—those who lived outside the village would have a more difficult time of it.

"Aye, it's only a half day's work lost," said Alasdair Smith, the stillman, as they swung down their spades again to widen Will's path. Smith, a large, burly man with a red beard, was no relation to the Smiths of The Glenlivet but always made a point to tell new acquaintances that he had just as good a nose for whisky. "No self-respecting Hielander would let a bittie snow get the better o' him," he added, his teeth showing white against his beard as he grinned.

"It's a bad omen," said John MacGregor, the excise man, "I'm telling ye, such a blow this early in the year." MacGregor was a sharp-nosed, precise man, and kept his distance from the others, as was usually the case with the government officers. But Will had always found him kind, in his fussy way, and MacGregor had never minded taking the time to answer a boy's questions. Now, he said more quietly to Will, "It's a good thing your faither's safe in Edinburgh, laddie. He'd ha been in a right bother this morning—"

"But he's not in Edinburgh," interrupted Will, and the other men fell silent as he told them of his father's arrival in the night. "And now he's burning with a fever," Will added, "and his throat paining him somethin' fierce."

Seeing the look Smith shot at MacGregor, he said, "What is it?" When the men hesitated, he barked, "Tell me!" The note of command in his voice surprised him— for a moment, he had sounded like his father.

"Och, laddie, it's nothing to worry ye," said Smith, but his eyes didn't meet Will's. "It's just somethin' I heard up at the Pole—seems there's a fever going round in Edinburgh . . ." The Pole Inn was the nearest public house, at the head of the Braes.

"It's bad, isn't it?" Will pushed him, knowing the answer even as he spoke.

Smith turned to his assistant, Kenneth Baxter. "You, Kenny, go back to the village, quick now, and fetch the nurse here. And you, Will," he continued, this time meeting Will's gaze, "you get back to the house. Your mam'll be needin' ye."

Gemma climbed slowly from the depths of sleep, shedding the disquiet of her dreams like layers of skin. Then, full consciousness arriving with the disorientation that often accompanies the first night spent in a strange place, she sat up.

Innesfree. The barn conversion. Hazel. The pieces clicked together, and she looked towards the other bed. There was no tousled dark head on the pillow, no sound from the bathroom. Hazel must have already dressed and gone out.

When Gemma had come in from her walk the previous evening, Hazel had been in bed, her light out. Although doubting that her friend was asleep, Gemma had been relieved not to talk further until she'd had a chance to sort out her reactions to Hazel's revelations. She'd rung Kincaid, hoping to talk with him, but much to her surprise, the line had been engaged.

Now she pushed her hair from her face and swung her legs out of bed, curling her toes against the chill of the tiled floor. What had she been thinking last night, to encourage Hazel to pursue her relationship with Donald Brodie? It was not just mad, but dangerous. Not that Tim Cavendish would ever hurt Hazel, Gemma told herself in an effort to still the sudden thumping of her heart, but she'd seen marriages disintegrate too often to take the possibility of violence lightly.

Glancing at the clock, she saw that there was still an hour to breakfast. She had plenty of time to talk some sense into her friend.

Showered and dressed, Gemma stepped out and looked around her. Yesterday, she had only seen the property in the fading light of early evening. Now, it lay before her, golden and gleaming in the morning sun. It was still cool, wreaths of mist drifted up from the river, and birdsong trilled up and down the scale. The air had a fresh, evergreen scent to it, and when Gemma breathed, it felt like wine slipping down into her lungs.

There was no one visible in the garden, and on an impulse, Gemma turned away from the house and took the path leading towards the river. The track ran along the outer edge of the pasture that lay between the river and the road, winding through a stand of birch and rowans. It was still and silent beneath the trees, and after the first few yards, the thicket enclosed Gemma in a green and dappled world. Looking down, she saw the tightly curled fronds of fiddlehead ferns, and a stand of bluebells. Enchanted, she knelt to examine the flowers more closely. The rich scent of damp earth tickled her nose, and a closer inspection of the ground revealed a shiny beetle making its determined way over a fallen log. *Kit would love this,* Gemma thought as she rose, and was struck by a wave of longing for her family.

That thought brought back her concern for Hazel in full force, and as she walked on, Gemma mulled over what she might say to her friend. The woods gave way to heather and tussocks, then the path angled sharply to the right to follow a lightly wooded fence line towards the river. Here the Spey widened in a gentle curve, and the shallow water near the shore grew thick with reeds and marsh grasses.

As Gemma stepped gingerly up to the bank, a duck took flight from the cover of the reeds with a sound like a shot. Gemma started reflexively, jumping back and stepping in a boggy spot. She'd begun to laugh at her own case of nerves when she caught a glimpse of motion off to the right. Two people stood farther down the shore, half-hidden by a clump of trees. Hazel, and Donald Brodie.

They stood a foot apart, their heads bent towards each other, and as Gemma watched, Donald raised his hand to Hazel's cheek. The murmur of their voices reached her, carried by a shift in the wind. Hazel shook her head and stepped back; Donald reached for her but didn't pull her closer.

Gemma hesitated, torn between her desire to call out— to stop Hazel being such a fool—and reluctance to interrupt such obvious intimacy. Then Donald bent down, taking Hazel's face in his hands and pressing his mouth to hers. After a moment, Hazel's arms slipped round his neck.

Feeling the blood rise to her cheeks, Gemma turned away and started back to the house, all pleasure in the day forgotten.

*   *   *

When Gemma reached the B&B, she found Louise Innes in the vegetable and herb garden at the back, snipping sprigs of thyme into a basket.

"For the breakfast plates," explained Louise, indicating her handiwork, "and mint for the fruit." She straightened up and tucked her clippers into a pocket in the apron she wore beneath her cardigan. "Did you have a nice walk?"

"Yes, thanks," answered Gemma, looking round at the neat garden. The smell of frying bacon drifted enticingly from the house, but she'd lost her appetite.

Louise studied her, then gestured towards the toolshed at the bottom of the garden. "You look a bit peaky. We've a few minutes before breakfast. Come and have a cuppa."

"What? Out here?" asked Gemma, puzzled.

"It's my retreat." Louise led her into the shed. A small window set in each side provided filtered morning light, benches held tools and potting equipment, and on a camp stove, a kettle bubbled merrily. "That's the downside to running a B&B, I've discovered—lack of privacy. Even though we don't open our bedroom to the guests, we're still always on call. This gives me at least the illusion of getting away."

"It's like a doll's house," Gemma said delightedly. "And I'm honored to be invited." She looked away from the intricate spiderweb decorating one corner, repressing a shudder.

Louise took two mugs from a shelf, wiped them out with a corner of her apron, and removed two tea bags from a canister. While the bags were steeping, she pulled a stool from beneath the bench and overturned a pail. "You take the elegant seat," she said, motioning Gemma to the stool. "It's a bit primitive, but then I don't usually entertain out here."

Gemma accepted a mug as she watched Louise tip the

tea bags directly into a compost pail. "Did you garden before you came here?"

"Not in Edinburgh. We lived in a tenement building, where the most I could manage was a pot of geraniums in the kitchen window. But I helped my mum when I was a child."

Gemma thought of her own parents' flat above the bakery in Leyton. Her mother had never even managed a pot of geraniums. "You're English?"

"Yes, from Kent, originally. But my parents divorced when I was thirteen, and I went to boarding school in Hampshire. That's how I came to know Hazel."

Gemma came to a decision. "Louise, I'm really worried about Hazel. I know you're old friends—"

"You're talking about Donald, aren't you? I didn't approve of this arrangement, if that's what you mean. Home wrecker is generally not part of my job description." Some of the previous evening's edge had returned to Louise's voice.

"I'm sorry. I wasn't criticizing you. I just thought you might have been able to discourage her, if you knew—"

"I've had nothing from Hazel in ten years but a scribbled note on a Christmas card. I don't think my opinion would have counted for much. And besides, we can't afford Donald Brodie's ill will. He's too—"

A distant crack reverberated in the still air. This time Gemma had no doubt it was a gunshot. She jumped up, spilling her tea. "What—"

"It's just someone potting at rabbits," Louise said, but she stood and poured out her mug. "This is shooting country, after all, and one has to keep in trim for the Glorious Twelfth." Seeing Gemma's blank expression, she added, "The Twelfth of August. The beginning of grouse season."

"Oh, yes," Gemma murmured, still listening for an outcry, or another shot. She stepped outside and Louise joined her. "It's just that in London—"

"You'll get used to it," Louise assured her. "People here basically shoot anything that moves. Grouse, pheasant, ptarmigan, deer—"

John Innes came out the back door, looking around in visible agitation. "Louise!" he called, spotting them. "I've guests at the table, and the plates not ready."

"Sorry," Louise said to Gemma as she picked up her abandoned basket. "Duty calls."

When Louise had followed her husband into the house, Gemma stood alone in the garden, listening for the sound of another shot.

Saturday dawned clear and fair, and after a fitful night's sleep, Kincaid set about trying to make the best of the day for the boys. He prepared boiled eggs with soldiers, which Toby loved, and coffee with steamed milk, Kit's special Saturday treat. Although Toby happily dunked the toast strips into his egg, Kincaid caught Kit studying him as if puzzled by his industrious cheer.

When they'd finished the washing up, they all trooped outside for the promised game of football. Their tiny back garden backed up to a gated communal garden, an advantage they could not ordinarily have afforded in London, if not for their good fortune in leasing the house from his guv'nor's sister. Both boys and dogs had spent many hours playing under the spreading trees, and there was enough lawn to lay out sticks for their football goalposts.

They chose sides, Kincaid against the boys, and for half an hour, he was able to lose himself in running and shouting, and in expending some of his anger in vicious kicks at the ball. The dogs ran alongside them, barking excitedly. At last a particularly fierce scramble for the ball brought them all down in a tangled heap of arms and legs. Toby, spying a friend at the other end of the garden, jumped up and raced off with a four-year-old's energy, while Kincaid and Kit lay panting in the sun.

Knowing he must grab the opportunity, Kincaid plunged in. "Kit, I've had a letter from your grandmother—or rather from your grandmother's solicitor."

"Solicitor?" Kit sat up, his face going pale beneath its rosy flush.

"She sent a copy to Ian as well. It seems she thinks you'd be better off in her care. She—"

"You mean live with her?" Kit was already shaking his head, his breath coming fast. "I won't! You know I won't. I'd rather—"

"Hold on, Kit." Kincaid put a restraining hand on the boy's shoulder. "Let me finish. Yes, that's what she wants, but that doesn't mean it's going to happen. You know I want you here with me—with us—always. But in order to ensure that, we're going to have to plan our response, and that means talking things out. Okay?"

Kit nodded, slowly, but his eyes were still wide with shock.

"Okay. Good lad." Kincaid smiled at him. "I rang Ian last night." He'd sat up late at the kitchen table, rereading Eugenia's letter and drinking too many cups of tea from Gemma's teapot. His ex-wife's mother had always been difficult, but after her only child's murder her behavior seemed to disintegrate beyond reason. Although she claimed to have Kit's interests in mind, she tormented the boy mercilessly, blaming him for his mother's death, and both Kincaid and Ian had severely limited her visitations. Vic's father, Robert Potts, was a mild-mannered man who seemed unwilling—or unable—to stand up to his wife's bullying. Now it seemed Eugenia was prepared to carry out the threats she'd been making for months.

Although Kincaid had been sorely tempted to ring Gemma, in the end he'd decided there was no point in spoiling her weekend with worry when there was nothing she could do.

When the hands on the kitchen clock crept round to midnight, he had picked up the phone and called Ian Mc-Clellan in Canada, catching him just home from his classes at the university. Kincaid explained the latest development, then, when Ian had finished swearing, he'd asked, "Could you write a letter giving Kit permission to live with me, and stating your reasons? You might have it notarized for good measure."

"I can do that," Ian agreed, "although I don't think any halfway decent family judge would give Eugenia the time of day. I'm sure at Kit's age his wishes would be considered paramount. Still . . ."

"You think we should consult a solicitor? We'll have to act together on this." Kincaid and Ian had developed an odd but workable relationship over the past year, rather like ex-spouses sharing custody of a child. Except, of course, that Kincaid had no legal rights.

"I think we'll have to," Ian said with a sigh, leaving Kincaid wondering if he were replying to the question or the statement. "Look, Duncan . . ." Ian paused for a long moment. "We've tiptoed around this for a good while, but I think now we're going to have to talk about it. Vic and I never did. We just let it fester, and I wish—well, things might have been different if we'd got it out in the open. What I'm saying is—it's not that I don't want to take responsibility for Kit, but if you were to prove paternity, there'd be no question of Eugenia interfering."

Of course, Kincaid had considered the possibility of testing but had been unwilling to subject Kit to the emotional stress such a procedure would entail, unless it was absolutely necessary—but that seemed to have come to pass.

Now, he said, "Kit, there is one simple way we could put a stop to this. We can prove you're my son."

"You mean . . . a test?"

At the look of horror on the boy's face, Kincaid hastened to reassure him. "Don't worry, it's painless. They just take a bit of saliva, a swab from inside your cheek—"

"No. I don't want to do it."

"It's nothing, I promise—"

"No, it's not that. I—I wouldn't want Ian to think I—"

"It was Ian's suggestion, Kit. He wants what's best for—"

"No," Kit said again, shaking his head more emphatically. He rose into a crouch, like a runner in starting position. "I'm not having any test. And I'm not going to live with the old witch. I'll run away first. Tess and I could manage on our own."

Kincaid tried to push aside the sudden vision of Kit living on the street, dirty and emaciated, curled up on a curbside blanket with the dog, but his worry and exasperation got the better of him. "Kit, don't be ridiculous. It's not going to come to that. If you'll just—"

"No." Kit pushed himself to his feet and looked down at Kincaid. His mouth was set in an implacable line that reminded Kincaid very much of Vic at her most stubborn. "You're always telling me to take things on faith," he said. "Well, now you can take me on faith, or not at all."

*   *   *

The group gathered after breakfast in the farmhouse kitchen, a large room that John Innes had equipped with a commercial range and a spacious center work island. Open racks on the walls held plates, the original cast-iron sink was set beneath the windows, and bunches of Louise's dried herbs hung from the ceiling. Between the kitchen and the back door was a scullery, with a glass-fronted gun case on one wall, while shelves on the other wall held Louise's flower baskets and a row of muddy boots.

The kitchen was a pleasant room, with space for the class to work comfortably together. John had divided them into pairs; Gemma with Hazel, Heather with Pascal, leaving Donald partnered with Martin Gilmore. If Brodie was unhappy with the arrangement, he concealed it, joking with Martin as they strained the broth John had put on to simmer the night before.

They were to prepare the first and last courses for that evening's dinner. First, a Brie and celery soup, a combination of ingredients that made Gemma wrinkle her nose in doubt, but John assured them it would be delicious. Beside her, Hazel chopped celery with quick efficiency.

"This soup is usually made with chicken stock," John explained, "but in deference to Hazel, we're using a veggie stock today."

Louise, passing through the kitchen on her rounds of tidying, gave him an *I told you so* look.

Shrugging, John said, "Och, the wee woman's always right. She told me yesterday to be prepared for vegetarian guests, and I paid her no mind."

"Oh, I find that women are occasionally wrong." Brodie's teeth flashed in his red beard as he smiled. "And it's the poor wee lads that suffer the consequences."

Hazel flushed, her fingers tightening on the knife.

"You do eat fish, don't you, Hazel?" put in John, with a quick glance at his friend. Looking relieved when she nodded, he added, "Tonight we're going to make it up to you. A grilled salmon with basil and red pepper pesto; *mange-tout,* blanched, then sautéed in a garlic butter sauce; scalloped red potatoes with sun-dried tomatoes and goat cheese." John's usually sallow complexion had taken on the glow of enthusiasm. "This is wild salmon, of course, caught just this morning. Wouldn't dream of using farm-raised."

"Farm-raised salmon provides jobs," interjected Martin, who obviously wasn't letting the acceptance of his brother's hospitality interfere with his freedom of expression. "Not just sport for the rich."

"It's not just the tenants who fish the rivers," corrected John. "It's the local folk as well."

"Martin does have a point," Donald said mildly, looking up from the onion he was now dicing. "How many stretches of the river can you name that aren't leased for the season?"

John scowled at him, unmollified. "Nevertheless. We're talking about cooking, and the farm-raised salmon has no taste." He unwrapped the large wedge of Brie he'd pulled from the fridge. "We'll remove the rind and cube the cheese," he told the group, "but we won't add it to the soup until just before serving." He sliced a chunk of butter into a large pot. "Onions and celery in now, please," he directed them when the butter began to bubble. "And the herbs," he added, nodding to Heather, who had been chopping fresh thyme and marjoram from the garden.

Heather Urquhart had exchanged last night's sleek, black suit for jeans and a pullover, and had tied back her hair with a businesslike cord. "Yes, sir, please, sir," she said, rolling her eyes at John as she scraped the herbs into the pot with the flat of her knife. "I'll just be tugging my forelock, sir."

"That's the first rule of the kitchen," replied John, good-naturedly. "The chef expects absolute and immediate obedience from the staff. But seeing as I'm a benevolent despot, I've arranged a lunchtime outing for ye."

"*You* have?" queried Donald, his eyebrows raised.

"Well, with a wee bit cooperation from Donald," admitted John. "But I did the food myself—a cold pheasant pie—for a picnic at Benvulin. And Hazel, I didn't forget about ye. I'll put together something special for you before you go."

"It's all right, John," Hazel assured him, with the first smile Gemma had seen all morning. "I'll be just fine with an apple and a biscuit. Now what do we do?" She gestured at the pot.

John instructed Pascal to stir a few tablespoons of flour into the sautéed vegetables, before slowly adding stock. Then he gave them a challenging look. "Now, while that simmers for a bit, we're going to make pastry."

"Highland whisky crèmes," John had pronounced, gazing at them expectantly.

Gemma, looking round at the blank expressions on the others' faces, ventured, "Whisky in a dessert? Is this a traditional Highland thing?"

"Highlanders can put whisky in anything," Donald Brodie said with a chuckle, "but I've no idea what this particular beastie might be." Brodie wore a kilt in muted greens and blues rather than the brilliant red Brodie tartan he'd worn the previous evening, with a woolen pullover that looked more suitable for stalking in the heather than cooking.

"It's shortbread, topped with an ice cream made with fresh cream and flavored with whisky and honey—local honey, of course." John sounded a bit put out at their ignorance. "Now we'll be starting with the shortbread—"

"We're going to *make* shortbread?" interrupted Heather, whose earlier patience seemed to be evaporating. "Why on earth would we make shortbread when Walker's is just down the road?"

"Because there's no comparison between shortbread made in a factory, however good it may be, and pastry made by hand," John admonished her briskly, setting out a bag of flour and several sticks of butter on the slab of marble set into the work island. "That's like asking why you would drink single malt whisky when you could have a blend."

"Ouch. That's vicious, lass," said Donald, grinning at Heather, and Gemma saw Hazel give her cousin a sharp glance. Were Donald and Heather more than business associates? But if so, why the elaborate scheme to get Hazel here? Although, Gemma mused, that might account for Heather's obvious animosity towards her cousin.

"The secret to good pastry is to handle it gently," continued John as they creamed butter and sugar together, Heather grumbling under her breath all the while. "Unlike a woman," he added, "the less you touch it, the more tender it will be."

"But is that true?" asked Donald, with a glance at Hazel that made her blush and look away.

"Theoretically," said John, seemingly unaware of the sudden rise in tension. "But in practice, I wouldn't take a wager on it."

By the time the shortbread was cooling on racks, and the ice cream safely stored in the freezer, Gemma was more than ready to break for lunch. Cooking, she'd found, was harder on the feet than walking a beat.

Donald had organized the transport to Benvulin; Pascal and Martin with Heather, Gemma and Hazel in his Land Rover, along with the picnic baskets. The early morning mist had cleared, and the day was fine and warm. John and Louise stood on the back steps of the B&B to see them off, like proud parents waving their children off to school, but just as the picnic party reached their cars, Hazel stopped and put a hand on Gemma's arm.

"Gemma, I think I'll stay behind," she said softly. "I— I've a headache."

Keys in hand, Donald turned, his kilt swinging. "But—"

"I'm sorry. I know you've gone to a lot of trouble." Hazel didn't meet his eyes. "But I just don't think— I'm really not up to it."

Donald took a step towards her, then seemed to realize they had a rapt audience. He gave a curt nod to Heather, who shrugged and herded her contingent into a black Audi. When the car had pulled out of the drive, Donald turned back to Hazel. "Aye, dinna fash yerself, hen," he told her, putting on the broad Scots. "We'll bring you a dram, for auld times' sake. You take care of yourself, have a nice lie-down."

"Hazel, I can stay with you," offered Gemma. "I don't mind—"

"No. It's all right. I wouldn't have you miss this, and I'll be fine." She gave Gemma the ghost of a smile. "I promise."

In Hazel's absence, Gemma found herself in the passenger seat of the Land Rover by default. Glancing surreptitiously at Donald as they drove, she was aware of his large, capable hands on the wheel, and of the strong profile of his nose above his bearded lips.

"Bloody hell," she swore under her breath. The man radiated a woolly sort of sexual magnetism. And if she weren't immune, she could imagine what Hazel must be feeling.

"Sorry?" said Donald, having—thankfully—not understood her muttered curse.

"Um, your kilt," Gemma blurted out as he glanced over at her curiously. "I was wondering about your kilt. I thought the one you wore last night was your clan tartan."

"This is Hunting Brodie. The hunting tartans are never as bright."

"Sort of like camouflage?"

"Exactly. The hunting tartans usually replace the background color of the tartan with blue, green, or brown."

"Have you always worn the kilt?"

"Oh, aye. Fits the image, you see, of the owner of an ancient distillery." His tone was lightly mocking. "And as a rule, I find the kilt more comfortable than breeks."

"There's no real tradition, then?" asked Gemma, genuinely interested now.

"I'd not like to disappoint ye." Donald smiled at her, and her pulse leapt. "There is a tradition, right enough, but it owes more to Sir Walter Scott and the Victorians than to authentic clan history. There's not even real evidence that early tartans were associated with specific clans. And as for the kilted Highlander marching into battle," he added, warming to his subject, "the original kilt was merely a belted plaid, and most of the time the soldiers took it off for ease of movement when fighting."

"A plaid is different from a tartan?" she asked.

"A plaid is just a woolen fabric. The early plaids were

long rectangles of cloth, about sixteen feet by five. A man would lay it out on the ground, pleat it, then lie on top of it and belt it on."

"It sounds very awkward," Gemma admitted. "And not the least bit romantic."

"Och, well, I'll try not to spoil all your illusions. Look." Donald pointed as he slowed the Land Rover. "There's Benvulin."

If Gemma had imagined an industrial site, similar to breweries she'd seen near London, she had been very much mistaken. Before them, an emerald green field rolled down towards a broad sweep of the Spey. In the foreground, a dozen shaggy Highland cattle raised their massive heads to stare at them as they passed. Beyond that, the distillery buildings clustered at the edge of the bluff overlooking the river.

The buildings were weathered gray stone, and in the center rose the distinctive twin-pagoda roofs of the kilns, complete with rustic waterwheel.

"Oh," breathed Gemma. "It's like a storybook."

"It is, arguably, the prettiest distillery in Scotland," Donald admitted. "Tho' I am a wee bit biased."

He pulled the car up in front of the house that sat to one side of the distillery complex. Heather's Audi already sat empty in the drive. "Come on; we'll join the others," he said, pulling the baskets from the back of the Land Rover.

"This is your house?" Gemma slid out of the car without taking her eyes from the prospect. Built of the same weathered gray stone as the distillery, the house was a conglomeration of gables, turrets, and rooflines that echoed the pagoda shape of the kilns. It should have been hideous, she thought, but somehow it wasn't.

"Neo-baronial excess," said Donald, following her gaze. "Built by my great-great-grandfather in 1885."

Gemma followed him as he headed, not towards the front door, but around the side of the house. "I think it's marvelous."

"You don't have to pay the central heating," Donald answered lightly, but she thought he was pleased.

As they came round the corner, Gemma saw a green lawn flanked by rhododendrons and, at its edge, the bluff overlooking the river.

The rest of the party had already spread traveling rugs on the lawn, and Heather called out, "Hurry it up, then. We're famished."

Donald and Gemma joined the group, and as they unpacked the picnic baskets and tucked into their lunch, Gemma watched Heather Urquhart curiously. The other woman seemed relaxed, without the sharpness Gemma had noticed in Hazel's presence, and her exchanges with Donald had the easy familiarity Gemma had noticed earlier.

Along with the fruit, cheese, and the wedges of cold pheasant pie provided by John, Donald had brought a bottle of whisky and a half-dozen squatty, tulip-shaped glasses. The bottle, however, carried not the Benvulin logo that Gemma had already come to recognize, but a simple paper label with a handwritten number.

"This is a single cask whisky," Donald explained as he handed round the glasses and poured a half-inch in each. "Do you know the distinction?"

She shook her head. "That's different from a single malt?"

"A single malt comes from one distillery," put in Heather, with more patience than Gemma had expected. "But the whisky is drawn from many different casks, to achieve a uniformity of taste—a style. A single cask, on the other hand, is just what it sounds, a whisky bottled from one single cask. Each cask is wonderfully unique, and once it's gone, it can never be replicated exactly."

"It's also very strong," cautioned Donald, "and so should be drunk with care." He held up his glass. "First, look at the color. What do you see?"

"It's a pale gold," Gemma ventured. "Lighter than the amber one we drank last night."

"That pale color means it was aged in American bourbon oak. The darker colors usually mean the whisky has spent some time in a sherry cask. Now"—he nodded towards Gemma's glass—"sniff." He demonstrated by holding his own glass under his nose. "What aromas jump out at you?"

Gemma inhaled gingerly. "Um, a sort of spicy vanilla."

"Verra good. Now take a tiny sip—you don't want to burn your tongue."

Complying, Gemma found that although her nose prickled, her eyes didn't tear as they had last night. "It's sharp, acid. With a sort of burnt-sugar taste."

"Brilliant. Now we're going to add some water, and taste again." Donald pulled a bottle of spring water from the basket and poured a few drops into her glass.

Gemma sipped, holding the liquid on her tongue and frowning in concentration before letting it slide down her throat. "It's much more flowery now," she said in surprise. "With a hint of . . . could it be peaches? And honey—it definitely tastes like honey."

"That's very good." Donald beamed at her as if she were a prize pupil. "And the more you taste, the more complexities you'll be able to discern. We'll turn you into a whisky connoisseur yet." He splashed water into the other glasses, then raised his own. "Slàinte."

This time, Gemma took a more generous swallow and felt the warmth work its way down into her belly, then out towards her fingers and toes.

They finished their drinks in companionable chat, and although Martin stretched out and promptly went to sleep, Gemma found that rather than experiencing the groggy sleepiness often induced by wine, she felt vibrantly alive and alert. "Could we see the distillery?" she asked.

"Of course," replied Donald. "We'll take a wee tour."

"I think I'll pass," said Heather, lazily. "That's too much like work."

"And I, as well," echoed Pascal, pouring himself another finger of whisky and lying back on his elbow.

"Right, then. I don't think we'll disturb young Martin." Donald stood and held out a hand to Gemma, pulling her to her feet as if she weighed no more than a thistle.

She snatched her hand back and rubbed it against her jeans as she followed him across the lawn, trying to dispel the lingering warmth of his touch.

Donald turned back to her as they reached the distillery buildings. "The kilns and the mill are just for show now, of course. The gristmill has been steam-powered since the turn of the century, but my father restored the mill wheel to working order. It impresses the visitors."

"And the kilns?" asked Gemma, admiring the twin pagodas.

"Almost all Scottish distilleries now buy malt from professional maltsters, although each distillery specifies the amount of peat smoke required." He led her into the large building behind the kilns. "We do still grind the malt here—that's the gristmill," he added, pointing at a large, steel box with a funnel-shaped bottom. He lifted a handful of barley grains from a bowl on a display table.

"The barley goes in like this"—dipping into a second bowl, he held out what looked like coarse-ground oatmeal—"and comes out like that. Grist."

Gemma touched the coarse meal with a fingertip, then followed Donald upstairs onto a steel mesh catwalk. They stopped before an enormous vat with a wooden cover.

"The grist is conveyed up here into the mash tun, where hot water is added to it." He lifted a section of the cover, and Gemma peered in. The vat was half filled with a frothy liquid that smelled good enough to eat.

"What is this?"

"It's called wort. The successive washes of hot water leach the sugars from the barley, leaving a sweet barley water. As children, we were given it as a treat. It's nonalcoholic at this stage."

"And over there?" Gemma gestured towards the series of smaller tubs she could see across the room.

"Those are the washbacks. That's where yeast is added to the wort, and it begins to ferment. The brewer in my grandfather's day used to say it was nae whisky if ye didna chuck a rat in the wash to give it a boost, but we don't do that these days."

"Rats?" Gemma couldn't repress a shudder, although she was sure he was teasing her.

"Aye, the vermin were everywhere, living off the malt. There were always a few wee cats on the distillery payroll." This time the twinkle was unmistakable.

"Well-fed cats, I should think," Gemma rejoined.

"As well as well-watered staff. The distillery crew was allowed three drams a day, straight from the still. Must have had cast-iron stomachs, those lads."

He led her back down the stairs at the far end of the platform, into a large, high-ceiling room that appeared dwarfed by the four huge, copper stills. "Once it's fermented, the wash goes into the wash stills—that's the pair in the front—then into the spirit stills. Those are the smaller stills in the back. The middle portion of that second distilling goes into the cask; the rest is redistilled."

"It's all very neat, isn't it?" said Gemma, gazing up at the graceful copper swan necks.

"Aye, if by that you mean tidy. The treacly residue from the kilns is mixed with the leftover barley to make animal feed—many distilleries used to have prize-winning cattle herds. But then the Scots have always had to be frugal. And patient. There's a good deal of waiting involved in the making of a good malt whisky."

"You'll be no stranger to that, then," said Gemma, thinking of Hazel.

Donald gazed at her a moment, as if considering his reply, but said merely, "Let me show you the warehouse."

They crossed the lawn to a stone building with high windows, and Donald unlocked the door. "There are two more buildings behind this one, actually, but this is the original."

Gemma beheld a long aisle lined with rows of casks above an earthen floor, and the air held a heady perfume. "Oh, what a lovely smell," she said, closing her eyes and inhaling again. There were notes of oak and alcohol, along with more subtle scents she couldn't identify.

"Up to thirty percent of the contents evaporate over the life of a cask. It's called the angels' share. Hazel loved this—she said she could never enter a warehouse without being instantly transported to her childhood."

Gemma jumped at the opening he'd given her. "Donald, look. I know you and Hazel have a history; she told me a bit of it last night. But do you realize what she's risking by seeing you? Her marriage, her child, a lovely home—"

"Aye, I know that. But if she were happy, she'd nae have come—"

"She's confused, and you're taking advantage of that—"

"Gemma, Hazel belongs here," he broke in, shaking his head. "It's that brought her back, as much as any feeling for me."

"If that's true," Gemma countered stubbornly, "why has she never talked about it? She's hardly mentioned Scotland in all the time I've known her."

"Because it would have been like opening the lid on bloody Pandora's box—all that longing—"

"And now you've let it out."

"Aye."

They stared at each other, stalemated. After a moment, Gemma said, "It will pass, if you'll let her go."

"And that's what you'd want for your friend, to be half alive? Half the person she was meant to be?"

"I-It's you who doesn't know her as she really is." Memories of all the cozy times spent in Hazel's kitchen came back to Gemma with a rush, and she felt the sting of tears behind her eyelids. Hazel had been the calm anchor in a turbulent world, and only now did Gemma realize how much that had meant to her.

"It's yourself you'll be thinking of," said Donald, with unexpected acuity. "Not that I can blame you, but that's hardly fair, now, is it?"

Unwilling to admit he'd come so near the mark, Gemma changed tack. "Donald, if Hazel was willing to see you at Innesfree, why did she refuse to come here?"

He looked away from her, gazing at the tiered casks as if they might provide an answer. At last, he sighed and said, "It was here we told my father we meant to marry. He would nae hear of it. He told her never to set foot on Benvulin land again. And—" He hesitated again.

"And what?" prompted Gemma.

"And he said he would cast me out if she did."

5

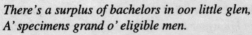

There's a surplus of bachelors in oor little glen,
A' specimens grand o' eligible men.

— ANONYMOUS

Carnmore, November 1898

"CATARRH," PRONOUNCED NURSE *Baird as she sat back from examining her patient. The rash flushing Charles Urquhart's fair skin indicated a particularly virulent fever, and a single look at his throat had confirmed her worst suspicions.*

"He'll be all right, then?" Livvy Urquhart asked, relief flooding her voice.

"It's a powerful infection, Livvy—you'll know that," cautioned the nurse. And the poor man was already weakened from his ordeal in the snow. Well, she would do what she could, as it would be days before the doctor could get there from Tomintoul.

Why was it, Nurse Baird wondered, that birth, death, and illness always chose to coincide with the worst conditions?—If that were the Lord's will, she'd have given him credit for more sense.

At the height of the storm, she'd been helping Mrs. Stuart give birth to her ninth, and that on the heels of easing the passage of old Granny Sharp at the opposite end of the village. She had just got back to her own fireside and her cat, Sootie, when Kenny Baxter had come hammering at her door with the news that Mr. Charles was taken ill.

Charles Urquhart had been a scrawny bairn when she'd delivered him nigh on forty years ago, in a snowstorm as fierce as this one, but he had survived. Perhaps he would show the same fortitude now.

She added crushed willow bark and wild garlic to the pot of hot water Livvy had brought her, then set the concoction aside to steep. At least Olivia Urquhart was a sensible woman, and fortunate in possessing some medical training from her physician father. By Livvy's directive, the room was clean and tolerably warm, and Charles had been well covered and fed warming drinks to soothe his throat.

But if Livvy Urquhart was sensible and competent, she was also much too beautiful for the hard life of the Braes. A hothouse flower, Nurse had thought when Charles first brought her to Carnmore, with her dark curls and fair skin. Nor had Livvy faded—if anything, she had become lovelier. It was as if the births of her children and the death of her little daughter had both tempered and refined her. A rose on a steel stem, that's how Nurse thought of her.

She wished she had the same confidence in Charles. He'd been delicate from a lad, with a drive that pushed him past the limits of his constitution.

Now, studying Will, Nurse thought she saw signs of the same delicacy. The boy had grown too fast, so that the skin seemed stretched too tightly over the sharp angles of his bones, and high spots of color flared in his cheeks. He was vulnerable, she thought as she filtered the herbal brew into a cup. *This infection could be highly contagious—she would do well to watch the boy as well as treat the father.*

Early that morning, Callum had watched Donald and the dark-haired woman emerge from the woods and wend their way along the meadow path towards the river. Through his binoculars, he could see Donald speaking urgently, and the woman shaking her head, as if she were not convinced by his arguments. As they reached the river, someone else came out of the copse, a slender woman with a long, boyish stride. Her hair, the color of copper beech leaves, was pulled away from her face, revealing strong bones and a slightly upturned nose.

The redhead reached the river's edge, then, turning to survey the shoreline, gave a start of surprise as she spied Donald Brodie and his companion. She observed the couple for a moment, as if hesitating, then spun round on her heel and retraced her steps along the path.

Callum watched a little longer, long enough to see Donald's kiss returned in full measure. Then he slipped the binoculars back into their case and adjusted the gun strap over his shoulder. He had seen enough.

It was past noon by the time Callum had ferried the trekker's baggage to the B&B in Ballindalloch and finished up his chores round the stables. Then, having made sure his father was dozing harmlessly in front of the telly, he drove the van into Aviemore.

He parked in the pay-and-display next to Aviemore Police Station and commanded Murphy to stay in the car. Ignoring the Labrador's look of reproach, Callum started down the hill, easing his pace to accommodate the Saturday shoppers strolling the other way. It was a strolling sort of day, with the sky a clear blue behind the Cairngorms and the steam train from Boat of Garten chugging merrily into the Aviemore station. Callum had no thought for the scenery, however, as he reached Tartan Gifts and pushed open the door.

The shop was busy, with Mrs. Witherspoon helping two well-padded women who were waffling over Bonnie Prince Charlie tea towels, while another couple browsed among the heather-filled paperweights. At the till, Alison was ringing up one customer while another queued impatiently.

Callum waited, fingering the monogrammed bookmarks while he avoided Mrs. Witherspoon's gimlet eye. It was stifling in the close confines of the shop, the air overheated and heavy with the odor of candles and Alison's distinctive perfume. He could feel himself sweating, could smell the oily, woolly scent of his own sweater, warmed by his body.

When Alison had finished with the second customer, he stepped with relief up to the register. "Come away outside," he whispered. "I need a word with ye."

"Are ye daft?" hissed Alison. "Can ye no see I'm busy?" In a louder voice, she added, "And what can I be doing for you today, Mr. MacGillivray?"

"Let me buy you a coffee," he persisted.

"That'll not be necessary, Mr. MacGillivray." Alison gave him a bright smile, then leaned forward to adjust something on the countertop, whispering, "Just bugger off, Callum. You'll get me sacked."

"Make an excuse," he urged softly. "This is about Donald."

Callum could see her hesitate, torn between irritation and curiosity. Then she jerked her head towards the door. "All right. Go on. I'll meet you outside."

He did as instructed, and a few moments later, Alison came out of the shop. She hurried down the hill, her heels clicking on the pavement, until she was well out of sight of the shop windows.

"I've told the auld cow I had to check on Chrissy," she said, "so be quick about it."

"Where is Chrissy?"

"She's at home. Where did ye think she would be? And why is it any business of yours?"

"I thought you might bring her for her riding lesson."

Alison shook her head impatiently. "Never mind about that now. Has something happened to Donald? Is he all right?"

"Depends on your point of view, doesn't it?" asked Callum, enjoying an unaccustomed sense of power. "You said he told you he had a business meeting this weekend."

"So? What of it?"

"It's an odd sort of business, then. He's staying at the Inneses'." Seeing Alison's blank expression, he asked, "Did he never introduce you to John and Louise Innes? They bought the old farmhouse just down the road from the stables. Turned it into a posh bed-and-breakfast."

"Donald's staying at a B&B so near his house?"

"And not alone."

Alison blanched beneath her makeup, her face looking suddenly pinched. "But—"

"She's verra pretty. Dark hair—"

"How do you know it's not a business meeting?" Alison protested. "He could—"

"There's no mistaking what I saw between them."

Alison glared at him. "I don't believe you. How did you—Where did—"

"I fish with John Innes. He told me what Donald was about. So I kept an eye out."

Alison looked away from him, crossing her arms beneath her small breasts as if she were cold. For the first time, Callum realized how tiny she was, her bones fragile as a sparrow's. And he saw what her makeup and bottle-blond hair usually disguised—her resemblance to Chrissy.

The pleasure he'd felt in his momentary victory evaporated. "I'm sorry, hen. I didna mean to hurt ye."

"Then why did you tell me?"

"Because it's not right the man should lie to you. You deserve better—you and Chrissy."

"And you're going to give us that?" challenged Alison, her belligerence returning.

"I—"

"If you ever have more to offer than stable muck, Callum MacGillivray," she scoffed at him, "you're very welcome to let me know. But in the meantime, you can bloody well keep out of my business."

Louise had thought that a quiet spell with the house empty would settle her nerves, but when the guests had left for Benvulin, she found herself pacing from hall to dining room to lounge, needlessly tweaking the flower arrangements and running the hem of her apron over already dusted furniture.

She'd seen Hazel turn away at the last minute and go back to her room in the barn, and she couldn't help but speculate as to the cause. It looked as if things between Donald and Hazel were not going well, but the satisfaction this occasioned Louise was overshadowed by her worry over John.

He had disappeared, as soon as the others had gone, on another of his manufactured errands. This time it was to pick up some necessary dinner ingredient from the grocer in Grantown—an ingredient Louise suspected he had deliberately forgotten when doing yesterday's marketing.

And not only did John make excuses to be away from the house, he also vanished without explanation at odd hours of the night and early morning. He must be seeing someone. There was no other explanation. But who?

The stem of a recalcitrant rose snapped in her fingers. Swearing, Louise felt the jab of pain behind her eyes that signaled the onset of a stress headache. Her lungs felt compressed, as if she were trying to breathe underwater. She must get out of the house or she would suffocate.

Crushing the broken rose into her apron pocket, she ran out the scullery door and across the lawn, sinking to her knees in front of the perennial border. She took great gulps of air and focused her gaze on the pink bells of the foxgloves before her until she felt calmer. Plants were something you could depend on, she'd found, unlike people. If anyone had taught her that, it had been Hazel.

Louise glanced at the barn into which Hazel had run with the urgency of one desperate for solitude. What did she know of this woman who had once been her friend?

She thought back to their first year at boarding school, both new girls, both suffering from personal upheavals. Hazel had been a dark, bright bloom among a field of bland anemic blondness, her soft Scots voice an exotic contrast to the other girls' flat English vowels.

While Louise suffered from the trauma of her parents' divorce, Hazel had been entirely displaced, her history and connections severed as cleanly as an amputation. Hazel had survived by taking on camouflage, becoming more English than the English, her accent fading year by year.

But as Hazel became more popular, she had not abandoned Louise. And as Louise's mother drifted into far-flung affairs, alighting less and less often on English soil, Hazel had taken her friend home with her on holidays. Home to Newcastle, to the dark and formal suburban house that seemed less a home than boarding school, to parents as gray as Newcastle skies. Shadow people, Louise had thought them, transplants that had not taken root in alien soil.

The girls had remained friends past school-leaving, Hazel studying psychology at university, Louise working at an insurance company. Then one day Hazel had rung, inviting Louise to come with her to Scotland, just as she must have rung this new friend, Gemma. But Louise had had to wait until her August holiday, and by then, Hazel had met Donald Brodie.

In spite of the fact that the two of them were so obviously a couple, Donald had extended the umbrella of his charm over Louise as well, and the three of them had become inseparable.

When Louise's holiday finished, she had resigned her job in London by post. She and Hazel worked together catering for shooting parties, and when business dwindled with the end of the season, the girls had found jobs in an estate tea shop. It had seemed as if they might go on forever, the three of them.

And then Donald had asked Hazel to marry him, and within a day, Hazel had vanished from their lives.

Heather Urquhart had made an excuse of needing a change of clothing, forcing Donald to take Pascal and Martin back to the Inneses' in his Land Rover, along with Gemma James. Gemma had had quite enough tête-à-tête with Donald already, in Heather's opinion, back at Benvulin.

Not that she was protecting Donald's pursuit of her

cousin, Hazel, by any means—it was his courting Gemma round the distillery that got up Heather's nose.

Crossing the wide expanse of the Spey at Boat of Garten, she soon reached her bungalow. She pushed the automatic opener that caused the heavy wooden gates to swing open, then closed them again as she stopped the car in the drive. Thick hedges of arborvitae surrounded the front of the house, and in back the garden ran down to a small, reedy loch. The house, a snug structure of white stucco with natural wood trim and a deep, overhanging tile roof, was her refuge.

Her job was demanding, requiring constant interaction with both the distillery staff and the public. When she entertained professionally she used the distillery premises, or local restaurants; in her private dalliances, she saw only men who were willing to share *their* beds. She seldom invited anyone to her home, male or female.

Turning her key in the lock, she felt the usual rush of pleasure as she stepped into the house. A tiled entrance led to an open-plan kitchen and a sitting room, fitted and upholstered in white. The contemporary furnishings were unmarred by paintings or knickknacks. A few large potted plants drew the eye to the glass wall at the back of the sitting room that framed the view of garden and loch.

Heather went straight to the kitchen and put the kettle on. After the rich lunch and the whisky at Benvulin, a cup of tea would clear her head. She needed to think.

How odd it had felt to see Hazel again. It had been what—ten years? Since her aunt's funeral in Newcastle, that had been the last time. Hazel had come with her newly acquired husband, Tim Cavendish, and he'd served as an effective buffer between the cousins.

The kettle clicked off at the boil, and after brewing a

cup of green tea, Heather took it into the sitting room. She sank into her favorite chair and curled her legs beneath her, gazing out at the loch as she tried to recall Tim Cavendish's face. He'd been a bit quiet and studious-looking, a far cry from Donald Brodie's large exuberance, as if Hazel had been deliberately going against type. But if Hazel had been so determined to erase Donald Brodie from her life, why had she come back after all these years?

Of course, Heather could understand Donald's allure—she'd not been entirely immune—but she'd been too fiercely ambitious to allow herself to fall in love with him.

The real question Heather had to consider, however, was what Hazel's return meant to Benvulin. If Hazel decided to stay, could she be won over to Heather's view of the distillery's future? Benvulin was still a limited company, with Donald holding the majority of shares, but if Heather could convince him to sell to Pascal's French group, it would give her more control. Should she try to win Hazel over, make an ally of her?

No. She set her cup down with a thump. She'd worked too hard for this to depend on anyone else, and the last thing she wanted was to be beholden to her cousin. It would be much better for everyone concerned if Hazel could be convinced to go back to London, and Heather was prepared to make that happen—whatever it took.

Donald decanted his passengers in Innesfree's graveled drive with less ceremony than he'd have accorded a halfway decent bottle of wine, Gemma felt sure.

"I've some things to attend to at the distillery," he called through his open window. "There's only a skeleton crew on the weekend. But I will be back for drinks, and to taste the fruit of our efforts," he added with a salute as he pulled away.

And did he consider Hazel one of the fruits of his efforts? wondered Gemma. A just dessert?

Martin and Pascal set off immediately for the house, Martin a little groggily, as if he hadn't quite recovered from his whisky-induced nap, Pascal with the firm step of a man with a purpose.

Gemma, however, stood a moment longer, surveying the house and garden in the flat light of midafternoon. It was the merciless time of day, when blemishes stood out from the hazy camouflage of morning and evening—a pile of timber against one side of the barn, proof of unfinished construction; a half dozen clumps of dandelion rising above the smooth surface of the lawn; a patch of crumbling harl above the scullery door. She found it comforting somehow, this evidence of ordinariness amid the B&B's manufactured perfection.

Real life was waiting at home, for her and for Hazel. She took a deep breath and headed for the barn, determined to pin Hazel down this time, to make her see reason.

But when she entered their room, it was empty. Both beds were neatly made, the duvets puffy. Hazel's overnight case was closed, her few toiletries on the dressing table neatly arranged. Only a used and rinsed teacup betrayed the room's recent habitation.

At least Hazel wasn't with Donald; Gemma could be assured of that much. She would look for her in the house. But first, she took her phone from her handbag and punched in her home number. Suddenly too anxious to sit, she paced as it rang, sounding tinnily distant.

Where were they? Thinking of Duncan and the boys in the park, or perhaps at Otto's for afternoon tea, she felt a stab of longing, and beneath that, a nebulous worry.

Why had Duncan been on the phone so late last night? And why had he not answered his mobile? Had there been an emergency at the Yard, and all their plans for him to spend the weekend with the boys gone for naught?

Or had something else happened? But, in that case, surely Duncan would have rung her, she reassured herself. Still, a nagging instinct told her that something was wrong. She should have kept trying last night; she should have rung again first thing this morning.

She should never have left them.

Gemma let herself into the house by the front door, closing it gently behind her. The hall smelled of flowers and furniture polish, but the house was quiet, as if still deep in afternoon slumber.

Peeking into the sitting room, she found it empty as well. The fire was laid but cold, the cushions restored to plumpness after last night's lounging. The room might have been a stage set, waiting for the action to begin.

Gemma had headed towards the kitchen, thinking the class might have begun to congregate, when she heard the murmur of voices from the dining room. One she recognized instantly—Hazel. The other was female, English, and clipped with anger. Louise.

"I know you didn't approve of my coming," Hazel was replying, "but surely you can understand—"

"Understand?" Louise shot back. "Oh, I understand that you think you can waltz back into our lives as if you'd never been away. And that we're all supposed to welcome the prodigal with open arms, no matter how much damage you left in your wake the last time."

"But I— Louise, you don't understand. I had no choice—"

"Didn't you?" Louise's voice was sharp as an ice pick. "Or did you just take the easiest course? Run away, and don't think about the consequences."

"But—Donald—Donald had the distillery—"

"Donald was devastated. And you left me to try to explain to him why the woman he loved had left him without a word of explanation—"

"Donald knew— He didn't need me—"

"Didn't he? You're always so sure of yourself, Hazel, but this time you were wrong. I don't think he's ever recovered. Did you not wonder why he never married?"

"Donald? But Donald—I just assumed—Donald always had women queued up—"

"When did that ever matter?" Louise laughed. "Did you think love was a commodity? And now you're going to inflict the same sort of damage on your new family, and you want my approval?"

There was a moment's silence. Gemma stood rooted in the dining room, afraid to breathe, unable to move forward or back without betraying her presence.

Then Hazel's voice came again, softly. "Louise, whatever else happened, I never meant to hurt *you*." Footsteps echoed, faded away, and then came the slam of the scullery door.

Hurriedly, Gemma slipped out the front door, making as little noise as possible. She didn't want to confront Louise, didn't want to appear as if she'd been eavesdropping. And she must talk to Hazel.

She found her friend standing at the edge of the back garden, looking out towards the river, twisting her hands together.

"You heard, didn't you?" said Hazel, without looking at her.

"Yes." Gemma waited, watching a few horses grazing leisurely in the far pasture. "Are you all right?"

"I've been so stupid. So stupid about everything, and so dishonest," Hazel said, as if she hadn't heard the question. "I managed to convince myself that I could come back here and dabble my toes in the water, just testing it to see if it was still as nice as I remembered, and no one would get hurt." Her lips twisted in a grimace of disgust. "I told myself I could always back out—choose not to act, and my life would just muddle on. But the truth is—Oh, Gemma. I'm not sure I *can* give it up. Can I go back to living a shadow life, when I know what I'm missing? Nothing's changed between us, not in thirteen years. I've never felt this for anyone else . . ."

She turned to Gemma, her face tear-streaked. "I'm a fraud, Gemma, a bloody charlatan. I make my living telling people how to sort out their lives. When they make a balls-up of it I'm gently patronizing, as if I had all the answers." She shook her head. "But this . . . this I don't know how to fix."

They dressed for dinner in silence, Gemma shivering a little as she pulled a moss green sweater over her head. The evening chill had come in early, and the central heating in their room had not yet come on.

Earlier, when John had called them into the kitchen to finish preparing dinner, Hazel had begged Gemma to make her excuses, saying, "I can't face either of them just yet."

"Donald and Louise?" When Hazel nodded, Gemma said, "Right, then. Migraine it is. And I'll come and fetch you when it's time for drinks."

No one questioned Hazel's headache, but to Gemma's

discomfort, Donald immediately snagged her as his cooking partner. Together, they had stuffed fistfuls of basil into the food processor, along with peeled cloves of garlic, deep green olive oil, roasted red peppers, and toasted pine nuts. This mixture they spread over the salmon fillets, leaving John to grill them at the last minute. They stirred the cheese into their celery and Brie soup, strung and sautéed the *mange-tout*. She and Donald worked well together, quickly establishing a rhythm, and by the end of the session she found herself smiling in spite of herself.

When they'd finished, John had dismissed them with a reminder that the evening would be festive, and to dress accordingly.

Donald, walking out with Gemma into the dusky garden, had stopped her with a touch on her arm.

"Gemma, put in a good word for me, will you?"

Feeling an unexpected sense of regret, she said, "You know I can't. She's my friend, Donald. I won't encourage her to ruin her life. I'm sorry."

He had shrugged ruefully and patted her shoulder. "Didna fash yerself, lass. I thought it wouldn't hurt to ask. I'm glad she has such a good friend."

Now, taking her turn in the bathroom, Gemma scrubbed her hands in a futile effort to remove the odor of fish and garlic. Defeated, she rubbed lotion on instead, pulled her hair up into a loose topknot, brushed a little shadow on her eyelids, and swiped a bronzy pink lipstick across her mouth.

Then she gaped at herself in the glass, lipstick suspended in midair. Whom did she mean to impress with all this primping? Donald?

Flushing with shame, she blotted her lips and brushed her hair back into its usual single plait.

When she came out of the bathroom, she found Hazel sitting at the dressing table, her mobile phone clutched in her hands.

"There's no one at home," Hazel said, looking up at her. "I thought . . . if only I could hear Holly's voice . . ."

Gemma frowned. "I've been trying to ring Duncan, too. No one's home, and he seems to have turned off his mobile phone. Do you suppose they've all met up and joined a cult?"

Seeing Hazel's stricken look, she hastened to reassure her. "I'm only teasing. I'm sure they're all fine." She'd been whistling in the dark to combat her own worry; she hadn't meant to aggravate Hazel's.

Gemma sat down on the edge of the bed, facing her friend. "Have you decided what you're going to do, love?"

"I'm going home on Monday, and I'm not coming back," Hazel said reluctantly. "But I'll have to tell Tim the truth—"

"The truth? That you love someone else and you're only staying with him out of duty? Hazel, you can't do that—you can't expect him to live with that sort of knowledge."

"No. I suppose you're right." Hazel looked up at Gemma, despair in her dark eyes. "But how do I go on, pretending nothing's happened to me?"

"You make the best of it," Gemma said, with more certainty than she felt. If Hazel thought herself a fraud, was *she* a hypocrite? What if she were faced with staying with a man she didn't love—Toby's father, Rob, perhaps, if the circumstances had been different—or being with Duncan? Would she find her choice so easy?

"What about Donald?" she asked.

"I'll tell him tonight," said Hazel. "What else can I do?"

* * *

When Gemma and Hazel entered the sitting room, they found the other guests assembled, except for Donald. The fire crackled, a lively Celtic air played softly in the background, and John was making the rounds with a bottle of single malt and a tray of cut glass tumblers. From the dining room came the clinking of china and cutlery—Louise setting the tables.

"Aberlour, eighteen-year-old." John raised the bottle towards them in greeting. "Thought everyone should taste a bit of the competition."

"You must be feeling very expansive tonight, John," Heather Urquhart said with a malicious glint. She wore deep red and had chosen the chair nearest the fire. "I'm sure Donald would approve."

Martin Gilmore sat opposite Heather, watching her with the fierce intensity he had fixed on Gemma the previous evening. If Pascal Benoit felt threatened by the young man's interest in Heather, he betrayed no sign of it. Wearing toast-colored cashmere, he looked relaxed and deceptively teddy-bear-like.

"Where is Donald?" asked Gemma, taking the proffered glass from John.

"Hung up at the distillery," replied John. "He rang up and said he'd be along shortly. Feeling better, are you, Hazel?" he added solicitously.

"Yes. Thanks." As Hazel smiled up at him warmly, reaching for her drink, Louise came in. Louise froze in the doorway, as if arrested by the fleeting glimpse of intimacy between Hazel and her husband.

Hazel's smile faltered, dimmed. "Oh, Louise . . ." She took the glass from John's hand too quickly, or he let it go too soon. Whisky sloshed over the rim, and the room smelled suddenly of fermenting pears and butterscotch.

Pascal offered Hazel a handkerchief to mop her hand, and the awkward moment passed, but silence still hung like smoke in the room. The plaintive wail of bagpipes came clearly from the CD player.

Martin held aloft his tumbler and leaped into the conversational breach. "Bloody good stuff, John. I could get used to this."

Louise gave him a look that said he'd better not bank on it, but before she could speak, the front door slammed and Donald came into the room. He brought with him the scent of woodsmoke and cold air, and beamed round at them with all the bonhomie of an auburn-bearded Father Christmas. "Started without me, have you?" He carried a bottle tucked in the crook of his arm like a baby.

"Everything all right?" asked Heather.

"Just had a wee root round in the cellar," answered Donald, still standing, still cradling the bottle. Although Gemma craned forward to read the label, she couldn't make it out. He turned to Louise. "Could you fetch us another tray of glasses, Louise? I've a little surprise." Turning back to the others, he added, "Put aside whatever swill John's seen fit to serve ye before you spoil your palates."

"What are you up to, Donald?" asked Heather, sitting up with an alertness that belied her sleepy-cat pose, but he merely shook his head.

Not until Louise returned with a tray of clean tumblers did he transfer the bottle to both hands, and then his manner became suddenly hesitant. "Aye, this is a rare treat for anyone lucky enough to taste a dram, but . . . it's for Hazel that this has a special meaning." He turned the bottle outwards, and Gemma saw that the label was handwritten like the one on the bottle he had brought for the picnic. "Carnmore, 1980. A sherry cask, unusual for Carnmore. It was the last issue."

"Don't tell me you bottled the Carnmore, Donald," Heather said, her face going pale. "That cask is worth a bloody fortune. You know—"

"Twenty-three years is long enough in the cask. And what better occasion than to mark Hazel's return to the Highlands?" He pulled the cork from the bottle, poured a half-inch in each glass, and handed them round. "When this cask came up for sale from a private collector a few years ago, I thought it well worth the investment."

Gemma held the glass to her nose and breathed carefully, as Donald had taught her. Toasted hazelnuts and . . . was it chocolate? "I don't understand," she said. "Why is this so special?"

"My family's distillery," Hazel said, her voice choked. "Up near Glenlivet. The last year of its operation was 1980. Donald, I-I don't know what to say."

"You don't have to say anything," he answered gently, and for a moment the two of them might have been alone in the room. "Just drink."

Hazel raised the glass to her lips, and Gemma followed suit. The whisky was rich, oily, like melted butter on her tongue, and it left shimmering ripples on the inside of the glass.

"Donald," Hazel whispered. "You shouldn't have done this. Not for me. I—"

The doorbell rang, a clamor in the hushed room. Louise, whom Gemma noticed had stood with lips tight and drink untasted, disappeared. The muted sound of voices came from the hall, then Louise came back into the room.

"Donald. There's someone to see you."

"To see me?" He sounded startled.

"You'd better go."

A look of apprehension crossed his face at Louise's

tone, but he smiled at Hazel and made a graceful exit. After a moment the murmur of voices came from outside, one Donald's bass rumble, the other a shrill female counterpoint.

The sitting room drapes were not yet drawn, although the light had faded to a pale charcoal illuminated by the pink glow in the western sky. Propelled by curiosity and a nameless unease, Gemma rose and went to the window. As she peered out, a movement at her shoulder told her Hazel had joined her.

Donald stood in the drive, talking to a blond in a very short skirt. The woman held a small girl by the hand, the child's face a pale blur in the dusk. Every line in the woman's taut body shouted her fury while Donald shook his head, his hands upraised in placation.

A movement along the driveway's edge drew Gemma's eye from the confrontation. Half hidden in the shadow of the hedge, a slender, kilted man stood perfectly still, watching.

6

O whistle, and I'll come to you, my lad:
O whistle, and I'll come to you, my lad:
Tho' father and mither and a' should gae mad,
O whistle, and I'll come to you, my lad.

        —ROBERT BURNS,
  "Whistle, and I'll Come to You, My Lad"

IT WAS THE longest meal in Gemma's memory. John and
Louise had hustled them all into the dining room while
Donald was still in the drive, on the grounds that the cel-
ery and Brie soup should be eaten immediately.

"As soon as the cheese melts, that's the secret," John
pronounced, with more urgency than any soup warranted.

They were halfway through the first course before
Donald returned. "Sorry about that," he said, sliding into
his seat beside Hazel, but his smile looked strained.

No one gave in to the temptation to ask him the
woman's identity, nor did he offer any explanation, and
the clinking of spoons against china grew unnaturally
loud. Heather watched him with open speculation, Martin with frank curiosity, Pascal with a detached amusement. Hazel didn't look at him at all.

But when John and Louise came in to take the soup plates, Louise smiled at Hazel, touching her shoulder lightly as she reached over the table. Was there a thawing of sympathy in that quarter, Gemma wondered, now that Hazel appeared to be the party wronged?

And was there a certain smugness to Heather Urquhart's smile? How much did she know about Donald's relationship with Hazel? Could she have engineered a deliberate sabotage? Not that it hadn't been in Hazel's best interest to see Donald in his true colors, Gemma reminded herself. But the sight of her friend's face, tight with misery, made her doubt her own judgment.

John brought in the grilled salmon, which was indeed as good as he had promised, but Gemma, watching Hazel push her portion about on her plate, found she had lost her appetite.

Rather to Gemma's surprise, Martin Gilmore made a valiant effort at conversation, questioning her about her job, and Pascal about his interest in moths, with more sensitivity than she had credited him with. The atmosphere eased a bit, and Donald joined in with an occasional comment, although Gemma noticed his wine consumption was more than generous.

"What about your kids?" asked Martin, turning back to Gemma. "You said you had boys?"

She nodded, her lips curving up in an involuntary smile. "Kit's twelve, and Toby's four."

Martin's eyes widened. "You can't possibly have a twelve-year-old. You're—" He stopped, a blush creeping up to the roots of his hair. "That sounded dreadfully rude. I only meant—"

"I'll take it as a compliment," Gemma told him. "And although I could have a twelve-year-old, Kit's my . . . partner's . . . son." She was never sure what to call Kincaid. *Partner* seemed rather stiff and formal, *significant other* as if he were an object in a shop, *boyfriend* made her feel like a giggly teenager, *lover* somehow didn't seem appropriate for polite company. But whatever she called him, she wished he would ring her or answer his bloody mobile phone. She was beginning to wonder if he was deliberately avoiding her, but she couldn't imagine why.

"A blended family?" said Pascal. "How very modern of you."

Gemma shrugged. "Hectic might be a better description. I never realized how much more complicated life was with two children rather than—" Too late, she caught a glimpse of Hazel's face and wondered if she was thinking of the woman and child who had come to see Donald. But before she could rectify her mistake, Martin compounded it.

"You have a child, too, don't you, Hazel? A daughter, I think you said. Have you a photo?"

"I— She—" With a wild look at Donald, Hazel stood, rocking the table so that the wineglasses sloshed precariously. "I— I'm sorry. Not feeling well," she blurted out, and ran from the room.

Hazel was out of the house and into the garden, gulping cold air as if she were drowning. The light had almost gone, but the sky still glowed palely in the west.

Fool, she told herself furiously. She'd been a fool to come here, and now she was making it worse by the minute. And Gemma, what must Gemma think of her? Why had she ever listened to Donald?

At least he'd made leaving easy for her, the bastard. She would go now; Gemma would understand. And Donald— a door slammed and she heard footsteps behind her.

"Hazel, will ye let me explain?"

"You've no need to explain anything to me." She tried to say it calmly, reasonably. "I came to Scotland for a weekend, and I'm going home in the morning. End of story."

"Hazel, we need to talk. If you'll just let me—"

Whirling around to face him, she found she was shaking with fury. "All right, then. Who is she, that woman?"

"Her name's Alison. But she's not important—"

"Not important! And was that your child? Some other little unimportant thing you forgot to mention?"

"God, no." He sounded genuinely shocked. "You think I would keep something like that from ye? Alison—she's just someone I went out with a few times, and she took it a wee bit too seriously—"

"Women have a habit of taking you a bit too seriously—I should know."

"Can ye no forget what happened thirteen years ago?" He was angry now as well, his tone no longer beseeching. "You never gave me a chance, Hazel. I told my father I didna want the bloody distillery. I walked out. Did ye know that? But you were gone, without a word, without an address. When I rang your parents, they wouldna speak to me—"

"That was only fitting in the circumstances, don't you think?" She knew she sounded like a shrew, but anger kept her safe, kept her from taking in his words. "So if you walked away from Benvulin, why are you still there?"

"My father died and left his shares to me. What did you expect me to do? Go live in a bloody monastery? You'd married—"

"How did you know?"

"Heather. But you didna say two words to your own cousin at your mother's funeral, and you didna ask about me."

"I—" The sound of voices drifted out to them from the house—the rest of their party had moved into the sitting room for coffee.

"We can't talk here," Donald said urgently, as if he sensed her weakening. "Come back with me, to Benvulin."

"No! How can you ask that, of all things—"

"Then walk with me." With a feather touch on her arm, he guided her towards the path that led into the wood."

"Donald, no—"

"Don't be afraid. I know the way, even in the dark."

The trees swallowed them, and at the first turn of the path, the lights of the house vanished from view.

When he stopped, she whispered the question that had consumed her. "When you learned where I was, why didn't you come to me then?"

"And you newly wed? I thought you'd made your choice."

"Then why did you change your mind, these last few months?"

He looked away, his profile clear in the faint light that filtered through the trees. "Did you dream about me, Hazel?" he said softly. "Over and over again? Did you have to stop yourself calling out my name when you were in your husband's arms?" When she nodded, reluctantly, he went on. "It was that way with me. And I began to see it wasna going to change, no matter how hard I tried— and I did try. We were meant to be together, whether we like it or no."

"It was no accident, that day in London, was it?"

"Well, I couldna verra well ring your doorbell, could I?" He took her hand in both of his, raised her palm to his lips. "You canna deny this, Hazel. And it's more than the flesh, whatever this is that draws us together."

She made a last desperate stand. "But my daughter—I can't do this to her—"

"What kind of life are you giving your daughter, lying to your husband and yourself? What kind of wife will you be, knowing what you felt when I kissed you this morning? And do you think I wouldna love your daughter as my own?"

She was lost. She knew it before he pulled her to him, knew it before her body responded of its own will. She knew it as they slid to the ground, the smell of crushed ferns rising around them in the darkness.

Carnmore, November 1898

IT WAS WELL *past midnight when Will's mother sent him for the priest. He'd seen the look that passed between his mother and the nurse, seen his mother nod and turn her face away.*

In spite of Nurse Baird's care, his father's condition had gradually worsened. Charles labored for every breath, and it seemed to Will that in the last few hours the flesh had sunk away from his bones.

It had not snowed since the storm two nights earlier, and the night was still and clear. The diamond-hard air seared his lungs as he slipped and slid his way down the track towards the village. In the sky above, the stars blazed, looking near enough to touch. God's eyes, his mother had told him when he was small, watching over them all. The idea had frightened him, and on nights when the starlight fell upon his bed he'd hidden his head beneath his blankets.

Now he tried to find some comfort in the idea of God looking down on his father, but it only made him wonder if God knew his father had not been a very good Catholic.

Oh, he'd gone to Sunday mass, had even donated towards the building of the new chapel, but that was an expected part of life in the Braes. Had it ever been more than a social duty on his father's part?

Will thought of his dad as he had seen him most often, in his office at the brewery, spectacles sliding down his nose, reading the books he brought back from Edinburgh. These had not been books of which the church would approve, Will suspected—Darwin, Huxley, Robert Owen, Haeckel. And once, when Will had questioned him about the Jacobites, his father had said that Catholicism was responsible for a good part of Scotland's grief. That was the sort of opinion one kept to oneself in this part of the Highlands, when one's family's loyalty in the '45 was a matter of honor, and Will had never repeated it. But God, now, what if there were no keeping secrets from God?

The track leveled out and Will quickened his pace, more surefooted now. Would it matter if he prayed? Could he intercede for his father? And what if Father Mackenzie prayed as well?

He ran now, into the village, down the path to the chapel house, snow flying under his boots, and slid into the door with a thump. Panting, he banged hard with his fist, the words in his mind forming a silent chant. Please don't *let him die, please* don't *let my father die.*

He waited until Louise's breathing steadied and slipped into what it would infuriate her to call a snore, then he eased out of bed. Pullover and trousers he'd left within easy reach on a chair, but he'd been careful to remove his belt and empty his pockets as a preventive against telltale jingling.

Once dressed, John crossed to the window, taking care to step over the creaking floorboard. He cranked open the

casement and perched on the sill, leaning out to light his
cigarette. It was a vice he seldom allowed himself, but
considering the evening, he felt he deserved some small
compensation.

A bloody disaster, the whole thing, and just when he
needed Donald's good will more than ever. Damn Callum! It must have been Callum who had told the woman
where to find Donald, but why would he have done such
a stupid thing?

Not that John had ever fathomed what made Callum
MacGillivray tick. He gazed down at the moonlit garden.
All was still and quiet. The lights were out in the barn
and the other bedrooms in the house, although he hadn't
heard Donald come in.

Well, he'd have to chance it. He flicked his fag end into
the flower bed below and drew back into the room, listening. Louise slept on, making tiny whuffling noises in her
dreams. John stopped once, holding his breath as the house
made an infinitesimal shift, then he slipped out the door. It
was getting late, and he had an appointment to keep.

Carnmore, November 1898

WILL WAS TOO *late. He knew, the instant he saw his
mother's bowed head and the nurse's comforting embrace, but he refused to believe it. Dropping to his knees
beside his father's couch, he shook the unresisting body,
shouting, "No! Wake up!" But his father's face, blue-
white as the marble Madonna in the church, remained
still.*

*It was the priest who disengaged his hands and led him
to a seat by the fire. "It's all right, son," Father Mackenzie said gently. "This is what God intended for your father. You'll learn to accept it, in time."*

Watching as Father Mackenzie took the unguent from his case and knelt beside his dad, making the sign of the cross, Will felt his anger sink deep inside him, hardening into a fiery core.

What use had he for a god who would take his father from him? There was no justice in it, and no pity. His father had been a good man, a kind man, who had lived by his principles and bettered the lives of those around him. If that had counted for nothing, if God had chosen to punish him for his beliefs, then Will was finished with him. He would have no part of such a god.

Gemma drifted in and out of troubled dreams in which a phone rang endlessly as she searched for Duncan and the children. She *had* tried ringing home again before she went to bed, but the line had once more been engaged. Nor had her wait for Hazel's return proved any more fruitful, although she had outlasted all the other guests in the lounge before finally giving up and making her way back to the barn alone.

Now she rose towards the surface of awareness, sensing Hazel's presence in the room, but she could not quite rouse herself to full wakefulness. Sleep claimed her again.

Some time later, she heard a door close—or had that been part of the dream as well?

The early dawn had come when the sound of a gunshot echoed in the fringes of her consciousness. *Just someone potting rabbits,* a dream voice reminded her, and reassured, she sank deeper into the clinging fog. Then, a few minutes later, she came fully awake with a gasp.

Had she heard a shot? She sat up and turned on the light. Hazel's bed was empty, although the indentation in the duvet indicated that she had at least rested there. But her overnight bag was gone, as were her bits and pots on the dressing table.

Gemma jumped out of bed, barely noticing the frigid flagstones beneath her feet, and checked the bathroom. No toothpaste, no toothbrush, no shampoo hiding in the corner of the tub. Back in the bedroom, she pulled aside the curtains and peered at the still-shadowed drive. The red Honda was gone as well.

Fighting the beginnings of panic, she shoved on jeans, sweater, and boots, then looked round the room once more for a note. Surely Hazel wouldn't have abandoned her without leaving a note? Unless she'd gone to Donald Brodie's for a spot of illicit sex . . . but then why take all her things?

She grabbed a jacket and went out into the drive. The sun hovered behind the screen of trees to the east, casting deep shadows in the garden. There was no sign of life from the house, and she hesitated to knock anyone up so early. Her fears would sound absurd, surely, if she voiced them to anyone else.

Donald's Land Rover, she saw, was still parked in the drive—had he gone with Hazel in the hire car?

She rocked on her heels for a moment, trying to decide what to do. Well, she could at least investigate the gunshot, put her mind to rest on one score, and perhaps by the time she came back the house would be astir.

Starting towards the track that led into the woods, she pushed away the nagging fear that Hazel and the gunshot were somehow connected. Pure paranoia, she told herself firmly, but her mouth went dry and her heart gave a painful squeeze.

Gemma slowed her pace as she entered the trees, listening, scanning automatically for signs of a disturbance. Halfway along the path she found something, an area of crushed bracken and bluebells, as if something heavy had lain there. But there was no sign of violence, and she breathed a bit easier as she came to the end of the wood.

From that point, the path was bordered on one side by the meadow and, on the other, by a tussocky mix of bracken and heather. She almost turned back, almost convinced herself that her fears had been groundless, but she couldn't quite silence the nagging disquiet.

And then she saw something, a few yards farther along the track, a flash of red half hidden in the heather. An abandoned sweater or jacket, Gemma told herself, but a wave of dread made her stomach lurch. Realizing she had halted, she forced herself to go on, one deliberate step at a time. And as she drew nearer, other shapes began to attach themselves to the splash of scarlet—a white strip here, a brown patch there.

Suddenly, the shapes shifted and coalesced, and she knew what she was seeing.

The red was a kilt, the scarlet Brodie tartan, and below it were dark green hose and sturdy brown boots. Above the kilt, an Arran pullover that had once been cream, but now bore a stain of deep red in its center. And the face, auburn-bearded, Donald's face . . .

"Oh, no. Please," Gemma whispered, only then aware that she had clamped her hand to her mouth. She felt her knees give way and she sank to the ground, unable to tear her gaze from the sightless eyes staring into the morning sky.

7

So lying, tyne the memories of day
And let my loose insatiate being pass
Into the blackbird's song of summer ease
Or, with the white moon, rise in spirit from the trees.
—ROBERT LOUIS STEVENSON,
"A Sonnet on the Ross of Mull"

BREATHE. GEMMA KNELT, eyes closed, fighting the slickness of nausea in the back of her throat. *Get it under control,* she told herself. This was a crime scene. You didn't sick it up in the middle of a crime scene. A murder.

Unless . . . It was unusual, but she had seen a chest-shot suicide once before. Forcing open her eyes, she scanned the immediate area. No gun visible. Not suicide, then.

Someone had shot Donald Brodie with a shotgun, and at point-blank range, by the tight circumference of the wound and the singeing of the wool round its edges. Not an accident.

How long had it been since she'd heard the shot? An hour—no, longer—she'd drifted back to sleep for at least a few minutes. Suddenly, the hair rose on the back of

Gemma's neck. Could Donald's killer still be close by? The rustle of the rising morning breeze through the heather seemed unnaturally loud; the call of a curlew overhead made her heart thud painfully in her chest.

No. It had been too long, the risk of discovery too great for the killer to stay. Still, she felt exposed, vulnerable. She must get help, and quickly. The sooner the police were called in, the greater likelihood of catching the shooter.

A fly buzzed past her ear, then another—the morning was warming, soon the air would be thick with them. Already they were clustering over the chest wound, their black bodies iridescent in the sunlight. Shuddering, Gemma wiped the back of her hand against a tickle on her cheek, felt unexpected moisture. Had she been crying? She saw that her hand was trembling, tucked it firmly under her arm.

The gesture strengthened her resolve. She had left her phone in the room so she'd have to go for help. But first she would have one more look, before the scene was damaged or interfered with. She might see something that would later be missed.

Gemma forced herself to sit back, to examine the body as if it were not someone she knew . . . not Donald. What struck her?

If Donald had been shot at close range in the chest, he must have seen his killer. Had he been afraid? There was no sign of defensive posture, and the gunshot was dead center—he had not even tried to turn away. Had he known his killer, considered him a friend?

Had he realized what was happening to him, in that instant before his heart stopped? Had he thought of Hazel in a last flash of consciousness?

"Oh, dear God," whispered Gemma. She would have

to tell Hazel. And then she remembered that Hazel was gone, vanished in the wee hours of the morning without a word of explanation.

The fear that had driven Gemma to search the woods flooded back. Where *was* Hazel? Had something happened to her, as well?

No. Gemma shook her head. Why would someone murder Donald *and* Hazel? And besides, she had heard only one shot, and Hazel must have taken the car well before that. Hazel was safe, Gemma told herself, and she would find her.

She stood carefully, trying to minimize her impact on the grass and bracken beneath her feet. Examining the ground, she saw some evidence of trampling in front of Donald's body, but nothing so distinct as a footprint. The soil was rocky, and even if it were damp, it would not take a good impression. There was no obvious point of entry or exit from the crime scene, and no token or article of clothing had been obligingly dropped. Nor could she see an ejected shell casing, an indication that the shotgun had been single-barreled.

Moving forward a few steps, she sank down on the balls of her feet again. She was close enough now to touch him, and for an instant she was tempted to brush his cheek with her fingertips, or to close his eyes.

Instead, she stood slowly, hands firmly shoved in her jacket pockets. She couldn't risk contaminating Donald's body, and she knew that a last human contact would comfort no one but herself.

8

Had we never lov'd sae kindly,
Had we never lov'd sae blindly,
Never met—or never parted—
We had ne'er been broken-hearted.
—ROBERT BURNS, "Ae Fond Kiss"

GEMMA FORCED HERSELF to walk back through the woods by the exact same route by which she had come, stopping briefly where she had noticed the crushed ferns. Who had lain there, and when? A forensic examination might soon provide the answers.

She went on, carefully, but as she reached the last few yards of the path, she gave in to the crawling sensation between her shoulder blades and bolted out into the garden just as Hazel's hired Honda rolled into the drive.

As Gemma started towards the car, Louise came out of the garden shed, her arms filled with freshly pulled carrots.

Louise's ready smile of greeting faded as she took in Gemma's expression. "Gemma, what is it? Are you all right?"

"I— Did you—" Gemma stopped, unable to force any

further sound past her vocal cords, for Hazel had emerged from the car and was walking towards her.

"Gemma—" Hazel began as she reached her, "we need to talk—"

"No. I mean—" Gemma swallowed against the earthy, pungent smell of the carrots that suddenly threatened to choke her. She swung her gaze to Louise's puzzled face, then back to Hazel. "Hazel. It's Donald. I'm afraid he's dead."

"Dead?" Louise repeated blankly, as if she hadn't understood the word.

Hazel's eyes widened, the expanding pupils swallowing the irises. "Wh—"

"In the meadow. He's been shot," Gemma said, very clearly.

Hazel shook her head. "Oh, no. There must be some mistake. That's not possible—"

"There's no mistake. I—I found him. Hazel, I'm so sorry."

"No." Hazel shook her head more vehemently. "You're wrong. He can't be—"

"I'm sure, Hazel," Gemma said firmly. "Come on. We'll go inside—"

But Hazel jerked away from her outstretched hand. "No. I don't believe it. Donald can't be dead. Where is he? What meadow?"

"We need to go into the house, love," coaxed Gemma, but her involuntary glance at the path had betrayed her. She reached for Hazel again, but too late. Hazel was away, flying across the garden towards the path in the woods.

"Hazel, no!" shouted Gemma, but as she started to run, Louise called out to her.

"Gemma, should I ring for an ambulance—"

"No, the police. And hurry," Gemma answered, but the reply cost her precious seconds.

Hazel disappeared into the cover of the trees, and Gemma, hampered by her fear of damaging evidence, couldn't quite manage to gain on her. It was only when Hazel reached Donald's body that Gemma caught up.

Hazel stood, staring, both hands clamped hard over her mouth as if to stifle a scream. When Gemma put an arm round her, she seemed unaware of the contact.

"Hazel, it's all—" *All right,* Gemma had started to say. But it wasn't, and all the platitudes she usually called up to comfort the bereaved seemed suddenly senseless, absurd. It wasn't all right. It was not going to be all right.

"Hazel," she began again. "We need to go back to the house now. The police are coming."

"But . . . Donald . . . I shouldn't leave him. I shouldn't have left him. Last night. I should never have—" Hazel gave a convulsive sob and began to shake.

"Hush. Hush." Gemma comforted her as if she were a child. "There's nothing you can do. Come with me, now."

Hazel moaned, pulling back towards Donald's body, but Gemma managed to turn her back towards the house. They had reached the woods when Hazel sagged against her, then fell to her hands and knees, her body racked by vomiting.

The spasms ceased after a few minutes and she looked up at Gemma, bewildered.

"It's all right," Gemma reassured her. She lifted Hazel to her feet again and urged her on. "We'll get Louise to make us a nice cuppa when we get back to the house," she murmured, knowing it a ridiculous bastion against the horror of Donald's death, but knowing also that it didn't matter what she said, only that Hazel should hear the sound of her voice.

When they reached the garden at last, she saw Louise sitting on the bench by the kitchen door, her hands hanging limply between her knees.

Galvanized by their appearance, Louise jumped up and ran to meet them. "I've rung the police. And John."

"John?" asked Gemma. "He's not here?"

"No. He'd gone to one of the estates to pick up some free-range eggs for breakfast. He's on his way back now."

Breakfast? With a shock, Gemma looked at her watch and saw that it was only now just after seven. "And the others?"

"Still sleeping, as far as I know. I didn't—should I have wakened them?"

"No. You did exactly the right thing. Now, if you'll take Hazel inside, I'll wait for the police." Gemma squeezed Hazel's arm and Louise slipped an arm round her shoulder with unexpected tenderness.

It was only as Gemma watched Louise shepherding Hazel in through the scullery door that she remembered the gun cabinet. There had been at least one shotgun, but she hadn't looked closely—hadn't thought anything of it at the time. Would she know now if a gun was missing?

Her mind balked at following that thought any further. She didn't want to consider the possibility that someone in this house—someone she knew—had fired that shot—but she knew it was a possibility that had to be considered.

Should she examine the gun cabinet now? Hesitating, she realized that the sky had darkened, the clouds scudding in from the west on the rising wind. *Not rain,* she thought with dismay. Rain would play hell with the crime scene, diminish any hope of collecting trace evidence.

But it wasn't *her* crime scene, she reminded herself. She had no jurisdiction here, no official responsibility to investigate Donald's murder.

But she had liked Donald, had felt an unexpected connection to him in spite of her disapproval of his relationship with Hazel—Hazel, who had loved him enough to risk her marriage.

And someone had *shot* him, put an irrevocable end to his future, and to any future Hazel might have had with him—and they had done it right under Gemma's nose. She would help the police find the bastard responsible. She owed it to Donald—and she owed it to Hazel.

Thinking furiously, she walked round to the front of the house, but before she could collect herself, a car with the distinctive yellow stripe of the Northern Constabulary pulled into the drive.

As the officer emerged from the car, Gemma saw that she was young and female, with dark hair, very blue eyes, and a square face that might be pretty when she smiled.

Reaching Gemma, the woman whipped her notebook from her belt with no-nonsense efficiency. "Ma'am. Was it you that reported a death?"

"Yes. One of the guests here at the B&B. I found him in the meadow, just the other side of the woods." Gemma pointed towards the river.

"And you would be?"

Belatedly, Gemma fished in the pocket of her jacket for her identification. "Gemma James. Detective inspector with the Metropolitan Police. I'm a guest here as well."

If the officer was startled by this bit of information, she betrayed it only by the slight elevation of her eyebrows. She spoke unintelligibly into her radio before saying to Gemma, "Ma'am. Now, if you could just show me the deceased."

The journey across the garden and back through the woods seemed a nightmare to Gemma. Her legs began to feel as if they were mired in clay; the distance seemed to extend itself with each step. She stopped to point out the area of crushed ferns, then again to indicate where Hazel had vomited.

"One of the other guests saw the body," she explained, "before I could stop her. She was sick here, as I was taking her back to the house."

At the far edge of the woods, Gemma stopped, finding herself unable to go farther. "Just over there." With a nod, she indicated the tussocks of heather hiding Donald.

Gemma watched as the officer continued along the path, saw the moment of hesitation as the young woman came close enough to make sense of what she saw. But the officer went on, her posture more businesslike than ever, and squatted to make a cursory examination of the body. The yellow of her jacket stood out against the heather with the brilliance of a clump of gorse. She stood and spoke into her radio again before returning to Gemma.

"We're to wait here for the backup from Aviemore, ma'am," she said grimly. Her skin had paled beneath her makeup.

"What's your name, Constable?" asked Gemma, sympathy momentarily overriding her personal worries.

"Mackenzie, ma'am."

"You're from around here?"

"Carrbridge. That's just north of Aviemore, on the A9," Constable Mackenzie added, unbending a little, as Gemma had hoped.

"I don't suppose you see many fatalities," Gemma said gently, thinking that the young woman couldn't be long out of training college.

"The A9 is bad for motor crashes. And a few weeks ago, we had a pensioner wander off—died of exposure before we found him."

"You haven't worked a homicide before?"

The constable stiffened at this. "What makes you so sure it's a homicide, ma'am?"

"No gun," Gemma answered. "And I knew him, a bit. I can't believe he'd have shot himself."

Tucking a stray hair behind her ear, Mackenzie opened her notebook again. "The deceased's name?"

"Donald Brodie."

Mackenzie stared at her. "Brodie of Benvulin?" When Gemma nodded, the constable said, "But you told me he was a guest at the B&B."

"He was. It was a special cookery weekend." As Gemma explained, all the complications of the situation came flooding back. Where had Hazel been that morning, and what was she to say about Hazel's relationship with Donald?

Detective Chief Inspector Alun Ross knelt at the edge of his flower border, setting out a flat of lobelia. From the springy turf beneath his knees, moisture seeped through the fabric of his old gardening trousers, but he didn't mind—it made him feel connected to the earth. Tamping the four-inch plant into the rich, composted soil, he sat back to admire his handiwork.

The tiny, star-shaped blossoms of the lobelia were a brilliant blue against the pale pink of the compact azaleas just coming into bloom behind them. A few feet farther along the border, a stand of magnificent white iris were just showing their tightly furled buds.

Although it was still early on Sunday morning, the sun soaked into his back like warm honey, and a light breeze cooled the sweat above his collar. The sound of bells came faintly over the garden wall, and in his mind's eye he saw his tidy terraced house and square of garden as the jewel in Inverness's crown, and from it the tiered streets dropping down to St. Andrew's Cathedral on Ness Walk.

As a child, he had attended services there, and he imagined his mother's dismay if she could see him now, slacking on a Sunday morning. But *this* was his idea of heaven—why should he look any further?

Not that his wife had agreed with him, mind you—his ex-wife, he should say. She was married now to a fertilizer salesman who liked to dance.

It had served Ross right, according to his daughter, Amanda, who had told him he should have taken her mum out a bit more. But then his daughter sometimes seemed to him as incomprehensible as an alien species—and how could he have explained to either of them that the last thing he'd wanted after a day on the job was to go *out*.

What he wanted was his own small universe, house and garden, a world he could control, an order he could impose. He came home; if it was fine enough he would work in the garden—there was always something needed doing—and if not, he did his chores round the house, then he would settle by the fire with his gardening books and catalogs and his dram of whisky.

Now his routine was undisturbed by anyone's nagging, and he liked it just fine, thank you very much. He had seen his ex-wife not long ago, walking along Ness Bank. She'd looked like a tart, hair newly bouffant, makeup too heavy, skirt too tight and too short. He'd been cordial enough to her and her paunchy, balding husband, but he'd been glad to make his escape—and if he'd felt a stirring of the old desire, he'd quickly banished it.

Now, setting the last of the lobelias into its new bed, he stretched in anticipation of a well-deserved break. He'd make himself a cup of tea from the kettle he'd left simmering on the kitchen hob, then he'd sit in his gazebo and have a browse through the Sunday newspaper while the bees hummed beside him in the lavender.

But as he dusted off his knees at the kitchen door, he heard the phone ringing.

His heart sank. No one called him for a friendly chat at this hour of a Sunday morning. Looking out, he saw that the light in the garden had faded as suddenly as if someone had thrown a blanket across the sun. With a sigh of resignation, he crossed the room and lifted the phone from its cradle.

He should have known. He'd been a policeman too long to believe in such a thing as a perfect day.

The call came as Kincaid was trying to grind beans for coffee and butter Toby's toast simultaneously, a feat he had not quite mastered. Nor was his multitasking helped by the fact that both dogs were beneath his feet, barking madly at the grinder, while Sid, the cat, hissed and batted at them from his perch on the kitchen table.

He switched off the grinder, shouted at the dogs, slid Toby's plate precariously across the table, and grabbed the phone without glancing at the ubiquitous caller ID.

"This had better be good," he snapped, assuming the caller was Doug Cullen, his sergeant.

There was a silence on the other end of the line, then Gemma's voice, sounding more than taken aback. "Duncan?"

"Oh, sorry, love. I thought you were Cullen, ringing to nag me for the umpteenth time—"

"I've been trying to reach you all weekend. Either the phone's been engaged, or you haven't answered, and your mobile is going straight to voice mail." She sounded unexpectedly distressed.

"Doug's been bending my ear all weekend over this report I left with him," Kincaid explained. It was fudging the truth a bit, but he didn't want to discuss Kit over the telephone, especially when the boy might appear at any moment. The fact that Kit had not come downstairs after all the canine commotion was a clear sign that he was still shutting out Kincaid—and Toby.

When he was a boy Kincaid's mother would have called it "a fit of the sulks"—the description a little harsh considering Kit's circumstances. But Kincaid *was* beginning to find the behavior a bit aggravating.

"—and I left the spare battery for the mobile at the Yard," he continued to Gemma. "Why didn't you leave a message? I'd have rung you back."

"I didn't want to talk to the bloody machine," Gemma said, her voice rising in an uncharacteristic quaver.

"Gemma, what's wrong? Are you all right?"

"Yes. No. Not really. It's Hazel."

"Is she ill? What's happened?"

"There's been a death, a shooting, early this morning. I found the body. His name was Donald Brodie, and he and Hazel were lovers before she was married. She was thinking of leaving Tim—"

"Good God." Kincaid dumped Sid unceremoniously from the kitchen chair and sank into it. "She was having an affair with this Brodie?"

"Not exactly. At least, not until— The thing is, I don't know what happened last night, and now I can't talk to her. The police have everyone else sequestered in the house with a constable until the investigative team gets here from Inverness."

"And you?"

"They've let me stay in the barn conversion—that's where Hazel and I were sleeping. But she left sometime in the night, and only came back after I'd found him—

Donald." Gemma's voice broke, and Kincaid waited while she made an effort to get it under control. "If I'd just talked to her before the police arrived, then—"

"Gemma, I'm sure you did all you could. Look, I'll get the next train—or the next flight to Inverness—"

"What about the children?"

"I could get Wes to come, or take them to your parents—"

"No. Just wait. But could you see Tim Cavendish? Tell him what's happened? I don't mean about Hazel and Donald," she amended quickly, "just that there's been a death, so he'll be prepared."

"Gemma—surely you don't think Hazel could have shot this bloke?"

"No," she said sharply. "Of course not. But—if there's some connection—what if Hazel is in danger, too?"

9

So you are happed and gone, and there you're lying,
Far from the glen, deep down the slope of seas,
Out of the stormy night, the grey sleet flying,
And never again for you the Hebrides!
We need not keep the peat and cruise glowing,
The goodwife may put by her ale and bread,
For you, who kept the crack so blithely going,
Now sleep at last, silent and comforted.
      NEIL MUNRO, "The Story Teller" *(written on the*
                              death of Robert Louis Stevenson)

**From the Diary of Helen Brodie, Benvulin, 10
December 1898**

This morning's post brought the news of the death of
Charles Urquhart at Carnmore from a virulent fever,
contracted on his return from Edinburgh a fortnight
ago. Poor Charles! His constitution was never
strong, as I recall, and he was caught out in the bliz-
zard that has isolated us here at Benvulin. My heart
aches for his poor wife and son. What a loss, a need-
less loss, of a man in his prime.

I remember Charles as a serious lad, one who

preferred to sit in the corner at dances and talk about books. And yet there was a spark of humor about him, and a kindness in the eyes. For a time, I had thought . . . but that was before he met Olivia Grant. From then he had no thought for anyone else, and rumor had it that Livvy's father encouraged him, seeking a stable and well-connected marriage for his daughter.

How will Livvy Urquhart manage now, I wonder, with sole responsibility for the distillery? We must do something for her, and hope that Charles showed more wisdom in the matter of Pattison's than my dear brother.

That brings me to the day's other ill tidings. Not that it was unexpected, of course, but it still came as a shock to see it written in the Edinburgh newspaper. Pattison's, the Edinburgh firm of blenders, has indeed failed, due at least in part to the profligate spending of the Pattison Brothers.

What this will mean for Benvulin I dare not think.

Rab, like our father before him, has always been inclined to invest recklessly (although, unlike Father, Rab's weakness is the distillery itself, rather than the house) and he has committed to several "joint adventures" in which he has sold whisky to Pattison's without payment, in expectation of a price rise; a price rise that will now never occur.

I assure myself that we shall weather this crisis, as we have others, but I cannot help but wish that my brother had not spent his wife's funds quite so readily. Margaret, the belle of Grantown society little more than a decade ago, has become fat and indolent in the security of her marriage. She has no *knowledge of the business and no interest in anything other than the vagaries of fashion or the latest gossip.*

Nor does she give proper attention to the children, who have become wayward from lack of discipline or schedule. Rab plays only the occasional game of cricket with little Robert, and of poor wee Meg he takes no notice at all.

How different might things have been if he had followed his heart rather than his pocketbook? A woman who challenged his intellect and his character might have made a different man of him, and perhaps a different father as well.

The snow grows heavier as I write, and I can no longer see the river from my window. Benvulin will soon be cut off again in its own little world, a state I used to anticipate with pleasure as a child, but have come to loathe. Only early December, and already a second fierce storm afflicts us. I fear this is a harbinger of a bad winter.

The knock came just as Gemma was ending her call to Kincaid. Opening the door, Gemma found Constable Mackenzie hovering on her doorstep, her hand raised to knock again.

"Ma'am—"

"Has the investigating team arrived?" Gemma asked. Among the police cars parked half on the lawn, leaving a clear path for the scene-of-crime and mortuary vans, she saw two new unmarked cars. *Poor Louise,* she thought with a pang of sympathy as she noticed the tire tracks in the soft turf.

"Yes, ma'am," Mackenzie answered. "It's Chief Inspector Ross, from headquarters in Inverness."

"He'll be wanting to talk to me, then. I'll just—"

"Ma'am." Mackenzie colored slightly. "The chief inspector's asked that I escort you to join the other guests."

"Escort?"

"Yes, ma'am. They're all in the sitting room of the main house. If you'll just follow me."

"But—" The protest died on Gemma's lips. The constable's embarrassment was obvious, and there was no use making things difficult for the young woman. She would have the opportunity to talk to the chief inspector soon enough, and in the meantime, she wanted to see Hazel.

But as she meekly followed Mackenzie around the house to the front door, she thought that Chief Inspector Ross from Inverness had made it quite clear that he had no intention of treating her as an equal.

Another constable stood at parade rest just outside the door of the sitting room, his broad face impassive.

John Innes jumped up as Gemma slipped into the room. "Gemma! What's all this about? They've said Donald's been . . . killed. Surely that's not—"

"Shot," said Hazel, with the clear articulation of the very shocked. She sat crumpled in the wing chair near the fire, hugging herself and rocking gently. "I told you. It was so neat, so tidy . . . I'd never have thought . . . There was hardly any blood at all."

Gemma couldn't tell her that the blood would have pooled beneath his body, his back a mess from the force of the pellets' exit. But Hazel was at least partly right—there would not have been much bleeding, even from the exit wound, because Donald's heart must have stopped pumping instantly.

The room, heated by the morning sun, smelled of stale

ash and, faintly, of sweat. On the table by the window, the heads of the mauve tulips drooped as if they, too, were grieving.

Louise gave Hazel a concerned glance and whispered, "I've tried to get her to drink tea, but she wouldn't touch it."

"So it is true." John began to pace. "Donald's really dead." He shook his head as if he couldn't quite comprehend it. "But why would someone kill him? Donald, of all people? Everyone loved Donald. And why herd us in here and put a guard on the door?"

"The police will be treating it as a suspicious death," Gemma explained. "It's routine procedure, until everyone has been questioned and the initial search completed."

"Oh, right. You would know, wouldn't you?" said Heather Urquhart from the other corner of the sofa. Although she sat with her feet tucked up beneath her in her usual feline pose, the tension in her body erased any grace.

Pascal and Martin gave Gemma wary looks, as if they'd just remembered her job, and she swore under her breath. Damn the woman.

"Have they sent you in here to spy on us?" added Heather, her voice rising. Her skin without makeup was blotchy, her long hair tangled and carelessly tied back.

"Is there some reason you think they should have?"

"No, of course not." Heather gave a dismissive shrug, but her eyes slid away from Gemma's.

"Look, I've no special privileges here," Gemma told them. "I'm a guest, just like you, but you can't expect me not to apply my experience."

Pascal studied her. "How can you be sure it was not an accident?" He looked rumpled, as if he had dressed hurriedly in yesterday's clothes. "These things happen, even with the most experienced hunter, a stumble—"

Had Gemma been in charge of the investigation, she'd have put the constable in the room, rather than outside it, to prevent just this sort of speculation and exchanging information. But since Chief Inspector Ross had not done so, she might as well take advantage of her position. "The gun was missing," she said, watching as their expressions registered varying degrees of surprise.

Martin Gilmore spoke for the first time. "But . . . what if someone was shooting and didn't see him—"

"Not if the wound was neat," interrupted John. "That means the gun was close, maybe only inches—"

Louise was shaking her head at him, miming towards Hazel.

"Oh, sorry," faltered John. "I didna think . . ." His accent was more pronounced than usual, making Gemma think painfully of Donald.

"Did anyone see anything?" she asked. "Or hear anything?"

"You know we were sharing a room," volunteered Martin. "I heard Donald go out this morning."

"What time was it?"

Martin shook his head, as if sorry to disappoint her. "I'm not sure. I remember pulling the pillow over my eyes, so it must have been light. And the bloody birds were singing."

When no one else spoke, Gemma turned to John. "John. Your gun cabinet. You haven't checked—"

John halted his pacing and stared at her. "My guns? But why would—"

"Jesus Christ!" Heather uncoiled herself with unprecedented speed, her feet hitting the floor with a thud. "You're not suggesting it was one of us?"

"I'm not suggesting anything," said Gemma. "It's the first question the police will ask once they've had a look round the house."

John rubbed his hand across the stubble on his chin, and it seemed to Gemma that the smell of sweat grew stronger. "I went out through the scullery door this morning," he said, "but I didna look— The cabinet was locked— I always lock it—"

Gemma turned to Louise. "You were here, Louise, in and out of the kitchen. You didn't notice?"

"No. I—" Louise stopped, frowning with the effort of recall. Slowly, she said, "I picked up my gardening things from the scullery, that I remember. And then afterwards, with Hazel—I never thought—"

At the sound of her name, Hazel looked up, blinking. "Oh, God. What have I done?" she whispered.

"It's all right," Gemma reassured her swiftly, but she was aware of a sharpening of attention in the room. How could she prevent Hazel from saying things that could be so easily misinterpreted? Crossing the room to Hazel's side, she said softly, "Hazel, you haven't done anything. You mustn't say things like that. Do you understand?"

"She should never have come." The words were harsh, the voice stretched to breaking. Turning, Gemma saw that Heather had stood. Her hair had come loose from its binding and spilled wildly over her shoulders and across her face. With her trembling hand pointed at Hazel in accusation, she might have been an ancient prophetess. "We were all right before she came. And now Donald's dead. I can't believe he's dead. What am I going to do without him?" She began to cry, with the dry, racking sobs of someone who didn't often allow such release and had never learned to do it gracefully.

To Gemma's surprise, it was not Pascal who went to

comfort her, but John. "It's all right, lassie," he crooned, easing her back into her chair. He reached for the whisky on the sideboard and poured her a stiff measure. "Have a wee dram for the shock. We'll all have a wee dram." Pouring another for himself, he drank it off in one swallow.

Louise reached out, as if to stop him. "John, are you sure that's—"

"I don't care if it's *wise*, woman. He was my friend, a good man. And he's dead." He began splashing whisky into the round of glasses on a tray.

Taking one, Gemma went back to Hazel and knelt beside her. The sharp odor of the whisky reached her, lodging in the back of her throat. "Have a sip, love," she whispered. "John's right. It will do you good." Hazel's hand trembled as she took the glass, and her teeth knocked against the rim. "Hazel," Gemma continued softly, urgently, as the conversation rose around them, "where did you go this morning, in the car?" She had to know before she talked to the police.

"The railway station. I was going to go home, without saying good-bye. I couldn't face Donald again, after last night—"

"You didn't see him this morning?"

"No. Not until—not until you told me—" Hazel pressed her fist to her mouth and began to cry soundlessly, the tears slipping unchecked down her cheeks, but Gemma sat back, dizzy with the force of relief that washed through her.

After Gemma rang off, Kincaid abandoned his own breakfast and went upstairs to check on Kit, who had not yet appeared. He found the boy sitting cross-legged on his bed in an old T-shirt, rereading one of his Harry Potter novels.

"Finished with *Kidnapped,* then?" Kincaid asked, pulling the desk chair closer to the bed and sitting down. Any idea he might have had of drawing parallels between the orphaned heroes was put paid to by the sight of the photo of Kit's mother on the bedside table.

Gemma had given Kit the frame for Christmas, and until this morning the photo had resided unobtrusively on a corner of Kit's desk.

Kit shrugged and kept his eyes on his book, although Kincaid could see that he wasn't reading.

"You didn't come down for breakfast," Kincaid said, trying again. "You're not ill, are you?"

"I'll get cereal in a bit." Kit still didn't look at him. "Where's Tess?"

"Begging toast off Toby. I'm not used to seeing you without your familiar," Kincaid quipped, and was rewarded by a twitch of Kit's lip, a stifled smile. "Listen, Kit," he went on, encouraged, "I've got to go out for a bit this morning, to see Tim Cavendish. There's been an accident—"

"Not Gemma! Or Aunt Hazel!" Kit's face went white and his book slipped from his fingers, its pages fluttering.

Cursing himself for his clumsiness, Kincaid said hurriedly, "No, no. It was a man—another guest at the B&B. Gemma had a chance to ring and wanted me to let Tim know before he saw it on the news, so that he wouldn't worry."

Kit seemed to relax, but Kincaid could still see the pulse beating in the fragile hollow of the boy's throat.

"Can they come home today, then?" Kit asked. "Gemma and Hazel?"

"I don't know. I expect they'll have to stay on for a bit, at least until the preliminary questions are answered."

"This man— It was a murder, wasn't it? Not an accident."

"I'm afraid it looks like it, yes."

Kit studied him for a moment, his expression unreadable. "You're going to go, too," he said, making it a statement.

Kincaid thought of his offer to Gemma, so quickly rebuffed. "I hope it won't come to that." He reached out and tousled his son's fair hair. "But in the meantime, will you look after Toby while I'm out?"

He knew he was going to have to talk to Kit again about his grandmother, but first he had to tackle Tim Cavendish.

The weather had held fine through the weekend, and deciding that he might as well enjoy the drive across London, Kincaid pulled the canvas cover off the Midget. Although the little red car could be called a classic, in reality it had sagging springs and sometimes-unreliable parts. He hadn't driven it for weeks, but for once the battery had held its charge and the engine puttered cooperatively to life on the first try.

He'd always maintained that Sunday was the day to drive in London for pleasure, but when, a half hour later, he found himself idling behind a queue of buses in the Euston Road, he wondered if he had been a bit precipitous.

Looking up at the ugly blocks of flats to his right, he thought of his sergeant, Doug Cullen, who lived nearby, and recalled uneasily the small falsehood he had told Gemma. He *had* spoken to Doug several times over the weekend—he'd only been stretching the truth a little when he'd said it was Doug who'd kept the phone line engaged.

But he knew well enough that even little lies, however kindly meant, had a way of assuming monstrous proportions, and he wished that he had been honest with Gemma from the beginning. Now, in the light of what had happened in Scotland, his omission was going to be even more awkward to explain. He would, he resolved, tell her as soon as he spoke with her again.

When, a few minutes later, he turned north from Pentonville Road into the sedate crescents of Islington, he realized it was the first time he'd been to the Cavendishes' house since Gemma had moved out. He had to remind himself not to pull round to the garage in the back. Although he knew that Hazel now used the flat as an office, he found it impossible to imagine it other than it had been, stamped by Gemma's and Toby's presence. Would he someday come to feel the same way about the Notting Hill house? It seemed to him that their full possession of the place was still marred by the emptiness of the nursery.

Pushing such thoughts aside, he parked in front of the Cavendishes' house, a detached Victorian built of honey-colored stone, unexpectedly situated between two Georgian terraces. As he climbed out of the car, he noticed that the garden, previously a model of tidiness, looked weedy and neglected.

The house seemed quiet, turned in upon itself, the front drapes still drawn. Kincaid wondered if Tim had gone out—no one with an active four-year-old slept in until midmorning, even on a Sunday—but the pealing of the bell brought quick footsteps in response.

The door swung wide, revealing a pleasant-faced woman in her sixties with smartly bobbed graying hair. "Can I help you?" she asked with an inquiring smile. She wore a raspberry shell suit, and her features seemed vaguely familiar.

"Is Tim at home? I'm Duncan Kincaid."

"Oh, you're Toby's dad," she said with obvious delight. "I've heard so much about you." Holding out her hand, she added, "I'm Carolyn Cavendish, Tim's mum."

Kincaid clasped her well-manicured fingers. "Nice to meet you." He had not quite got used to being referred to as Toby's dad, and he felt an unexpected flush of pleasure.

"Come in, won't you?" Stepping back, she ushered him into the house. "Holly is quite smitten with you."

"And vice versa." Kincaid looked round, prepared for the onslaught of Holly's usual enthusiastic welcome, but the child didn't appear.

"I've just made some coffee," said Carolyn Cavendish, "if you'll join me?"

As Kincaid surveyed the familiar array of slightly worn furniture and children's toys, the magnitude of what Gemma had told him that morning truly registered for the first time. How could Hazel, of all people, have possibly been having an affair?

He had never known anyone so contented, so at home in her domestic environment. He caught sight of the piano, music still open on the stand as if Gemma had just finished practicing, and felt a pang of loss for a time that had been innocent at least in memory.

Realizing that Mrs. Cavendish was watching him curiously, he brought himself back to the present with an effort. "Thanks. I'd like to wait if Tim won't be long—"

"Oh, but Tim's gone." Leading the way to the kitchen, Mrs. Cavendish pulled two mugs from a rack above the cooker. "But I'm glad of the company." As she pressed the coffee already standing in the pot, she added, "Tony—that's Tim's father—has taken Holly for a swing on the school playground, and I had nothing on my agenda more pressing than the Sunday papers."

Kincaid accepted the mug and sank slowly into a seat

at the scarred wooden table where he had spent so much time with Hazel, Gemma, and the children. The kitchen looked much the same; the old glass-fronted cabinets were still stained a mossy green, the walls sponged peach, and a basket of Hazel's knitting sat on the table end.

"Tim's out?"

"Away for the weekend," she corrected. "Well, it was such lovely weather, and it was no trouble for us to come from Wimbledon. Usually, Holly comes to us, but she had a birthday party here in the neighborhood yesterday. One of her school friends. Not that Hazel would have approved of all the sugar," she added ruefully. "You should have seen them, little savages—"

"Mrs. Cavendish." Kincaid abandoned his manners in his rising anxiety. "Where *is* Tim?"

"Walking. Some friends rang on Friday, after Hazel had got the train, and invited him to go. It seemed the perfect opportunity. He hasn't had a holiday in ages, poor dear."

"Where are Tim and his friends walking?" he asked carefully, trying not to betray his dismay.

"Um, Hampshire, I think he said. The Downs."

"Do you know when he'll be back?"

"Sometime this evening." She frowned slightly. "Is there something wrong?"

"Can you get in touch with him? Did he take his mobile phone?"

"No, I don't believe he did. He said they were planning a real getaway. Has something happened?"

He forced a smile. "I'm sorry, I didn't mean to alarm you. It's just that there's been an accident at the B&B where Hazel and Gemma are staying—Hazel's fine, don't worry—but I thought Tim should know as soon as possible."

"An accident?"

"One of the other guests," Kincaid explained. "He's dead, I'm afraid. The police will have questions, and it's always possible that the story could make the national media. I didn't want Tim reading about it in the papers before Hazel had a chance to call him."

He finished his coffee and stood. "Will you tell Tim to ring me as soon as he gets in?"

"Yes, of course, but—" She touched his arm. "This man, you said there was an accident. What happened?"

"He was shot."

Mrs. Cavendish lifted a hand to her mouth. "Oh, my God. You're sure Hazel's all right? Did she—"

"Hazel's fine," he assured her again. "But that's all I know, Mrs. Cavendish. I'll let you know as soon as there's more news." He took his leave, but once in the car he sat for a moment, his unease growing as he thought over what he had heard.

Surely it was a coincidence that Tim Cavendish had had an unexpected invitation to go out of town on the very weekend Hazel had meant to see another man—the weather was lovely, after all. But although he didn't think of Tim as a close friend, they had spent a good deal of time in idle chat, and he had never once heard Tim mention an interest in walking.

That could well be coincidence again—perhaps the subject had just never happened to come up. But Kincaid had learned over the years to distrust coincidence—especially when there was murder involved.

God, how he hated outdoor crime scenes. Chief Inspector Alun Ross had acted quickly to initiate the tedious and painstaking process of securing the scene and gathering evidence, but since he'd arrived, the sun had disappeared behind an increasingly ominous bank of cloud and chill spurts of wind eddied through the trees and bracken. If the rain held off another hour, they would be lucky.

At least the police surgeon, Jimmy Webb, arrived quickly. Giving Ross no more than a nod of greeting, he suited up and knelt over the body. Although the heavy-jowled Webb was taciturn, he was direct and efficient, and Ross was always glad to find him on duty.

Webb soon finished with his poking and prodding, and shucked his white coverall like a mollusk sliding out of its shell. "You'd best get your tarps up," he said, glancing at the sky as he came over to Ross.

"The lads are fetching them now." Ross gestured at the team of uniformed officers emerging from the woods, carrying awkward bundles of canvas sheeting. "What can you tell me?"

"Cause of death is obvious enough, but I can't be definite about the size of the gun. The pathologist should be able to tell you more when he gets him on the slab." Wadding up his coverall, Webb handed it to the nearest constable. "I can tell ye that it's my opinion the body hasn't been moved."

"Time of death?"

"Sometime after midnight." Web smiled at Ross's grimace. "Well, what did ye expect, man? Miracles?" He shook his head. "It's a shame, that. The man made good whisky."

And that, thought Ross as the doctor stumped away, was surely the highest compliment a Highlander could give.

He directed a team to set up shelter over the trysting place in the wood as well, but there was no way he could protect all the area that needed to be covered in the fingertip search. The officers would just have to do the best they could if it rained. It wouldn't be the first time they had worked in the muck, nor would it be the last.

Damn it! He needed more men, and soon, while the weather held off. He made his way back to the house and stopped at the garden's edge, looking for his sergeant, Munro. The graveled car park was a hive of yellow-jacketed activity, the officers' muted conversation providing a constant hum. But after a moment's search he spotted Munro, giving instructions to a newly arrived search team. Not that Munro would be easy to miss, Ross thought affectionately—the man was a head taller than anyone else, with a pale cadaverous face that concealed a quick wit and slightly malicious sense of humor.

Munro having acknowledged his presence with a nod and a lift of his hand, Ross surveyed his surroundings while he waited for the sergeant to finish. It was a nice old property, well situated, and he recognized the hand of a fellow gardener at work. But why, with his own grand house just down the road, had Donald Brodie chosen to stay the night at a B&B?

Nor would he be the only one speculating, thought Ross as he saw the first of the television vans pull up at the drive's end. The constable on duty refused the driver entry, but this one was merely the first of many—soon the media would be thick as maggots on a corpse.

While he waited for Munro to join him, Ross examined the list of the B&B's residents and guests compiled by the first officer on the scene. Mackenzie, her name was, and a bonny wee lass who had no business in a man's uniform. She was sharp enough, though, and according to her report, the woman who had discovered the body was a London copper, CID, no less.

Well, he supposed even the Metropolitan Police deserved a holiday now and again, but still, it struck him as odd to find another copper at a murder scene. He would definitely interview Detective Inspector Gemma James first.

She sat across from him at the dining room table, her posture relaxed, her hands clasped loosely in her lap. He found something slightly old-fashioned about her face, and he wondered briefly if her background was Scots. She reminded him a bit of his daughter, Ross thought as he studied her, not so much in looks or coloring, but in her direct and confident manner. Her hair was the deep red of burnished copper; her face bore a light dusting of freckles; a wide, generous mouth; hazel eyes with flecks of gold in the irises. She was attractive rather than beautiful, he decided, with an air of friendly competence—and he found that he thoroughly distrusted her.

He'd begun by asking her to relate the events of the morning, while behind him, Munro took notes from a chair in the corner. With the ease born of practice, Inspector James told her story with a conciseness marred only by the occasional furrowing of her brow as she added a detail. Once or twice she paused to allow Munro to catch up, and he saw his normally lugubrious sergeant tighten his lips in what passed for a smile.

Deliberately, Ross refrained from using her title. "Miss James, your friend that was sick in the woods—I understand you're sharing a room?"

"Yes."

"And yet you alone heard the shot—or what you thought was a shot? And you alone went to investigate?"

"Yes. That's right."

No elaboration, Ross thought. She would know well that unnecessary elaboration could trip one up, lead to careless disclosure. His interest quickened.

"And yet it was this same friend"—he glanced at his notes—"Mrs. Cavendish, I believe?"

"Yes, Hazel."

"It was this same friend who was sick on seeing the body?"

"Yes." Gemma James's posture didn't change, but he thought he saw a faint heightening of the color along her cheekbones.

"But she wasn't with you when you made the initial discovery. Was she still sleeping?"

"No. She'd gone for a drive. She arrived back just as I was about to ring the police."

"I see. And you told her where you had found Mr. Brodie?"

"No—I—I said I'd found Donald in the meadow. And that he was dead."

"Then you took her to see the body?" Ross allowed disapproval to creep into his voice.

"No! Of course not," she retorted with the first hint of defensiveness. "She ran—she looked before I could stop her."

"Then you must have told her which meadow," Ross suggested reasonably.

"No. It was a natural assumption. Everyone walked that way."

"You've been here how long, Miss James?" Ross shuffled his papers again.

"Two days." She compressed her lips, as if unwilling to be drawn further. He could hear her accent more clearly now—London, but not Cockney, and not posh.

"In two days you've learned everyone's habits?" he asked, combining admiration with a dash of skepticism.

"No." This time her flush was unmistakable. "But I'm

observant, Chief Inspector, and as I said, the path was obvious."

Ross thought for a moment, considering what she had told him—and what she had not. "About your friend, now, wasn't it rather early for someone to be going for a drive?"

Gemma James shifted in her chair for the first time. "I don't know. You'll have to ask her."

This was the least cooperative response she'd given so far, and Ross had the distinct impression that she'd both dreaded the question and rehearsed the answer. There was definitely something fishy here, and not just the piscine parade on the wall. And Hazel Cavendish had vomited—not a surprising response under the circumstances, but was there more to it than the shock of unexpected and violent death?

"You said you and your friend came for a cookery weekend. Was Mrs. Cavendish previously acquainted with Mr. Brodie?"

"Yes, she knew him. She also knew Louise Innes— they were at school together—and Heather Urquhart is her cousin."

Cozier and cozier, thought Ross. He didn't like it at all. "What was the nature of Mrs. Cavendish's relationship with Mr. Brodie?"

"I believe they were old friends." Gemma James gazed at him with such limpid candor that he suspected he would get no more out of her and changed his tack.

"Tell me about the others," Ross said, settling back in his chair. "And how they were acquainted with Mr. Brodie."

"Well, there are the Inneses, who own this place. John cooks, and Louise runs the house and does the gardening.

I believe they came here from Edinburgh a couple of years ago, and, um . . . I think perhaps they cultivated Donald Brodie for his contacts." She looked uncomfortable as she added this, as if she felt disloyal.

"Then there's Martin Gilmore. He's John Innes's half brother, and he's interested in cooking. I don't think he'd ever met Donald before this weekend.

"Pascal Benoit, the Frenchman, had some sort of business dealings with Donald, but I don't believe he ever said exactly what they were. And Heather Urquhart, Hazel's cousin, is Benvulin's manager, so she probably knew Donald better than anyone. I think she's quite cut up by his death."

"Thank you. That's very helpful." Ross heard Munro shift behind him, as if preparing to close his notebook. He lifted his hand slightly in a halting gesture and focused all his attention on Gemma. Deliberately, he used her title for the first time, calling on her professional instincts. "Now, Inspector James. Have you seen or heard anything that leads you to believe one of these people might have had reason to kill Donald Brodie?"

She studied her clasped hands for a moment before looking up at him. "No. I've no idea why anyone would have wanted to kill Donald. But . . . I did see . . . something. Yesterday evening. A woman came to the house, with a child, to see Donald. He went out to her, and from the window I could tell that they were arguing. And there was another man, standing back in the shadows. The rest of us went in to dinner, and after a few minutes Donald joined us. I don't know what happened to the woman or the other man."

"And no one questioned Mr. Brodie about it?"

"No. It was . . . awkward."

"You don't know who this woman was?"

"No." She looked away from him, out the window at the police cars now flanking the drive, and she seemed to come to some decision. "But I had the distinct impression that Heather Urquhart did."

10

❧

The wild roses had just come into bloom, pink roses and white, and the broom was yellow as meadowland butter with an eddy of scent now and then that choked the brain like a sickly sweet narcotic.

—NEIL GUNN, *The Serpent*

CALLUM HAD BREAKFASTED early before going to pick up the trekkers' luggage from the guesthouse in Ballindalloch. Aunt Janet would guide the group back to the stables by a different route, with a stop for a picnic lunch. For a moment, he envied them their amble along the wooded trails, with pauses to gaze into the trout pools that lay like jewels along the Spey.

Once, it had been enough, evenings with his feet stretched towards the fire in his cottage as he read about the exploits of his Jacobite forebears. Then Alison had come into his life, and with her the worm of discontent.

Suddenly, a wave of exhaustion swept over him. He pulled the van onto the verge, just where the road curved to reveal the sweeping meadows of Benvulin. Gazing at the view, he tried to form in his mind the things he loved rather than think of Donald Brodie—the scents of wild thyme and pine on a still summer's day, the clusters of red berries on rowans in the fall, the black tracks of ptarmigan on the winter snow. Callum had lived easily in the rhythm of his life, and if he had felt socially awkward with women, he had enjoyed his guide duties, telling the tourists about the terrain as they rode, the plant and animal life, the history that seemed to breathe from the rocky land.

His eyelids drooped and he jerked himself awake. The previous night's lack of sleep was beginning to tell on him, but it had been worth it. Everything he had done, he had done for the best, for Alison, and for Chrissy. Surely, now that Alison knew the truth about Donald, she would see things differently. Checking in the rearview mirror, he pulled the old van into the road again. He would pay Alison a visit that evening, but first he had responsibilities to meet.

He had only gone a few miles when he saw the flash of blue lights ahead. Rounding a curve, he braked hard. Police cars lined the road, and a crowd milled in the verge. His first thought was of his father—he and Janet worried constantly about Tom's weaving progress down the narrow, winding road, but at least walking was safer than letting him behind the wheel of an automobile. Had the old man tempted fate once too often and stumbled in front of an oncoming car?

But as Callum drew nearer, he realized that the thickest part of the mob had gathered in front of the Inneses' gate. He spotted a van bearing the familiar logo of Grampian television. Dread gripped him. He pulled the van off onto the verge, and when he pulled the keys from the ignition, he saw that his hands were shaking.

He pushed his way through the crowd to the gate but

found his way blocked by a uniformed constable. "What is it? What's happened?" he asked.

"Sorry, sir. I'm not at liberty to say."

"But I'm a friend of the Inneses. Are they all right?" Callum moved forward, and the constable stepped sideways neatly, blocking his path. "Sorry, sir. Can't let you through. Orders."

Callum hesitated, wondering if he might push his way past, when he felt a hand on his shoulder. It was Peter McNulty, the stillman at Benvulin. McNulty motioned him aside, out of the constable's hearing.

A dark-haired, blue-eyed Celt, McNulty usually displayed a debonair charm, but now his eyes looked bloodshot, and he was white and pinched about the mouth. Callum gripped his arm. "What is it, Peter? What's happened here?"

"It's Donald Brodie. Someone's bloody shot him," McNulty said hoarsely. He wiped the back of his hand across his mouth and took a sip from a flask.

"Brodie? He's dead, then?" Callum stared at him.

"Aye." McNulty passed him the flask. "I've a wee cousin on the force. He saw the body."

"But—" Callum stopped, still trying to take in the implications.

"He was a good man, a good boss." McNulty sounded near to tears. "Better than his father. God knows what'll become of us now with *her* in charge."

"Her?"

"Bloody Heather Urquhart. She's a cold bitch, that one, who cares for nothing but her own power. She'll try to convince the board of directors to sell to one of the large holding companies, because she thinks they'll make her managing director. It's not her family's business at stake, and if you want my opinion, she'd like nothing better than to see the Brodies done for." McNulty swigged from the flask again, but absently. "French, Japanese, Americans, Canadians—soon there won't be anything left in Scotland owned by Scots."

There had been a McNulty as stillman at Benvulin since Donald Brodie's great-great-grandfather's time. While Callum knew what it would mean to Peter to see Benvulin pass out of the Brodie family, he had more urgent concerns.

"But who could have killed him, Peter? Do ye think it was Heather Urquhart?"

Peter considered for a moment, his eyes bleary. "No," he said slowly. "She's a serpent, that one. Not her style to shoot someone point-blank in the chest."

"Oh, Christ," Callum muttered, trying to banish the image. "Look, Peter, I've got to go." Turning away, he blundered his way back to the van and climbed inside. He sat there, trying to think things through.

He had been up early that morning, walking Murphy down towards the river. He *had* heard a shot, he remembered, but had thought nothing of it. And then he had seen—no, that was bollocks.

Surely it had been a trick of the morning light, the mist rising from the river, a twist of his imagination. Callum shook his head as if to clear it, but it didn't help. For the first time in his life, he doubted the evidence of his own senses.

Like a priest, Ross had seen them in all their affliction— those dazed and befuddled with grief; those who went sharp and prickly with it, as if they could defend themselves; those who collapsed, like jellies taken too soon from the mold.

Perhaps that was why he had stopped attending the

church. He had had little confidence in the comfort tradi-
tionally offered to the bereaved, and even less in God's
ability to punish the wicked.

On this morning, he called the suspects—and they
were all suspects to him until proven otherwise—in what
seemed to him the order of least importance. Of course,
such initial impressions could be misleading, and it was
only by a careful piecing together of their stories that he
would be able to form a truer picture.

He began with Martin Gilmore. The young man came
in with an air of suppressed excitement, and Ross had the
impression he was struggling to rearrange his bony features into an expression of appropriate solemnity.

Having ascertained that Gilmore had shared a room
with Brodie, and that he had heard Brodie go out about
daybreak, Ross said, "You must have had some conversation with the man, then. What did ye talk about?"

Gilmore shrugged. "I don't think he took me very seriously. Oh, he was friendly enough, but he was an Alan
Breck sort of character—you know, all Highland disdain
for someone who came from the city. If you weren't born
stalking stags and gaffing salmon and drinking whisky
with your mother's milk, you weren't in the same club."

"But he signed up for this cookery weekend."

"Not that he had much real interest in the cooking. It
was more of a lark for him." Gilmore paused for a moment, as if wondering how much he should say. "And I
think he had another . . . agenda. There was something
going on between him and Hazel—Mrs. Cavendish."

Ross raised an eyebrow. "What sort of something?"

"I'm not stupid, you know," the young man said, his
eyes gleaming with sudden malice. "They've all treated
me like an idiot. There were all these awkward silences
and loaded glances. And after that other woman came last

night, you could have cut the tension with a knife. They went out together—Donald and Hazel—after dinner, and you could tell there was a row brewing."

"Did you hear them argue?"

Gilmore looked disappointed. "No. They must have gone round to the back of the house."

"Did you see either of them after that?"

"No. The rest of us sat round next door, in the sitting room, and after a bit I went to bed. There's no telly," he added, as if inviting Ross's disbelief.

Ross thought a moment, then backtracked. "You said a woman came here?"

"Just before dinner. Rang the bell and asked to speak to Donald, apparently. She had a child with her."

"Any idea who she was?"

"Not a clue. A bit tarty, though, from what I could see. Made me laugh, everyone trying to have a gander without being obvious about it."

"Did anyone say anything?"

"No. All too bloody polite, weren't they?"

"All right, Mr. Gilmore. If you'll just go and give your statement to the constable in the kitchen."

Martin Gilmore stood. "Can I go after that?"

Glancing at his notes, Ross said with casual friendliness, "Keen to get back to work tomorrow, are you?"

Gilmore flushed an ugly, mottled red. "I'm out of work just now. Temporary setback."

When he had left the room, Ross muttered to Sergeant Munro, "At least he had the grace to feel embarrassed about it. Most of the layabouts these days seem to find being on the dole a reason to brag."

"Weel, I'd say he'd got himself free meals and a comfortable billet for the weekend," reflected Munro. "What do you wager he's still here tomorrow?"

*   *   *

Unlike Gilmore, Pascal Benoit seemed genuinely sad-
dened by Brodie's death; nor did Ross detect any uneasiness in his manner. Even if the man had dressed hastily,
his clothes spoke of wealth, and he had the unmistakable
assurance of one used to power.

"I'm not quite sure I understand what it is that you do,
Mr. Benoit," said Ross, when they had got the formalities
out of the way.

"I represent a French company with multinational interests, Chief Inspector. In the last few years, we have acquired three distilleries in Scotland, all of which have
performed quite well. We would be interested in adding
another such property to our portfolio, and as there are
few family-owned distilleries still operating, we cultivate
an ongoing relationship with those that are."

And that was business-speak for hovering like vultures
waiting for a corpse, Ross thought. Schooling his face
into an expression of pleasant attentiveness, he asked,
"But did you have a particular interest in Mr. Brodie's
distillery?"

"Benvulin would make the jewel in our crown," admitted Benoit. "We had hoped to convince Mr. Brodie of
the benefits of such an arrangement. While we would
have assumed financial responsibility for the distillery,
he would have been encouraged to remain as managing
director."

"I take it Mr. Brodie had not yet agreed to this plan?"

"No. It was only a friendly discussion. And now,
well . . ." Benoit gave a shrug. "This is a terrible tragedy.
Donald's death will be a great loss to the industry."

"What will happen to Benvulin?"

"That I can't say, Chief Inspector. I imagine any such
decisions will be made by the board of directors."

"Is there no family member to take on Mr. Brodie's position?"

"I'm afraid I've no idea. I'd suggest you ask Miss Urquhart."

Making a note to do just that, Ross excused him. The man was far too canny to admit that his firm might benefit from Donald Brodie's death.

As Benoit left the room, the constable on duty in the hall stepped in. "Sir, we've found a gun cabinet in the scullery. It's not locked, and it's possible there's a gun missing."

"What's the owner's name?" Ross glanced at his list.

"Innes, sir."

"Take him to look at the cabinet, then bring him in here."

As they waited, Ross heard the first sharp spatter of rain against the windowpanes. He swore under his breath, and Munro stood and looked out the window.

"I think the worst of it will hold off a bit yet." Munro stretched his long neck and cracked his knuckles, a habit Ross found profoundly annoying.

"Will ye stop that, man," he snapped. "How many times do I have to tell ye?"

"Sorry, Chief," said Munro, looking more doleful than ever. "I get the cramp in my fingers."

They sounded like an old married couple, Ross thought with a glimmer of amusement, although Munro was much better tempered than Ross's ex-wife. Before he could apologize, the door opened and the constable popped his head in.

"Mr. Innes says there is a gun missing, sir, a small-bore Purdy."

"Send him in, then."

"I don't know how it could have happened," John

Innes said as he entered the room. A large man with thinning hair, dressed in a pullover that had seen better days, he seemed to vibrate with agitation. "That was my grandfather's gun. I always lock the cabinet, always. I don't know how—"

"Sit down, Mr. Innes, and let's begin at the beginning. I'm Chief Inspector Ross."

Innes hesitated for a moment, as if unsure what to do with himself in his own dining room, then pulled out a chair.

"Now, that's better," Ross continued. "Why don't you describe the gun for me."

"It's Purdy lightweight, a twenty-gauge. A scroll and vine pattern, made before the Great War."

Ross blanched. In good shape, a gun like that could be worth thousands of pounds. How could the man have been so careless? Making an effort to keep his temper, he said, "This gun cabinet of yours, Mr. Innes, who would have access to the key?"

Innes took a breath. "I keep mine on my key ring. It's usually in my pocket, except at night, when I put them on the dressing table."

"Is that the only key?"

"No. My wife has a copy. Louise usually hangs her keys on the hook by the scullery door when she's at home."

"So you leave the key to the gun cabinet in plain sight, in the same room?"

Flushing, Innes said, "This is the country, for God's sake. We run a guesthouse. We'd never have done that in Edinburgh, but here, you don't think—"

"You are legally responsible for the security of your weapons, Mr. Innes. Do you understand that you can be prosecuted? Or at the very least, fined?" Ross persisted, but wearily. The man had a Highland accent; he had probably grown up in a household where guns were kept as casually as dogs.

"Tell me, Mr. Innes, who had access to the gun cabinet?"

"Access? The guests normally go in and out through the front, but I hold my cookery classes in the kitchen, and there's nothing to stop anyone going in and out as they please." He rubbed his fingers across the stubble on his chin, the rasping clear in the quiet room. "But surely you don't think Donald was shot with *my* gun?"

"I think it beggars coincidence that a man was found shot dead on your property on the same day as your gun turns up missing."

Innes's sallow skin blanched. "But you can't think it was one of my guests! Someone could have come in and taken the gun—you've just said so. What if I did leave the cabinet unlocked, and some tramp saw his chance—"

"And why would a tramp be shooting Mr. Donald Brodie in your field in the wee hours of this morning?" asked Ross, giving free rein to his sarcasm.

Innes went quiet at that. When his protest came, it was feeble. "I don't know, do I? But it *is* possible."

"Aye. The Loch Ness Monster is possible. But it's not verra likely, is it, Mr. Innes? Are you telling me now that you left your cabinet unlocked?"

"No!" A film of sweat had appeared on Innes's brow. "I'm sure I locked it. I just meant it's a habit, the sort of thing you don't really think about doing."

"Have you seen anyone in the household near the gun cabinet?"

"If you mean have I seen anyone lurking suspiciously in the scullery, no. But the entire class was in the kitchen much of yesterday."

Ross considered what he had learned so far. "Mr.

Innes, were you aware of a special relationship between Mr. Brodie and Hazel Cavendish?"

"No!" The response was too quick, too emphatic. "I mean, I knew they were friends, Louise and Hazel and Donald, from a long time ago. It was meant to be a sort of reunion, this cookery weekend, a surprise for Hazel."

"Do you mean that Hazel didn't know Donald would be here?" asked Ross, deliberately using their Christian names.

"I—I'm not sure. It was Louise who arranged it."

"And what about this other woman who turned up with her child to see Donald yesterday evening? What can you tell me about that?"

"I've no idea who she was. I didn't see her. It was Louise who answered the door."

"You didn't look out the window?" Ross asked with a hint of disbelief.

"No. I was in the kitchen, getting the meal ready." The uncertainty that had characterized Innes's earlier answers seemed to have vanished, and Ross suspected he was telling the truth.

"But Hazel and Donald had a row about this woman, during dinner, was it?"

"I don't know anything about that. I was in the kitchen, and serving the food."

"I understand they went out together, after the meal."

"Neither of them came into the sitting room for coffee, that's all I can tell you. I didn't see them go out."

"You didn't hear them arguing?"

"No."

Ross sat back with a sigh. Innes's answers had become not only firm, but mulish. Was it Hazel Cavendish the man was protecting? And if so, why? "I think that's all for now, Mr. Innes," he said. "A constable will take your statement."

"I'm free to go?" Innes sounded as if he'd expected to be hauled off to the nick.

"For the moment, unless you've something else to tell me?"

"No. I— Is it all right if I fix the breakfast now?"

Ross's stomach rumbled in response to the thought of food, and he thought regretfully of the breakfast he had forgone early that morning in favor of gardening.

"This is aye a murder inquiry, Mr. Innes," he said testily, "and there are more important matters to attend to than food." Ross sensed Munro's suppressed smile behind him, which made him all the more irritable. Munro knew, from long experience, that he got cross when he was hungry.

"I'm sorry." Innes looked abashed. "God knows I didn't mean any disrespect to Donald. But I thought it might help, you know, with the shock, if everyone had something to eat. It's my remedy for all ills, cooking."

The man was right, Ross had to admit. It never failed to amaze him that, in the midst of tragedy, the human body kept on demanding food and drink and sleep—even sex, often enough. "The constable is taking statements in the kitchen," he said a bit more kindly. "You'll have to wait until she's finished, and your scullery will remain off limits for the time being."

When Innes had left the room, Ross said to Munro, "That wee mannie is hiding something, but I'll be damned if I know whether it has anything to do with the murder."

"Do you want to see the wife next, Chief?" asked Munro, rising.

"No. I think we'll have a word with Miss Heather Urquhart."

*   *   *

She would be a striking woman under other circumstances, thought Ross, with the contrast between her pale skin and her mass of long, dark hair. But now the hair was carelessly matted, the rims of her eyelids red from weeping.

They had established that she had worked for Donald Brodie for ten years, beginning as his personal assistant and working her way up to distillery manager, and throughout the questioning she had been tightly abrupt, as if she didn't dare give rein to her emotions.

Now Ross said thoughtfully, "Miss Urquhart, was your relationship with Donald Brodie romantic in nature?"

She stared at him with an expression of intense dislike. "That's none of your business."

"Oh, but I'm afraid it is." He leaned forward, saw her instinctive recoil. "Your employer, Miss Urquhart, was brutally murdered, and that makes everything about Donald Brodie my business. Have you ever seen a shotgun wound?" he added, deliberately cruel, meaning to shake her cold self-possession. "Not a pretty sight—"

Her hands flew to her face, as if she could shield herself from his words with her long, pale fingers. "Stop, please," she said shakily. "No. The answer is no. Donald and I were friends—good friends—but that's all."

"Then maybe you can explain the woman who called on him last night, the one with the child."

Nodding, Heather lowered her hands to her lap again, but not before he saw the tremor. "Her name is Alison Grant. That was her little girl, Chrissy. She's a cripple." Her voice held a faint distaste, as if the child had displayed bad table manners. "Donald had seen Alison a few times, but I think lately he'd been trying to avoid her."

"So she came looking for him?"

"I don't know how she'd have known he was here," said Heather, sounding puzzled. "I don't think he'd have told her. I certainly didn't."

"Do you know where can we find Alison Grant?"

"She has a flat in Aviemore; I don't know the address. But she works in the gift shop on the main road, just down from the railway station."

Ross made a note. "Did she argue with Mr. Brodie last night when she came here?"

"I don't know. He only spoke to her outside."

"And you didn't discuss it with him afterwards?"

She shook her head. "No. There was dinner, and then . . . then he went out."

"With your cousin, I believe, Hazel Cavendish."

"I couldn't say."

"Couldn't, or won't?"

"I can't, Chief Inspector. What either of them did after they left the dining room, I've no idea."

"But there was a relationship between your cousin and Donald Brodie?"

"At one time, yes. But it was before I went to work for Donald, and I wasn't privy to any details."

"You weren't close to your cousin?"

"No," Heather said sharply, and then as if afraid she'd been too abrupt, she added, "not since we were children. Her family moved away when we were in our teens."

"Then perhaps you can tell me what will happen to the distillery, with Mr. Brodie gone."

"I—I'm not sure. Donald's sister is dead—you'll know about that. His parents divorced before his father died, and his mother has remarried, so she has no claim on the estate. I've no idea what provision Donald made for his shares."

"You'll have the name of Mr. Brodie's solicitor?"

"It's Giles Glover, in Grantown. They were school friends."

Ross took this down, then dismissed her.

Munro spoke up from his chair against the wall. "Prone to tragedy, the Brodies, I'd say, with what happened to the father and daughter, and now the son."

"I remember reading something in the papers—"

"Climbing accident on Cairngorm. Snow came down suddenly, cut them off. It was days before they found the bodies."

"A bad business," Ross agreed. "But I don't see how there could be a connection."

Munro looked disappointed, but rallied. "It seems to me the lassie was verra weel informed about Mr. Brodie's affairs, for all her protest to the contrary."

"Maybe, maybe not, considering her position in the firm. We'll see the solicitor first thing tomorrow. But now, let's light the fire in this bloody room. Then we'll see what Mrs. Innes has to say."

Louise Innes reassured them, with more confidence than her husband had shown, that she had not seen any member of the household near the gun cabinet, or any strangers in the garden or near the scullery. She couldn't remember when she had last glanced at the cabinet, nor could she tell that her key ring had been tampered with in any way.

"What about last night, Mrs. Innes?" asked Ross. "I understand it was you who answered the door to the young woman who came calling for Mr. Brodie."

Pursing her lips in disapproval, Louise Innes said, "She was really quite rude. She demanded to see Donald. I was afraid she was going to make a scene right there on the doorstep."

"What did she say, exactly?"

Louise considered for a moment, then said carefully, " 'I want to see Donald. Tell him I know he's here. There's no use him skulking about, the lying bastard.' " Shaking her head, she added, "And in front of the child, too."

"You'd never seen her before?"

"No. She wasn't our sort." Louise Innes seemed to feel no need to apologize for her snobbery.

"Did you overhear any of her conversation with Donald?"

"No," Louise said, with what might have been a trace of regret. "I was getting the dining room ready, and helping John with the food."

"I was under the impression that the guests did the cooking on a cookery course."

"The class did most of the preparation yesterday, but John likes to do the last bits himself. He thinks that if people are paying to stay, they should have a little pampering—or at least that's what he says. If you ask me, I think he just can't bear to give up that much control of the kitchen."

Ross gave her an encouraging nod. "Now, about your friend Hazel Cavendish, Mrs. Innes. Did she have some special understanding with Donald Brodie? A relationship?"

"Oh, not for years. But— Well, it was Donald who wanted to invite Hazel this weekend. I told John from the beginning I thought it was a bad idea," Louise added, with the self-righteousness of the justified.

"You thought there might be trouble?"

"Oh, no—of course I never imagined anything like this! It's just that—well, no matter what Donald wanted, Hazel *is* married. He couldn't expect . . ."

"Are you telling me that Donald Brodie was still in love with Mrs. Cavendish? Were they having an affair?"

"No! I don't— Donald wanted to see her, that was all. For old times' sake."

"But Mrs. Cavendish knew he would be here, when you invited her?"

"Well, I did mention it, of course." Louise smoothed already immaculate hair behind one ear. "She didn't seem too concerned one way or the other."

"But she was angry last night, after the young woman called for him?"

"I—I don't know. I wasn't in the dining room much at all."

Ross had the distinct feeling she was prevaricating. "Mrs. Innes, I know you mean well, but it really is best for everyone if you cooperate fully. Withholding evidence in a police inquiry is quite a serious matter."

Louise Innes tucked her hair behind her ear again, then clasped her hands, rubbing the ball of one thumb over the top of the other. "There's nothing, really. It's just that . . . after dinner, when I went to take the rubbish out to the big bin, I heard them in the garden. They seemed to be arguing."

"Did you hear what they said?"

"No, just raised voices. It was dark by then, and I couldn't be sure exactly where they were. I hurried back inside—didn't want to be caught eavesdropping."

Ross found it interesting that she hadn't said she didn't want to eavesdrop; only that she didn't want to be caught. "Mrs. Innes—"

"You're not thinking Hazel had something to do with Donald's death?" She gazed at him, her hand lifted halfway to her mouth. "That's just not possible! Hazel would never hurt anyone. And besides, Martin said Donald came back to their room last night, so even if Donald and Hazel *were* together last night it doesn't mean—"

"No, it doesn't, but Mrs. Cavendish's movements are unaccounted for this morning, and that is the crucial time period."

"Oh." The pupils of Louise Innes's pale blue eyes dilated. "But . . ."

"Did you see Mrs. Cavendish this morning?"

"No. Not until after . . . her car was gone when I first went out into the garden. She drove up just as Gemma . . ." For the first time, Louise looked near to tears.

"Did you hear the gunshot?"

She shook her head, the bell of her hair swinging with the motion. "No. At least I don't think I did—I might not have paid any attention. I was in the kitchen for a bit, making coffee, doing my usual morning chores, making a good bit of noise, I suppose. But after John left, I went out into the garden. I would surely have heard it then."

"Your husband left this morning?" Ross's interest quickened. Behind him, he heard Munro shift position and knew his sergeant had caught it as well. "I don't remember your husband mentioning going anywhere this morning."

"He ran to one of the neighboring estates to pick up some fresh eggs for breakfast—they keep free-range hens. What's the harm in that?"

"Do you know what time this was?"

"I— No, I didn't notice. You don't think—you can't think *John* took the gun," she went on, her voice rising in horror. "He couldn't have. I was in the kitchen when he left."

"He could have put the gun in the car earlier—perhaps during the night."

"You are surely joking, Chief Inspector," Louise said flatly, as if she would not have it be otherwise. "Even if it were possible that John could do such a thing, how could he have known that Donald would be walking in the meadow this morning? How could anyone have known?"

Ross wasn't sure what he had expected, from what he had heard of Hazel Cavendish—a glamorous woman, perhaps, sophisticated in the manner of her cousin Heather Urquhart.

Instead, he found himself facing a slight woman with an appealing heart-shaped face made more striking by her dark eyes and curly dark hair. She wore a yellow, fuzzy pullover, and her face was swollen from weeping.

Resisting an unexpected urge towards gentleness, he said, "Mrs. Cavendish, were you having an affair with Donald Brodie?"

"No." The word was a whisper. "No," she repeated more firmly, with obvious effort.

"But you had been lovers?"

"That was a long time ago, Chief Inspector." She sounded weary beyond bearing. "It was another life."

"But Donald hoped to renew your relationship, isn't that right?" When she didn't answer, he went on. "Is that why ye argued with him last night?"

Her eyes widened. "I— He—he brought up some old issues between us. It wasn't an argument. It can't have had anything to do with Donald's death."

"Aye, well, I canna be so sure about that, now can I? I had the idea you were angry over the wee lassie who called on him before dinner."

"I don't know anything about that." Her mouth was set in a stubborn line.

"And what about this morning, Mrs. Cavendish? Can you tell me where ye went in the car?"

She swallowed and took a sharp little breath, as if readying something rehearsed. "I drove to Aviemore. I was worried about my daughter. I'd never left her for so long, before this weekend, and I thought I should go home. But there was no train that early. So I came back."

She hadn't had much practice at lying, thought Ross, and she did it remarkably badly. "What time did you leave the house?"

"I'm not sure. It was light. Before five, I think."

"And yet you returned at"—he checked his notes—"around half six, according to Mrs. Innes. The drive to Aviemore takes only a few minutes."

"I sat at the station for a while, deciding whether to wait for a train."

"Did anyone see you?"

"I—I don't know. The ticket office was closed. I didn't speak to—"

There was a tap at the door, and the duty constable came in. "Sorry to interrupt, sir, but one of the crime scene technicians thought you'd want to see this."

Ross stood up and took the clear evidence envelope by its corner.

"He said they found this in the trampled area in the wood," the constable continued, "along with traces of semen."

"Thank you, Constable." Ross looked at the wisp of pale yellow yarn he held in his hand, then at Hazel Cavendish.

"You're not serious." Gemma faced Constable Mackenzie across the work island in the Inneses' kitchen. "You want to do a metal trace test on *me*?" Her voice rose in a squeak

of outrage in spite of her attempt to control it. Having given her statement to another constable seated in the corner, she had then been passed on to Mackenzie.

"I'm sorry, ma'am." Mackenzie's brow was furrowed with distress. "It's orders from the chief inspector. Everyone in the household, he said, no exceptions. I'm to take a footprint, as well."

"The bastard," swore Gemma under her breath. Feeling her face flush with telltale warmth, she turned away for a moment, trying to master her temper. Would Ross have treated Kincaid this way, she wondered, or would Kincaid have been respected as a fellow officer—even deferred to?

Of course, there was the matter of rank, she told herself, attempting to be fair, but even that didn't excuse Ross's behavior.

Nor was it Kincaid's fault that he was male and automatically a member of the club, she reminded herself, curbing the unjustified flash of anger she felt towards him. In its place, she felt a sudden longing for him so acute that it caught at her chest like a vise.

He'd have Ross wrapped round his finger in no time, and she—she wouldn't feel so afraid. The law had always been her friend, her protector, and now she found herself on the other side of the wall.

Damn Ross. Well, if he wouldn't work with her, she saw no reason why she should cooperate more than regulation demanded. But that, at least, she would have to do. Summoning a smile for Mackenzie, she turned back and held out her hand. "Right, then. Let's get on with it."

As Mackenzie swabbed each of her fingers in turn, Gemma gazed out the window. The rain had come on, softening the outline of shrubs, drive, and barn. God, what a mess. She should be glad this wasn't her scene, her case, her responsibility, she told herself. And so she might be, if she could just rid herself of the nagging uncertainty she felt over Hazel.

A movement in the drive caught her eye. Two uniformed officers had emerged from around the corner of the house, a third figure between them. As Gemma watched, one constable opened the door of a marked car and eased the third person into the back, protecting the top of the dark, curly-haired head from the doorframe with a large hand.

Gemma jerked her hand away from Mackenzie, reaching out as if she could stop the car door closing over Hazel's white, frightened face.

11

I wave the quantum o' the sin,
The hazard of concealing;
But och; it hardens a' within,
And petrifies the feelin!
    ROBERT BURNS, "First Epistle to John Lapraik"

Carnmore, April 1899

IT WAS ONLY *after Charles had been buried in the Chapeltown churchyard that Livvy began to realize all griefs were unique.*

She had lost her mother at sixteen, to a lingering respiratory illness that not even her physician father had been able to cure. Livvy's grieving had been wild and hot, punctuated by racking sobs and waves of such hollowness that she thought surely her body must collapse into this interior abyss.

But with Charles's death, she'd felt a surprised numbness, and a cold that grew daily, settling into bone and flesh like the weight of the snow that lay across the Braes. She felt dull, diminished, as if her soul had become a hard, heavy thing inside her.

And secreted inside that brittle shell, a kernel of guilt; for Livvy knew Charles's death to be her fault.

She had not loved him enough. She had liked him, respected him, admired him even, and between them had grown a comfortable intimacy and dependence. But there had been no passion on her part, and it was that missing bond that might have held him tethered, to her and to Will. Had he seen her failure, when he'd looked in her eyes for the last time?

In late March, the snow turned to rain. The already saturated ground became spongy with moisture; water seeped and trickled down the hillsides into the fast-flowing Crombie Burn. The village children came out to play, like rabbits emerging from their burrows, and the men began to talk about the spring planting.

Livvy began to feel a painful anticipation, as if possibilities waited alongside the green shoots in the earth, and it frightened her. So she tried not to think at all, throwing herself into the running of the house and, with Will, the business of the distillery.

She practiced holding each moment, like a pearl in her hand, but one by one they slipped inexorably away. And then on a morning when the sun shone and the breeze blew soft from the east, an auburn-haired man came riding up from the village on a bay horse, and she knew him.

Louise slipped out the front door while John was cooking a belated breakfast for the guests. There were still two white-coveralled technicians working in the scullery, and the guests were milling about in the hall and sitting room—no one seemed to want to face the dining room, where they had been interrogated by Chief Inspector Ross.

She'd had to ask John for the keys to the old Land Rover—letting go her car had been just one of the sacrifices they'd made when they came to this godforsaken place. When he'd questioned her, she'd told him they needed biscuits for tea that afternoon, and she'd offered no explanation to anyone else. The constable on the porch nodded but didn't stop her.

The rain fell in a mist so fine and heavy that it felt as if she were walking through water, and she had forgotten an umbrella. By the time she reached the car she was sopping, bedraggled as a water rat.

There was English rain, she had discovered, and there was Scottish rain, and Scottish rain invariably made you wetter and colder.

Whatever had possessed her all those years ago, to give up life in London and come here? It had been Hazel, of course, the one person she had ever truly thought of as a friend, and now Hazel had come back and turned everything topsy-turvy once again.

How could they have taken Hazel away? Every time Louise thought of it, she came up against a wall in her mind, as if this shock on top of all the others had formed an impenetrable barrier. It couldn't be happening—none of this could be happening. Donald couldn't be dead. She saw the square shape of the mortuary van at the edge of the drive and looked away, her throat closing convulsively.

And John, where had John gone that morning? It shouldn't have taken him more than half an hour to buy eggs, yet he had been gone a good deal longer than that. He was terrified, she could smell it on him, and this wasn't the first time he'd disappeared without explanation.

Louise backed the Land Rover up and drove to the gate, rolling to a stop as a constable came up to the window. His yellow-green jacket was slick with rain, the water beaded on the bill of his cap. As she lowered the window, drops splattered on the sill of the car door.

"Ma'am," said the constable, "you're not to—"

"Chief Inspector Ross said we were free to go."

Stepping back, he spoke into the radio on his shoulder. After a moment he nodded at her. "Sorry, ma'am."

The crowd milling about on the verge was not so obliging. Louise eased the car forward, avoiding eye contact with those who looked vaguely familiar, and when a man held a news camera up to the window she shook her head violently and pressed on the accelerator.

The bodies scattered and she was free, the car skimming along silently except for the rhythmic squeak of the wipers against the windscreen. A mile down the road, she slowed and turned to the right, bumping into a drive heavily rutted by the wheels of horse vans. A weathered sign on a post identified the MacGillivrays' stable.

The house looked deserted, not even a wisp of smoke from the chimney visible in the rain. Nor was there any sign of Tom, Callum's father, for which Louise was grateful. She couldn't have coped with the man's drunken ramblings, not today.

She drove down to the barn and got out, shielding her face from the rain as she ran in the open door. The air inside the barn smelled warm and ripe, even in the wet. Two horses looked at her over their stall doors with mildly curious expressions, and she recognized one as Callum's horse, Max. She called out Callum's name, her voice tentative in the echoing space.

When there was no answer, she went out and looked down the hill towards the old crofter's cottage that lay between the barn and the river meadow. She knew Callum lived there, rather than in the main house, but she'd never been inside. They had developed an unexpected friendship in the past year, based at first on their common interest in native plants. Callum was odd, Louise had to admit, but in a way it was this very oddness that had allowed her to feel comfortable with him, to open up with him in a way she seldom did with other people. With Callum, there was no fear of not measuring up, of giving herself away as not belonging.

Until now, however, she had not visited him in his cottage. As she hesitated, wondering if she should have come, a light flickered faintly in the window.

Before she could change her mind, Louise ran down the pebble-strewn path and knocked lightly on the door. A dog barked sharply, making her jump, and Callum's voice called, "Come in with ye, then."

Louise stepped in, holding out a hand for Murphy, Callum's Labrador retriever, to sniff. There was only one room, she saw, warmed by an old stove and lit by a paraffin lamp standing on a scarred table. There Callum sat, pouring over what looked like account books.

Glancing up, he said, "Louise! What are ye doing here? I thought you were my father." He stood, closing the topmost book.

"Have you heard?"

"It's true, then, about Donald?"

She nodded. "How did you—"

"I saw the crowd round your gate. I stopped, but they wouldn't let me through. It was Peter McNulty told me Donald had been shot!"

Louise felt suddenly faint, as if the reality of what had happened had finally caught up with her body. It must have shown in her face, because Callum hurried towards her.

"Sit ye down, Louise." He pulled out a chair at the oak table. "I'll make ye some tea."

Obeying, she looked round the cottage in an effort to

focus on something other than the turmoil of her thoughts. The black iron stove, where Callum was putting a kettle on to boil, stood on a raised tile hearth. To one side of it stood a deep farmhouse sink, with a handmade rack holding cups and plates; on the other, a tatty armchair and a small side table stacked with books, and what looked like a tin hip bath. There did not seem to be any indoor plumbing, except for the sink.

The two deep front windows let in little light, but she could see the outline of an alcove bed against the far wall, as well as a notched rack holding half a dozen fishing rods, and pegs hung with oilskins and tweed caps.

Murphy, apparently deciding the excitement was over, returned to a cushion near the stove and flopped down with a sigh, his black coat gleaming in the lamplight. The room smelled of peat smoke and warm dog.

Callum set a steaming mug before her, adding a dash of whisky from the bottle that stood on the table. "Drink up, now. You'll feel better."

He gave her a moment to sip, then said, "Tell me what happened."

Haltingly, she related the events of the morning, ending with Hazel's being taken for questioning.

"They took your friend? Do you think she can have done such a thing?"

"No! But if it was John's gun . . . Who else could have taken it? And after . . ." She glanced up at him. "Callum, that woman last night . . . I saw you, watching from the hedge. Did you bring her to see Donald?"

He hesitated, spreading his fingers on the tabletop, and for the first time she noticed how large his hands were. "I didn't bring her exactly, but aye, I did tell her where Donald was."

"But why? Who is she?"

"She's a friend of mine. Her name is Alison Grant. She's been going out with Donald, and I thought she should know he wasna telling her the truth about this weekend. He told her he had a business meeting."

"But why would you—" Louise stopped, seeing the obvious. "*You're* interested in her, this Alison? But she's—" *A slag,* she had started to say, and caught herself just in time. "Callum, how did *you* know it wasn't just a business meeting?"

"It was himself who told me." Callum's accent grew heavier under stress, she noticed, as did John's.

"Himself? You mean Donald?"

"Aye. All about the woman of his dreams."

"And look where it bloody got him," Louise burst out, choking back a sob. She gulped at her tea, feeling the whisky bite at the back of her throat, and managed to say, "He never had any sense where Hazel was concerned."

"But, Louise, you canna be sure it had anything to do with her. You don't know why the police took her in?"

She shook her head. "He's cold, that detective. A calculating bastard. He—he frightened me."

"You've no reason to be frightened." Callum reached out and gave her an awkward pat on the shoulder. "Whatever happened, it's nothing to do with you."

"But this could ruin our business, don't you see? And John—" Now that she had come to it, the words stuck in her throat. She forced herself to go on. "Callum, you didn't see John this morning, did you? He went to buy eggs, but he was gone for a long time."

"John?" Callum stared at her. "But you canna think—"

"It's not what I think—it's what the police will think," she said urgently. "Do you know where he was this morning?"

There was a moment's silence, then Callum said, a bit

too heartily, "No, Louise, I didna see him. I'm sure he will have some explanation—have you asked the man himself?"

"There was no chance, and now he's got everyone in the kitchen, cooking for them." She couldn't keep the irritation from her voice.

"Aye, that's his way," said Callum, with a note of disapproval at her tone. That was a typical man, thought Louise—couldn't bear to hear another man criticized. "Hadn't you better be getting back?" he added. "They'll aye be wondering where you've gone."

Louise stood, stung by what seemed to her a dismissal. "Yes. All right."

"I'm sorry, Louise," said Callum, standing as well. "I didna mean to be crabbit with ye. It's just that I'll have to tell Alison, ye see. She goes to her mam's in Carrbridge on a Sunday afternoon, but she'll be back soon, and I'm fair dreading it."

"It's okay," she told him, mollified. "And you're right, of course you're right. I'd better go."

It was only as she turned to the door that she saw a shotgun standing beside it, as if it had been set down carelessly after a walk. Beside the gun sat a pair of heavy boots, streaked with what Louise could have sworn was drying silt from the river.

Gemma caught Chief Inspector Ross as he was getting into his car. "What do you think you're doing?" she shouted at him, ignoring the rain streaking her face. "What do you mean by taking Hazel away?"

Ross turned to her, his hand still on the open car door. "She's helping us with our inquiries, Inspector. That should certainly be obvious to you," he said, with exaggerated patience.

"But you can't believe she had something to do with Donald's death!"

"She had motive—they were heard arguing. She had means—access to Mr. Innes's shotgun. And she had opportunity, as far as I'm concerned, unless she can prove her unlikely account of her movements this morning."

"But there must be more than that—"

"You also know that I can't discuss details of the investigation with you, Inspector. Now, if you don't mind"—Ross grimaced and brushed at the water beading on his shoulders—"it's a wee bit wet."

He got into the car and his sergeant pulled away, leaving Gemma standing in the drive. She stared after him, momentarily paralyzed by fury. Pulling herself together, she sprinted across to the hired Honda, found it locked, and swore aloud. Hazel must have taken the keys with her—she'd had no opportunity to return to their room. Nor could Gemma search the room in any case; all the bedrooms in the B&B were off limits until the forensics team had finished with them.

Gemma pushed a sodden strand of hair from her face and tried to think calmly. First, she had to find out where they had taken Hazel. If she could just manage to get a word with her, tell her not to say *anything* without counsel. Not that she thought Ross would give her access, but she might be able to pull rank on someone with less authority.

Going in search of Constable Mackenzie, she found the officer in the scullery, packing up her test kits. "Do you know where the chief inspector will be conducting his interviews?" she asked from the doorway, trying to sound casual.

"They're setting up an incident room at Aviemore Police Station, so I should think all inquiries would proceed from there." Mackenzie hesitated a moment, then added awkwardly, "I'm sorry about your friend, ma'am."

Gemma forced a smile, touched by the young woman's consideration. "Thanks. But don't worry. I'm sure it will be sorted soon."

As the technicians were still taking prints and collecting trace evidence in the scullery, Gemma went round the house again and in through the front door. She found the group assembled in the sitting room, picking with varying degrees of enthusiasm at plates of bacon, eggs, and toast.

John turned from the salvers he'd trundled in on a cart. "No one wanted to eat in the dining room," he explained. "Here, I'll get ye a plate."

Shaking her head, Gemma said, "Oh, no. I couldn't possibly." Her stomach felt tied in knots, and a sense of urgency gnawed at her. "What I wanted was to know if I could borrow a car. Hazel has the keys to our hired car, and I need to get to the police station in Aviemore."

"You've just missed Louise, I'm afraid. Otherwise she could have given you a lift."

"Louise is gone?" Gemma asked, startled.

"She ran out to the farm shop for a few things for tea. We'll miss lunch, I think, with breakfast so late, so I thought we'd do a proper afternoon tea."

What the hell difference did it make, Gemma wanted to shout—lunch, high tea, low tea—with Donald dead and Hazel taken off to the nick?

Biting her lip, she said as evenly as she could, "Is there anyone else who could give me a lift, or loan me a car for a bit?"

"Sorry," said Martin Gilmore, looking up from his empty plate. "I left my old banger in Dundee. John collected me at the station."

Gemma looked at Heather, who was pushing un-touched eggs round her plate with a fork. "I've got to get to the distillery," Heather responded, a tremor in her voice. "And I'll need Pascal's help."

"Then I shall ride with you," said Pascal, "and Gemma can drive my car." Like Martin's, Pascal's appetite seemed undiminished by the tragedy, nor had he lost his manners. He stood, fishing a key from his trouser pocket. "It's the black one, a bit of a beast."

Gemma had noticed the car, a new model BMW, pol-ished to perfection. Under other circumstances she would have hesitated to drive such a car, but she accepted the keys with alacrity. "I'll be careful," she promised, and wished that scraping Pascal's paint were the worst of her worries.

Retracing the drive she'd made less than two days before with Hazel, it looked to Gemma as if she'd entered a dif-ferent world. The mountains that had floated hazily in the distance now seemed to brood, their peaks wreathed in cloud, and the river that had sparkled silver in the sun-light now flowed sullenly against its banks.

And if she had thought Aviemore less than charming on a golden evening, the drizzling rain rendered it less salubrious still. There were a few fine Victorian houses along the main street, but they were overshadowed by the souvenir and coffee shops, and the mock chalets hawking ski wear.

Gemma found the police station without difficulty, a new building of honey-colored stone next to the car park. The sergeant on duty was a good-looking man with sil-very blond hair, a lilting Highland accent, and a helpful manner, but Gemma soon discovered that the public-friendly policing went only so far. Not even the production of her identification convinced him to let her talk to Hazel, and after an hour's wait in the anteroom, she went out into the street again, seething with frustration.

Ducking into a restaurant across the street from the station, she took a table by the window. When she'd ordered coffee and a sandwich to mollify her suddenly protesting stomach, she took out her mobile and rang Kincaid. To her relief it was he who answered, rather than Kit or Toby. She didn't think she could bear to talk to the children at the moment.

She poured out what had happened since she'd spoken to him earlier that morning, her voice rising until she caught a few other patrons staring at her. Shifting her body towards the window, she forced herself to whisper. "He must have something else, some sort of evidence, but he won't tell me what it is, and he won't let me see Hazel—"

"Gemma, calm down," Kincaid said soothingly in her ear. "I'll admit your chief inspector hasn't been very accommodating, but you really couldn't expect him to share forensic information with you. Whatever he's got, I'm sure there's an explanation. It will just take—"

"But Ross could bully Hazel into something. I'm telling you, you haven't met him. She needs some sort of representation. Is Tim coming?" Of course, Tim would have to be told about Hazel and Donald, but she only hoped he would support her, considering the seriousness of her situation.

There was a moment's silence at Kincaid's end, then he said quietly, "I didn't speak to Tim. He'd gone away for the weekend, and there was no way to contact him."

"Gone away?" Gemma repeated, wondering if she'd misheard. "What do you mean, gone away? What about Holly?"

"His parents came to stay at the house. I spoke to his mother. Apparently, Tim had a last-minute invitation to go walking with some friends. He won't be home until this evening."

Gemma watched the rain falling in the street, glistening on the hoods and umbrellas of the few resolute shoppers hurrying by. "I don't believe it," she said at last, flatly. "Tim's so conscientious; he always makes sure he can be reached in case of an emergency." Her imagination raced. What if Tim had somehow learned about Donald, decided to do something stupid—no, she couldn't voice that fear, even to herself. "You've got to find him, Duncan. Talk to him—"

"I'll go back tonight. If he hasn't turned up by then, I'll put Cullen to work on it. In the meantime, Gemma, you're not doing Hazel any good by staying in Aviemore. Go back to the B&B, talk to the others, see what you can learn. And Hazel has family there—a cousin, didn't you say? Maybe there's a family solicitor who would act on Hazel's behalf."

"Yes, but—" Gemma stopped, unable to come up with an argument. She knew Kincaid was right, but she felt suddenly deflated and near to tears. Her determination to storm Ross on his own patch had kept her going, in spite of her fear and her shock, and she was afraid to let it go. "All right," she said quietly, making an effort to keep her voice steady. "Ring me tonight, then."

"I will. Don't worry, love," he added, with an easy affection that came near to undoing her. "And, Gemma, I'm catching the early train tomorrow. I should be in Aviemore by midafternoon."

"Up ye go," then," said Alison patiently as she climbed the stairs in Chrissy's wake. She knew better than to offer to

help her daughter in her slow progress, or to pass her by, even though her hands were smarting from the weight of the supermarket carrier bags.

It was their usual Sunday routine. A trip to the supermarket for the week's shopping, and before that, a visit to her mum in Carrbridge, complete with a tea of bread-and-butter sandwiches and store-bought cakes. Chrissy loved her grandmother and never seemed to tire of the fare, but today her usual sunny chatter had been subdued.

Alison knew it was last night's row with Donald that had upset her, and she was furious with herself for having taken Chrissy to the bed-and-breakfast. She hadn't meant it to turn into a shouting match; hadn't meant even to ring the bell. She'd only wanted to see the place, to see if Donald was there, to see if what Callum had told her was true.

But then she had caught a glimpse of Donald in the lamplit sitting room, pouring his precious whisky for the pretty, dark-haired woman, gazing into her eyes like a lovesick sheep.

She remembered Chrissy tugging at her hand as she strode towards the door, but she was past reason then, burning to tell the bastard what she thought of him. All her dreams had gone up in smoke in that moment, and it was knowing herself for a fool that made it harder to bear.

Now it was all clear, all the little slights and excuses. He had been ashamed of her, and she had been too stupid to see it. He'd never meant to move her into the house at Benvulin, never intended anything more than for her to warm his bed and pass the time until something better came along.

And then last night she had burned her bridges by telling him off. She'd no hope of salvaging anything now, not even a parting guilt-induced gift.

Chrissy reached the top of the stairs and unlocked the door with her own key. The flat was cold and smelled faintly of the cabbage that seemed to constitute the daily diet of their downstairs neighbor. From now on, thought Alison, this would be their life; tea with her mum, shopping at the supermarket with an anxious eye on every penny, a week's work under the cold, fishy eye of Mrs. Witherspoon—and then it would start all over again.

Then, as Alison watched Chrissy putting away the cornflakes in the cupboard and carefully placing apples in a bowl, her little face intent, she felt ashamed. She had Chrissy, that was what mattered, and somehow they would get on.

"We could watch a video tonight," she suggested brightly. "Something special. And hot cocoa. You'd like that, wouldn't you, baby?"

Chrissy turned and looked at her, her gaze unexpectedly solemn. "It's all right, Mummy. You don't have to pretend. You don't have to make up for Donald."

"But . . . I thought . . . I thought you'd be disappointed. The pony . . ."

Chrissy shrugged her thin shoulders and slid a carton of milk into the fridge. "I never really believed it. It was like a story in a book. It's okay, really it is."

"But, baby . . ." Alison brushed at the sudden tears threatening to smear her mascara.

"Can we watch *Spirit: Stallion of the Cimmarron*?" Chrissy asked, closing the subject.

"Again?" asked Alison, choking back a half laugh, half sob. When Chrissy glared at her she added, "Okay, okay. I know I promis—"

The knock on the door made her jump. "What the hell . . . ," she muttered, crossing the room and yanking the door wide.

Callum MacGillivray stood on the mat, looking exceptionally clean and brushed in MacGillivray tartan, his expression pinched and anxious.

Alison felt the blood rise in her face. "What do ye think you're doing here?" she said furiously. "Go to hell, Callum. I don't want to see you."

"Alison—"

"Could ye not have left me to make a fool of myself in my own time?" She started to slam the door, but Callum thrust out a strong arm. "Alison, I've got to talk to ye—"

"You've done enough damage. I've nothing to say."

"Alison, I've something to tell ye. It's bad news."

The fear swept over her then, clenching her gut. Her knees seemed to dissolve and she found herself clutching the doorframe, unable to speak.

"Chrissy, I think maybe ye should go to your room," Callum said gently, but Chrissy shook her head and stepped closer to her mother.

"No," she whispered. "It's not Max, is it, Callum? Or Grandma?"

Some small detached part of Alison's mind almost laughed at her daughter's priorities. Would she, she wondered, have the dubious honor of coming before the horse?

"No," she said, in a calm voice that seemed to come from somewhere outside herself. She forced herself to focus on Callum. "It's Donald. He's dead, isn't he? And you bloody killed him."

12

The sharp constraint of fingertips
Or the shuddering touch of lips,
And all old memories of delight
Crowd upon my soul tonight.

     —ROBERT LOUIS STEVENSON,
    "I Saw Red Evening Through the Rain"

Carnmore, April 1899

WILL STOOD IN *the door of the warehouse, gazing at the ranks of casks. He had discovered in the past few months that this was the one thing that gave him a sense of satisfaction, of completion. Some of these casks now were his, his legacy, as the ones before had been his father's.*

He breathed in the scent of oak, of hard-packed earth, and even on this cold April day the ever-present vapor of maturing whisky. This was his life, his world, embodied in barrels and hogsheads, stamped with the Carnmore seal. He had put away his books, and along with them his dreams of university in Edinburgh, of studying medicine. The promise he had made his father bound him more

*tightly than any physical constraint, and he had deter-
mined that he would commit himself well.*

*Will poured over his father's ledgers and account
books, he questioned the men, absorbing details of the
distilling process he had never thought to notice. They
were patient with him, these men who had been his
friends since childhood, and he noticed that as time
passed they listened more and more readily when he offered an opinion. He could only hope that he would live
up to their expectations.*

*Closing and locking the warehouse doors, he started
out across the yard towards the office. He had paperwork
to do, there were orders to be filled, but just for a moment
he stopped at the edge of the yard and looked out across
the Braes.*

*They were strip-burning the heather up on the moors—
late this year because of the persistent rains in March.
The smoke rose in curls, and he caught the smell of it,
sharp and acrid on the dry air.*

*Since he had put aside his books, he had begun to feel
the land like a living thing, a presence that never left him.
The life and rhythm of it pulsed in his blood, in his skin,
the tips of his fingers, the soles of his feet. When the first
buds appeared on the trees, he'd felt the hard nodules on
the ends of his fingers, masked by velvety skin. He felt the
water moving through the earth, the green shoots pushing upwards, the delight of the lambs frisking in the
fields.*

He told no one, afraid they would think him mad.

*It was the same in the distillery. He felt the whisky at
every step, from the malting of the barley to the final dis-
tillate—and he knew when it was right. He began to wonder if his father had found grace with God after all, and
so been allowed to bestow a last gift upon his son. What*

other explanation was there for what had happened to him?

This uncanny awareness did not extend to people, however. Watching his mother as she went about her daily tasks, he was unable to penetrate her reserve. It was not that she seemed desperately unhappy, but that his father's death had changed her in some basic way that Will couldn't fathom.

And then Rab Brodie had come calling from Benvulin. It was almost fifteen miles from the Speyside distillery to Carnmore, and Will wondered if the condolences Mr. Brodie had come to offer merited such a ride. Brodie had walked round the distillery with an assessing eye that made Will uncomfortable, but it was the man's easy condescension that made Will's skin prickle.

He knew from the men's gossip that Benvulin had not fared well in the Pattison's disaster, and if Brodie was struggling to keep his own distillery afloat, what possible interest could he have in Carnmore?

After another futile visit to the police station, where even the friendly sergeant's patience seemed to be wearing thin, Gemma retreated to the car. She considered going round the town, trying to find a witness who had seen Hazel early that morning, but she had to admit that the likelihood of finding anything on her own was slim.

She knew she should take Kincaid's advice and go back to the B&B, but it galled her to do it. She couldn't banish the thought of Hazel, alone in an interview room, or worse, being badgered by Chief Inspector Ross, after what she had already been through that day.

Gemma made an effort to put herself in Ross's position. Wouldn't she have done the same, with the information Ross had?

No, she couldn't summon the detachment, she was too close, and yet the effort brought with it a small worm of doubt. What *had* Hazel done last night? Had she argued with Donald? And why had she left so precipitously this morning? Where had she been at the moment Donald was shot? Two days ago it would never have occurred to Gemma that Hazel might hide secrets. How well, she wondered, did she really know her friend?

Unwilling to follow that train of thought any further, Gemma started the car and drove out of Aviemore, heading north towards Innesfree. As she crossed the bridge over the Spey, she realized that her wipers were squeaking. The rain had stopped. Looking up, she saw that a clear ribbon of sky had appeared beneath a dark and forbidding bank of cloud. In the distance, the hills glowed impossibly green, and it suddenly seemed to Gemma that the morning's violence had been a dream.

How could such a thing have happened in this place, where beauty took the breath away? She shivered, as if someone had walked over her grave, and turned up the car's heater.

As she neared the B&B, she saw that the crowd had dispersed except for a few stragglers and an isolated television van. Slowing for the turn, she remembered that Heather had meant to go to Benvulin. Why not go there and talk to her, ask about the solicitor as Kincaid had suggested?

Gemma drove on, finding that it seemed logical to go on to Benvulin, but she knew that what drew her most was the chance to return to the place where she had felt closest to Donald Brodie.

Graced by the late-afternoon sun, Benvulin looked much as it had the day before, except for the two police cars parked in the drive alongside Heather's Audi. Deciding to try her luck first in the office, Gemma went up the steps and entered the small stone building next to the old mill.

This was not included in the visitors tour, Gemma quickly surmised. It was a real, working office, crammed with file cabinets, computer desks, and the piles of paperwork that any business generated. There was no one in the first room on the right, but from the size of the desk and the memorabilia on the walls, she assumed the office was Donald's. A large, carved sideboard held an array of Benvulin whiskies and a tray filled with crystal tumblers. For an instant, Gemma imagined Donald sitting in the leather-backed chair, half turned towards the window so that he could survey the domain he had so loved. She blinked, shook her head to dispel the vision. Donald Brodie was gone.

She went on, and in the next room along the corridor she found Heather Urquhart. The woman sat hunched over her desk, her face covered by her long, slender fingers. At the sound of Gemma's footfall, she looked up, startled, and snapped, "What are you doing here?"

Heather looked so miserable that instead of making a retort, Gemma sat down and said gently, "You must be having a dreadful time of it. What are the police doing here?"

"Searching the bloody house. For what, I don't know." Sarcastically, Heather added, "A note inviting Donald to a secret assignation in the meadow, signed with the murderer's name?"

Gemma had to smile. "They should be so lucky."

"Well, then, what *are* they looking for?"

"Details," Gemma said slowly. "Details of a life. All the bits and pieces that make up the whole, and they hope that when they put it all together, they'll see a pattern that will point them in the right direction."

"They've taken away the computers. You'd think they'd realize we still had a business to run."

Gemma hesitated, then said, "I can't speak for Chief Inspector Ross, but it's not usually the aim of the police to make life difficult for those trying to deal with a tragic death. They just want to solve the case—and so do you. The consequences of not succeeding are terrible for everyone concerned with the victim. Trust me on this."

"So you're saying we should cooperate?"

"Yes, and cooperate fully, rather than grudgingly. That's when the little, innocuous things come out that can glue the entire case together."

"But I can't abide that man," Heather protested, her earlier hostility towards Gemma apparently forgotten. "He makes me feel guilty even though I haven't done anything. Do you know I actually started thinking about the time I stole a bag of marbles from the novelty shop when I was six?"

"I hope you didn't confess," Gemma said, grinning. "But I know what you mean. He's rather terrifying."

Heather's answering smile was fleeting. "You went to Aviemore—what about Hazel? Did you see her?"

"Ross is still detaining her, and no, I wasn't able to see her, I'm afraid. She should have a solicitor. Is there someone you could call?"

"There's Giles Glover, the firm's legal adviser. But I've rung him already. He's out of town for the weekend, won't be back until tomorrow morning. About Hazel—I hope—you don't think Ross took her in because of something I said?" Heather twisted her hair into a careless knot.

"What did you tell him?" asked Gemma, making an effort to keep her voice even, friendly.

"Only that Donald and Hazel had had a relationship, but years ago. I didn't say—you'd think he'd have taken in that Alison woman. I mean, she was the one screaming at him like a fishwife last night—"

"Her name is Alison? I had the impression you knew her," Gemma added, with some satisfaction.

"Alison Grant." Heather made a grimace of distaste. "She lives in Aviemore, works at the gift shop there. It was nothing serious between her and Donald, at least on his part."

"So do you think someone told her Donald had another . . . um . . . romantic agenda for the weekend?"

"Someone must have, but I've no idea who." With a return of her former prickliness, Heather added, "It wasn't *me*."

"No, no, I didn't think it was. Where's Pascal?" Gemma asked, hoping to diffuse the tension. "I thought he was coming with you."

"He did. He's in the stillroom with Peter McNulty, the stillman. Peter showed up here this afternoon already half pissed, and is now proceeding to drink his way through an eighteen-year-old bottle of Benvulin. It seemed the least I could offer," Heather said bitterly. "He was devoted to Donald. Everyone was devoted to Donald."

"Including you."

Heather's eyes filled, and she swiped angrily at the tears. "Yes. Including me. God, what a bloody mess."

"What will happen to the distillery? Will you stay on?"

"It will depend on the disposition of Donald's shares. And on the board of directors. I've rung them with the news."

"And the house?"

"It belongs to the distillery, not Donald personally. Donald's father mortgaged it when the distillery had a cash shortage back in the eighties. Donald's mother has no claim. She remarried shortly after she and Bruce divorced, and lives in California now. I've rung her as well."

"What was he like, Donald's father?" asked Gemma.

"Bruce Brodie was . . . difficult. He bullied Donald, as hard as that is to imagine." Heather's smile was fleeting. "When he was killed—that was not long after I came to work here—I'd almost say Donald was . . . relieved."

Gemma sat up a bit, her interest quickening. "He was killed?"

"Did Hazel never tell you? It was a climbing accident, on Cairngorm. Almost ten years ago, now. Donald's sister, Lizzie, died, too."

"How dreadful!" exclaimed Gemma. "How did it happen?"

"An early snowstorm. It was four days before Mountain Rescue found their bodies. The weather forecast had been a bit dicey, but Bruce ignored it. He was always reckless. And Lizzie . . . Lizzie would have followed her father to the end of the earth. I suppose you could say she did."

"I'm so sorry," said Gemma, wishing she had more comfort to offer. "It must have been very hard for you, especially if you and Donald were close."

"Do you mean if we were lovers?" said Heather, hostility back in full force. "At least you had a little more tact than Chief Inspector Ross. Why does everyone find it so hard to believe that men and women can be friends?"

"I'm sorry. You're right, it was stupid of me." Even as she cursed herself for her clumsiness, Gemma noticed that Heather had not answered the question directly.

Heather stood abruptly and went to the window, where she stood with her back to Gemma, looking out.

Taking advantage of the opportunity, Gemma got up and examined the photos on the wall behind Heather's desk. There were many of Heather, or Heather and Donald, in the distillery with various members of the staff.

Another picture caught Gemma's eye, Heather and Donald in evening dress at a banquet. It must have been an affair honoring whisky, as bottles marched down the center of the table. Heather looked happy in a way Gemma had not seen before.

Among the business shots, Gemma spied a framed photo of a slightly younger Heather with an older couple Gemma took to be her mum and dad. And then she noticed an unframed snap, stuck into the corner of a corkboard, half covered by papers. She peered at it, trying to make out the details. It was a distillery, but not Benvulin. The buildings were spare and white-harled, and looked bleak against a snowy ground and barren moors.

There were two girls, off to one side, in the shadow. One was surely Heather, the long, dark hair distinctive even then, and the other, half-hidden by the corkboard's edge—was it Hazel?

"It's Carnmore." Heather had turned round and was watching her. "My family's distillery."

"Your family? But I thought Hazel's father—"

"My father was the younger brother. It should have come to him, but he wasn't in a financial position to take on the business when Uncle Robert decided to sell," explained Heather, her tone once again bitter.

"Did you and Hazel spend much time together?" asked Gemma, still studying the photo.

"We were inseparable. I never imagined things would turn out the way they did." Heather moved to the corkboard and touched the snapshot with a fingertip. "Losing Carnmore was bad enough, but I thought Hazel would write, that she'd come back for the summers. I never dreamed she would just disappear."

Was this the source of Heather's ambition? wondered Gemma. A longing for a childhood idyll, rather than a passion for the whisky itself? "It might have been hard for her to come back," suggested Gemma. "To be reminded of what she'd lost."

"I know that now. But I didn't at twelve. Look . . ." Heather turned to face her. "What I said this morning, about what's happened being Hazel's fault. I don't really believe that. But why—after all this time—would someone choose this particular weekend to shoot Donald?"

When Kit learned that Kincaid had arranged for Wesley to come and stay from Monday afternoon, he had gone ominously quiet.

First, Kincaid tried determined cheerfulness, but as the afternoon wore on and Kit's attitude did not improve, he called the boy into the study, a cozy room that held not only Kincaid's desk but also a squashy sofa and the television.

"Kit, what's the problem, here? I thought you got on with Wes—"

"It's nothing to do with him." Kit stood before the desk, hands shoved in his pockets, spots of color high on his cheekbones. "I just don't see why we need anyone—"

"I thought we'd already had this argument. I don't know how long I'll be away, and I'm not leaving you and Toby alone without an adult in the house. That's just not an option." Leaving Kit alone really would give Kit's grandmother ammunition to accuse him of improper care, Kincaid thought with a shudder, but he wasn't going to remind Kit of that. He tried to curb his exasperation. "Now, why don't we take the dogs for a run before—"

"Then let me go with you. Toby can stay here with Wesley."

"Kit—"

"I can help you. I could do all sorts of things for you."

Kincaid had a sudden flash of understanding. "Kit, if you're worried about Gemma and Hazel, I'm sure they'll be fine. There's no—"

"How can you say that? A man's dead. Someone they knew. That means Gemma could— Hazel could—"

To Kincaid's horror, he saw that Kit was fighting back tears. Thinking of how close they had come to losing Gemma just a few months earlier when she had miscarried and subsequently hemorrhaged, he said with more certainty than he felt, "Kit, I promise you Gemma and Hazel will be all right. That's why I'm going to Scotland, to make sure of it. And I need you to help Wesley keep things running smoothly here."

Kit shook his head and bolted from the room, but not before Kincaid had seen the accusation in his eyes.

They both knew what Kit had not said—that safety was illusory, and that promises could be broken. For Kincaid had failed his son once before, when he had let Kit's mother die.

"Sod it," muttered Kincaid, sitting once more in the traffic on the Euston Road. Sod Hazel Cavendish for having got them into this mess. Sod Tim Cavendish for having done a bloody runner over the weekend.

But his anger couldn't quite mask his worry. He kept replaying his confrontation with Kit, and remembering Gemma's fear that Hazel might be in danger, too. The only way he could assure Hazel's safety was by learning why Donald Brodie had been killed, and in the meantime, he was just as happy to have Hazel safely in the Aviemore nick.

Neither Tim nor Carolyn Cavendish had rung him back over the course of the afternoon, and when he had called the Cavendishes' number, he'd got the answer phone. After the third try, he'd made the boys their tea and climbed back in the car, this time without any of the morning's pleasure at the prospect of the drive.

His uneasiness was confirmed when he turned into Thornhill Gardens. Tim Cavendish's mud-bespattered car was parked in its usual spot in front of the house. Kincaid got out and rang the bell. When there was no answer, he walked round the corner to the garage flat and went in through the garden gate.

Tim sat in one of the white iron patio chairs, a beer in his hand, while Holly dug in the sand pit at the bottom of the garden. Under other circumstances, a scene of perfect normalcy, but on this evening it jarred on Kincaid like a note out of place. Something here was very wrong.

"Tim!" he called out. Tim looked up but didn't speak while Holly dropped her trowel and came running to him, clinging to his leg like a limpet.

"Duncan!"

"Hullo, poppet." Kincaid swung her up to his hip and hugged her, finding unexpected comfort in the damp-child smell of her.

"Where's Toby? Is Toby with you?"

"No, sweetheart, not this time," he said as he carried her across the garden. Someone, he noticed, had carefully plaited her unruly dark hair, but strands had sprung loose to float about her face. "I've come to see your dad," he added as he reached the patio and set her down.

"Duncan," said Tim at last, looking up at him.

Tim Cavendish had shaved the beard he'd worn when Kincaid had first known him, and it struck Kincaid now that his face looked naked without it, defenseless.

"Holly, go finish your barn while I talk to Duncan." Tim's tone brooked no argument, and Holly trudged obediently off towards the sand pit, dragging her feet to express her displeasure.

Kincaid shifted a chair round to face Tim and sat down. "Tim—"

"Have a beer?" Tim gestured vaguely towards the kitchen. There was no slur to his words, Kincaid thought with relief—at least he wasn't drunk.

"No, thanks. Tim, your mother must have told you I came by—"

"She's been playing farm," interrupted Tim, watching his daughter. "My mother bought her a set of barnyard animals. Spoil her rotten, my parents."

"Tim. I told your mother there was a shooting at the B&B in Scotland. A man named Donald Brodie was killed. What I didn't know this morning was that Hazel's been taken in for questioning."

"Hazel? They think *Hazel* shot him?" Tim looked squarely at him for the first time. Kincaid saw the dark circles under his eyes, the lines cutting grooves about his mouth. The man was clearly exhausted. "My wife is capable of many things," Tim added, his tone meditative, "but I think even she would draw the line at that."

He knew, Kincaid realized. Tim knew about Hazel and Donald. "Tim—"

"You don't have to spell it out for me, you know. I'm not stupid—or at least not anymore. So why do the police think my wife shot her . . . lover?"

Denials ran through Kincaid's head—there was no

proof, after all, that Hazel had done more than renew her friendship with Brodie—but he knew at heart that anything he said would be cold comfort to Tim Cavendish. "I don't know. The officer in charge of the case wouldn't speak to Gemma. I'll take the train up in the morning, see what I can find out."

"Bully for you. Duncan to the rescue." Tim took another swig of his beer, then held up the bottle and squinted at it in the fading light.

"Come with me. Holly can stay with Wesley and the boys. We'll get this sorted out—"

"No. You can't fix this," Tim said fiercely. "I can't fix this, and I'm not traipsing up to the bloody Highlands to make an even bigger fool of myself. Hazel made her own bed—excuse the metaphor—let her lie in it."

"Tim, you can't mean that," Kincaid argued reasonably. "She's still your wife, and Holly's mother. Do you realize the seriousness of the situation? If she's accused of murder—"

"She'll have to get a lawyer, then, won't she?" said Tim, tapping his empty bottle against the flagstone.

"Tim, you can't make these kinds of judgments when you don't have all the facts. You've too much at stake—"

"Facts? What's between Hazel and me isn't a police case, Duncan. What I know for a fact is that my *wife* lied to me, and that she went to Scotland to meet a man who had been her lover. If it were Gemma, wouldn't you put two and two together?"

"Not without talking to her," Kincaid protested, but he couldn't help but wonder how he would feel in Tim's shoes. "Surely, you can—"

"No!" The bottle in Tim's hand shattered against the patio.

Holly, Kincaid saw, had stopped digging and was sitting very still, her face turned away from them. Deep shadow had stolen over the garden, and the lightless house seemed desolate without Hazel's presence.

"Okay, Tim," Kincaid said quietly. "Just take it easy. You're scaring Holly. Let her come to us—"

"She's my daughter," Tim responded, but kept his voice down. "She stays here with me. Now why don't you just sod off, Duncan, and play knight somewhere else?"

"All right, I'll go. But first tell me one thing: Where were you this weekend?"

"Why should I?"

"The police will get round to asking you, you know. Why not tell me, if you've nothing to hide?"

Tim gazed out across the garden for a moment, then shrugged. "I went walking. My mum told you."

"With your friends?"

Kincaid saw Tim hesitate before he said, "No. That fell through. I went on my own."

Had there ever been any friends? wondered Kincaid. "Where did you go?"

"Hampshire. I needed to think."

"Did you see anyone?"

"A few sheep," answered Tim.

"You must have gone in a pub, a petrol station—"

"Daddy." Holly had given up her digging and edged her way back to the patio. She watched her father from a foot away, her brow creased with worry.

"Baa." Tim reached out and gathered her to him, burying his face in her dark hair. "Can you say 'baa,' sweetheart?"

Holly pulled away. "Daddy, when's Mummy coming home? I want Mummy."

"We'll manage just fine on our own." Tim stood and

lifted her up. "I'm going to make you macaroni cheese. How would you like that?"

Kincaid didn't see how he could continue questioning Tim without upsetting Holly further. "Tim, ring me if you change your mind," he said reluctantly, and went out the way he had come in.

Walking round to the front of the house, he stood for a moment, looking back at the darkened windows. He didn't like leaving the child alone with Tim, but he had no authority to do otherwise. The little girl was obviously sensing her dad's anger, and missing her mother. Tim Cavendish was a therapist, he told himself, a man who understood the fragility of children, but he feared Tim's judgment was compromised by his emotions.

Could he contact Tim's parents, ask them to come back? Tim would protest, he felt sure, but perhaps they'd have more leverage with him.

Had Tim really gone to Hampshire? Kincaid ran a finger over the rain-speckled boot of Tim's dark blue Peugeot. The south of England had been dry the entire weekend.

Ross had always been one for expending the least effort necessary to get results, and so he had left Hazel Cavendish alone in an interview room for the afternoon. Oh, he'd sent in sandwiches and coffee—no one could accuse him of ill treatment—but he'd been happy enough to let her stew in solitude while he organized the gathering of information. In his opinion, there was nothing like a few hours in an empty room to induce a confessional state of mind.

In the meantime, he had set in motion a house-to-house inquiry along the Inneses' road, although the scattered nature of the properties made the results less than promising. He'd assigned an officer to enter all the data collected into HOLMES, and a family liaison officer to trace Donald Brodie's living relatives. As well as the team working at Innesfree, he had a team searching Brodie's house and business, and another team had been delegated to canvas the railway station and nearby shops in Aviemore, in an effort to substantiate Hazel Cavendish's early-morning movements.

And he had spoken to the press, who had followed him from the crime scene to Aviemore Police Station like vultures after a carcass. Although he knew rumors as to the victim's identity were flying, he had asked the media to keep such speculations to themselves until any next of kin had been notified.

Only then had he felt ready to interview Hazel Cavendish. He summoned Munro, who appeared looking even more lugubrious than he had earlier in the day. Eeyore the donkey, thought Ross, that's who Munro reminded him of—although Munro's nature was surprisingly optimistic considering his countenance.

"Two things, sir," said Munro as they clattered down the stairs. "We found Alison Grant's address here in Aviemore, traced her phone and electricity services. A constable went round, but there was no one at home. He'll try again in a bit."

"Why don't you go, Sergeant?" suggested Ross. "I'd rather trust your judgment on this one. What else?"

"John Innes's gun, sir. It's not licensed. His other two shotguns are, but not the little Purdy."

Ross was not surprised. "Damn family guns," he muttered. "Just because there's no record of purchase, people can't be bothered. Well, I'll throw the book at him on this one." They had reached the interview room. He stopped and automatically straightened his tie. "Now, let's see how our wee birdie's getting on."

Hazel Cavendish stood up abruptly at their entrance, sloshing coffee over the table, then looked round wildly for something to mop it up.

"Sergeant, see if you can grab a kitchen roll," said Ross. When Munro had gone, he studied the woman before him. Time and isolation had taken their toll, he noticed. The flesh seemed to have molded itself more tightly to the bones of her face, leaving the planes and hollows more pronounced. And he saw that her hands were trembling, although she clasped them together to hide it. The remains of her sandwich lay in the open plastic box, shredded to bits. Ross couldn't tell that she had actually eaten any of it.

He shook his head disapprovingly. "Ye need to eat, lassie, keep up your strength."

"What I need," she countered, facing him across the table, "is to go home and see my daughter."

"Weel, the sooner you answer our questions satisfactorily, the sooner ye can go—although you may be obliged to stay in Scotland for a few more days." To his delight, it did not seem to have occurred to her that she could refuse to talk to him until she had a lawyer's counsel, and as he had not actually charged her, he was not obliged to advise her of her rights.

Munro came back, his arrival silencing her protests for the moment. While Munro swabbed the table, Ross turned on the recorder, stated the date and time, and identified the participants.

"Can we get ye some more coffee, Mrs. Cavendish?" he asked as he sat down. "Munro can fetch it from the machine—"

"No, please, I don't want anything, except to go home. I don't understand why you've brought me here."

"Ach, weel, why don't we start at the beginning, then.

Tell me about your relationship with the deceased, Donald Brodie."

She twisted her hands together in her lap but met his gaze directly. "We were close once, years ago, before I was married. But I hadn't seen him in years."

"Then how do you explain your row with him after Alison Grant came calling at the B&B last night?"

Her hands tightened, and he heard the small catch of breath in her throat. "You're mistaken, Chief Inspector. We didn't argue."

"Is that so?" He smiled at her. "Weel, I have it otherwise from a number of sources. How do you explain that, Mrs. Cavendish?"

"I—I don't know."

"You and Mr. Brodie went out together after dinner, and you were heard shouting. Now, I would call that a row, myself."

"I—I was worried about the child. She had a child with her when she came to see him."

"Alison Grant?"

Hazel nodded. "I was afraid he'd made promises to the woman—to Alison—that would hurt the child."

"A very noble sentiment, Mrs. Cavendish. And it was that worry drove you to have sex in the woods with Mr. Brodie?" Ross thought it worth the gamble that the DNA test on the semen sample found in the woods would give him a positive identification. He knew Hazel Cavendish had been there from the fiber match, and it seemed highly unlikely that she'd been meeting someone else.

Her eyes had widened. "Oh, God," she whispered, covering her face with her hands.

"It will go easier for ye, lass, if you'll just tell us the truth," encouraged Ross at his most sympathetic.

"It wasn't like that—what you said." She dropped her

hands, gripping the table edge as if it might anchor her. "He'd asked me to come. Donald. He wanted me to leave my husband. It wasn't until I saw that woman and her child that it really hit me what damage we were contemplating. Not just my husband, my daughter, but this woman who cared about him, and her child, and then I saw that it would ripple outwards from there.

"We did argue. I was angry with him, but even angrier with myself. I told him it was never going to work out between us. What we did then . . . in the woods . . . I suppose it was a good-bye."

"And this morning?"

"I couldn't face seeing him again. I thought I'd just pack and leave, but there was no train. I decided I had to face up to things, so I came back. And that was when . . . Gemma told me . . ." She lifted a hand to her mouth, pressing her fingers against quivering lips.

"Why didn't you tell us this from the start?"

"I was so ashamed. And I suppose I was hoping it wouldn't have to come out, that my husband wouldn't have to know."

That was it, thought Ross, feeling a firecracker fizz of inspiration. That was the reason that made the pieces fit. Of course she hadn't wanted her husband to find out, not if she'd made up her mind to go back to him.

"That's all very plausible, Mrs. Cavendish," he said. "But I think that's not quite how it happened. I think you met Mr. Brodie again this morning, and that when you told him you meant to go back to your husband, he threatened to expose you. Then you found some excuse to take the gun—no, wait." Ross frowned, working out an even better scenario. "I think you told him last night, and he threatened you then. Was that why you argued? And the sex, you were placating him. Did you invite him to meet you this morning, a romantic rendezvous? He would never have thought you meant to harm him—"

"No!" Hazel pushed away from the table and stood. "I would never have hurt Donald! How could you even think—"

"Sit ye down, Mrs. Cavendish," soothed Ross. Having failed to shock her into a confession, he knew he had little hard evidence to support his theory. "If you'll—"

There was a knock at the interview room door. Munro got up, and as he went out, Ross glimpsed one of the officers assigned to the Aviemore detail.

A moment later, Munro looked in again and said, "Sir, a word with ye . . ."

Ross switched off the tape recorder and joined him in the corridor.

"You'd better hear what P. C. Clarke has to say," Munro told him quietly, "before you go any further."

The constable nodded at him. "Sir. Someone from the car hire office in the railway station recalls seeing a woman matching Mrs. Cavendish's description early this morning. He remembered because it was odd to see someone turn up, bags and all, two hours before the scheduled train. He said she sat in the waiting area for half an hour, then went out again."

"Did he remember the time?" asked Ross, his heart sinking.

"Getting on for six o'clock, sir. He had come in to arrange an early car pickup."

"All right," Ross growled. "Get a statement. Then have him make a definite identification." He turned away, swearing under his breath. That would make it just about the time Inspector James had reported hearing a gunshot, and he bloody well couldn't make a case on the premise that Hazel Cavendish had been in two places at the same time.

Gemma left Benvulin when the team arrived to search the offices. With a last glance back at the house, set like a jewel above the river, and the distinctive twin pagodas of the distillery, she got into the BMW and eased the car into the drive. When she reached the road, she hesitated a moment, then turned left, away from Innesfree.

Heather had said she'd bring Pascal back to the B&B to collect his car later on, so Gemma had no reason to hurry. Nor was she sure the forensics team at the B&B would have finished their search of the room she shared with Hazel, and the thought of being on the premises while someone went through her belongings made her skin crawl.

But there was more to her reluctance than that, she realized—she just wasn't ready to face the others, to answer their questions about Hazel, to see those she had considered friends as suspects.

She drove on, absently watching the light and shadow play across the hills, through the hamlet of Nethy Bridge, and then across the Spey and into the planned Victorian town of Grantown-on-Spey. Finding a spot in the car park, she carefully locked the BMW and walked down to the High Street.

Most of the shops were closed, it being a Sunday afternoon, but the newsagents and pubs and cafés seemed to be doing a brisk business. There were people walking purposefully along the pavements, which suited Gemma—she felt the need to be near people doing ordinary things, but she didn't want to speak to anyone. "Wallpaper," Kincaid would say accusingly to her when she got into such a mood. "You want human wallpaper."

Imagining the sound of his voice made her throat tighten with longing, and she felt a wash of relief as she thought of his arrival tomorrow.

Damn her pride—she must have sounded an ungrateful cow on the phone earlier. Not that she had exactly protested, but he must have heard the reluctance in her voice. How could she have even considered letting her desire to do it all herself—and to get the better of Chief Inspector Ross—get in the way of anything that might help Hazel?

She walked on, trying to put her mind into neutral, admiring the tidy symmetry of Grantown's High Street, which opened out into a large green at the top end. The town was ringed by the hills that rose above it on the north and west, and by the heavily wooded valley of the Spey on the southeast. It gave the place a secure feel, and as lights began to glow in the windows of the large houses facing the square, she found herself enchanted.

The imposing edifice of the Grant Arms Hotel anchored the square. Gemma was just crossing the greensward to have a better look when the sky darkened and a squall of wind and stinging rain blew up out of nowhere.

Sprinting for the hotel entrance, she darted inside and stood in the lobby, panting and shaking the water from her hair like a drenched dog.

Although she had seen tour coaches parked outside, the hotel appeared comfortably elegant. The woman from the reception desk crossed the lobby, and in a friendly, Highland voice she asked Gemma if there was anything she needed.

"A cup of coffee would be grand," admitted Gemma, still shivering slightly from her unexpected soaking. "The rain caught me by surprise."

"That's the Highlands for you," the young woman said with a smile. "We pride ourselves on our unpredictability. The restaurant's closed until dinner, but I'll just fetch you a cup from the kitchen, if you don't mind having it in here."

Having accepted gladly, Gemma wandered about the lobby as she waited, discovering a small plaque detailing the history of the hotel. When the receptionist returned with her coffee, Gemma said, "I see you had Queen Victoria as a guest."

"In 1860." The young woman grinned. "That was the greatest moment in Grantown history, if you can believe it. Still," she added a bit wistfully, "it must have been grand in those days—all the balls and dinner dances. And the clothes must have been lovely."

"And bloody uncomfortable," offered Gemma, and they both laughed. "Can you imagine corsets?"

When she'd finished her coffee, the rain had stopped. She went out again onto the green and stood for a moment, looking up at the hotel in the gathering dusk, imagining the square filled with carriages and traps and the chatter of excited voices.

With a sigh of regret, she turned away. She had no business indulging in a fantasy of a happier time. Returning to the car, she phoned the police station in Aviemore and inquired about Hazel. There was a different—and much less accommodating—sergeant on duty, who told her only that he believed Mrs. Cavendish was still with Chief Inspector Ross.

Gemma then rang the bed-and-breakfast and spoke to Louise.

"You're coming back for supper?" Louise said, an appeal in her voice. "John's put together a goat cheese tart. He thought it would suit Hazel . . . he was hoping . . ."

"Don't count on me," Gemma told her evasively. "I've a few more things to do, and I wouldn't want to hold you up." The idea of sitting in the Inneses' dining room, facing *two* empty chairs, suddenly struck her as an impossible feat.

But the truth, she realized as she drove slowly out of Grantown, was that she had nothing to do, and her frustration at her lack of control was interfering with her ability to think clearly. She somehow had to let it go, to find a different perspective. She'd stop somewhere, have a pub meal, think things through.

Once on the main road, she passed up the turning for Nethy Bridge and took the next, the route to the village of Boat of Garten. The receptionist had recommended the bar meals in the Boat Hotel there. She found the place easily enough, but as she climbed out of the car, she caught a glimpse of her reflection in the car window. For the first time that day, it occurred to her that she was unwashed, uncombed, and still wearing the clothes she had thrown on before six that morning. Oh, well, she thought, shrugging as she tucked a strand of hair behind her ear, she would just have to do.

Entering the bar, Gemma gave her order and took a table by the window. Over her solitary meal of cock-a-leekie soup, she tried to sort out the events of the day in her mind. So accustomed was she to having Kincaid as a sounding board that she felt handicapped without his presence.

But it was more than that, she admitted to herself as she finished her half pint of cider and walked back out to the car park. It wasn't her lack of authority in the investigation that had her stumbling round so ineffectually, nor was it the absence of her usual intellectual give-and-take with Duncan. It was her doubts about

Hazel that were keeping her from approaching the case in a logical way.

She thought of all the times Hazel had been there for her, a calm center when she'd struggled with crises at work and at home, an unwavering support through the loss of her baby. Hazel might be more complex, and less perfect, than Gemma had realized, but she was still her friend, and Gemma owed her the same support. She would put away her doubts, and start from there.

Looking up, she saw that the long dusk was fading into night, and the last remnants of clouds had been swept away by the wind. Lights had begun to wink on in the comfortable houses lining the village street. Below the hotel, the locomotive belonging to the steam railway that went from Aviemore to Boat of Garten sat on the track like a great black slumbering beast, and beyond the little railway station, the ever-present River Spey flowed silently, cold and deep.

Chiding herself for her fancies, Gemma was nonetheless glad to shut herself in the close warmth of the car. When her mobile phone rang, she jumped as if she'd been bitten, and her heart gave an irrational flutter of fear.

But it was Kincaid's voice she heard when she answered, and a smile of pleasure lit her face.

"Any news, love?" he asked.

Sobering quickly, she said, "No. Hazel's still at Aviemore Police Station. But I can't believe they'll keep her much longer, unless Ross actually means to charge her."

"What about getting a solicitor?"

She told him about her conversation with Heather Urquhart. "Heather said she'd tell Mr. Glover as soon as he rings in the morning."

"Can you trust her to do it?"

"Yes," answered Gemma, rather to her surprise. "I think so."

"Good. I'll be getting the seven o'clock train. Can you pick me up at Aviemore at half-past two tomorrow afternoon?"

"What about Tim? Did you see him? Is he coming with you? Holly could stay—"

"Gemma, I did see him," Kincaid said flatly. "But he's not coming."

"Not coming? But—"

"He knows about Hazel and Donald. I didn't ask him how he found out. He says he won't help her. He doesn't want to see her at all."

There was silence on the line as Gemma tried to come to grips with this latest disaster.

"You'll have to tell Hazel," Kincaid said, breaking into her thoughts. "And, Gemma, I'm not at all sure Tim's telling the truth about where he was over the weekend."

Her stomach knotted as the implication sunk in. "No. I can't believe Tim had anything to do with this. Not Tim—"

"He's got motive. He's got no witnesses to his movements. He's obviously distraught. And his car's muddy. It didn't rain in Hampshire."

"It did here," Gemma said slowly, unwillingly. "But even if Tim drove to Scotland—and that's a long shot—how could he have walked into the B&B in the middle of the night and taken John Innes's gun?"

"They haven't proven that Brodie was shot with that gun."

"No," mused Gemma. "But I can't believe that John Innes's small-bore shotgun would mysteriously disappear at the same time Donald was killed with a *different* gun. That's stretching coincidence a bit too far. And how would Tim have known who Donald was?"

"Tim left London on Friday. He could have been watching her the entire weekend."

Gemma thought of the scene between Donald and Hazel she had witnessed by the river on Saturday morning, and of the nest she'd discovered in the woods. She felt cold.

"Gemma, you'll have to tell your Scottish detective. It will be up to him to follow through."

"But this is Tim! How can I give Hazel's husband to the police as a suspect?" She was near shouting.

"How can you do otherwise, when Hazel herself is a suspect? Don't kill the messenger, love," he added, sounding as weary and discouraged as she felt. "I'm only telling you what you already know. And if you're lucky, if your chief inspector is doing his job properly, he might beat you to it." Kincaid paused a moment. "Gemma, about Tim . . . Hazel may not thank me for interfering, but after I left the house tonight, I rang Tim's parents and asked them to go back. Tim's mother seems a sensible woman. She said they'd take Holly home with them."

"You told Tim's mother—"

"As little as I could. That it was a stressful situation, and I thought Holly might be better with her grandparents. Will you tell Hazel? And I'll ring you from the train in the morning."

"Wait." The rush of her anger had drained away, leaving her feeling shaken and hollow. "I'm sorry. I didn't mean to snap at you. It's—it's been a beastly day."

"I know." His voice was gentle. "Get some rest, love."

"Tell the boys I miss them."

There was the slightest pause before he answered. "Right . . . They miss you, too."

When he'd rung off, she sat for a moment, wondering

if she had imagined his hesitation. Another sliver of worry lodged itself in her heart. Was there something wrong at home that he had failed to tell her?

On reaching the B&B, Gemma drove past the front of the house and parked near the barn. She'd seen the pale blur of faces through the uncurtained sitting room window, but she was determined to freshen up a bit before she returned Pascal's keys. And she wanted to check on her room, see what sort of mess the forensics team had made.

They had left the lights on, she thought with a flicker of irritation as she stepped inside. Turning, she gasped in surprise. Hazel stood by the bed, her suitcase open, a half-folded nightdress clasped against her chest.

"Hazel! You're back. I've been so worried—"

"He had to let me go. Someone saw me in the railway station this morning, just at the time you reported hearing a gunshot."

Relief flooded through Gemma. "Thank God." Then she remembered what she had to tell Hazel, and her heart sank. "Hazel—"

"I'm going home. There's a late train." Hazel put the nightdress carefully into her case. "Chief Inspector Ross said I could."

Gemma pulled out the dressing table chair and sat down. "Hazel, there's something you have to know," she said reluctantly, knowing there was no way to cushion the news. "Duncan went to see Tim this evening. Tim knows about you and Donald."

"Oh, Christ." Hazel sank down onto the bed as if her knees had given way. "But how—"

"He didn't say. I'm sorry."

Hazel gazed into space, her expression desolate. "I had

meant to tell him, but in my own way, and in my own time. But now . . . how am I going to face him?"

Gemma felt a moment's qualm at the idea of Hazel going home to her angry and disillusioned husband. But surely she was safer there than here, where Donald had been murdered. "Don't," she told Hazel. "Go back to London, but don't see Tim just yet. Pick Holly up from Tim's parents and go to our house. Then, when Tim's calmed down a bit, you can meet him on neutral ground."

"That's good advice." Hazel's smile held a bitter irony. "I might have given it myself, once. What about you?"

Gemma hadn't reconsidered her own plans. With Hazel cleared by the police and off to London, there was nothing stopping her from going as well. She could ring Duncan tonight and tell him not to come—she could, in fact, pack her things and get on the train with Hazel.

Except that she found she couldn't. She had known Donald Brodie, and had liked him, and someone had murdered him, had shot him while she slept a few hundred yards away. She could not—would not—leave it in other hands.

"I think I'll stay," she said slowly. "At least another day or two. If John and Louise can't keep me here, I'll find a room somewhere else. I want to see things . . . wrapped up."

Standing, Hazel went to the bedside table and picked up a bottle of Scotch Gemma hadn't noticed. It was, she saw, the last-issue Carnmore that Donald had given Hazel the previous night. Hazel cradled it, as if it were a living thing, stroking the label with a fingertip. "You intend to find Donald's killer yourself," she said quietly, not meeting Gemma's gaze. "Do you think I would do less for him?"

"No, of course not, but—"

"As long as I know Holly's all right, I'm staying, too." She looked up, and Gemma saw an unexpected resolution in her eyes. "I'll see Donald buried—I owe him that."

13

❦

The friends are all departed,
The hearthstone's black and cold,
And sturdy grows the nettle
On the place beloved of old.
— NEIL MUNRO, "Nettles"

Grantown-on-Spey, May 1899

EVERY YEAR, SINCE *Livvy had left her father's house to marry Charles Urquhart, she had come back to Grantown in May and September for an extended visit. Usually, both Charles and Will had accompanied her, but as Will had grown older, he and his father had several times made their own expeditions.*

These annual fortnights had been a necessary and much-anticipated element of Livvy's life. There was shopping for staples and household goods not readily available in the Braes or Tomintoul, the refurbishing of their wardrobes, the time spent cloistered with her father in his study, the visits with her two aunts and her father's neighbors, the catching up on the latest in fashion and gossip. Always Livvy had made the transition from coun-

try to town easily enough, but this time, on their arrival in Grantown in mid-May, she found herself restless and out of sorts, unable to settle to any of her ordinary pursuits.

First, there were the condolences to be got through, trial enough, so many months after Charles's death, even if kindly meant. But as the days regained their ordinary pattern, she felt more alien, rather than less. She began to realize that although she and Charles had not spent much time together on these visits, she had been unconsciously aware of the solidity of his presence, and it was this that had kept the two parts of her life linked together. Now she was adrift.

She had moved back into the room she'd occupied as a girl, hoping to find some connection with the person she had once been, sufficient unto herself, but that long-ago girl eluded her. The days were lengthening, and she found it difficult to sleep, as she always did at this time of year. But now, she felt feverish as well, stretched, her senses raw with exhaustion.

Her father insisted that she and Will should accompany him to an upcoming dance at the Grant Arms Hotel, so she filled her time with sewing, making over a gown of her aunt's. It was a dusky purple, a suitable color for a widow. Livvy reduced the puff of the sleeves and added a bit of lace to make it more stylish; this would, after all, be her first formal outing without Charles.

Her father took Will to the local tailor's shop to be fitted for evening clothes, his first, and in the evenings Livvy helped him practice his dancing. Will was now, after all, the man of the house. If it was time for Livvy to face the world on her own, it was time for Will to give up boyish pursuits and take his place in Highland society.

None of these preparations, however, eased Livvy's

discomfort as the night of the dance arrived. It had been seventeen years since she'd appeared in public without the armor of a husband at her side, and she felt as awkward as a girl. She stood just inside the door of the ballroom, watching the dancers glide by in a shifting blur of pattern and color. The air was filled with the scent of perfume, of warm bodies and hot candle wax, a tincture as dizzying as laudanum.

Will swung by her, looking quite the beau with old Mrs. Cumming on his arm. When had he grown so tall? He had become a man in this last year, in more than looks, and Livvy felt a rush of pride. The girls would be noticing him soon, if they hadn't already. In fact, Livvy saw one of the Macintosh daughters cast a simpering eye his way, but Will fortunately seemed oblivious. He caught her eye over Mrs. Cumming's shoulder and smiled, his usually serious face alight with his pleasure.

Then Livvy felt ashamed of herself for indulging her own vanity. She was thirty-five years old, and widowed; she should be past worrying about such things. It was Will that mattered now, with his life spread before him.

But then Rab Brodie spun by her, with his angular sister, Helen, and her pulse quickened in spite of herself. When Rab returned after the next interval and offered her his arm, she hesitated only a moment. There was no impropriety, after all, in dancing, and if a little voice whispered in her ear that by such small steps the mighty are fallen, she pretended not to hear.

Gemma woke to the sound of whimpering. Her first thought was of the children, then, as consciousness came flooding back, she remembered where she was. She sat up, blinking.

It was past daybreak; a pale light filtered in through the

drawn curtains. In the next bed, Hazel tossed restlessly, moaning now. Then the moan rose to a scream, and Hazel sat bolt upright, panting, her eyes open but unfocused.

"Hazel!" Gemma leaped from the bed and crossed the gap between them, grasping Hazel's shoulder.

"No. No!" Hazel cried out, flinching, and it was only when Gemma shook her firmly that she seemed to realize where she was. She looked up at Gemma, her face streaked with tears.

"It was just a dream," soothed Gemma, patting Hazel as she would one of the boys. "Try not to think about Donald—"

"No, it wasn't Donald," Hazel said, shaking her head. "Oh, Gemma, it was the strangest thing. I was in our old house, at Carnmore, except that it wasn't exactly our house. Some things were the same, but others weren't." She frowned. "The kitchen was red, I remember that, and there was a rocking chair by the stove." Rubbing at her bare upper arms, she began to shiver. "I know that doesn't sound frightening, but I was terrified. It was as if I was seeing things through someone else's eyes, and I couldn't get back to myself. And then—" She stopped, swallowing hard. "Then I was in the distillery, and there was a fire—maybe it was the kilns. I'm not sure, but I was frightened—not as myself this time, but as her—"

"Her?"

"Yes." Hazel nodded, looking surprised. "I'm sure of it, I don't know how. *She* was afraid, and then there was shouting, and blood, and the smell of whisky . . . the smell of whisky everywhere." She shuddered. "God, I feel sick."

"What you need is a cup of tea," Gemma said briskly, padding over to the kettle. She sloshed it, decided there was enough water for two cups, and switched it on. "It's only natural you should have nightmares, after what's happened."

"Yes, but it . . . it was so *real*. Not like a dream at all, yet at the same time I knew I was dreaming. I've never experienced anything quite like it."

Gemma put two tea bags into the comfortably mismatched flower-patterned cups Louise had provided. "Was there ever a fire in the distillery?"

"Not that I know of."

As Gemma made the tea, she thought of the photo she'd seen in Heather Urquhart's office, and of the little that Heather had told her about the distillery. "I have an idea," she said, handing Hazel her cup. "Will you take me to see Carnmore?"

"What?" Hazel stared at her. "Now?"

Gemma glanced at the clock on the bedside table, then opened the curtain until she could see out into the garden. It was not yet seven, and the sun was shining. "Yes. Why not? We'll skip breakfast. We could pick up something on the way."

"But— What about—" Awareness of what the day would hold flooded back into Hazel's face. "Shouldn't we be doing something—"

"There's nothing we can do this morning but wait." Gemma had stayed awake, worrying into the wee hours of the morning. As she considered each angle of the case, she ran smack into her own helplessness. *She* couldn't call on the firm's solicitor to learn the disposition of Donald's will; *she* couldn't attend the postmortem; *she* couldn't query the forensics results, or the findings of the house-to-house inquiries. Any little morsel of official information would have to come by the grace of Chief Inspector Ross, and Gemma suspected she would do well to get a crumb.

There was a bright spot—Heather had promised to ring

her when she'd heard from the lawyer, and that information might give her something to go on with. And she would chat up the other guests, but she sensed that would be better done when she could get them on their own, and once the police had finished with the property. The presence of the team completing the search of the area would not exactly invite confidences.

As for suggesting that Chief Inspector Ross inquire into Tim's movements, she had decided to wait at least until Kincaid arrived after lunch, in hopes that Ross would be thorough enough to request London's help without her having to interfere.

She had rung Kincaid before going to bed, letting him know that Hazel had been released but that she and Hazel both intended to stay on a little longer.

"You don't have to come," she'd added, but without much conviction.

After a moment's thought, he'd said, "You're determined to have a hand in this case, aren't you, whether the local force likes it or not."

"Something like that," she'd admitted. "There's another thing—Hazel wants to stay for Donald's funeral, and I won't leave her here on her own."

"I don't suppose it will make any difference if I remind you that it's inadvisable, and that if the Northern Constabulary complains to your chief, you're going to have a hard time talking your way out of this."

"Um, no. I'll call Notting Hill first thing in the morning; tell them I've been delayed. I can afford to take a few personal days."

Kincaid had given a barely audible sigh. "Right, then. If you're staying, I'm coming up. We might as well put our heads on the block together. And, Gemma," he'd added before ringing off, "do be careful."

Turning now, she saw Hazel gazing into space, her teacup tilting absently, her face already pinched with strain. "Sitting round brooding is the last thing you need to be doing," Gemma said decisively. "Can we get to Carnmore and back before lunch?"

"Oh, yes, I should think so." Hazel's expression seemed to brighten a bit at the prospect.

Gemma was already pulling on her clothes. "Good. While you get ready I'll leave word where we'll be."

As John, having assured Gemma that she and Hazel could stay a few more days, insisted on giving them toast and more tea, it was close to an hour before they got away. The morning was still fine, however, and when Gemma cracked open the car windows, the air had a rain-washed, flinty sharpness and smelled faintly of peat smoke.

Following Hazel's instructions, she drove through Nethy Bridge, as she had the previous day, but this time she turned right before she reached Grantown, taking the way that led up into the hills, away from the gentle valley of the Spey. "It wouldn't be so far if you could travel as the crow flies," Hazel said. "But then, it's seldom possible to do things directly in Scotland."

The road snaked as it rose, and within a few miles the landscape had changed entirely. To Gemma, the moors seemed wild and desolate, alien as the moon—and yet she found them unexpectedly, searingly beautiful. The scene touched something in her that was both new and ancient, awakening a longing she hadn't known she possessed. For the first time, she wondered how Hazel could have borne leaving.

Beside her, Hazel sat silently, picking at the hem of her pullover. They hadn't discussed Donald or Tim since the night before, but Gemma knew there were things she must ask.

"Hazel, do you mind telling me what happened between you and Donald on Saturday night, after you left the dining room? Did he tell you about the woman who came to see him?"

"Alison. He said her name was Alison. We had a row over her. I told him I couldn't believe he'd asked me to come here, to risk my marriage, when all the while he was keeping someone on a string." She shook her head. "What a hypocrite I am, as if I hadn't been holding on to Tim as a sort of insurance."

"But you—the place in the woods—I thought that you and Donald—"

Hazel flushed. "So you saw that, too. The police found a thread from my sweater—that's why Ross took me in. Oh, Donald talked me round. He was always good at that." She gave Gemma a look of appeal. "That was the first time, you know, since all those years ago."

"But if you—then why did you leave yesterday morning—"

"I couldn't face seeing Donald again. I'd made up my mind that it couldn't go on, that I had to go back to London and sort things out with Tim. But Donald could be so persuasive . . . I was afraid he would talk me out of it. So I ran away. I should have known it was too early for the train."

When she'd negotiated a particularly hair-raising pass, Gemma said, "Hazel, about Tim— Did you see him this weekend?"

"See Tim?" Hazel gave her a startled look. "How could I have seen Tim? He was in London."

"The thing is . . . Tim may *not* have been in London. He had his parents come and stay with Holly over the weekend. He said he went walking in Hampshire, but when Duncan asked him about it, he was rather . . . vague. There were some things that made Duncan think he might have come to Scotland."

"Tim?" This time Hazel gaped at her. "You think Tim was here?" The implication sank in. "You think *Tim* killed Donald? You can't mean that!"

"No, of course not," Gemma reassured her. "But I'd feel better if I was sure Tim went off for a weekend on his own in Hampshire. Hazel, how do you suppose he learned about Donald?"

"I don't know. There was nothing— I didn't—" Hazel clapped a hand to her mouth. "Oh, how could I have been so stupid? There was an old photo. I left it under my office blotter, along with Donald's card. But even if Tim saw those, why would he have thought anything of it? I mean . . ." She looked away, as if embarrassed. "I tore up Donald's notes, and there was nothing else . . ."

"Did Tim know about your past relationship with Donald?"

"Well, yes," Hazel admitted. "I'd told him a little when we first met. You know how you do, recounting life stories. That was why he never liked me to talk about Scotland, or the past."

"So Tim's always been jealous?" Gemma asked, her unease growing.

"I suppose you could say that," Hazel agreed reluctantly. "Although I never really thought of it that way. It wasn't like he thought every man I met was trying to have it off with me."

"Just Donald," Gemma said flatly. "But he didn't say anything when you told him you'd planned to come back to the Highlands for the weekend?" When Hazel shook her head, Gemma added, "Did he seem as usual before you left?"

"I suppose so. A little edgy, maybe," Hazel admitted. "But I know Tim would never hurt anyone. No matter what I did." Hazel's voice held just a touch too much conviction.

The road had dipped, risen again, and now ran through a cleft of rock that looked as if it had just been scooped out by a giant hand. Then, to Gemma's surprise, a valley opened before them. At its bottom flowed a river, willow lined, pasture flanked, a scene of pastoral perfection set amid the blasted moor.

"Where are we?" Gemma asked, glad to change the subject.

"It's the River Avon. Some of the best fishing in the Highlands. Donald and I used to come here. He always liked to picnic," Hazel added, her voice expressionless. "How typical of the man—he could seat twenty in his dining room, but his ideal meal was outside on a blanket. It was the whole Victorian legacy, the gentry sporting in the fresh air."

"Was that so bad?"

"Donald's family were farmers originally, like mine. It was just that they gave themselves airs." Hazel fell silent, picking at her pullover again, and Gemma sensed constraint between them.

"Hazel, about Tim— It's just that when something like this happens, you have to consider all the possibilities."

"You may, but I don't, and that's one I refuse to think about. It's just not possible."

"Hazel—"

"Look, we're coming into Tomintoul," Hazel said, and Gemma realized there was no point arguing with her.

Glancing about her, she had an impression of a village built all of a piece, set round an airy square, a little island of civilization in the wide expanse of moorland.

"It's the highest village in Scotland," Hazel continued. "Built by the duke of Gordon after the Battle of Culloden, when this was still a major military thoroughfare for the Hanoverian armies." She pointed ahead, towards the end of the village. "You turn left at the junction."

"Carnmore is farther still?" Gemma heard the hint of dismay in her voice, and saw Hazel's fleeting smile.

"Another ten miles. Often in winter you can't get from Tomintoul to the Braes. And the stretch of road that runs through the Lecht Pass, between Tomintoul and Cockbridge, is the first in Scotland to be blocked by snow every winter." This said Hazel with the native's pride in extreme weather.

Gemma took the turn Hazel indicated, and within moments, the village disappeared from her rear view as if it had never been. "Didn't you go mad, snowed in for months at a time?"

"No. I loved it, to tell the truth. It's as if the world shrinks . . . everything seems more focused somehow . . . Life can be hard here, but people are amazingly tough and self-reliant—at least until you uproot them. My father—" Hazel shook her head. "It wasn't so bad for my mother when they left here; she came from Braemar, near Balmoral. But my father had spent all his life in the Braes. I watched him wilt and die, and I swore that would never happen to me."

"Is that why you were so determined to sever your connections, why you didn't keep in touch with Heather, or come back to visit?"

"Poor wee girl," Hazel said softly. "She was always intense; even as a child, she took things to heart. And she loved Carnmore with a passion rare in a child, even more than I did, I'm afraid. I don't think she ever forgave my father—or me."

"But if your father had no choice—"

"Adult choices don't mean much to a child. And choice is relative, isn't it? There was a slump in the whisky industry, yes, but my grandfather, Will, survived much worse without giving up."

Glancing at her friend, Gemma said, "You never forgave your father, either."

Hazel considered this. "No, I suppose I didn't. We Scots are notorious for holding grudges."

"That's the first time I've ever heard you refer to yourself as a Scot."

Hazel didn't meet her gaze. "Here's the Pole Inn, the last outpost of civilization as you enter the Braes. You'll turn to the right."

A beckoning wisp of smoke rose from the chimney of the pub, but Gemma obeyed Hazel's direction. They entered a single-track road that wound round a conifer-covered hill, then followed a bubbling stream through farm pastures and into the small hamlet of Chapeltown. There was a scattering of houses, a church that Gemma assumed gave the village its name, and a whitewashed distillery. Pointing, she said, "Is this—"

"No. That's Braeval. Built by Chivas Regal in the seventies, to make whisky for their blends. Unlike Carnmore, they could weather the changes in the market, with corporate might behind them."

"And the church?"

"Our Lady of Perpetual Succor. Built on an old site around the turn of the century. This was a Catholic stronghold," Hazel explained. "A haven for Jacobites and smugglers."

"Smugglers?" asked Gemma, intrigued. "What did they smuggle?" The paved road had come to an end, and at Hazel's affirmative nod, she nervously eased the car along a rutted track that seemed destined to dead-end in the hills rising before them.

"Illegal whisky. These are the Ladder Hills; they're honeycombed with smugglers' paths. We used to follow them in the summer . . . Heather and I, always hoping to find a working still. It was our version of cowboys and Indians—smuggler and excise man."

"Were your family Catholic, then?" asked Gemma, thinking about what Hazel had told her.

"Nominally, yes. But my grandfather Will didn't hold with religion, so my father wasn't brought up in the church, and my mother was Presbyterian."

"Did you know your grandfather?"

"No. I wish I had. But he married late, and my father and uncle weren't born until he was in his fifties. He died before I was born."

They passed farms, their yards filled with rusting implements, as the track twisted and turned, following the curve of the hill.

Then, as they rounded a bend, a house and outbuildings appeared before them, white-harled, tucked into the fold of the hill Hazel said was called Carn More. "There it is," she whispered now. "Carnmore."

Gemma climbed out of the car, looking curiously about her. On closer inspection, she saw that both the house and the distillery buildings behind it were unoccupied. No smoke came from the chimneys; broken windowpanes gaped like eyes; nettles covered what had once been a neatly cobbled yard.

Hazel stood staring at the desolation, hugging herself as if she were cold. "I'd no idea it would be so bad." She sounded appalled. "Donald and I came here once, but my father was still alive then, and the house was rented."

"Your father didn't sell the property?"

"People don't move *into* the Braes," Hazel said dryly. "If they've any sense, they move *out*."

Gemma turned to her in surprise. "Hazel, do you still own this place?"

"Oh, God. I suppose I do. I never went through all the papers when mother died . . . I couldn't face it. Tim took care of things—" She saw Gemma's look and shook her head. "Tim couldn't have sold it without my knowledge, if that's what you're thinking. And besides, it's not worth anything."

"Except to you."

Hazel gave a rueful shrug. "I'd never have admitted that . . . until now." She tried the door of the farmhouse, found it still locked, then peered in the windows. "There'll be water damage, at the least."

"What about the distillery?" Unlike Benvulin, the buildings looked basic and uncompromising, built for the work they were meant to do without thought for aesthetic appeal. There were no charming, pagoda-roofed kilns here.

"Dad sold off all the equipment to other distilleries, and the stock, of course. These buildings are just husks now, without any heart. Donald had dreams, I think, that when we were—that *if* we were married, we might restore it together." Hazel walked slowly towards the distillery, and Gemma followed.

The sun peeped in and out of a building bank of cloud, making shadows race across the hills, and birds called out in the heather. Hazel stopped by a rowan tree that stood midway across the yard, fingering the leaves. "I always loved the rowans, especially in the fall."

"Hazel, you said Donald's father didn't approve of your relationship. It sounds as though you and Donald talked of marriage—Were you actually engaged?"

"Ah, there's the rub," said Hazel with an effort at irony,

but her eyes reddened. "For a day, a glorious day, ring and all. Then Donald took me home to meet his father.

"Bruce Brodie's temper was notorious, with good reason. Not only did he tell me quite literally never to darken his doorstep again, he told Donald he'd disinherit him if he went through with the marriage. It was more than bluster—he meant it, and Donald saw that he meant it."

"And then?" Gemma prompted gently, when Hazel didn't continue.

"Donald hesitated. I saw the terror in his face—I knew what it would mean to him to lose Benvulin. And I knew that if I forced him into such a choice, he would never forgive me. I couldn't live with that." Hazel turned to Gemma, a plea in her voice. "You can see that, can't you?"

"You left, didn't you?" said Gemma, understanding. "You never gave him the chance to choose."

"I felt I couldn't bear it either way. To be rejected outright, or to cost him what he held most dear. But he told me—" Hazel stopped and took a breath. "Donald told me, on Saturday night, that he had refused his father. He told Bruce to go to hell, and he came after me, but I was gone. If I had—"

"No." Gemma took Hazel by the shoulders and gave her a shake. "Don't go there. You can't know what might have been. You did what you thought best at the moment." As she thought back over the time she'd spent with Donald Brodie, she added, "And for what it's worth, I think you were right. Donald may not have been happy without you, but he wouldn't have been whole without Benvulin, either. It was his father that was at fault, not you or Donald. But what did Bruce Brodie have against you, against your family?"

"I don't know," said Hazel. "But I always suspected Donald knew more than he told me."

* * *

They drove back to the bed-and-breakfast in silence, Gemma growing more anxious as the morning progressed and her mobile phone did not ring.

They stopped only once, for a quick lunch at a tearoom on one of the local estates.

"Changing times," commented Hazel, gazing out at the garden center and wildlife trails visible from the café windows. "This was a grand place when I was a child, but these days they do what they have to in order to survive."

"Could your father have stayed at Carnmore, if he'd been willing to compromise, perhaps by selling an interest to one of the big distillers?" Gemma asked thoughtfully as she nibbled at her sandwich.

"I don't know. I think it would have proved inevitable at some point."

"And inevitable for the Brodies, as well?"

"Benvulin has had a charmed life—the Brodies have a history of overextending, of making poor financial decisions, but somehow they've always managed to hang on by the skin of their teeth. I suppose it was a combination of stubbornness and the ability to turn a blind eye to reality, neither of which my father had. I'll hate to see Benvulin lose its character." Hazel's eyes filled with the tears she had not shed at Carnmore.

When they returned to Innesfree, Hazel went straight to their room, saying she intended to rest. Gemma sought out Louise, whom she found in the back garden with a hand trowel, trying furiously to repair the damage done to the lawn by the police vehicles.

No, Louise confirmed, no one had rung the B&B with a message for her. The police forensics team was still working in the house itself, and search teams were still combing the river meadow.

According to Louise, Heather and Pascal were at the distillery, and John had taken Martin to Grantown on some undisclosed errand. "I can't do anything in the house," Louise had complained, wiping a muddy hand across her brow. "And I've had to cancel all our bookings for the next week. A death in the family, I told them. How could I explain what's happened? And there's no way of knowing how much longer this will go on." She sat back on her heels, her eyes widening as she seemed to realize what she'd said. "Oh, God. I must sound horribly selfish. It's just that—I know how trivial it is compared to Donald's death, but it's been hard to get this place going, and we've just begun to get on our feet the last few months. We were fully booked for the first time, and now—" Her gesture took in the police cars parked in the drive.

"I understand," Gemma told her. "Life goes on, and most people feel guilty because they can't suddenly stop being concerned with it. But it's perfectly normal."

"Thanks." Louise reached up and squeezed Gemma's hand. "You've been a great help. Without your calming influence, I think we'd all have gone round the bend. We might yet," she added, attempting a smile. "You are bringing your friend back for dinner, aren't you?"

"Duncan?" Gemma had told John and Louise that morning that Kincaid was coming up from London, to "lend a bit of moral support," but she hadn't reminded them of his rank. "Yes, I suppose so. I hadn't really thought about it. Are you sure it's not too much trouble?"

"John has something special planned. That's his way of coping with things, poor love, and I'm afraid we've not been very cooperative. Heather's going home tonight, and Pascal intends to stay at Benvulin. He feels someone should be there until the lawyers get things sorted out, and Heather just didn't feel up to it."

"That's kind of him. But then I take it his interest is more than personal?"

"Well, we have wondered," said Louise. "I mean, Heather and Pascal have become quite friendly recently. But I can't imagine she'd have got involved with anything that would have harmed Benvulin. She and Donald were so close . . ."

"Was there ever a romantic attachment between them?"

"Not that I know of. But, of course, Heather had worked for Donald a long time before John and I came here."

Dropping down beside Louise, Gemma idly smoothed the turf with her fingers. "But then, you knew Donald before, when he and Hazel were together. Tell me, did Hazel and Heather have any contact in those days?"

Louise frowned, then said slowly, "I remember seeing Heather once or twice, but I think she must have been away at university then."

"What about Heather's father?" asked Gemma, recalling her conversation with Heather the previous day. "Did you ever meet him?"

"No. I think he worked for one of the big whisky distributors, but I always had the impression that he wasn't terribly successful."

Not in a way that had mattered to Heather, thought Gemma, because he'd been unable—or unwilling—to save Carnmore, and that seemed to be the criterion on which Heather had based all judgments.

Gemma had felt an unexpected sense of kinship with the woman when they talked yesterday, but could she trust her own instincts? And could she trust what Heather had told her, including her identification of the woman who had come to see Donald on Saturday night?

It was all jumbled up together: Donald's relationships, Hazel's family, the distilleries. Gemma knew there was a pattern, if only she could get enough perspective to see it. Suddenly she wondered about Martin Innes—how did he fit in?

"Louise, I can see why Pascal would stay on, but what about Martin? When is he going back to Dundee?"

"You'll have to ask him." Louise looked irritated again. "I can't imagine why he would want to stay, after what's happened. But as we've had to cancel the next few days' bookings, John doesn't seem inclined to boot him out of the room. I'm surprised at his sudden attack of brotherly affection."

She *would* ask Martin, Gemma thought, as soon as she had the chance. But in the meantime, she could get to Aviemore with an hour to spare before Kincaid's train, if she left now. Standing, she said, "Louise, I've got to go. Could you keep an eye on Hazel for me? See if she needs anything?" The thought of Tim Cavendish nagged at her.

She made up her mind that, no matter how disloyal it felt, as soon as Kincaid arrived they would have a word with Chief Inspector Ross about Tim's whereabouts over the weekend.

When she reached Aviemore, she parked in the now-familiar car park and, with only a glance at the police station, began to investigate the shops along the main street. A gift shop, Heather had said, but *gift shop* was a loose term, and she made two false starts before she struck gold.

Tartan Gifts could not be described as anything *other* than a gift shop, she thought as she peered in the window at the tartan tea cozies and heather-emblazoned coasters. And she recognized the young woman behind the cash register, last seen in the shadows of the drive at Innesfree.

There were a few people in the shop, so Gemma went in, pretending to browse while surreptitiously examining her quarry. She had the pale, unfinished look of a woman unaccustomed to going without makeup, her blond hair appeared carelessly combed, and her eyes were swollen and red-rimmed. This was one instance, Gemma realized, when she would not have to be the bearer of bad news.

When the other customers had made their purchases and gone out, Gemma approached the register and said quietly, "Are you Alison? Alison Grant?"

"What's it to ye?" The woman gave Gemma a belligerent stare. "Look, if Callum's sent you, you can tell him—"

"No. I just want a word with you. It's about Donald Brodie."

There was a flash of vulnerability in Alison Grant's face before her expression hardened. "What about him? And who are you to be asking?"

"My name's Gemma James." Gemma had contemplated using her police identification but decided that pretending an official status was unwise as well as unlikely to benefit her. "I was staying at the B&B with Donald this weekend. I was there when you came to see him, and Heather Urquhart told me you and Donald were close—"

"What would *she* know about it? I canna believe that woman ever had feelings for anybody, the cold bitch. And that still doesna tell me what it has to do with you." Alison's accent had grown broader as her voice rose.

In an effort to calm her, Gemma said, "Look, Alison, is there somewhere we could visit? I could buy you a cup of coffee."

"And I could lose my job," Alison hissed, a note of hysteria in her voice. "My boss is on her lunch hour; I

canna leave the shop. And if the auld biddy comes back
and finds me talking to you, she'll likely take it out o' my
wages."

"Okay, okay," soothed Gemma. "I'll buy something if
she comes in." She picked up a picture of a Highland
sheep that stood near the register and held it ready. "Now
can we talk?"

"All right," Alison said sullenly. "What do ye want to
know?"

Gemma hesitated for a moment, then plunged ahead. "I
came up for the weekend with my friend Hazel. She had
known Donald for a long time—they were engaged once.
You seemed angry with Donald when you came to see
him. Had he told you he was seeing Hazel?"

"Sod all, that's what he told me, the bastard," said Alison, but her swearing lacked conviction. "A business
weekend at Benvulin, he said, and he'd ring me if he had
the chance. And there was me sitting by the phone like
some gormless idiot, waiting for him to call."

"But you found out it wasn't true—did someone tell
you, then?"

"It was Callum, the mad bugger. I didna believe him at
first, but he kept at me, and so I thought I'd go along to the
bed-and-breakfast and prove him wrong. More fool me,"
Alison added bitterly.

"Who's Callum?" asked Gemma, her pulse quickening. It was the name Alison had mentioned when she first
came in.

"Callum MacGillivray. He and his auntie Janet own
the stables just down the road from your bed-and-
breakfast. He was jealous of Donald. I'd not put anything
past him. I told thon police sergeant last night—"

"The police have been to see you?"

"Aye. Munro, that was his name. I told him he should

be asking wee Callum what *he* was doing yesterday morning."

"Let me get this straight. Callum fancies you, so he told you Donald had lied to you about his plans for the weekend, thinking it would make you go off Donald." Gemma remembered the shadowy figure she'd seen in the drive on Saturday night. "Is he a tall bloke, fair, wears the kilt?"

"Aye."

"Did you know that he was watching you, when you came to the B&B? I saw him in the drive, half-hidden in the hedge."

"No." Alison looked suddenly frightened. "I'm telling ye, he's daft. I've said I want nothing more to do with him, but he won't hear of it. He claimed he was sorry about Donald, but I didna believe him."

"He claimed? Alison . . . was it the police who told you about Donald?" Gemma knew that Ross had managed to keep Donald's name from the media, although she doubted he could hold out much longer.

"Nae, it was Callum."

"And did he say how he knew?"

Alison shook her head. "No, and I didna think to ask. I didna really believe it until the policeman came to the flat."

Gemma had to assume that Heather Urquhart had told the police about Alison, but how had Callum MacGillivray known of Donald's death? She knew rumor traveled fast, and the fact that Callum was the Inneses' neighbor made it even more likely he'd have heard the news despite Ross's precautions. But still, it seemed as if the man had motive—and so, she thought, did Alison Grant.

Deciding there was no subtle way to phrase it, Gemma

said, "Alison, did the police ask you if you had an alibi for the time of Donald's death?"

Alison gave her a look of dislike. "You've a lot of bloody cheek. But I'll tell you the same thing I told them. I was in my flat, and there's no one to prove it except my nine-year-old daughter, who was fast asleep in her bed."

Gemma reached the railway station with a few minutes to spare. She sank onto a bench on the platform and watched as the little steam train to Boat of Garten chugged cheerfully out of the Aviemore station, like the Little Engine That Could. Beyond the tracks, the still-snowcapped peaks of the Cairngorms rose in the distance, and she found it hard to believe that just that morning she had stood in the foothills of those same mountains.

But her mind darted back to her recent interview. She might not have made an ally of Alison Grant, but she had at least gleaned some useful information. She and Duncan could pay a visit to Callum MacGillivray, once they'd finished their business in Aviemore.

Her stomach gave a flutter of nervous anticipation as she thought of seeing Duncan. It had only been a few days, but with everything that had happened, it seemed a lifetime, and she suddenly felt as breathless as a girl awaiting a first date.

Then she heard the distant thrum of the approaching train, and a moment later the diesel locomotive was squealing into the station on a whiff of hot oil and scorched brake linings.

Standing, she watched the passengers spill from the compartment doors. She saw Kincaid step down from the last car, a head taller than his fellows. His unruly chestnut hair fell across his forehead; he wore his favorite

scuffed, brown leather jacket, and swung a duffel bag
from one hand.

His face lit in a grin as he spied her through the crowd,
and in a moment he was beside her. Dropping his bag, he
gathered her into his arms. Her cheek fit into the familiar
hollow of his shoulder.

For a moment, Gemma allowed herself to feel the solidity of his body against hers. She inhaled the mingled
scents of his leather jacket and the bay rum lingering
from his morning shave.

"Hullo, love," he said against her hair, his voice gentle.
"I can't let you out of my sight, can I, without your getting into trouble?"

14

*One thing in life calls for another; there is a
fitness in events and places.*
— ROBERT LOUIS STEVENSON,
   "A Gossip on Romance"

I SUPPOSE YOU could say the place has a sort of rakish
charm," Kincaid commented as he and Gemma walked up
Aviemore's main street. His eyes strayed from the ski
shops and cafés to the mountains rising beyond the town,
formidable even in late spring. He had been to Scotland
several times as a child, visiting Kincaid relatives in
Strathclyde, and had made one memorable trip to Oban
and the Isle of Skye, but he had never been to this part of
the Highlands.

"It does grow on you," agreed Gemma, but her smile
seemed to take an effort. Her freckles, he saw, were no-
ticeable against the pale background of her skin, always
a sign that she was tired, or under stress.

"I've missed you," he said, slipping an arm round her
shoulders and giving her a squeeze. "How's Hazel?"

"Holding up fairly well, under the circumstances.
Have you talked to Tim again?"

"I've been ringing him since I got on the train this morning, and I've sent Cullen by the house. He's not answering the door or the phone. I've spoken to his mum; they haven't heard from him since they picked Holly up last night."

"What the hell is he playing at?" said Gemma, and he felt her shoulders tense under his arm. "We'll have to speak to Ross, then, as little as I like it." She shook her head. "I keep thinking of all the times we've spent together, the four of us. Tim's our *friend*—"

"All the more reason the matter should be out of our hands," Kincaid told her, more firmly than he felt. "Let the Met—"

"Do you think he's all right?" Gemma stopped and turned to face him, impeding the flow of pedestrians along the pavement. "You don't think— I still have a key to the house— I should have gone back— What if—"

"Gemma, you can't be in two places at once. I'm sure Tim's fine." Kincaid didn't voice the fears he'd been trying to pass off since the previous night. "But we can suggest to the man here that he have the Met send along a couple of uniforms, a welfare call, if they can't get CID there right away. Now, where do we find this dragon of a chief inspector?"

"The police station is just past the car park. We can put your bag up first." They reached the car park a few yards farther along, and she led him to the sleek-looking red Honda and unlocked the boot. Earlier, she'd taken time to extend the car hire.

Kincaid tossed his bag in, then hesitated before closing the boot. With a glance at Gemma, he unzipped the holdall and pulled out a sheet of paper. "Toby sent you this," he said, handing it to her. "He worked on it all weekend."

It was the much-embellished crayon drawing Toby had begun on Friday, depicting Gemma and Hazel on the train. He had since added frisking lambs, red long-horned cows, a blue river, and in the background, purple mountains with snowy caps.

"He wasn't too far off the mark, was he?" Kincaid said, gesturing at the peaks of the Cairngorms, clearly visible through the open space beyond the car park.

With a sudden glint of tears, Gemma folded the drawing and tucked it carefully in her handbag. "Sorry," she said, sniffing. "You know how I hate maudlin mums. It's just that with everything else that's happened—"

"I know." Kincaid decided he had better take his chance. "Listen, Gemma. There is something I need to tell you— No, it's all right, the kids are fine," he added hastily, seeing the panic flare in her eyes. "It's just that I've had a letter from Kit's grandmother."

"Eugenia?"

"None other. She's sent a copy to Ian as well, saying she's suing for custody. She's alleging that Kit's not being cared for properly."

Gemma gaped at him. "You're not serious."

"I am, unfortunately."

"Well, that should be simple enough to deal with. It's past time you had a paternity test—"

"Simple, yes, except that Kit refuses to do it. Look, we can't talk about this just now. But I thought you should know."

"Why doesn't Kit want to be tested?"

"I don't know. He won't talk to me."

"I can't believe you didn't tell me this," Gemma said, her voice rising. "You *were* avoiding me over the weekend, weren't you?" she added. "You didn't *want* to tell me."

"Am I so transparent?" He snapped the boot shut, trying to make light of it. "I didn't want to spoil your weekend."

"Spoil my weekend?" She faced him, hands on her hips, her eyes bright with anger. "You can't keep things from me. Not for my own good. Not for any reason."

"Gemma, I only wanted—"

"No." Her voice shook. "Not if we're in this together—a family. You have to promise me."

"But—"

"It's the crack in the ice, Duncan. Don't you see? It could happen to us, what's happened to Hazel and Tim, and that's how it starts. A little deception, a little something kept back. It could happen to us," she repeated.

And he did see. She was right—he should have told her. It was a learned habit, sharing, and one at which he had not had much practice. He had been on his own for too many years, but before that, he should have learned his lesson with Vic. "No, it won't," he said, and ignoring the stares of passersby, drew her to him. "We won't let it."

"Inspector James." The fair-haired sergeant was on duty again. He smiled at her in recognition, then glanced curiously at Kincaid.

"This is Superintendent Kincaid, from Scotland Yard," said Gemma. "We need to see Chief Inspector Ross."

"He's out, I'm afraid. If you'll just—"

"But it's urgent. If you'll tell him—"

"He really is out, ma'am," the sergeant said, apologetically. "He's in Inverness, at the hospital."

Of course, Ross would be attending the postmortem, Gemma realized, and she felt a moment's thankfulness that it wasn't she performing that duty. "What about Sergeant Munro?"

"With the chief inspector."

"Can you give the chief inspector a message, then?"
She passed the sergeant her card. "Ask him to ring me on
my mobile, as soon as he can. I have some information
for him."

"Is it something I can help you with?" offered the sergeant, his very blue eyes alert and speculative.

Gemma hesitated before replying. "No. I think I'd better talk to Chief Inspector Ross. But ta just the same."
She flashed him a grateful smile.

When she and Kincaid reached the street again, he
grinned wickedly at her. "The man fancies you."

"What—the sergeant? Bollocks!"

"Plain as day. Unless that's what they call community
policing up here."

Gemma gave him her most severe look. She knew he
was deliberately trying to charm her, to smooth over the
difficulty between them, but she was flattered nonetheless. "It's too bad my feminine charms didn't impress
Chief Inspector Ross."

"Shall we wait for him?" Kincaid asked as he reached
the car. "I must say I'm looking forward to meeting the
man who could resist you."

"No." As she slid behind the wheel, Gemma debated
bringing up Kit again but decided it would be better to
wait until they had some uninterrupted time.

Now she needed to bring Kincaid up-to-date on what
she had learned about Alison Grant and her unwelcome
suitor. They could pay a call on Callum MacGillivray on
the way to the B&B. "No, we can't afford to put ourselves at Chief Inspector Ross's convenience. We've
other fish to fry."

In spite of the fact that he wore nothing but a kilt and
boots, at close quarters Callum MacGillivray was not as

romantic a figure as Gemma had imagined from her glimpse of him on Saturday night.

At the sound of their car bumping down the track to MacGillivray's Stables, he had come out of the barn and stood watching them, pitchfork in hand. When they got out and approached him, she found he smelled, quite literally, of horseshit. Nor did he seem particularly pleased to see them.

"If ye want to make a booking, ye'll have to talk to my aunt, and she's away the noo," he said curtly. But in spite of the less-than-welcoming statement, he peered curiously at Gemma, as if trying to place her.

Gemma caught a glimpse of Kincaid's amused expression and knew he would tease her about making another conquest. Making an effort to ignore him, Gemma focused on Callum MacGillivray and found herself staring at his bare chest. Although not a heavily built man, he was well muscled, and his fair skin gleamed with sweat.

Hurriedly, she raised her eyes to his face and said, "No, it's you we've come to see. You are Callum MacGillivray, right?" Kincaid had agreed that they could not identify themselves as police officers—they were courting Ross's ire even with their unofficial questions—so they'd decided the simplest approach would be best. "We were friends of Donald Brodie," she explained after giving their names, fudging the truth only a little. "And since your property is next to the Inneses', we thought you might have seen something."

"What sort of thing?" Callum leaned on his pitchfork, looking wary.

Kincaid extricated himself from the thorough sniffing administered by Callum's dog, a sleek black Lab. "Someone doing something out of the ordinary . . . or someone doing something ordinary at the wrong time."

"And why should I tell ye if I had? The police have been here already, nosing about."

"I was staying at the Inneses'," countered Gemma. "I saw you on Saturday night, watching Alison Grant. And I've talked to Alison—she says it was you who told her Donald would be there."

"What if I did? There's no crime in that."

"Alison says you were jealous of her relationship with Donald—"

"Och, you canna believe everything the woman says," Callum said with obvious exasperation. "She had no relationship with Donald. I only wanted her to see the truth of it."

"That was a bit brutal, don't you think?" asked Gemma, in a tone of friendly inquiry.

"I told her time and again. She wouldna listen to me."

"Did you think she would thank you for it?"

"Aye, weel, I suppose I wasna thinking past the moment," Callum admitted, with less assurance. He picked up a fleece pullover thrown carelessly across a wheelbarrow and pulled it over his head, as if the cold had suddenly struck him. "I didna realize she'd be angry with *me*."

"But you knew she'd be furious with Donald—which she was. Did you not think she might take it further than a shouting match?"

"Alison? I'll tell ye what I told thon policeman; Alison wouldna hurt anyone."

"She seemed pretty tough to me." Gemma raised an eyebrow.

"You havena seen her with her wee daughter, Chrissy. She's a good mother." Callum's defense was earnest, but so ready that Gemma suspected he had been called on to repeat it more than once. And it might be true, she thought, but good mothers could be fierce, especially if their children were at risk. Remembering what Heather Urquhart had said about Alison's daughter being crippled, she wondered if Donald had somehow threatened the well-being of the child.

Kincaid, she saw, had gone back to fondling the dog, making himself inconspicuous so as not to disturb the rapport she'd established with Callum. She knew he was listening intently, however, in spite of his relaxed posture.

"Callum, how was it you knew about Hazel—my friend—coming to see Donald for the weekend?"

"It was when we were fishing, the three of us. I'd never heard Donald talk that way about a woman before. He took them for granted, the same as he did Alison."

"The three of you?" asked Gemma, curious.

"Aye. Donald and John and me." Callum looked suddenly uncomfortable. "We would go out, on the occasion."

"Salmon good along here, is it?" asked Kincaid.

"Nae. It's mostly the trout." Callum reached for his pitchfork again, as if to terminate the conversation.

"There's something I don't understand," Gemma said quickly, to forestall him. "You and Donald were friends, weren't you?"

"Aye. Since we were at primary school together."

"Did Donald know that you were fond of Alison?"

Callum leaned down to stroke the dog, which had come back to his side. "I knew her first, through the shop. My aunt orders bits and pieces for the trekkers. But when Alison met Donald at a party, she had nae more time for me. A posh bloke, she said, that owned a distillery. It didna take long to worm it out of her."

"And you didn't warn Donald off, once you knew?" Kincaid asked.

Callum colored. "And have him laugh at me, because I couldna keep a girl?"

"There is that," Kincaid agreed. "But when you told Alison about Donald and Hazel, did you not think it unfair to rat on a mate?"

"He didna need Alison," Callum said defensively. "I saw him with her—your friend from London," he added to Gemma. "On the Saturday morning, down by the river."

Had he been watching, wondered Gemma, when she had seen Donald and Hazel together? And in that case, had he been watching the next morning as well? Carefully, so as not to sound as if she were accusing him, she said, "Callum, do you walk along the river path?"

"Aye. Sometimes." He answered casually enough, but his hand on the dog's neck grew still.

"And yesterday?"

"Yesterday I had to go early to Ballindalloch."

"You didn't go out along the river?"

"Nae, I've told ye," he said shortly, rising. "And now I've the horses to see to, if ye don't mind."

Gemma didn't see how they could push him further. They had thanked him and turned to go when Gemma stopped. Prompted by something she didn't quite understand, she fished a card from her bag and turned back to him. "Callum, wait. I came here on holiday, but at home I *am* a police officer. If there's anything you . . . remember . . . or you just want to talk, you can ring me."

She saw the small flash of shock in his eyes, but after a moment he took the card from her with a nod.

Rejoining Kincaid, she waited until they were on the road again before she said, "John Innes would have told him anyway, if they're friends."

"If they're friends," Kincaid answered thoughtfully, "he would know where John Innes kept his guns. You said he was at the house on Saturday night; maybe he nipped round to the back and into the scullery while the rest of you were in the dining room."

Gemma shook her head. "John and Louise didn't sit down to dinner with us. They were in and out of the kitchen constantly."

"Early the next morning, then, before anyone was up and about?"

"I suppose that's possible," Gemma admitted. "But why would he bother shooting Donald when he'd already sabotaged Donald's relationship with Alison? And how would he have known he'd have a chance to kill Donald before anyone noticed John's gun was missing?"

"Maybe they'd made an appointment to fish together."

"Then where's Donald's fishing tackle? It wasn't found near his body."

"The same place as the gun?"

Gemma smacked the flat of her hand on the steering wheel. "Bloody hell, I hate this! We'd have found the gun, if we'd had access to the crime scene."

"That's hardly fair, love. That gun could be in England by this time, for all we know."

She shot him a look as she slowed for the turn into the B&B. "If you mean Tim, I still don't believe— Look, that's Heather's car."

Heather and Pascal were just getting out of Heather's Audi as Gemma pulled up beside it. The other parking spaces, Gemma saw, were filled by a crime scene van and several police cars, so the police had not yet finished their search. A blue-and-white crime scene tape had been stretched across the entrance to the path at the bottom of the garden, its ends fluttering in the rising breeze. The temperature had dropped, and Gemma fastened a button on her jacket.

"I'm glad you're here," said Heather, coming to greet her as she got out of the car. "I was just going to ring you." Heather wore a black trouser suit that made the contrast between her pale skin and dark hair more striking than ever, but on closer inspection, Gemma noticed that she looked almost blue about the lips, and that the hand she held out to Kincaid was unsteady.

"Heather, are you all right?" asked Gemma.

"We had to— I didn't know he would look like that," Heather said hoarsely. She touched her throat with her long fingers. "I've never seen anyone dead before, and Donald . . ."

Having shaken Kincaid's hand, Pascal turned to Gemma. "We had to identify Donald's body for the pathologist. It was difficult for Heather, but as there was no other family . . ." He shrugged, and Gemma saw that the day had taken its toll on him as well. His button-bright eyes were shadowed, and his round face had acquired unexpected hollows under the cheekbones.

"I'm so sorry," said Gemma, berating herself for not having realized Heather would be called upon to perform that task. But it was unlikely Ross would have accepted her as a substitute, even had she volunteered. He would have wanted to watch Heather's and Pascal's reactions when confronted with Donald's corpse, because they were potential suspects.

It was a cold-blooded business, policing, thought Gemma, and for the first time, the knowledge that it had to be done did not make it seem more palatable.

"Come in the house, why don't you," she added, searching for some means of comfort. "I'm sure John or Louise will make us some tea." It was the old standby, certainly, but it fulfilled the human need for activity, and ritual, in the face of shock.

"No, wait." Heather touched Gemma's arm when she would have turned away. "I've something to tell you. Giles Glover, the solicitor, was waiting for us when we got back to Benvulin. He'd had a look at Donald's will. It was dated shortly after Donald's father died. Donald— Donald left all his shares to Hazel."

"What?" Gemma stared at her, not sure she'd heard correctly. "To *Hazel*? But— Are you sure—?"

"It is true," Pascal assured her. "They were his, to do with as he wished."

"He held the majority?" Kincaid asked.

"Yes." It was Heather who answered, and Gemma sensed the effort it was costing her to keep her voice steady, her face composed. She had given Donald Brodie ten years of utter dedication, and he had not left her a crumb. "It's a limited company, with the shareholders owning forty-nine percent, so Donald's was the controlling interest. I'll have to inform the board, but first, I have to tell Hazel. Where is she?" Heather looked round, as if just realizing Hazel's absence. "I thought she would be with you."

"She's here." Gemma nodded towards the barn. "She wanted some time on her own while I picked Duncan up at the railway station. Heather, do you want me to tell her?"

Heather hesitated, then shook her head. "No. We're going to be working together—that is, if Hazel sees fit to keep me. We might as well start as we mean to go on."

Postmortems always left a bad taste in his mouth. Ross had wondered over the years if the phenomenon was caused by the odors of the morgue permeating his skin—

a fanciful and unscientific notion, true, but he had noticed that it only went away after he'd showered.

He'd had Munro stop at a petrol station on the A9 between Inverness and Aviemore so that he could buy breath mints, which he disliked, and his mood had not improved by the time they reached the Aviemore Police Station.

The postmortem had told him nothing he had not expected: Donald Brodie had been shot in the chest at near point-blank range with a small-gauge shotgun loaded with bird shot; Brodie had no other injuries and had been in good physical health at the time of his death. The pathologist had judged time of death to be consistent within an hour or two of the time of the gunshot reported by Inspector James, which helped Ross not at all.

Heather Urquhart's effort at control as she identified the body had been visible, but again, such a reaction was not unexpected. The Frenchman, Benoit, had been solicitous in a rather formal way that Ross characterized as "continental," but not out of the ordinary.

Nor had forensics turned up any interesting trace evidence on Brodie's clothing or body, or at the crime scene.

The surprise of the day for Ross had come earlier, when he had stopped briefly in Grantown to interview Donald Brodie's solicitor. Of course, he had seen strange bequests in the course of his career, but that hadn't prepared him for the fact that Brodie had left his shares in the distillery to Hazel Cavendish, who claimed not to have seen him in a dozen years. And as the distillery owned Benvulin House, the solicitor had explained, that meant that the shares made up most of Brodie's estate. How, Ross wondered, was Mrs. Cavendish going to explain this rather awkward acquisition to her husband?

As they entered the temporary incident room at

Aviemore station, Ross saw there were half a dozen officers still working, organizing the results of the various
inquiries. The room smelled stale and had begun to ac-
quire its quota of empty soft drink cans and crisp pack-
ets—an incongruous complement to the crime scene
photos pinned on the board.

The officer in charge greeted him with a stack of mes-
sages. The top three were requests from Inspector James
to return her call. Well, he thought, irritated, he would
deal with her in his own time. What could she want with
him, now that her friend had been released, except to tell
him how to run his investigation?

Ross sat down at the desk allotted to him, removing
someone's half-drunk cup of tea and wiping with his
handkerchief at the damp ring it had left.

Munro had apparently been following his own train of
thought. "What if Heather Urquhart *thought* Brodie had
left her his shares?" he asked as he sat opposite.

"Then I'd say she had a verra nasty shock when she
heard from Mr. Glover this afternoon. I suppose Brodie
could have led her to think she would benefit, as a way of
increasing her loyalty and commitment to the distillery."

"The same would be true of the Frenchman," mused
Munro. "If he thought Urquhart would sell out to his
company if she gained control."

"Aye. But," Ross said, tapping the pile of statements on
his desk, "according to these, both Urquhart and Benoit
were still in their rooms when the police arrived. How
could either of them have taken the gun, got out of the
house, killed Brodie, and got back in without being seen
by either of the Inneses?"

Rubbing at the five-o'clock stubble appearing on his
chin, Munro said, "I'm beginning tae think it's like that old
Agatha Christie film, where they were all in it together."

Ross sighed. "Such things dinna happen in real life, man, thank heavens. Imagine trying to put such a case before the Procurator Fiscal."

"Then I'd put my money on young Alison Grant," offered Munro. "She's a tough wee baggage, and she had a good motive, if ye ask me. I'd the impression she saw Brodie as her Prince Charming, and then he let her down."

"We've nothing linking her to the scene, and I think it's highly unlikely she'd have nipped into the Inneses' house and nicked their shotgun."

"We don't know for certain that it *was* John Innes's gun," said Munro, playing devil's advocate.

"Then where did she get a gun? A shotgun is not the sort of thing an ordinary shopgirl keeps lying about, especially with a child in the house."

"From a friend?" Munro suggested. "There's the bloke who told her about Brodie and the other woman, Callum MacGillivray." Munro stood and sifted through the pile of reports on Ross's desk. "Here it is. MacGillivray has a license for a twelve-gauge—what's to say he didn't keep another unlicensed gun, like John Innes?"

"And she says, 'Oh, please, can I borrow your shotgun? I need to kill somebody'?" said Ross, with practiced sarcasm.

Munro was undaunted. "Maybe they were in it together. MacGillivray says, according to this"—he waved the paper—"that he drove to Ballindalloch yesterday morning, but he didn't arrive there until well after Brodie was killed."

"That's verra neat," Ross said with a smile. "She gets rid of her unfaithful lover; he gets rid of his rival—two birds with one stone, so to speak. I'm beginning to think you've got conspiracies on the brain."

"I suppose it is a wee bit far-fetched." Munro folded

himself back into the spindly desk chair, his face creased with disappointment.

Ross relented. "We'll have another word with the lassie. And with Callum MacGillivray. But in the meantime"—Ross pulled the reports towards him again and thumbed through them—"I'm curious about Mr. Innes." After Innes's wife had told them during their initial interview that her husband had been out when Brodie's body was found, Munro had talked to him again. John Innes had confirmed his visit to the farm shop on a neighboring estate but added that he wasn't sure exactly what time he'd left the B&B. Ross now saw, however, that when an inquiry team had questioned the clerk at the shop, she'd told them Innes had not come in until almost seven o'clock.

Yesterday Ross had not taken the man too seriously as a suspect, but then he'd had Hazel Cavendish in his sights. Meditatively, he said, "We know John Innes left the house some time before the body was discovered, because Mrs. Innes had been working in her garden when Inspector James told her the news. Why did it take him so long to run to the farm shop?"

"Did he do something else, maybe dispose of the gun?" Munro suggested. "If he stopped along the road and approached Brodie through the wood, he could have put the gun back in the car and got rid of it anywhere."

"Wipe the smile off your face, man," Ross said crossly. "That's a dismal prospect. We canna search the whole of Invernesshire."

"Aye. Except that, since Brodie was shot at such close quarters, some blood or tissue might have transferred itself to the barrel of the gun—"

"And from there to the car," agreed Ross. Trust Munro to see the bright side. "It's worth getting a warrant to have forensics go over Innes's Land Rover. But why would John Innes want to kill Donald Brodie?" Inspector James had said she thought the Inneses might have cultivated Brodie for his connections, which matched Ross's own impression. "Is there some way the Inneses could benefit from Brodie's leaving the distillery to Hazel Cavendish?"

"That I canna tell ye. But I thought yesterday that the man was nervous about more than the discomfort of his guests."

"Aye," Ross said, remembering John Innes's sweaty agitation, and his insistence on getting back into his kitchen. That, in turn, reminded Ross of his own empty stomach. It was getting on past teatime, and he had begun to think longingly of his dinner and a dram, not necessarily in that order, when another report caught his eye.

"Well, I'll be buggered," he said, skimming the page. "It seems John Innes's wee brother has a record. Why didna someone point this out to me yesterday?"

He had fixed a beady gaze on Munro when one of the female constables appeared at his elbow. Mackenzie, he thought her name was. She had been first on the scene.

"Sir."

"What is it, lass?" Ross prompted when she didn't continue. "I havena got all day."

"It's the gun, sir. They found a gun in the river, and it matches the description of Mr. Innes's Purdy."

15

❧

Hunger lives here, alone with larks and sheep.
Sweet spot, sweet spot.
                              —ROBERT LOUIS STEVENSON,
                                   letter to Sidney Colvin

JOHN INNES CAME out to greet them, and when he had been introduced to Kincaid, led them into the kitchen through the scullery. The police, he explained, had finished with their tests earlier that afternoon.

Gemma noticed Kincaid's interested glance at the gun cabinet as they passed through, but he made no comment. Turning back, she saw that the hook above the back door, where Louise had been in the habit of leaving her keys, was now empty. A bit late for instituting safety precautions, she thought, a classic case of locking the barn door after the horse had escaped.

"Come in," John urged them as they filed into the kitchen. "I'll put the kettle on." He bustled about, filling the kettle, pulling two stools out from a little nook under the work island. There were two chairs at the small table under the window where Gemma assumed John and Louise took their own meals.

"Nice kitchen," Kincaid said with a whistle. To Gemma's amusement, since he'd refinished the kitchen in his Hampstead flat, he had become a connoisseur of cabinets and cookers.

"Functional," John agreed. "Although I have to admit I miss the old oil-fired cooker. We lived with it for about a year while we were doing the refurbishing. Cozy, but not practical for the cookery class—besides the fact that cooking on the bloody thing is a challenge in itself."

Gemma was about to agree, for the much-prized Aga in their Notting Hill kitchen drove her to distraction, when she thought of all the help and encouragement Hazel had given her as she tried to master the cooker. Following her miscarriage, it had provided an excuse for the comforting time spent visiting in the kitchen with her friend. Swallowing, she searched for a change of subject. "Where's Louise?" she asked, looking round.

"Gone for a walk," John told her. "She should be back soon. What about Hazel and Heather? Will they be joining us?" His eyes flicked towards the barn, so Gemma guessed he'd been watching from the window.

"I don't know," she said honestly, and saw Kincaid and Pascal Benoit look at her sharply. "They've—they've some catching up to do." It wasn't her business to break the news to anyone about Hazel's inheritance; Hazel and Heather could share that information when they were ready.

Kincaid slid onto a stool with the graceful economy of movement Gemma always found surprising in a man his height. "Something smells wonderful," he said, sniffing, and Gemma focused on the cooking aromas that had been tickling the edge of her awareness . . . onions, floury potatoes, smoky fish.

"It's Cullen Skink." John chuckled at her startled expression. "That's not as bad as it sounds, believe me. It's a Scottish fish soup or stew, made with smoked haddock, potatoes, and milk. Martin and I drove to the east coast this morning to get a real Finnan haddock. There are several small smokehouses that still prepare the fish in the traditional way; that's a slow, cold smoking with no artificial colorings or flavorings added. We bought fresh mussels as well; they'll go into the pot at the last minute, along with butter, fresh parsley, and pepper." The electric kettle had come to a boil, and as he spoke, John spooned loose tea into a large crockery teapot.

"You've gone to a great deal of trouble for us," Kincaid said. "All this must be hard for you."

John had his back to them, reaching for the mugs hanging on a rack. He hesitated for a moment, hand in the air. Then he seemed to collect himself and, lifting down a mug, said without turning, "Yes. Donald was a good friend. I still can't believe he's gone." He busied himself with the tea things. "Have ye any idea when they'll release his . . . body . . . for the funeral? Christ—I never even thought—did Donald go to church?"

"Heather will know," said Pascal, lowering himself a little stiffly into the chair next to Gemma. "It is Heather who will have to make the arrangements for the funeral, yes?" He shook his head. "It is too much, I think, but there is no one else."

How terribly ironic, Gemma thought, that Donald had not seen fit to remember Heather in his will, when it was she who must act on his behalf. Why had Donald left her nothing? Was it mere carelessness on his part, as he had been careless of Alison Grant's feelings? Or had he felt betrayed by Heather's relationship with Pascal? Had Heather's pressuring him to sell the distillery to Pascal's company angered Donald?

Perhaps even more to the point, thought Gemma as she accepted a steaming mug from John, was not why Donald had left Heather out, but rather why he had chosen to make such a grand gesture towards Hazel. It was one thing to seduce a former lover—it was quite another to leave her the controlling interest in your family's business. And why had he done it so long ago? If he had meant to make up for his father's treatment of Hazel, he had gone a bit over the mark.

". . . soon, I should think," she realized Kincaid was saying, "if they've finished with the postmortem and the forensics testing."

Beside her, she heard the sharp intake of Pascal's breath as he shifted in his chair.

"Are you all right?" she asked softly, seeing him wince.

"Yes. It's just my back. It's playing up a bit." The Englishness of the last phrase sounded odd in Pascal's accent.

She was about to compliment him on his fluency when the back door banged open and Louise came in through the scullery, her arms filled with green boughs.

"Oh, I didn't realize . . ." Louise came to a halt, and Gemma had the impression she wasn't terribly pleased to find an unscheduled gathering in her kitchen.

"Let me get you a cup of tea, darling," John put in quickly. "This is Gemma's friend, Duncan, come up from London."

"Oh, of course," said Louise as Kincaid stood and gave her his friendliest grin. She glanced down at her burden as if wondering how to free a hand.

"Let me help you," offered Gemma, jumping up.

"We'll just dump these in the sink." Louise smiled her thanks as Gemma took some of the greenery.

"Mmmm . . . What are these?" asked Gemma as the scent reached her nose. "They smell lovely."

"Rowan, juniper, and elder." Louise dropped her portion into the deep farmhouse sink. "According to my gardening books, the ancient Celts brought these branches into the house in May, to celebrate Beltane, the Celtic rite of spring. They're considered protective trees."

"As in warding off evil spirits?"

"Well, yes." Louise blushed a little. "I know it sounds silly, but they do smell nice, and I thought I could arrange them in vases, instead of flowers."

"I think it's a brilliant idea." As Gemma watched her sort the boughs, she noticed that Louise's hands were dirty and bleeding from several small scratches, and she had broken a nail. As careful as Louise was in her appearance, it surprised Gemma that she would go out without gloves.

"Did you know that the hazel tree was special as well?" asked Louise. "It was the Druids' Golden Bough. They believed it was the root and symbol of wisdom."

"A hard name to live up to, then," suggested Gemma.

Louise glanced up at her in surprise. "Yes. I suppose so. But Hazel does have a way of making you think she's invincible, doesn't she? Where is she, by the way?" Louise added, glancing round the room.

"In the barn, talking to Heather."

Louise raised an eyebrow at this but merely said quietly, "Has she heard from her husband?"

Gemma was saved from answering by John Innes setting a cup of tea at his wife's elbow. As Louise turned to him, asking if he had made all the arrangements for dinner, Gemma heard the faint sound of a piano.

"Is that coming from the sitting room?" she asked John.

"Aye. That'll be Martin. He can bang out a tune or two."

This was more than a tune or two, Gemma thought, listening. The notes wandered up and down the scale, segueing into snatches of melody that teased her memory.

After giving Kincaid a quick glance, she asked John, "Is there enough tea for Martin?"

He nodded towards the pot. "I was just about to take him a cup."

"I'll do it for you."

Mug in hand, Gemma wandered into the sitting room. Martin sat at the old upright piano, his back to her, his hands moving across the keys as if of their own accord. Bars of late-afternoon sunlight fell across the carpet, illuminating the muted tartan.

"Martin," she said softly, "I've brought you a cuppa."

He jerked as if stung, twisting round to look at her. "Jesus. You gave me a fright." The color drained from his already sallow face, leaving the blemishes on his cheeks an angry red.

"Sorry." She held up the mug. "Didn't mean to startle you."

"No, I'm sorry," he apologized. "I'm just a bit jumpy these days, that's all." He started to get up, but she waved him back to his seat.

"Don't stop on my account, please. It was lovely. I didn't know you played." Crossing the room, Gemma set his mug next to the dog-eared sheet music on the upright's stand.

"Bloody thing needs a good tuning." Martin turned back to the keyboard. "My mum gave me lessons. All part of a proper middle-class upbringing," he added, with a note of derision. His fingers moved over the keys again, picking out a faintly Scottish air.

"But you play by ear, don't you?" asked Gemma, the

certainty forming as she listened. "That's not something you learn from lessons." She looked at him with sudden envy, forgetting his spottiness, his youth, his awkward behavior, seeing only a gift she would have made a pact with the devil to possess. Perching on the edge of the chair nearest him, she said, "Is this your job, back in Dundee?"

Martin snorted. "There's no money in this. Oh, I pick up a few bob, filling in on a gig, but it's not going to pay the rent."

Why was it, she wondered, that people never seemed to appreciate what they had? Martin had shrugged off his talent as if it were no more worthwhile than sweeping floors. Nor had he answered her question about his job, she realized, and that aroused her curiosity.

"Martin, I know it's none of my business, but I'm surprised you haven't gone home. I mean, it's not as if you knew Donald . . ."

"Nor did you, before this weekend, and you're still here." His glance was sharper than she'd expected. Shrugging, he added, "I thought I'd lend John a bit of support. It's not as though he'll get it from any other quarter."

"You mean Louise?" Gemma studied him. "Is there a particular reason you two don't get on?"

"Besides the fact that she's a bitch? She's always treated me as if I were a bug that needed squashing. What bloody right has she? He's *my* brother."

"Yes, but it is her house, too."

Martin flushed at the note of reproof in Gemma's voice. "You mean I should be grateful for her charity?"

"No, I mean you should have better manners. This is about more than a weekend cookery course, isn't it?"

Martin gazed down at the keyboard as the silence

stretched. "It's just that I've got no place else to go at the moment," he admitted at last. "And I don't like being made to feel a nuisance."

"No place to go? You mean—"

"I lost my bloody flat, okay? And my job. Actually," he amended, "it was the other way round."

"Oh, that's rotten luck," said Gemma. "It could happen to anyone." She thought back to their earlier conversations. "But you must have some other options. I thought you said your mum lived in Dundee. Couldn't you—"

"My mum's not speaking to me. I'm not exactly in her good books at the moment, but at least she doesn't seem to have shared her feelings with Louise. There's no way Louise would have passed up ammunition she could have used against me."

Gemma frowned. "Wait a minute. What ammunition?"

Martin gave her a sideways glance. "Why should I tell you?"

Gemma considered for a moment, tilting her head, then said, "Because it sounds to me as though you could use a friend, and I don't think you're as tough as you make out. And because"—she reached out with her right hand and played a bar of the first thing that came into her head, which happened to be *Jesu, Joy of Man's Desiring,* the piece she had been working on at her last piano lesson—"we have something in common."

"Ouch," Martin said, falling in with the next measure. "That was a low blow. I think it's been scientifically proven that one can't behave badly while listening to Bach."

Gemma grinned. "Then stop it and tell me what happened."

He looked up at her, his hands still. "I worked in a music shop, in Dundee. It was all right, but then I got busted for selling X-tabs to some of the customers. It was stupid, I know," he added, as if to forestall her. "My boss fired me. When I couldn't pay my rent, I lost my flat. And I've got no way to pay for legal counsel when my trial comes up."

Refraining from agreeing with his own assessment, Gemma asked, "Does John know?"

"Yeah. He's been really good about it."

"You never were interested in cooking, then, were you?"

"No, that's not true," Martin said, sounding hurt. "There's this bloke I know that might take me on at his restaurant. I thought if I could learn something from John, I'd have a better chance at it."

"And what about Louise? Does she know?"

"What do you think? You don't imagine she'd let someone less than perfect take up space in her precious house? What surprises me," Martin added thoughtfully, "is that she ever condescended to take on John."

"John? Why wouldn't—" Gemma stopped, listening as the low murmur of voices coming from the kitchen suddenly rose in volume. She recognized Heather's clear alto. Hazel and Heather must have come in from the barn.

Then, the sound of car tires on gravel snapped her attention back to the front of the house. Looking out the window, she recognized the car, an unmarked Rover. Bloody hell. It was Ross, and she didn't want to talk to him about Tim Cavendish in front of Hazel.

"Martin, sorry," she said, giving him a fleeting pat on the shoulder. "I've got to have a word with the chief inspector," she added, already half out the door.

"You won't tell him about me?" Martin called after her.

"I'll wager he already knows. You should have told him yourself."

She ran out into the drive as Ross and Sergeant Munro were getting out of the car. "Chief Inspector. I left you a message," she said a bit breathlessly. Skidding to a halt on the gravel, she lowered her voice and added, "It's about Tim Cavendish, Hazel's husband. Have you requested that the Met interview him?"

Ross looked at her with disfavor. "Inspector James, I'm perfectly capable of—"

"Have you?" she repeated, past caring if she was rude. "Because he wasn't in London over the weekend, and he doesn't seem able to verify his movements." She saw Ross's hesitation as he took this in, and pressed her point. "And he knew Hazel was planning to see Donald Brodie over the weekend."

"Och, all right," Ross said with obvious reluctance. "Munro, call in and have them ask London to run a check on the man. Now, Inspector, if you don't mind—"

"There's more. Tim's not answering the phone or the door, even to his family."

"I can't say I blame the man for not wanting to talk to his wife." There was a note of bitterness in Ross's voice.

"It's not just that. He won't talk to his parents, and they're keeping Holly, Tim and Hazel's little girl. I haven't said anything to Hazel; I didn't want to worry her unnecessarily."

"You just wanted to worry me," Ross said, sounding aggrieved.

Gemma stared at him. Had she actually seen the corners of his mouth turn up? He looked tired, she realized as she studied him. Even his graying hair seemed to have lost some of its bristle.

"I'll request a welfare check," he told her. "And now, if you don't mind, lassie, I'd like to see John and Martin Innes."

Carnmore, August 1899

LIVVY HAD JUST *rolled out a fresh batch of oatcakes for the girdle when the knock came at the kitchen door. As in most country houses, the front door at Carnmore was seldom used. Wiping her hands, still slightly greasy from the bacon fat she'd kneaded into the oatmeal, she called out, "Come in!" Will had gone down to the burn with his fishing rod, taking a well-deserved hour off from the distillery, and Livvy assumed it was one of the hands with a question.*

"Livvy?"

For a moment, she saw only a shape in the doorway, framed by the bright light of the August afternoon, but she would have recognized the voice anywhere. "Rab! What on earth are you doing here?"

"Have I caught you at a bad time?" He stepped forward, his features gaining definition, and she saw that he was dressed for riding. She hadn't seen him since the night of the Grantown dance, and since then she had pictured him in evening clothes.

"Oh, no, come in, please. Forgive my manners. It's just that I was surprised to see you." She was suddenly aware of her disheveled hair and her workaday shirtwaist. Her hands were red and raw from scrubbing preserve jars, and she suspected she had smudges of flour on her nose.

"I had business in Tomintoul," Rab said, taking off his hat. "It seemed a shame not to pay a call when I was so near."

"So near! Rab Brodie, it must be all of ten miles from Tomintoul to the Braes," she protested, warm with pleasure.

"And a very pleasant day for a ride." He smiled at her, his eyes sparkling above the flush of sunburn on his

cheeks. His boots and trousers, she saw, were dusty from the road, and he had loosened his collar.

"You must be thirsty. Sit down and I'll make some tea. You've caught me in the middle of baking—I hope you don't mind yesterday's oatcakes."

"How are you keeping, Livvy?" he asked as he sat at the scrubbed oak table. "You look well."

"I've been berry picking this week with some of the women from the village," she said, laughing. "I'm as sunburned as a fishwife, but, oh, it was lovely, and I've berries to spare. I've made a blaeberry preserve, and we've fresh cream. We can have a bit with our tea, if you like . . ." She realized she was babbling and concentrated on setting out the best rose-patterned teapot, with the matching cups and saucers. The china had been her wedding gift from her father.

"That's a bit grand for the kitchen, isn't it?" asked Rab, nodding at the cup she'd set before him.

Livvy felt a rush of mortification. "Oh, how stupid of me. Of course we'll go into the sitting room. We have visitors so seldom—"

"Nonsense." Rab settled back in his chair. "I won't have you stand on ceremony for me, Livvy. This is a comfort I don't often enjoy at home, and I'd much rather be treated as a friend than as a guest."

Livvy doubted he ever set foot in the kitchen at Benvulin—nor did his wife, except to give instructions to the cook—but she acquiesced. She spooned still-warm fruit preserve into a dish and topped it with a ladle of cream from the jug. When she had set the dish before Rab, she sank into the chair opposite and watched him with anticipation.

"Don't tell me you're not joining me?"

"I've been tasting all day," she told him, although the

truth was, she didn't want to waste a moment of this visit in eating when she could be listening, and talking, and storing up the conversation to remember later. "I'm afraid I'll turn blue if I have one more berry." *Realizing she'd forgotten the oatcakes, she jumped up again and fetched a plate of the crispy, triangular cakes, then poured the tea.*

"Livvy, sit," *he commanded her, laughing.* "You remind me of a whirling dervish."

She complied, folding her hands primly in her lap. "All right, then, I'll be a proper hostess. How are things at Benvulin, Mr. Brodie? And Margaret, is she well?"

"Margaret's taken the children to London for a month. Her uncle has a house there, and she thought the children needed civilizing."

"And your sister?"

"Helen's managing admirably, as usual. She keeps me in line." *He spooned berries and cream into his mouth, closing his eyes for a moment as he savored the combination.* "Nectar of the gods," *he pronounced, with a grin.*

"Och, get away with ye, Rab Brodie," *said Livvy, more flattered than she would admit.*

Sobering, he said, "Seriously, Livvy, how are you getting on? Are you and Will managing on your own?"

"Will's been remarkable. Charles would have been so proud. But . . ." *For the first time since Charles's death, she gave in to the temptation to speak freely.* "But I know this isn't what Will wanted. It's a good life, but Will's had his choice made for him, and so early . . . We could hire a manager for the distillery, so that he could go to school in Edinburgh, but he won't hear of it."

"He could do worse. There are not many men who have everything they want, Livvy." *Rab gazed at her directly until she looked away, uncomfortable.*

"If Charles hadn't had the foresight to steer clear of Pattison's," Rab continued, making blue-purple swirls in the cream with his spoon, *"you might have lost everything."*

Livvy saw lines of strain in his face that she hadn't noticed before. Leaning forward, she touched his hand. *"I've heard rumors . . . about Benvulin . . . Is it really that bad?"*

He shrugged, his expression suddenly bleak. *"We'll manage, somehow. Margaret's trying to raise some money from her uncle—not that she cares about the distillery, but she'll not let her social status go so easily. At least it's been a good summer; we'll have barley to spare if we can stay in production."*

Livvy took a breath. *"Rab, if there's anything we can do . . ."*

"Duncan!" Hazel came straight to him and he enfolded her in a hug. She clung to him, burying her face against his chest. Her dark curls just brushed his chin, and compared with Gemma's, her frame felt delicate under his hands. He had never before thought of her as fragile.

"Have you spoken to Tim?" Hazel asked as she let him go. "Gemma said you saw Holly— How is she?"

"What shall I answer first?" he said with a smile, wanting to reassure her. "No, I haven't talked to Tim today, and yes, I saw Holly, and she was full of mischief as usual." Beyond Hazel, he saw Pascal glance at Heather in silent question, and Heather shrug in reply. Just how much did they have riding on Hazel's response to Donald's bequest? he wondered.

Before he could speculate further, the door to the hall swung open and a gangly young man came hurriedly into the kitchen. Kincaid surmised that he must be John Innes's younger brother, Martin, although he could see no resemblance.

"It's that policeman," the young man said. "He's here again."

There was an instant's pause in the room, as if a film had frozen at a single frame. Then John turned back to the cooker, saying, a bit too loudly, "I suppose I'd better put the kettle on again." Louise dropped the bough she'd been trimming into the sink and reached for a towel. Heather moved a little closer to Pascal's chair.

Only Hazel still stood without moving. "He won't— He can't take me in again, can he?" she whispered, her face pale.

"I shouldn't think so." Kincaid gave her shoulder a squeeze and urged her towards the stool he had vacated. "Gemma must be talking to him now."

Then he heard voices from the hall, and Gemma came into the kitchen, followed by a solid, graying man in a rumpled suit, and a tall, thin man with a cadaverous face. The shorter man had an unmistakable air of authority.

If he was going to pull rank, Kincaid thought, he had better do it now. He stepped forward, hand extended. "Chief Inspector Ross? My name's Kincaid. Superintendent, Scotland Yard." Someone in the room inhaled sharply, as if surprised at this news, but he couldn't be sure of the source.

As Ross gave him an assessing glance and a perfunctory handshake, Kincaid felt his usefulness being weighed, an unusual sensation. "If I can be of any help . . . ," he offered, and Ross made an indecipherable grumbling noise in his throat.

"And why exactly are you here, Superintendent?" Ross asked, casting a look in Gemma's direction.

"Gemma—Inspector James—and I are personal friends of Mrs. Cavendish."

"So you came to lend your support? Verra thoughtful of you," Ross said with only a slight grimace. It seemed he had decided to err on the side of caution. "But it's actually not Mrs. Cavendish I've come to see," he continued. "I've a wee matter to discuss with Mr. Innes. Sergeant"—he nodded at the tall man—"if ye'd be so good."

The other detective stepped forward, and Kincaid saw that he carried a folder. Ross took it from him and, clearing a space on the work island, laid the contents out before John Innes, large, glossy, color photos of a shotgun. "Is this your gun, Mr. Innes?"

"Oh, Christ." John Innes touched an unsteady finger to the top photograph. "I— It looks like it, yes. The scrollwork is fairly distinctive. But how— Where—"

"We found it in the river, fifty yards or so downstream from the body. It's possible the current dragged it along the bottom."

"No fingerprints, I suppose?" Kincaid asked, forgetting his role as observer in his interest.

"No, just a few wee smudges."

"Had the gun been wiped before being submerged?"

"It's difficult to say, Mr. Kincaid." Ross gave him a quelling glance. "But we can be sure that the gun used to kill Donald Brodie came from this house—"

"You can't be certain," interrupted Gemma. "There's no way to get an absolute ballistics match on a shotgun—"

"Inspector James." Ross scowled at her. "I find it verra unlikely that this gun just happened to end up in the river at the same time Donald Brodie was shot with a *different* small-bore gun." He turned back to John. "Mr. Innes, you'll need to come into the station to make a formal identification. You'll also need to do a much better job of accounting for your time on Sunday morning."

John stared at him blankly. "But I've told you. I went to buy eggs—"

"You didn't arrive at the farm shop until seven o'clock, after the police had been called to the scene, and yet, according to your wife, you left home some time before Inspector James discovered the body."

"No!" Louise took a step towards John. "I said I wasn't sure of the time. I didn't look at the clock—"

"How could ye not see the clock, Mrs. Innes?" Ross looked pointedly at the large-faced kitchen clock mounted on the wall above the table. "Especially when your business depends on keeping a schedule in the mornings?"

"Don't ye badger her," said John, his fists clenching. "It's nothing to do with Louise. I took a wee walk along Loch an Eilean, if ye must know. There's no crime in that."

"Then why didn't ye see fit to mention it?" Ross asked.

"I didna think anything of it." John appeared to be struggling for nonchalance. Louise was staring at him, her delicate brows lifted in surprise. "I often go there when I've an errand at the estate shop," John added.

"Did anyone see you?"

"I didna notice. Wait— There was a couple walking their dog, an Alsatian."

"That's very helpful of you, Mr. Innes," said Ross, with scathing sarcasm. "I'm sure we'll have no trouble verifying that. In the meantime, we've requested a warrant to have our forensics team go over your car—a Land Rover, isn't it? But if you were to demonstrate your cooperation by turning it over voluntarily, it would make things easier for everyone concerned."

As John glanced at him in mute appeal, Kincaid began to realize just how awkward a position he and Gemma had got themselves into. After a moment's hesitation, he nodded at John. Ross would have the car searched regardless, and John would do himself no good by trying to obstruct it.

"All right," said John, with a show of bravado. "Go ahead. I've nothing to hide."

"Good. That's verra sensible of you." Ross looked more weary than pleased. "Now, why don't ye come with us to the station, and we'll send a constable along to take charge of the car."

"Wait." Louise stepped forward. "I want a word with my husband, Chief Inspector."

"With all due respect, Mrs. Innes, I'd rather you didna do that until he's amended his statement. If you have something different to tell us, I'd suggest you do it now."

Louise hesitated, glancing at John, then back at Ross. "No. I— It was nothing."

Sergeant Munro gathered the photos together, then stepped back, gesturing at John to precede him.

As John reached the door, he called back, "The soup— Louise, you'll see to the soup?"

"Soup?" Louise wailed as the door swung shut. "How can he think of soup when—"

A babble of voices broke out as everyone began to comment, drowning her words. Kincaid put a hand on her arm and guided her into a quieter corner of the room. "Louise," he said softly, "do you know what John was doing yesterday morning—other than *not* walking around Loch an Eilean, whatever that is."

"It's a local scenic spot, near the farm shop. John's never mentioned walking there." She looked baffled. "I've no idea where he could have been—I didn't realize, until the chief inspector said, that he was away for so long." Frowning, she added hesitantly, "But there have been other times lately when he's disappeared without telling me, or been gone a good bit longer than an errand required." She looked up at Kincaid, color suffusing her fair skin. "And once or twice, I've awakened in the night and found him gone. I thought— But it can't have anything to do with Donald."

Kincaid was trying to think of some way to reassure her, a difficult proposition, as he had no idea what John Innes had been getting up to, when he realized Gemma had followed the detectives and John Innes from the room.

"Louise, I'm sorry, but I've got to catch Gemma up. We'll talk later, I promise."

He dashed through the house, and as he burst out the front door, he found his suspicions confirmed. John was safely tucked into the unmarked car with Sergeant Munro, and Gemma was standing in the drive, arguing with the chief inspector.

As Kincaid came up to them, he heard her say, "You can't rule out the possibility that someone outside the house had access to the gun—or that the gun was taken for another reason."

Ross seemed to be making a monumental effort to keep his temper in check. "And what reason would that be?"

"What if someone wanted to cast suspicion on John, or on the household in general?"

"Who?" Ross barked.

"I don't know," countered Gemma, without the least sign of being intimidated. "But you can't ignore Alison Grant and Callum MacGillivray. They both had motive, and neither had an alibi. And what about Tim Cavendish?"

Ross shook his head in disbelief. "Do ye *want* your friend's husband to be guilty of murder, lassie?"

"No, of course not!" said Gemma, sounding less sure of herself. She turned to Kincaid, as if for confirmation. "I just want—"

"Ye canna protect them all, lass. You must see that. Someone fired that shotgun into Donald Brodie's chest, and the odds are that it was someone in this house. Ye canna hide from the fact. Why don't ye take Mrs. Cavendish and go back to London? Ye'll be weel out of it."

"I—"

Whatever Gemma had meant to say was cut off by the ringing of Kincaid's phone. "Sorry," he said, turning away as he slipped the phone from his belt. It was about time Doug Cullen rang him back.

But it was not Cullen, and as Kincaid listened, his surroundings faded until he was aware of nothing but the cold dread squeezing his chest.

"No," he said at last. "No. Don't do anything yet. Let me make a few calls. I'll ring you back."

As he hung up, he felt the feather brush of Gemma's fingers against his arm. "Is it Tim?" she asked, clearly alarmed by his tone. "What's happened? Has he—"

"No." Kincaid forced himself to breathe, to meet her eyes. "That was Wesley. It's Kit. He's disappeared."

16

And I remember home and the old time,
The winding river, the white morning rime,
The autumn robin by the riverside,
That pipes in the grey eve.
    —ROBERT LOUIS STEVENSON, "The Family"

KIT WALKED AIMLESSLY for hours, only vaguely aware of his surroundings, his mind playing and replaying the events of the morning. He had been finishing a last-minute piece of toast before school when the phone rang. Wesley had already left with Toby, and he'd assumed it was Wes calling from his mobile phone with a last-minute instruction.

When he'd heard Ian's voice on the other end of the line he'd whooped with surprise.

"Dad! What are you doing ringing this time of morning? It must be the middle of the night in Canada." He felt awkward now saying *Dad*, but what else could he call the man he'd thought of as his father for almost twelve years? Absently, he tossed the dogs their ball and watched them scramble after it.

"It's almost two," said Ian, "a bit late for an old man

like me, I'll admit." Kit thought he sounded slightly tipsy. "But I wanted to catch you before you left for school."

Kit felt a little clutch of fear, and the last bit of his toast seemed to stick on the way down. "Why? Is something wrong? You know about the letter?"

"Yes, but that's not why I called, Kit. And nothing's wrong. In fact, I've got some rather good news to share with you. I wanted you to be the first to know."

Kit's heart leaped. "You're coming home? Back to Cambridge?"

"Um, no." Ian sounded suddenly hesitant. "It looks like I'll be staying in Toronto permanently. There are two things I had to tell you, actually, Kit. The house in Grantchester finally sold."

Kit's throat tightened. It was all he could do to speak. "That's . . . good. That's . . . that's what you wanted."

"I know the idea's going to be a little bit of an adjustment for you, but it had to be done. You do understand that, don't you, Kit?"

"Yeah, of course I do," Kit said, trying very hard to sound as if he did. The dogs had come back to him, panting, Tess the proud possessor of the ball, but he ignored them.

"I've got to make a new life. We both do." Ian paused again, clearing his throat. "That's the other thing I was going to tell you. That's why I was up so late. I've been at a party, celebrating my engagement."

"Engagement?" Kit said blankly. In the moment's silence, he heard the tick of the kitchen clock, and as he gazed at Gemma's black and red teapot, the colors swam before his eyes.

"She's a wonderful girl, Kit. I know you'll like her. Melinda—her name's Melinda—is really looking forward to meeting you. Of course, she is a bit young for me." Ian gave a chuckle. "But who am I to complain?"

"You're getting *married*?"

"That's what I've been telling you." Ian's patience sounded forced. "The first of July. Just a small ceremony—"

"How can you be getting *married*?" Kit shouted, taking it in at last. "Mum's only been dead a year—"

"Kit! That's enough," snapped Ian. "Look," he went on more gently, "I understand this is a shock, but you know your mother and I hadn't been on good terms for a while before she . . . died. It's time for me to move on, concentrate on the living. And this means you'll have a new home, in Canada, when you come to visit."

"I don't want—"

"That's the other thing, Kit. I know we'd talked about your coming at the end of June, when your term finishes, but Melinda and I will be on our honeymoon. I'm sure we can work something out later in the sum—"

Kit didn't hear the rest of Ian's plan because he had, for the first time in his life, hung up on an adult in the middle of a conversation. When the phone rang again, he was walking out the door. It was only after he turned the corner that the insistent burring faded away.

His feet had carried him along the familiar route to school of their own accord, but when he reached the gate he saw that the schoolyard was empty. The bell had rung, and it suddenly seemed to Kit as if walking into an already seated class and explaining his tardiness was a feat as far beyond him as walking on the moon.

He had turned round and gone the other way, back through the quiet streets until he'd reached Notting Hill Gate, and then into Bayswater Road. At some point, he'd taken off his school blazer and stuffed it into his backpack, for it was warm, and he was aware of the stare of the occasional passerby wondering what a boy his age was doing out of school on a Monday morning.

He kept thinking of some other family living in the cottage in Grantchester, but even though he'd stayed there again with Ian for a few months before moving to London, he couldn't get a picture in his head that didn't include his mother.

For an instant, when he'd thought Ian might be coming back, he'd imagined living there again. Not that he wanted to leave Duncan and Gemma and Toby—not at all—but he missed his old school and his friends, especially Colin. He had belonged, and that belonging had been part of him, as were his memories of his life before his mum had died.

Now it seemed Ian meant to take even that away from him. Kit didn't *want* another family; he couldn't bear to see Ian with another woman, a replacement for his mother. Was that why Ian had suggested the paternity test? Did he intend to put the past behind him, so that he could start his new life—his new family—unencumbered by the child he had never thought of as his own?

Kit went on, putting one foot in front of the other automatically, and it was only when he looked up and saw Marble Arch that he realized he'd walked the whole length of Hyde Park. Turning, he looked back at the park, and the sight of the people walking their dogs made him think of Tess with a pang.

But Tess would be all right, he assured himself. Wes would take care of her. He missed her, and Geordie, Gemma's cocker spaniel, but he could not face going back to the Notting Hill house. He couldn't sit calmly at the kitchen table and tell Wesley that his dad was getting married again. And what would he say when Duncan called, or Gemma? Even if he didn't tell them about Ian, he would have to explain why he had missed school, and what sort of excuse could he possibly invent?

A number seventy-three bus barreled by, turning the corner into Oxford Street, on its way to Euston and King's Cross Station.

King's Cross. Fumbling in his pocket, Kit pulled out the spending money Duncan had given him for the week and counted it. There was enough—at least for a single ticket, and just now he didn't care about the return. He wanted only to be someplace familiar, someplace that felt right, someplace where he could think things through.

He set off after the bus at a run.

"It's our son," Kincaid explained to Ross. "He seems to have taken advantage of our absence to play truant from school," he added, trying to make light of it.

"How old is the lad?" Ross asked.

"Twelve."

"Och, I don't envy ye, then," Ross said sympathetically. "It's a difficult age. Weel, I'll leave ye to get on with it. I'm sure you'll turn him up—or he'll come home of his own accord when he gets hungry." He got into the car, but as his sergeant began to reverse, he called out to them. "I didna realize the two of you were married. It's verra confusing these days, what with the women having different names."

"Of all the—" began Gemma as Ross drove off, then she shook her head. "Never mind. Tell me exactly what Wesley said."

"He started to get worried when Kit didn't come home at the usual time. After an hour, he rang one of Kit's mates at school, the boy he'd been partnering on his science project—his name's Sean, I think." He should know this, Kincaid told himself furiously. It was his business to know these things. He forced himself to go on. "Sean told Wes that Kit wasn't in school today at all."

"Did he leave a note?"

"Not that Wes could find."

"What about Tess?" asked Gemma. "Did he take Tess?" Kit seldom went anywhere without the little terrier he had befriended in the days following his mother's death.

"No. But his school bag is gone, so he must have started out—"

"Oh, God." Gemma had gone dead white. "You don't think—someone—"

"No." Kincaid pulled her to him in a fierce hug. "No, I don't think anything's happened to him. I think he was angry with me, and decided at the last minute to do a runner. I'm going to call Laura Miller."

Laura Miller had worked with Vic in the university's English faculty, and Laura's son, Colin, had been Kit's best friend at school. Kit had stayed with the Millers for several months after Vic's death and still visited Colin every few weekends.

"Right." Gemma gave him a shaky smile. "That's where he will have gone."

But when Kincaid got Laura on the phone, she said she hadn't seen Kit since the last time he'd come to visit. She promised to quiz Colin and to ring back if she learned anything.

When he related this news to Gemma he saw the flare of panic in her eyes. "We'll have to put out a bulletin," she said. "If he's been gone since first thing this morning, he could be anywhere—"

"No, wait." Kincaid held up a hand as a thought occurred to him. "Let me try one more thing." This time he rang a Grantchester number. Nathan Winter had been Vic's next-door neighbor and, briefly, her lover. A Cambridge biology professor, he had encouraged Kit in his love of science, and the two had become friends.

"Hullo, Nathan? It's Duncan—"

"It's all right, Duncan," came Nathan's familiar deep rumble. "He's here. I found him down by the river a half hour ago. I'm just taking some tea and sandwiches out to the garden for him—he was ravenous, poor lad."

Relief left Kincaid's muscles weak, but the emotion was quickly replaced by a rush of anger. What the hell had prompted Kit to go to Grantchester without telling them? And how was he going to get the boy home, if he couldn't trust him? Even if he had Nathan put him on the train, he'd no guarantee that Kit would do as he was told. "Put him on the phone, Nathan. I want to speak to him."

"Duncan, wait. Let him stay with me for a bit, let me talk to him. He wouldn't have come just on a whim. He muttered something about Ian having rung him this morning—"

"Ian?"

"That's all I've got out of him, so far. But perhaps I can help him sort it out, whatever's happened. I've a light day for tutorials tomorrow, and he can come with me."

Kincaid thought of the circumstances that had sent Kit running to Grantchester once before. Then, he'd been escaping from his grandmother's abuse. What could Ian have said to the boy to induce such a response? And if he had been home, would Kit have confided in him, instead of running away?

"All right," he said to Nathan at last, feeling as if he'd set the seal on his failure. "Perhaps for a day or two, until I can get back. But you should know what's been going on." He told Nathan about Eugenia's latest maneuver. "I've asked Kit to have DNA testing, to put paid to her once and for all, and Ian's agreed, but Kit won't consider it. Maybe you can talk some sense into him."

"I'll do my best. Look, I'd better go. He's coming in from the garden."

"Okay. Tell him he can stay tomorrow, at the least, and ring me when you've had a chance to speak to him. And, Nathan," Kincaid added, "don't let him out of your sight."

Dinner that night was a strained affair. Louise served Gemma, Kincaid, Martin, and Hazel in the dining room, Heather and Pascal having gone to Benvulin for the night.

Everyone seemed preoccupied with his or her own worries. Hazel had at last reached her mother-in-law, Carolyn Cavendish, who had told her that Tim was being questioned by the London police. Louise had not heard anything from John since Chief Inspector Ross had taken him to Aviemore, and both Gemma and Kincaid were concerned about Kit. Since his discussion with Nathan, Kincaid had been trying to ring Ian in Toronto, with no success.

Martin, to his credit, had offered to help Louise in the kitchen, but she'd refused him with a marked lack of graciousness, and he had been glowering at her ever since.

When Louise had set the last bowl of steaming fish stew before them, Hazel said, "Louise, come sit down and join us, please."

Louise stopped in the doorway, twisting the skirt of her apron in her hands. "Oh, no, thanks. I don't think I can bear to sit, to tell the truth, not until John's . . . I'll just get some more hot bread." She vanished back into the kitchen.

Gemma felt as if the painted fish swimming round the walls were staring down at her accusingly. With an apologetic nod at the largest trout, she took a bite of her stew and found it much better than she'd anticipated.

"How long can they keep him?" asked Martin, frowning at his soup bowl. "It's not like they can charge him with anything—can they?" The sudden appeal in his voice made him sound very young.

"I shouldn't think so," answered Gemma, "based on what Chief Inspector Ross said." She leaned forward, catching the fresh green scent of the boughs Louise had placed on the sideboard. "But, Martin, you have to understand that we're not privy to all the chief inspector's information."

"What sort of information?"

"Forensics results, witness reports—"

"You're saying he may have more evidence against John than he told us? But John can't have—John wouldn't—"

"Martin." Louise had slipped back into the room, unnoticed, a basket of sliced bread in her hand. "Just shut up. You don't know anything, and you'll only make things worse by going on about it."

"Worse?" Martin's voice rose to a squeak. "How could asking questions possibly make anything worse? Good God, Louise, anyone would think you believed John had done—" He stared at her, his eyes widening. "That *is* what you think, isn't it? You actually believe your own husband shot Donald!"

"You've no idea what I think." Louise bit the words off furiously. "And I'm bloody sick and tired of you swanning round my house as if you owned it, spouting your opinions, as if anyone actually cared what you thought. When John gets back—"

"Louise—" began Hazel, but Martin stood, rocking the table and sloshing soup on the tablecloth.

"Right. That's it. I'm going, and when John gets back, *you* can explain to him why I left." Martin brushed by

Louise and stalked out of the room. A moment later they heard his footsteps clattering up the stairs.

"Louise," said Hazel again, but Louise turned and bolted back into the kitchen.

The other three sat looking at one another for a moment, then Gemma said quietly, "He's got no place to go."

"Maybe I should have a friendly word with him." Kincaid's offer was given so swiftly that Gemma suspected he'd been looking for an excuse to leave the room and ring Ian again.

When he'd gone out, Hazel dropped her face into her hands. "And I should go talk to Louise," she said, her voice muffled.

"You've enough on your plate just now," Gemma told her gently. "Give her a minute to cool down and I'll go in. But in the meantime, I want a word with you." They hadn't had a moment alone since Hazel had spoken with Heather in the barn. "Hazel, Heather did tell you—"

"Yes." Dropping her hands, Hazel looked up at her with red-rimmed eyes. "I still can't believe it."

"Have you any idea why Donald left you his shares?" asked Gemma.

"No." Hazel shook her head in bewilderment. "Especially considering the way his father felt about me. I'm the last person Bruce Brodie would have wanted in control of his business."

"Could that have been *why* Donald chose you?"

"To show his father up? But Bruce has been dead for years."

"What if he felt his father had ruined his life by driving you away . . . a bit far-fetched, I'll admit," Gemma added with a sigh. She thought for a moment. "But what if Donald meant it as a gesture to prove his commitment to your future together? In which case, he must have intended to tell you what he'd done." Gemma's heart gave a lurch as she realized where her supposition led. "Hazel, Donald didn't tell you, did he?"

Hazel looked appalled. "Of course not! You can't think I knew—"

"No, no. I'm sorry." Gemma reached across the table and touched Hazel's hand. "That was stupid of me. But what if Donald told someone else?"

"You think someone murdered him because of it? But why would someone kill Donald because he'd left his shares to me?"

"Is there any way someone could profit from your ownership?" asked Gemma. "What about Heather?"

"No. Heather's the one who's lost most over this, after everything she did for him. Only if I—" Hazel looked down at her stew and seemed to focus great concentration on taking a bite.

"What? Tell me what you were going to say," demanded Gemma.

"Nothing. It was nothing. We should eat," Hazel added brightly. "The stew's getting cold."

"That's bollocks." Gemma caught Hazel's gaze, held it. "If you keep things from me, I can't help. You do want to find out who killed Donald, don't you?"

"You know I do." Hazel shut her eyes, and Gemma saw her shudder, as if she were recalling the sight of Donald's body. "All right," she said at last. "It's just that Heather made me an offer today. She said Pascal's firm would buy my shares outright, immediately. She said I could just walk away from the whole thing, easy as pie."

"That's what she wanted from Donald," mused Gemma. "But he wouldn't give it to her. Maybe she thought you'd be an easier mark."

"I don't believe that. She's my cousin, for God's sake. I've known her since she was a child."

"You don't know her now," Gemma argued. "You haven't seen her in ten years."

"That doesn't matter. I know she couldn't have shot Donald. She loved him— I don't mean they were lovers, but they were friends. She was like family to him."

Too often, Gemma had seen love mutate into violence, but she didn't have the heart to share that with Hazel. Instead she asked, "What are you going to do? Will you sell Pascal the shares?"

"How could I? That would mean betraying Donald— and how could I agree to profit from Donald's death? That's—that's obscene." Hazel pushed her bowl away abruptly, as if the smell made her ill. Her eyes filled with the tears she'd managed to hold in check for two days. "This is too much. And then, when I talked to Carolyn tonight . . ."

"Tim's mum?"

Hazel nodded. "We were friends, Carolyn and I, and now I've betrayed her, too. She kept trying to comfort me, telling me it was all some dreadful mistake and that things would be all right. But it's not going to be all right. If I'd had the slightest hope that Tim and I could patch things up, Donald giving me those shares put an end to it. How can I possibly explain this to Tim?"

"Right now it's more a question of Tim explaining where he was over the weekend," said Gemma practically. She couldn't shake the feeling that Tim had been there, perhaps close enough to touch, and yet she knew that was the last thing Hazel would accept.

"I'm sure he just wanted some time on his own. Why are the police talking to him, anyway, if they think Donald was shot with John's gun?"

"They have to be thorough," Gemma told her, feeling a twinge of guilt for having insisted that Ross have Tim interviewed.

"Not that I believe for a minute that John would do something like that," continued Hazel. "I mean, why would he have wanted to hurt Donald?"

Gemma thought of the usual motives for murder. There was jealousy, but John had never met Hazel until that weekend. There was greed, but she couldn't see how John had benefited from Donald's death. There was revenge, but as far as she knew, Donald had been a good friend to John. And then there was the desire to protect a secret.

"Hazel, what do you really know about John?" she asked. "You and Louise hadn't seen each other for years."

Hazel considered for a moment. "Louise met John after Donald and I split up—after I'd gone back to England—so I never knew him when Louise and I were living in Grantown. I don't think she ever really dated anyone seriously until she met John, come to think of it. Um, let's see." She chewed her thumbnail. "I know he sold commercial real estate in Edinburgh before they came here, and that he and Louise had a flat in the New Town. I know he always wanted to cook. And then there are the obvious things, of course—he's married to Louise; he has a much younger brother, Martin, from his mother's second marriage."

John did have another connection with Donald, Gemma realized, one she had forgotten. They had both been friends with Callum MacGillivray.

"This is dreadful," Hazel said suddenly. "These are my friends. How can I be sitting here, speculating about them?" She pushed her bowl aside.

"I'm sorry." Gemma could have kicked herself for being so insensitive. "You're right. I shouldn't have asked you. This is hard enough for me, and I've only known them a few days."

"No, I'm sorry." Hazel gave her a tremulous smile. "You're trying to help, and I snapped at you. And here you must be worried sick about Kit, and I've been no use to you at all."

"I'm certain he's all right with Nathan," said Gemma, reassuring herself as much as Hazel. She wondered what had happened to Duncan, and if he had succeeded in reaching Ian. "Why don't you go on to bed," she told Hazel, "and I'll give Louise a hand in the kitchen."

Hazel had protested, but without much force, and Gemma soon convinced her to go back to her room for a bath.

"You're not staying with me, are you?" asked Hazel. "I think Louise meant to put you and Duncan in Pascal's room."

"You're certain you don't mind?" Gemma still didn't feel entirely comfortable leaving Hazel alone, but she didn't want to worry her by saying so.

"Positive."

"Okay. I'll just pop in and get my things later on."

When she had seen Hazel out the front door, she stood in the hall for a moment, listening. There was a low murmur of male voices from upstairs. Duncan and Martin had obviously found something to talk about.

Collecting a stack of dirty dishes from the dining room, she carried them into the kitchen and looked around. There were cooking pots piled in the sink and an unfinished bowl of Cullen Skink on the small table, but there was no sign of Louise. Gemma thought she would have heard if Louise had gone up the stairs, so she stepped out through the scullery to have a look outside.

The garden was quiet, deep in the shadows of the late dusk. From somewhere nearby she caught the faint, pungent scent of tobacco smoke. As her eyes adjusted to the dimness, she noticed a flickering glow of light coming from the garden shed. "Louise?" she called out, crossing the lawn.

When she looked inside the shed's open door, she saw Louise sitting on a campstool, smoking a cigarette. On the potting bench burned a small spirit lamp. "Do you mind if I come in?" Gemma asked.

"Suit yourself. I had to get out for a bit." Louise had thrown a cardigan on over her kitchen apron but still hugged herself as if she were cold.

"I didn't know you smoked," Gemma said as she took the other stool.

"I don't, usually. These are John's. It's a little game we play. I pretend I don't know he smokes them, and then occasionally I nick one or two, but he can't say anything to me without admitting that he bought them in the first place."

Gemma smiled. "That sounds like one of those things that keep marriage interesting."

"I suppose you could look at it like that." Louise took a last drag on the cigarette, ground it out under her foot, then set the fag end carefully on the bench. "But you and Duncan aren't married, are you? Why not?"

"Oh, um, it's complicated," said Gemma, taken by surprise. "I was married before, and so was he, and neither of us was very successful at it. Maybe we're afraid to jinx what we've got."

"And the son who played truant today, he doesn't belong to both of you?"

"He's Duncan's son from his first marriage. Toby, the four-year-old, is my son from my first marriage." She couldn't help thinking of the child they had lost, the little boy who would have been due any day now, if he had lived.

"It sounds complicated," said Louise, bringing Gemma back to the present. "Blending a family like that."

"Sometimes. But no more complicated than most families, I think." Gemma saw an opportunity. "Louise, speaking of families, why do you dislike Martin so much? He is John's brother, after all."

"Half brother," Louise corrected, "and he presumes on it. He always has some sad story, although I don't know the whole of it this time. John's always taken care of himself—why should he feel obliged to bail Martin out of trouble time and again?" she added bitterly.

"I suppose John feels responsible because Martin's so much younger," Gemma suggested, privately wondering if it had something to do with the fact that John and Louise had no children of their own. "Louise, are you sure you don't have any idea where John was yesterday morning? Could it have had something to do with Martin?"

Louise frowned. "I don't see how. I saw John leave on his own, and Martin was here."

"You'd have seen Martin go out?"

"Well," Louise hesitated. "I think so. But I was working in the garden, and I was in and out of the shed, so I can't be absolutely certain. And I can't imagine what Martin and John would have been doing together at that time of the morning."

"Fishing?" Gemma said, remembering her conversation with Callum MacGillivray.

Louise looked at her blankly. "What are you talking about? John doesn't have time to fish."

"But Callum MacGillivray told me that he and John and Donald fished together."

"You've talked to Callum?" asked Louise, sounding surprised.

"Earlier this afternoon, after I picked Duncan up at the station. I saw Alison Grant, the woman who came to see Donald on Saturday night, and she said it was Callum who told her Hazel would be here."

"And what did Callum tell you?"

"He wanted to convince Alison that Donald wasn't serious about her." Gemma thought back to her conversation with Hazel in the dining room and saw an angle she hadn't considered. "Louise, do you know if John knew Alison Grant?"

The shadows from the spirit lamp flickered across Louise's face, making it difficult for Gemma to read her expression. "If he did," Louise said carefully, "he never told me."

Callum had sat through dinner with his aunt and his father in the farmhouse kitchen, picking at his food. From the worktop, Aunt Janet's old black-and-white television had relayed the local news, and they had all watched, transfixed by the fuzzy images. The police had released Donald's name, and the television producers had managed to unearth a tape showing Donald opening the previous year's local Highland Games. This they had juxtaposed with footage of Benvulin, of the crowd milling about the gate at Innesfree, and of the white mortuary van turning out of Innesfree's drive.

It had made Callum's throat tighten with renewed grief, and he thought with horror of Alison and Chrissy watching from their sitting room.

His father, befuddled with gin, kept repeating, "Is that Donald Brodie? I thought you said he was dead."

"He is dead, Tom," Janet said patiently. "That's just a film."

Callum fought against a rising tide of hysteria, unsure whether he was going to laugh or sob. He forced himself to kiss his aunt's cheek, and to nod a good night to his father, then he escaped into the stable yard with Murphy at his side.

They had eaten unusually late, having waited for the vet to stop by to see one of the horses, and now the gathering dusk was pooling in the yard's corners and crannies. Callum felt the cool darkness brush against his skin like velvet, and the scent of the river came to him for an instant. A curlew piped as it settled down for the night.

He felt his love for the land, and for this place, as an ache lodged in his chest, and for the first time he saw clearly the futility of his desire to share it with Alison.

How could he have been so stupid? It had to be bred in the bone, in the sinews, in the blood, and he could no more force it on someone else than he could take it out of himself.

Chrissy, now, she was different. He had seen it in her eyes the first, when Alison brought her to the stables. There was something about the way she stood so still, taking everything in, and in the expression of delight that slowly blossomed on her small, round face. She understood the language of the horses, and of the other animals; she listened when he told her the stories of the land, and of the men who had shaped it.

There was so much he could have taught her, but he had lost that opportunity when he had turned Alison against him.

Beside him, Murphy lifted his nose to the wind, sniffing, and the hackles rose along his back. Callum caught the scent a moment later, the faintest trace of cold metal and brine. The mild, clear evening was a treacherous de-

ception—there was snow coming, and before long, if he
was not mistaken.

Snow in May was not unheard of in the Highlands,
but always dreaded for the damage it did to plants and
animals alike. Callum felt a chill worm its way down
his spine, which had nothing to do with the weather,
and he was suddenly eager for the close warmth of the
cottage.

He made a last circuit of the barn, checking on the
horses, before going into the cottage and banking up the
stove. He fetched a mug and the distinctive dark green
bottle from the shelf above the sink, then settled himself
in the worn armchair. This was not mellow, honeyed Benvulin, but Lagavulin from Islay, redolent of peat fires, coal
tar, and sea winds. This was a night for a whisky that
would scour the soul.

Usually, he allowed himself only a dram in the evening—he had no wish to end up like his father. But tonight he poured an inch in the cup, stared at it, then
poured another. The bottle felt unexpectedly light. He
shook it experimentally, then upended it once more,
splashing the last few drops into the mug.

The first swallow bit into his throat, but after a moment
he felt the familiar warmth spreading from his belly, eras-
ing the cold as it coursed outwards towards his fingers and
toes. He drank steadily, seeking the drowsy oblivion that
would blot out thought and feeling.

He had almost drained the cup when he realized something was wrong. A strange, cold numbness filled his
mouth, then the room tilted sickeningly. This was not the
soft blurring of edges that came with drinking good
whisky, even too much good whisky. His heart gave a
thump of panic, but it felt oddly separate from him. Placing his hands on the arms of the chair, he pushed himself

up. The room spun, and then he was on his knees, without quite knowing how he had got there.

Help, he thought fuzzily, he had to get help. But his mobile phone, his one concession to modernity, was still in the pocket of his jacket, and his jacket was hanging on a hook by the door.

A wet, black nose pressed against his face. Murphy, thinking this was some sort of new game, had come to investigate. Callum pulled himself up again, carefully, carefully, using the dog and the chair for support. He managed to lurch halfway across the room before a wave of nausea brought him to his knees. He crawled the last few feet. Clutching at the jacket, he pulled it from its hook.

But when he managed to pull the phone from the pocket, he found the numbers a wavering blur. In desperation, he stabbed at the keypad, following the pattern imprinted in his tactile memory.

It was Chrissy who answered. Sickness filled Callum's throat, but he managed to choke out a few words. "Chrissy . . . something wrong . . . whisky. Ill. Get your mum."

Then darkness overtook him, and he remembered nothing else.

17

So, as in darkness, from the magic lamp,
The momentary pictures gleam and fade
And perish, and the night resurges—these
Shall I remember, and then all forget.
                    —ROBERT LOUIS STEVENSON,
                        "To My Old Familiars"

GEMMA SLIPPED INTO the double bed in the upstairs
bedroom, alone. It was a pleasant room, the bed covered
in a white, puffy duvet, the walls a deep, sea blue, the furniture simple farmhouse pine.

Leaving the small bedside lamp switched on, she lay
quietly, thinking over the events of the evening, feeling
the starched coolness of the sheets against her skin.

After their conversation in the shed, she'd insisted on
helping Louise with the washing up. They had almost
finished when they heard the sound of a car in the drive,
and a moment later John appeared in the scullery door.

"John! Thank God." Louise had spun round, the last
soapy dish in her hands. "Are you all right?"

"Aye." He came into the kitchen, then stopped, as if not
quite sure what to do next. His shirttail had come un-

tucked, his thinning hair stood on end, and to Gemma he seemed somehow shrunken, deflated.

"What happened? What have they done to you?" asked Louise, but still she didn't go to him.

"They've done nothing but ask me the same questions until I was fit to go mad, and keep me from my dinner," John told her wearily. "Is there soup left?"

"I've just put it up." Louise made a move towards the fridge, but he stopped her with a wave of his hand.

"Och, never mind. I canna be bothered. A drink is what I need."

Gemma dried her hands and faced him. "What about the gun, John?" she asked.

He met her eyes briefly, and nodded. "Aye, there's no doubt. My grandfather's initials are worked into the carving on the stock."

There was an awkward pause, and Gemma wondered if her presence was keeping them from speaking freely, or if the constraint in the atmosphere was due to John's reluctance to discuss the interview with Louise.

Louise broke the silence. "What about the car?" she asked matter-of-factly, turning back to the sink.

"The chief inspector said they would return it in the morning, when they've finished their tests. He had a constable bring me back and drop me off with a 'cheerio,' as if we'd been for an ice cream. I'm that fed up with this business."

"Not as fed up as Donald Brodie," Gemma said sharply. "We're inconvenienced; Donald is dead."

"Oh, Christ. I'm sorry, Gemma." John rubbed his hand across his darkly stubbled chin. "You're right, and I've been a self-absorbed boor. But I'm still going to have that dram. You can consider it my wake for Donald." With that, John had shambled out of the kitchen, presumably to join Kincaid and Martin in the sitting room.

Louise stared after him, her lips compressed, and had only made the barest response to Gemma's further attempts at conversation. Gemma could only guess at what was wrong between husband and wife. Did Louise suspect John of having something to do with Donald's death? Or did she merely suspect John of having an affair, perhaps with Alison Grant? But why had Louise seemed surprised when Gemma had mentioned John fishing with Callum and Donald? She couldn't imagine why John would have neglected to tell his wife such an innocent thing, nor could she see why Callum would have invented it.

When Louise announced, a few minutes later, that she was going up to bed, Gemma bid her good night and wandered into the sitting room. A half-empty bottle of Benvulin stood on the low table between the men, who were sprawled in the tartan chairs in varying degrees of inebriation. John's glass held a generous measure, and Martin's face was already flushed from overconsumption, but Kincaid, although a bit more bright-eyed than usual, seemed little the worse for wear.

"I'm not giving up until I get Ian on the phone," Kincaid told Gemma when she perched on the arm of his chair. "His secretary's promised he'll be back in his office within the hour. If you want to turn in, I'll join you as soon as I can."

"No, stay, have a drink." John, apparently having recovered enough to play the host, started to get up, but Gemma shook her head. Guessing that Kincaid meant to take advantage of the whisky-induced male bonding, she'd retired gracefully from the field.

But now, as she lay in bed, she realized how much she had missed Duncan, and how much she'd been looking forward to time alone with him.

A wave of homesickness swept over her. Earlier in the

evening, she'd called to talk to Wes and Toby, and Toby, after the momentary excitement of getting a phone call, had begun to cry. As much as he loved Wesley, he missed her and Duncan and Kit, and she was sure he had absorbed Wesley's anxiety over Kit's absence that afternoon. She'd done her best to reassure him, but now the sound of his small, tearful voice came back to haunt her.

Then there was Kit—was he all right at Nathan's? And what could have prompted him to run away? He was ordinarily a thoughtful and considerate boy; he must have been dreadfully upset to do something he knew would make them frantic with worry. She wished she could talk to him, but she'd agreed with Kincaid to wait until they had spoken to Ian.

At some point in her catalog of concerns she must have drifted off to sleep, her worries over her own family mutating into a dream of Holly, calling for her mother, and of Tim, reaching out for the child with bloody hands.

She woke with a gasp to a darkened room, and the feel of Duncan sliding into bed beside her. He smelled faintly of whisky, and his bare skin was cold. "What—what time is it?" she said groggily, trying to sit up.

"Shhh. It's late. I was trying not to wake you." He wrapped his arms round her.

"I didn't mean to fall asleep." Awareness came flooding back as the nightmare images melted away. "What about Ian? Did you talk to him?"

"I did." There was an edge of anger in Kincaid's voice. He rolled onto his back and stuffed a pillow under his head. "I was going to wait till morning to tell you, as I don't think it will improve your sleep."

Ian had never been an ideal parent, even before Vic's death, and Gemma had learned not to place too much confidence even in his good intentions. "Oh, no," she whispered, heart quailing. "What's he done now?"

"It took me a while to pry it out of him. Apparently, he realized he'd made a royal cock-up of things, after Kit hung up on him. First, he told Kit that the cottage in Grantchester had sold, which I think Kit could have dealt with, given a bit of time. He was expecting it, after all.

"But then Ian dropped the real bomb. He told Kit that he's getting married again, in July, and he canceled Kit's visit because he's going to be on his honeymoon."

"Married?" repeated Gemma, wondering if she'd heard correctly.

"Married. To a twenty-something Toronto socialite, one of his graduate students. Not that Ian doesn't have the right to get married again," Kincaid added, "but he could have broken the news to Kit a little more gently, and taken his feelings into consideration when he made the arrangements."

Gemma sat up in bed and pushed her hair from her face. "That's much too charitable. He's a bastard. Doesn't he realize that Kit's been planning this visit since Ian left for Toronto in December? To snatch that away from him would have been blow enough, after the letter from Eugenia, but to add marriage and a new stepmother on top of that—"

"I asked him if he could rearrange the wedding around Kit's visit, but he said Melinda's family had already made their plans."

"Melinda?" Gemma squeaked. "God, I hate her already. What are we going to do?"

"What can we do? We have no control over Ian—"

"We have to get legal custody of Kit," interrupted Gemma, with the decisiveness born of fury. "Ian has done enough damage; we have to make sure he can't suddenly decide he wants to impress this *Melinda* by moving Kit to Canada, or something equally daft. We have to insist on the DNA testing. Doesn't Kit realize we only want what's best for him?"

"Can you blame Kit for not trusting us, after twelve years with Ian?" Kincaid turned on his side and propped himself on his elbow so that he could look at her. "Gemma—you don't have any doubt, do you? That Kit is *my* son, and not Ian's?"

The moonlight spilled through the gap in the curtains, illuminating his face clearly and revealing a vulnerability he seldom expressed. His hair fell across his brow in a familiar question mark. Gemma reached up and brushed it back with a fingertip. "No. You can't see what I see, when the two of you are together. And it's not just the physical resemblance—it's in a gesture, a movement, an expression."

He nodded, once, then frowned. "But why should it make any difference? I don't mean for the obvious reasons, the custody issue, but in the way I feel. Why does it matter so much to me?"

"Maybe it's just human nature," Gemma said softly. "The desire for connection."

"Yes." He reached for her, pressing her back until her head touched the pillow, then rolled over and pinned her beneath him. "I'd agree with that." There was an unexpected hint of laughter in his voice.

"I didn't mean—"

"I know you didn't." Taking her face in his hands, he brushed his lips down her cheek until he reached the corner of her mouth. "But I do."

From the Diary of Helen Brodie, Benvulin, 1 November 1899

If I have neglected this journal in these past few weeks, my justification lies in the events that have overtaken the household. Margaret has once again taken to her bed, although the doctor can find no ailment. When he reproved her for feasting on sweetmeats rather than nourishing foods, she sent him away in a fit of pique, calling him useless—a case, I must say, of the pot calling the kettle black.

It is not so much that Margaret contributes to the household when she is up and about, but that her malingering causes much extra work and disruption for everyone else, particularly the servants.

And then there are the children. Since poor little Miss Andrews left so precipitously for London last summer, they have been without governess or tutor, allowed to run wild about the estate without discipline or routine. Little Robert had begun to show signs of temper, and Meg of aping her mother's vapors.

At last, I felt compelled to take matters into my own hands, and have hired a governess, a young woman of good family from Edinburgh, with whom I am well pleased. She has instituted a schedule of study for the children, with set times for lessons, music, drawing, and play. The change has been little short of miraculous. Within the space of a fortnight, the children have begun to show an improvement in character.

Rab, of course, seconded my decision, although he could not be pressed into taking the matter in hand himself. To give him his due, he has been much occupied with the distillery. Despite his frequent trips to Edinburgh and Glasgow in search of profitable connections, our situation has steadily worsened. Although our own barley harvest this autumn was more than sufficient to keep up pro-

duction, our stock sits in the warehouses, unsold.
The loss of Pattison's distribution has been a devastating blow, and I fear that before the winter is
out we will be without the funds to pay even the distillery workers.

I cannot help but wonder at the sudden blossom-
ing of friendship between Rab and Olivia
Urquhart. Not that I would suspect my brother of
an ulterior motive, but I know how much he both
admires and envies the manner in which Carnmore
has weathered this financial storm.

It is, perhaps, a blessing that Margaret felt herself unable to attend the Hallowe'en festivities
given by one of the Laird of Grant's tenants yesterday evening. Livvy and her son had come down
from Carnmore for the night, taking advantage of
the fair weather for one last sortie out of the Braes
before inclement weather closes them in.

Adults and children alike participated in the
reels and apple dooking and crowdie supping with
much hilarity. Amongst all the activities, there was
much sharing of glances and touching of hands for
those inclined to flirtation.

Margaret, for all her indolence, is sharp-eyed,
and she could not have failed to notice the attrac-
tion between Livvy Urquhart and my brother. Petty
vengeance is certainly within Margaret's capacity,
and she does possess the social connections required to set such retribution in motion.

Of Rab's reputation I have no fear—men of our
station have always regarded widows as fair game.
Livvy Urquhart, however, seems an innocent, unaware of the precipice looming beneath her feet.
She has not the social position or the élan to carry

off such an intrigue and would, I fear, reduce her-
self to the pathetic. And what of her son? What will
it do to his prospects if his mother compromises
herself?

Or are these only idle fancies brought on by the
lateness of the hour, and given rein by the self-
indulgence of expressing myself within these pages.
Why should I, after all, begrudge my brother a bit
of happiness, inside or out of the social conven-
tions? Is it merely the sour envy of a spinster turned
nearly forty years of age, with all hope of such
companionship behind her?

Alas, it might be better so, but my heart tells me
there is substance to my fears, and that we shall all
rue the consequences of Charles Urquhart's un-
timely death.

"Mummy!"

Alison woke instantly, a mother's response to a child in
distress. It was still dark as pitch in the bedroom, but she
could feel Chrissy shaking her shoulder. "Baby, what's
wrong? Are you sick?" She reached up and switched on
the lamp, blinking against the sudden brightness.

Chrissy knelt beside her on the bed, fully dressed, even
to her trainers. "No, it's not me," said Chrissy. "It's Callum. Mummy, you have to get up."

"Oh, Chrissy, no. Don't ye start that again." They'd
had a huge row earlier in the evening. Chrissy had answered the phone, then come to her with some tall tale
about Callum saying he was ill. Assuming this was some
strategy on Callum's part to get back in her good graces,
Alison had refused to give any credence to it, and she'd
been furious that he'd use such tactics on a child.

When Chrissy had added that Callum had said there

was something wrong with his whisky, and then the phone had gone dead, Alison had considered her theory proved. She'd ignored Chrissy's pleas and sent her to bed.

"I tried to ring him back," Chrissy said now. "He didn't answer."

"Well, of course he didn't answer." Alison looked at the clock and groaned. "It's past one in the morning."

"No, I've been trying ever since you went to bed. I couldn't sleep."

"Why, you wee sneak—"

"Mummy, please!" Chrissy insisted, her face pinched with misery. "I know something's wrong. Callum didn't sound like himself at all, and I could hear Murphy whining in the background. Please. We have to go."

"If you think I'm going to drive out to that bloody stable in the middle of the night . . . ," began Alison, but she didn't finish her well-worn tirade. Doubt had begun to set in. She had never seen her daughter so adamant, and Chrissy was not one for dramatics. What if—what if there was a remote possibility that Chrissy was right?

She could ring the police, she supposed—that would be the logical thing—but what would she say to them? That her nine-year-old daughter had told her that Callum MacGillivray had poisoned himself on bad whisky? They would think she'd gone off her head, and the same applied to ringing Callum's aunt Janet.

"Mummy—"

"Oh, all right." Alison peeled back the duvet and scooted Chrissy aside. She was desperate for a fag now, which meant going outside. At least a run in the car would give her a chance to smoke. "But just remember, you owe me big-time for this."

Chrissy gulped back a sob of relief and smiled.

"Right, go get your coat, then, while I get some clothes

on." God, she was daft, thought Alison as she hurriedly pulled on jeans and boots, as daft as Callum MacGillivray. She had not much petrol in her car, which was unreliable at the best of times; she had no mobile phone, because she couldn't afford one; and she had to open the shop in the morning, which meant being at work a half hour early.

She was worse than daft, she was mental.

Chrissy met her at the door, bundled into her pink anorak and carrying the small torch they kept in case of power failures. "Good girl," Alison told her, giving her a squeeze as they started down the stairs.

For a moment, she thought her old car would let her down, but the engine caught on the second try. The night had turned cold, but not so cold that Chrissy's teeth should be chattering. As they drove north out of Aviemore on the deserted road, Alison cranked up the heater, saying, "It'll be okay, baby. You'll see."

Chrissy said quietly, "Mummy, when you told that policeman that Callum killed Donald, you didn't mean it, did you?"

"No," Alison admitted after a moment's thought. "I don't suppose I'd be here if I did, not even to please you."

"Then why did you tell them he did?"

Alison shrugged. "Because I was angry with him. And because I was angry that Donald was dead." But . . . if she didn't believe Callum had killed Donald, who had? And what if that person had meant to hurt Callum, too? He'd told Chrissy there was something wrong with his whisky—what if it had been poisoned?

Alison's pulse began to beat in her throat, and she pushed harder on the accelerator, praying that she was wrong, that it *was* a hoax, after all.

The road seemed to swoop and curve endlessly

through the darkness, but at last Alison saw the stable's sign. She turned into the drive and stopped, halfway between the farmhouse and Callum's cottage. Both were in darkness.

"Okay, right," Alison muttered as they got out of the car. The bowl of the sky seemed enormous above them, and the silence of the night pressed down like a weight. Then a dog barked, a crack of sound in the darkness, and she and Chrissy both jumped.

"It's Murphy." Chrissy started towards the cottage, holding the torch out in front of her like a sword.

"Here. You let me go first," hissed Alison, catching her up and taking the torch. They could hear the dog clearly now, whining and scrabbling at the cottage door, but no light appeared in the window. If Callum were all right, wouldn't the dog have woken him?

When they reached the cottage door, Alison pushed Chrissy firmly behind her. "You stay back until I tell you." Taking a breath, she called out, "Callum! Are you in there?" There was no response except more frantic whining from the dog.

Alison tried the latch. It gave easily, but the door only opened an inch. Something was blocking it. She pushed steadily until Murphy's black nose appeared in the gap, and a moment later the dog had wriggled out. He jumped at them, whimpering, and Chrissy wrapped her arms around his sleek, black neck.

"Stay back," Alison instructed her again, and eased her body through the opening. The stench hit her like a wave—vomit and whisky. She clamped her hand to her mouth, swallowing hard, and shone the torch down at the object blocking the doorway.

It was Callum. He lay on his side, his head only inches removed from the pool of vomit. "Oh, bloody Christ," whispered Alison. Was he dead? She couldn't see his face.

Squatting, she grasped his shoulder and called his name. "Callum!" When he didn't respond, she forced herself to touch the exposed skin of his neck. His flesh felt slightly warm, but he didn't move. Alison leaned closer, listening. She thought she heard a faint, snoring breath.

"Mummy?" Chrissy called from outside.

"Hold on, baby," Alison shouted back. Bloody hell, she had to get some light, so that she could see what she was doing. She stood, searching for a light switch, then remembered Callum hadn't any electricity. "Daft sodding bugger," she muttered, scanning the room with the torch. There, on the table, was a paraffin lamp. It looked just like the one her granny in Carrbridge had had when she was a child.

She checked the lamp's reservoir. Empty. But the beam of the torch showed her a paraffin tin near the stove, and she quickly filled the lamp. She lit the wick with the lighter she carried in her pocket and stood back as the bloom of warm light illuminated the cottage.

Callum lay with one arm beneath him, the other curled over his head. A foot from his hand, she glimpsed the metallic gleam of his phone, but when she snatched it up, she saw that the battery had died. She knew that Callum only charged it in the van.

Swearing under her breath, she hurried to the door and slipped through. "Here, Chrissy. You take the torch. Go up to the big house and wake Callum's auntie. Tell her to ring for an ambulance."

Chrissy stared back at her, eyes enormous in her pale face. "But— Is he all right?"

"I don't know, love," Alison answered honestly. "We need to get help, a doctor. Go. Hurry."

Nodding, Chrissy started towards the farmhouse, her gait more uneven than usual over the rough ground. The dog, however, sat down by the door, accusing Alison with his gaze.

"What do ye expect me to do?" she said aloud, but she went back into the cottage. She was afraid to move Callum, afraid she might somehow make him worse. But she could cover him—*that* she remembered from her school first-aid lessons. Taking the tartan blanket from his narrow bed, she carefully laid it over him.

Her next instinct was to clean up after him, but as she went to the sink for a cloth, realization hit her. If there had been something wrong with the whisky, she shouldn't touch anything. She saw the green glass bottle on the tabletop, and on the floor beneath it, a pottery mug tipped on its side.

She'd never known Callum to drink much, and certainly not to the point of being insensible. God, why hadn't she listened to Chrissy? Callum was daft, and aggravating, but he had never lied to her—he'd only shown her things she didn't want to see.

Why had she thought he would invent an illness just to get her sympathy? He'd called her for help, and she'd refused him the kindness she'd have given freely to a stranger in the street.

If he died, she would never forgive herself. Worse yet, Chrissy would never forgive her.

18

❧

It's ill to break the bonds that God decreed to bind,
Still we'll be the children of the heather and the wind.
Far away from home, O, it's still for you and me
That the broom is blowing in the north countrie!

— ROBERT LOUIS STEVENSON, from a poem written to
Katharine de Mattos,
with a copy of *Dr. Jekyll and Mr. Hyde*

GEMMA PULLED HERSELF from Kincaid's arms reluctantly, loath to leave the cocoon of rumpled sheets and the scent of sleep-sweet skin for the harsh reality of day. But a cold, gray light shone mercilessly in through the window, and the house was stirring around them.

"What is it about holiday beds?" she asked, yawning. "It's never so hard to get up at home."

Kincaid regarded her seriously. "It probably has something to do with the fact that you kept me up half the night."

"Me?" She threw a pillow at him. "It was you kept me up!" When he covered his face with it in mimed sleep, she retaliated by snatching the duvet right off the bed.

"Hey, what do ye think ye're doin', hen?" he grumbled, in fair Scots.

She stared at him in surprise. "Where did you learn that?"

"I'm a man of hidden talents." He grinned at her, reclaiming the duvet. "And you haven't met my father. We really should remedy that someday soon."

Gemma sat on the edge of the bed. "We should. I'd like to see your mum again. And Kit would love it—Toby, too, of course." She hesitated, then added, "About Kit . . . Will we ring him this morning and make arrangements to get him home?"

Kincaid sobered. "I've been thinking. This business with Ian is not something I want to discuss with him over the phone—it needs to be face-to-face. If it's all right with Nathan, I think we should let Kit stay there for another day or two, until I can pick him up on my way back to London. We'll have to let his school know, of course."

"Um, right."

He must have detected some lack of enthusiasm in her response, because he sat up, frowning.

"What? You don't agree?"

"No, it's not that. But when *are* we going to get home, if something doesn't break on this case? Our hands are tied in every direction. We've no idea what's going on with Tim, and Ross is focused entirely on John Innes—"

"Can you blame him, considering the fact that Innes's gun seems to have been the murder weapon? Not to mention his dodgy alibi."

"No," she said, grudgingly. "I suppose not. But that doesn't mean I buy John as the shooter. I'll give you method, and opportunity, but not motive. Why would John Innes have killed Donald?"

"The truth is that you like John, and you don't want to consider him as a suspect."

"So?" Gemma countered. "That doesn't mean I'm wrong."

"Flawless logic, love," Kincaid told her, grinning. "But as it happens, I'm inclined to agree with you. I did make a little headway with John last night. After half a bottle of Scotch, he announced that since he didn't shoot Donald, he wasn't going to dig himself another hole just to provide the chief inspector an alibi."

"Is that all?"

"After that he descended into the maudlin. He told us at great length what a good friend Donald had been to him, and that he didn't see how he was going to manage without him. Martin and I had to help him up to bed."

"Would keeping an affair from Louise be worth the risk of being charged with murder?"

"People have killed for less," Kincaid reminded her.

"Maybe Donald threatened to tell Louise that John was having an affair," suggested Gemma. "But why would Donald have done such a thing? And I still can't see John as the Casanova type. He's much too domestic."

"You think men who cook don't have affairs? That's very sexist of you."

Gemma refused to take his bait. "None of this is getting us any further forward."

"So what would you do if you were Ross?"

Gemma considered for a moment. "I'd have another word with Callum MacGillivray. There's something not right there, although I'll be damned if I can see what it is. But for one thing, he was very slippery about what he was doing on Sunday morning."

"Then why don't we pay him a call, first thing after breakfast?"

*   *   *

By the time they had taken turns squeezing in and out of the tiny shower, Gemma could hear the hum of conversation from downstairs, and the tantalizing smell of frying bacon had begun to drift in under their door.

Not having packed for more than a weekend, she stared at the meager selection in her bag, attempting to decide which of her outfits to recycle. She had glanced out the window, trying to assess the temperature, when she saw Hazel in the back garden.

Pulling on a nubby, oatmeal-colored pullover without further deliberation, she told Kincaid she'd meet him in the dining room. She wanted to have a word with Hazel before breakfast.

Hazel stood at the edge of the lawn, looking out over the wood and, beyond it, the meadow where Donald had died. The crime scene tape still fluttered in the chill little gusts of wind, and the clouds massing in the west were the color of old pewter. Hazel clasped the edges of her cardigan together, as if she were cold.

"The weather's changing," Gemma said as she joined her.

"The Gab o' May. That's what they call it in the Highlands—the return of bad weather in mid-May."

"It's not unusual, then?"

"No. I can remember snow in the Braes in May, when I was a child." Hazel turned to her. "Gemma, I had the dream again last night. Well, not exactly the same dream, but the same sort of dream."

"The one where you were at Carnmore?"

Hazel nodded. "But this time there was a man, as well. It wasn't Donald, but there was something about him . . . Oh, it's such a jumble. It's as if the pieces of someone's life were put in one of those cheap kaleidoscopes we had as children, and shaken. I get fragments of experience, but I can't make sense of them."

"I'm not surprised, after what you've been through these last few days." Putting her arm round Hazel's shoulder, Gemma gave her a brief hug. "But it's just a dream—"

Hazel was already shaking her head. "I know that shock—and grief—do odd things to the psyche. But there's an urgency to these dreams that stays with me. I feel her fear— It's as if there's something I should do—"

A car door slammed behind them, interrupting Hazel. Turning round, Gemma saw Pascal getting out of his BMW. He moved stiffly, as he had for a moment the previous evening, but now he looked as if he were in real pain.

Gemma and Hazel hurried towards him. "Pascal, are you all right?" asked Gemma. "You don't look at all well this morning."

He grimaced. "It's my back again, I'm afraid. Yesterday I was helping Heather with Donald's things. I must have lifted too heavy a box. It's an insult to my vanity."

"Have you pulled a muscle?" Hazel asked, sympathetically.

"No, I have a bad disk," Pascal admitted. "Usually, it's manageable, but sometimes I have to take medication, and I seem to have misplaced my tablets. I thought perhaps I had left them in my room."

"Duncan and I had that room last night," Gemma told him. "But I don't recall seeing anything of yours left behind. We should ask John and Louise—" She broke off as another car came down the drive and pulled up behind the BMW. Gemma recognized it instantly as belonging to Chief Inspector Ross.

"A good day to ye," Ross called out as he and Sergeant Munro climbed from the car. He sounded too pleasant by half, thought Gemma, immediately wary.

"Something's happened," she whispered as Ross approached them.

"Sleep well, did ye?" Ross smiled, showing an expanse of teeth. "Mr. Benoit. Mrs. Cavendish. Inspector James." He nodded at each of them in turn, as if bestowing a pontifical blessing. "And where are the others this morning?"

"Just gathering for breakfast, I should think," answered Gemma, after glancing at her watch. It was getting on for half past eight. "Chief Inspector—"

"Why don't we go inside for a wee chat," interrupted Ross before Gemma could ask any of the half-dozen questions on the tip of her tongue.

Hazel grasped his arm as he turned away. "My husband, Chief Inspector— Have you—"

"I havena heard anything from London yet this morning, Mrs. Cavendish," Ross said more gently than Gemma would have expected. "Now, perhaps we could impose on Mr. Innes for a cup of coffee."

Hoping for enlightenment, Gemma glanced at Munro as they followed Ross towards the scullery door, but the sergeant's long face remained impassive. She had a suspicion that Ross was planning some sort of "gather the suspects in the library" interrogation—but why?

Ross did gather them all together, but in the dining room rather than the library. "I like to think of myself as an economical man," he explained, sitting down at the table and nursing his coveted cup of coffee. "I thought it would save me repeating myself if I talked to ye all at once— time management, I believe it's called."

Gemma doubted Ross's imitation of a naive rustic deceived anyone. Glancing round the room, she found Kincaid watching the detective with interest, while the others

NOW MAY YOU WEEP 331

looked as if they had unexpectedly encountered a cobra among the coffee cups. Pascal had eased himself into a chair. Martin had been seated when they came in, having already started on his cereal, while Louise had been helping John with the cooked breakfast in the kitchen. No one other than Pascal seemed inclined to join Martin and the chief inspector at the table.

Sergeant Munro had unobtrusively occupied the position he'd taken during their formal interviews, in the chair next to the sideboard.

"Now, then," Ross continued after taking another appreciative sip of his coffee, "there's been an interesting development since last night. I thought I should have another word with your neighbor"—he nodded at John and Louise—"Mr. Callum MacGillivray, as he was a bit vague as to his movements on the Sunday morning. Just in case he had seen more than he'd led us to believe, ye understand. Now, imagine my surprise this morning when I found, not Mr. MacGillivray forking hay into the horse troughs, but Mr. MacGillivray's aunt.

"She had just come back from the hospital in Inverness, where her nephew was admitted in the wee hours of the morning." Ross paused, appearing to savor the fact that he had their full attention. "It looks very much like someone tried to poison him."

"Poison? How? What happened?" asked Gemma, cursing herself for not acting immediately on her instincts. She'd felt sure that Callum had been hiding something.

"Is he— Is he all right?" Louise put a steadying hand on the sideboard.

"From the doctor's report, and a quick look round the cottage, it looks as though someone put a hefty dose of opiates in his whisky—a terrible thing to do to a good bottle of Lagavulin." Ross shook his head disapprovingly.

"The forensics laddies will be able to tell us more when they've had a go."

"But is Callum all right?" said John, echoing his wife.

"Weel, now, that's verra kind of you to be concerned, Mr. Innes. Especially as Miss MacGillivray told me you and your wee brother here paid a call on Callum early yesterday afternoon . . . and although Callum was out at the time, the two of you availed yourselves of his cottage."

"But— You can't think you're going to pin this on us? Just because we stopped by his cottage?" Martin leaned forward, a quick flush of anger suffusing his face. "We had nothing to do with—"

"Mr. Gilmore." Ross turned on him like a terrier after a rat. "It seems you neglected to tell us that you had been recently charged with the sale of illegal substances, ecstasy, I believe it was. Did ye think we wouldna find it out?"

"But it wasn't relevant," protested Martin. "That had nothing to do with Donald's murder—"

"That's for me to decide," snapped Ross. "And what I see is that a man has been poisoned with opiates, and that you had access to drugs."

"If by opiates, you mean morphine or heroin, I've never even seen the stuff. I wouldn't know where to get that sort of thing even if I wanted to—and it's a far cry from selling a few X-tabs to friends for a rave."

"So that's why you're hanging about," said Louise, giving Martin a look that could have curdled milk. "I should have known—"

"You say this man was given opiates?" Pascal interrupted, rising from his seat. "What sort of opiates?"

"I've not seen a copy of the hospital's lab results," Ross said. "Why?"

"I take a pain medication, by prescription. It's hydromorphone, a morphine derivative. I came round this morning because I had discovered my tablets were missing."

"If you mean Dilaudid," Munro said from his corner, "that's stronger than morphine. My wife was given it after a surgery a few years ago. The stuff made her sicker than a dog."

"Mr. Benoit, when did you last see these tablets of yours?" asked Ross.

Pascal thought for a moment. "Not for several days. I do not take them regularly, you see, but only when the pain is most severe. Last night, after I had moved to Benvulin, my back was very bad, but when I looked in my case, the tablets were not there."

"But you're sure you had them here, in this house?"

"Yes," Pascal answered firmly. "I remember I took one on Friday, after Donald had taken me fishing on the Thursday."

"Do you know how many tablets were in this bottle?"

"The prescription is for thirty—there were perhaps fifteen remaining. I cannot be exactly certain, you understand."

Ross looked round the room. "Weel, this puts a slightly different complexion on things. Anyone in this house could have put those tablets in Callum MacGillivray's whisky, but"—his gaze swung back to John—"it was you and young Martin here who were seen entering Mr. MacGillivray's cottage."

"I just wanted Martin to see the place." John sounded desperate to convince him. "I knew Callum wouldn't mind."

"Chief Inspector, you still haven't told us anything about Callum," said Louise, her face set with determination. She seemed to have decided to ignore Martin for the time being. "I don't know if you mean to be deliberately cruel, but Callum is our friend as well as our neighbor."

"I apologize, Mrs. Innes." Ross gave her his most gracious smile. "I didna mean to keep you in suspense. The doctors seem to think Mr. MacGillivray is out of the woods, but it will be a few hours before they'll let us question him."

Gemma was relieved but not surprised, as she'd suspected that if Callum had died Ross would have told them straightaway. She also felt sure Ross had neglected to mention that he would have a guard posted outside Callum's room, just in case someone decided to finish what they had started before Callum could talk.

"Thank God," breathed Louise, and Gemma saw John give her an odd look. Did John not think his wife should show such concern over their neighbor? Was there something going on here that she had completely missed?

Just as she was wondering if she and Kincaid could talk Ross into letting them see Callum, or if she could get Louise alone again, her phone vibrated. Excusing herself, she turned away and looked at the caller ID. To her surprise, it was a local number. She slipped from the room and answered the call.

"Gemma? It's Heather Urquhart here. Is Hazel with you? I've come across something I think she should see." Heather sounded hesitant and puzzled, quite unlike her usual confident self. "In fact, I'd like you both to come over straightaway, if you could manage it."

Kit had run away once before, from his grandparents' house, just after his mother had died. He'd come back to Grantchester then, too, searching for something that had eluded him. Why had he thought this time would be any different?

His mum was dead, his house belonged to someone else, and now Ian was gone, too. There was nothing left for him here.

He sat on the ground, inside the yew arbor that ran like a tunnel along one side of Nathan's cottage. A gate at either end gave the space an enclosed, cavelike feel, and Kit had often come here to think after he and Nathan had become friends.

That morning he'd awakened early, aware of the strange bed, the unfamiliar creakings of the house as it settled around him. A fierce wave of homesickness had gripped him—he'd had no idea how accustomed he'd become to the house in Notting Hill, to the sound of Duncan singing hopelessly outdated tunes in his morning shower, to Gemma murmuring to the animals as she moved about the kitchen, to Toby's little feet thumping up and down the stairs. Automatically, he reached for Tess, and patted an empty space on the coverlet.

How could he have left Tess behind? It was the first time he'd been separated from the little dog since he'd found her, and he felt as if he'd lost a limb.

Knowing he couldn't sleep any longer, he'd dressed and slipped out of the house, trying not to wake Nathan. He took the path that led from the bottom of Nathan's garden down to the Cam. From the morning mist that lay in the dips and hollows along the river, tendrils floated out like ghostly fingers. Reflections of the old trees swam insubstantially in the still surface of the water, and the air smelled of damp earth, and faintly of decay.

Kit walked along the river path until he could see into the back garden of his old house. The cottage's Suffolk-pink plaster glowed rosily in the morning light, but the grass in the garden was uncut, the patio empty. Perhaps the new family had not yet moved in, he thought, but then he'd heard a door slam, and seen a flash of movement at the uncurtained kitchen window.

For an instant, behind the streaky glass, he thought he

saw his mum's profile and the swing of her pale hair. Then he had turned and run, blindly, back to Nathan's, hiding himself away beneath the yews, trying to get the surge of his emotions under control.

The gate creaked, and Nathan's stocky silhouette filled the arbor's entrance.

"I thought I might find you here," Nathan said, coming to sit down beside him. That was one of the things Kit liked about Nathan; he never minded getting dirty. "Duncan rang a few minutes ago. He said he let your school know you'd be absent for a couple of days." Nathan rubbed a yew needle between his fingers, then added, "He also told me about Ian."

They sat in silence for a bit. That was another thing Kit liked about Nathan; he could sit with you in silence, without telling you what you should think about something.

"I'd been saving all term for that trip to Toronto," Kit said, when he thought he could trust his voice.

"Rotten luck. Or maybe I should say rotten timing, as far as Ian's concerned." Nathan smiled. "You know, Kit, just because people are grown up doesn't mean they always think through the consequences of things. I'm sure he didn't realize how much you were counting on that visit."

"He wants rid of me," Kit said thickly. "He said he was starting over, with a new life, a new family. I'm sure that's why he wanted me to have the DNA test."

Nathan thought about this for a moment. "And you don't want to have the test, right?"

"Right."

"But even if what you said about Ian were true—and I don't think it is, mind you—your life is with Duncan and Gemma now. Are you not happy there?"

"No, it's not that—well, school's not all that brilliant, really, but it's not that, either. It's just—" Kit rested his chin on his knees, struggling to put something he could barely get his mind round into words.

"Are you afraid the test won't prove Duncan's your father? Or that it will?" Nathan added softly, as if he'd suddenly understood something.

A spark of sunlight stole through the yew branches, illuminating the lace on Kit's shoe with a microscopic clarity. "Yes," Kit said. "Both. If Duncan's not really my dad, then I'd have to go away, and I don't—" He swallowed. "We're like family, you know. But if it proves that Ian was never my dad, then it means that everything that went before was a lie. Mum, and Ian, and me. This." His nod took in the cottage down the road, the village, everything that had been his reality for twelve years. "And that makes me . . . not who I thought I was."

Slowly, Nathan said, "Kit, no test, no configuration of molecules, can take your past away from you. That experience will always be a part of you, no matter what happens in the future, no matter where you live, or how many times Ian gets married. Those layers of living build up like a pearl in an oyster—you can't just slice them away . . . although sometimes it might be easier for people if they could."

"But what if— If I wasn't— What if Duncan didn't *want* me anymore?" There, he had said it. He felt suddenly lighter.

"Kit, I think Duncan wants to prove you're his son *because* he loves you and is proud of you, not the other way round. Does that make sense? But no one can make you have this test. You have to do what you think is right for you."

"But what about my grandmother?" Kit's voice rose as the panicked feeling set in again.

"You can go to the judge and tell him how you feel. In fact, you can tell him exactly what you've told me. You're old enough to have a voice in your own future, if you're strong enough to make it heard. It's what *you* want that matters now."

"Will they charge John?" Hazel asked from the backseat of the Honda as they sped towards Benvulin. Saying that Hazel was needed urgently at the distillery, they had left the chief inspector taking John once again over his visit to Callum's cottage. Ross had made no attempt to detain them, but when Pascal had offered to come with them, Ross had insisted he stay until he'd completed a written statement about his missing medication.

"He'd have charged him already if he had the evidence," Kincaid said, turning towards her. "He's just stirring things at the moment while he waits to see what the forensics team turn up in the car."

"I don't believe it," Hazel protested. "I simply can't believe John would have taken Pascal's tablets and poisoned this man—Callum."

None of the other options were any more palatable, Gemma thought as she slowed for the entrance to Benvulin, but she didn't say so. She was increasingly worried over the lack of news about Tim Cavendish. Hazel had spoken to her mother-in-law earlier that morning, and Carolyn had told her she'd had no word from Tim since the previous evening. Was he still "helping" the Met with their inquiries?

Kincaid looked round with interest as Gemma parked the car in Benvulin's drive. "What a lovely place—more fairy-tale than industrial. Is the design unique?"

"No." As they got out of the car, Hazel studied the distillery buildings as if seeing them anew. "The twin pagoda-roofed kilns were an innovation of a Victorian architect called Charles Doig, and the design was adopted by a number of Highland distilleries—but nowhere did all the elements come together quite so well as they did here at Benvulin. You can see why the Brodies loved it, sometimes beyond reason, I suspect."

"And Donald was no exception," Gemma murmured. She had started automatically for the offices when Heather came out the door of Benvulin House and waved to them.

Heather wore trainers and old jeans rather than smart work clothes. The others changed course, and as Gemma mounted the steps to the house, she saw that Heather had a smudge of dirt over one eyebrow.

"Heather, what's happened?" Hazel asked without preamble. "Is it something to do with the business?"

"No." Heather's manner seemed suddenly hesitant. "I've been going through Donald's personal papers. I've made a start on the funeral arrangements, and I was hoping to find something that would tell me what Donald wanted. And in truth"—she looked directly at her cousin—"I'd hoped I might find another will."

"Heather, you know I didn't want—"

"No, it's all right. It was silly of me, and unfair. I know this isn't your choice, but it's what Donald thought best, and I have to come to terms with it. But that's not why I called. Come and see for yourselves." Heather turned and led them inside, through a great hall and up a massive carved staircase.

Glancing into rooms as she passed, Gemma glimpsed richly faded Persian rugs and heavy velvet draperies. Stag heads loomed on walls, beside the gilt of ornate mirrors and framed portraits, and the house had an overall air of heavy, faded, and slightly shabby opulence.

"Scotch baronial at its finest," said Heather. "This place is a dinosaur, and horrifically expensive to maintain." She led them into a room at the top of the stairs. Its tall windows looked out, not on the distillery, but towards the gray sweep of the river.

Here was ample evidence of her endeavors; stacks of books and papers covered the floor as well as the old leather-topped desk. "I don't think Donald ever felt really comfortable in this room," Heather continued. "It reminded him too much of his father." Seeing Kincaid studying a watercolor of Benvulin hanging over the desk, she added, "That's a Landseer, a gift to Donald's great-grandfather, I believe. The painter was well known for dashing off a painting of his hosts' properties in return for their extended hospitality."

Hazel still stood in the doorway. "Heather, what—"

"Here." Heather touched a stack of cloth-bound books on the corner of the desk. "I found Donald's great-grandfather's sister's diaries. And I think I've discovered what caused the rift between the Brodies and the Urquharts, but I want you to read it for yourself."

Hazel stepped into the room with obvious reluctance just as Gemma's phone rang again. "Bloody hell," Gemma muttered, snatching it up. It was Alun Ross.

She listened for several moments, then said, "Yes, I'll tell him. Yes, right away. No, I can drive him." When she rang off, however, it was not Kincaid she looked at, but Hazel.

"That was Chief Inspector Ross." She took a breath. There was no way she could soften the news. "The London police found a receipt from a petrol station in Aviemore in Tim's car, dated Saturday. They're holding Tim for questioning. Tim's refused a solicitor—he says he won't speak to anyone but Duncan." She turned to Kincaid. "There's a flight from Inverness to London in a little over an hour. I said I'd have you on it."

19

❦

I have trod the upward and the downward slope;
I have endured and done in days before;
I have longed for all, and bid farewell to hope;
And I have lived and loved, and closed the door.
— ROBERT LOUIS STEVENSON,
"I Have Trod the Upward and the Downward Slope"

Carnmore, November 1899

LIVVY STOOD IN *the distillery office, her father's letter dangling from her nerveless fingers. She had been found out, her undoing a mere slip of the tongue by the banker, sharing a midday dram with her father. The banker, assuming her father privy to her affairs, had casually mentioned her withdrawal of funds from her account, and now she would have to deal with the consequences.*

She'd felt a nagging sense of foreboding for some weeks, but she'd put it down to the time of year. It was more than the upcoming anniversary of Charles's death; she hated the dark, the closing in of the days, the interminable nights with nothing but her few books and a bit of sewing to keep her thoughts occupied. Not even to herself had she been willing to admit how much she dreaded the curtailing of Rab's visits, which would inevitably follow on bad weather.

The shooting season had brought Rab frequently to Carnmore's door, as he was on friendly terms with the duke of Gordon and was often invited for a day's sport at the duke's lodge in Tomintoul. Their tea and conversation at her kitchen table had quickly become her cornerstone, the events round which revolved the rest of her existence.

It was no more than Highland hospitality, she told herself, ignoring the whispering of her neighbors, as she did Will's increasingly obvious dislike of Rab. She prided herself on her status as Rab's friend, and she'd listened to his tales of Benvulin's troubles with increasing distress.

Other distilleries were suffering, she knew; some had already closed their doors, and as the weeks went by she became more and more worried that Benvulin would share that fate. If the same thing were to happen to Carnmore, she and Will could at least fall back on her father—Rab had nothing. She'd wished desperately for some way to help him, but it was not until her autumn visit to her father in Grantown that she'd conceived a plan.

Both she and Rab had attended a recital at the home of a Grantown dignitary. Aware of Rab's absence during the dinner buffet that had followed the musical performance, she'd slipped away from the dining room to search for him. When she'd found him at last, he'd been sitting alone in the small conservatory, his head in his hands.

He looked up at the sound of her entrance. "Livvy! You shouldn't be here. People will talk."

"I don't mind," she said, going to him as he stood. "Rab, what is it?"

He'd touched her cheek. "You're too kind, Olivia, do

you know that? I've no intention of spoiling your evening with my troubles. Go back to the buffet, before someone notices your absence."

"Not until you tell me what's troubling you."

"Blackmail, is it?" he said, giving her a crooked smile. "Well, I suppose I might as well tell you, as everyone will know before long. I don't think I can keep Benvulin going any longer, Livvy. I've had a hint of a buyer for some of the stock, from a grocer in Aberdeen who's selling his own blend—"

"But, Rab, that's good news—"

"It would be, except that it will take several months to complete the arrangement—if it materializes at all—and in the meantime, I can't pay the men's wages. Not that it's likely another distillery can take them on, but they can at least try to find some sort of work that will feed their families. I can't see that I have any choice but to close the doors."

"Rab, what about your family?"

"Margaret has gone back to her uncle's in London— leaving the sinking ship, I fear—although I don't know how long he will keep his patience with her spending habits. I've kept the children here, but it looks as though I'll have to let the governess go soon, as well."

"And your sister?"

"Helen will stand by me until the bloody end, I think. She loves Benvulin almost as much as I do. And she has nowhere else to go."

"Rab . . ." Gazing at him, Livvy realized the seed of an idea had been germinating for weeks. "Is there any way you can hold out a bit longer?"

"I could sell some of the pictures, and the silver, I suppose, but if I do, there may be nothing else to keep us."

"Do you trust me?"

He looked at her in surprise. "Of course. You've been a good friend these last few months, Livvy. If things were different . . ."

It was the first time either of them had spoken of what lay between them. She swallowed and glanced away. Wishful thinking would get them nowhere, and she couldn't let it distract her from what she could do.

She had money, left to her by her mother. It was hers to do with as she wished, but she knew Rab would never agree to take it if she told him what she meant to do.

"Rab, promise me you won't take any action yet. Wait just a bit longer, even if it means selling a punch bowl or two."

He smiled at that but quickly sobered, taking her shoulders in his hands. "Do you mean to work miracles, Livvy? I fear that's not possible."

"Wait and see," she had told him, and slipped back to the party.

It had taken some maneuvering on her part to remove the money from the bank without Will's or her father's knowledge, but on the evening of the harvest-home given by one of the Laird of Grant's tenants, she had pulled Rab aside and presented him with the banker's draft.

He had looked up from the paper he held, his usually ruddy complexion gone pale with shock. "Livvy, you can't be serious. I can't take this."

"You can," she said earnestly. "It's not for you, Rab, it's for Benvulin. Consider it a loan. You can pay it back as soon as things improve."

"I—"

"Don't ye argue with me, Rab, my mind's made up. It's my money, and I want to help you. It will be our secret."

And so it had remained, until now. Her father's outrage had leapt from the page in the quick, bold strokes of his handwriting. She had betrayed his trust, he said; she had compromised her family, and he meant to take steps to learn exactly what she had done with the funds.

Livvy's cheeks burned with humiliation. She very much feared that her father would have no trouble coaxing further indiscretions from the banker . . . and that meant she'd have to find some way to warn Rab before he faced the onslaught of her father's wrath.

Gemma could think of no innocent reason why Tim Cavendish would have been in Aviemore over the weekend. Nor had she been able to offer much comfort to a stricken Hazel, who had at first insisted on flying back to London with Kincaid.

"There's nothing you can do in London until we know more," Gemma had told her. "At least here you can help Heather. I'll come straight back from the airport, and Duncan will phone us as soon as he's seen Tim."

Hazel had seemed too shocked to offer much protest. "Tim can't have shot Donald," she had whispered as they were leaving. "There must be some other explanation. There must be."

Now, as they passed the turnoff for Culloden Battlefield, Gemma said to Kincaid, "Do you suppose Ross is wrong about the gun, then?"

He looked up from the map he'd been studying and absently ran a hand through his hair. "Of course, it's possible. But in that case, there's no logical explanation I can see for John Innes's gun ending up in the river. And how would Tim have laid hands on a gun? He's not exactly the sporting type."

"I'd never have imagined Tim Cavendish spying on Hazel, or lying about what he'd done, or refusing even to speak to her. What's one more improbable thing to add to the list?"

"But if Tim shot Donald, who poisoned Callum MacGillivray?" argued Kincaid. "We know Tim was in London yesterday. Are we looking at two different perpetrators, two unrelated crimes?"

Frowning, Gemma slowed for the exit onto the A96, the route to the Highlands and Islands Airport east of Inverness. "I suppose it's possible," she said, echoing Kincaid's earlier comment. "Could someone have been taking advantage of the suspicion Donald's murder cast on John?"

"To lay another murder at his door?"

"Or . . ." Gemma drummed her fingers on the wheel. "Could Callum have attempted suicide? His effort to win over Alison Grant by shopping Donald failed miserably. He must have been distraught . . ."

"And invisible, if he walked into the Inneses' and took Pascal's tablets without anyone noticing."

"True," admitted Gemma. "Bugger. That puts us back to square one." But as she slowed for the airport exit, an idea struck her. She glanced at the map still open on Kincaid's lap. "What we need is to talk to Callum. I wonder . . . Did I see the hospital, not too far off the Aviemore road?"

Kincaid looked down. "Raighmore Hospital, yes. Just off the A9. We must have passed within half a mile of it. You're not thinking of trying to see Callum, are you? Ross would never agree."

"Who says I have to ask him?"

"Gemma, you can't just waltz in and demand to interview Callum MacGillivray. Ross will have a coronary."

Gemma pulled up in the passenger drop-off lane. Leaning over, she kissed Kincaid on the cheek. "Then he should take better care of himself."

*   *   *

It was easier than she'd expected. And she didn't exactly lie; she merely told less than the truth. Flashing her identification at the constable guarding Callum's door, she'd said, "Inspector James, Metropolitan Police, here to see Mr. MacGillivray." The constable's eyes had widened and he'd ushered her respectfully in.

Gemma felt thankful for the benefits of rank and hoped she'd still have hers if Ross found out what she'd done and reported her to her guv'nor. Now she just had to pray that Ross himself didn't show up within the next few minutes.

Callum MacGillivray lay in the hospital bed, his long, fair hair spread out on the pillow, his eyes closed, his face waxen. For a moment Gemma was reminded of a Viking warrior laid to rest on a bier, then Callum opened his eyes and blinked fuzzily at her.

"Callum?" Gemma pulled a chair up to the side of the bed and sat down. "Do you remember me? It's Gemma James. I came by to see you yesterday."

"The copper," he whispered hoarsely. "Sorry." He touched a finger to his throat. "They tell me my throat hurts because they put a tube down it, but I don't really remember it." An IV drip ran into his arm, and he looked oddly defenseless in his hospital gown.

Gemma grimaced. "That's probably just as well. How are you feeling now?"

"Still a bit groggy," he said more strongly.

"Can you remember anything at all about what happened to you?"

"Yeah. I meant to finish a bottle of Islay malt—my own private wake for Donald. But after that, nothing, really. They say it was Alison and Chrissy who found me." There was a note of wonder in his voice. "Otherwise, I might have died."

"How did Alison know you were ill?"

"She told the doctors I phoned them, but I dinna remember that, either."

"Callum, do you know that someone put a drug into your whisky, a form of morphine?"

He met her eyes and nodded, but didn't speak.

"Have you any idea who would have done such a thing to you?"

He picked at the hem of his sheet. His hands, Gemma saw, were large and callused. "I canna think. Do the police believe it was the same person who murdered Donald?"

"They're not sure. But they do know that John and Martin Innes stopped in your cottage yesterday, while you were out."

"John Innes?" Callum stared at her as if she'd lost her wits. "They canna think John tried to poison me?"

"He doesn't seem to have a very good explanation for what he was doing in your cottage, or for what he was doing at the time Donald was shot on Sunday morning."

"Och, it was the fish," said Callum, shaking his head. "The man's a wee fool, not to have said."

It was Gemma's turn to look astonished. "Fish? What fish?"

"The salmon." Callum looked away but added reluctantly, "John and I, we've been doing a wee bit of illegal fishing. At night, mostly."

"You mean you've been *poaching*?"

"That's not a word I care to use. Shouldn't a man have the right to catch a fish in his own river, or shoot a deer on the moor?" He gave a little shrug. "But aye, I suppose you could say we were poaching. John needed the cash to keep the B&B afloat, until he could recoup the cost of the refurbishment. And I—I wanted to fix my place up a bit.

I thought Alison . . ." His hands grew still. "It was a pipe dream, I see that now. I dinna know what possessed me."

"Callum, are you telling me that John was *fishing* on Sunday morning?"

"No, it was the Saturday night, late. He'd come across to me, and we'd taken a half-dozen good-size salmon from the Spey. On the Sunday morning, he would have been selling them to a customer, one of the hotels. It was Donald who set up the clients for us, although he didna take a cut. He had the connections, you see."

"I do see," Gemma said slowly. "John didn't want to admit where he was because he was doing something illegal, and he didn't want to compromise you, or Donald."

"Or the buyer," Callum added. "But I suspect there was more to it than that—he didna want Louise to find out."

"And yesterday, when he came into your cottage?"

"He left me my share of the money from Sunday's sale. He made the sales, and I kept the books. Because he couldn't."

"Not without Louise finding out. I wonder how he explained the extra cash." Gemma frowned, remembering the way Louise had watched her husband. "Louise thought he was having an affair. I'm not surprised, with him sneaking about in the middle of the night."

She mulled over what he had told her for a moment, and an inkling of the truth began to dawn. "Callum, if John was at a hotel selling the fish on Sunday morning, where were you?"

He was silent for so long that she began to wonder if he had drifted off, but then he said quietly, "I was out along the river with the dog, the same as most mornings."

Gemma leaned towards him, touching his hand. She hardly dared to breathe. "You saw something, didn't you? Someone? But not John."

"Not John." Callum met her gaze, and she saw the sudden brightness of tears. "I didna think anything of it, at first. She sometimes goes out potting for rabbits; they're a bloody nuisance in the garden. And then, when I heard about Donald, I didna want to believe it—I couldna think she would do such a thing. We were friends."

"She? But, Callum, why would Alison—"

"Och, no, it wasna Alison." He shook his head. "It was Louise."

From the Diary of Helen Brodie, 20 November 1899

Dr. Grant of Grantown, Olivia Urquhart's father, came to call just after luncheon today. Rab was away, gone to Tomintoul for a day's shooting, so I entertained the doctor myself.

The man made no pretence of civility, refusing my offer of refreshment, but told me a preposterous tale, accusing my brother of extorting money from his daughter. Her inheritance from her mother, he said, withdrawn from the bank, and paid to my brother by draft.

Of course, I told Dr. Grant I would not listen to such nonsense, and I sent him away with a promise that Rab would call upon him as soon as he returned. Afterwards, I paced in the drawing room for an hour, recounting all the things I might have said to defend my brother's honor. But then, my suspicions overcame my sense of injury, and I went to the distillery office and began to look over the books.

Where did Rab get the money to pay the men's wages and the outstanding accounts? The records show only a paltry income these last months, much less than is needed to pay the distillery's expenses.

The financial situation is much worse than I had feared—I should never have trusted Rab to tell me the truth.

I dare not think that my brother would have accepted money from Olivia Urquhart, and yet I can see no other explanation for our sudden solvency. To what lengths would he go to stave off disaster?

And, I must ask myself, now that I have seen the ruin almost upon us, would I not have been tempted to do the same myself?

Benvulin, 21 November

The snow began yesterday at teatime. It came across the river in a white, billowing curtain, and in no time we could see no farther than a few feet from the door. I can only assume that Rab has stayed overnight with his acquaintances in Tomintoul. If the men were caught out on the moors, they will have had a difficult time of it.

Benvulin, 26 November

It snowed without stopping for twenty-four hours. If we had such weather here, in the valley of the Spey, I shudder to think of the conditions in the hills.

I have entertained the children as best I could, but they are old enough to miss their father's presence, and to worry.

Yesterday, the thaw had progressed enough that I thought it safe to send one of the grooms out on horseback, but he returned some hours later, sodden and exhausted. Drifts still block the road to Tomintoul. I can only assume that Rab is enjoying the extended hospitality of friends.

Benvulin, 28 November

A spell of clear, bright weather has rendered the roads passable, although the moors are still buried in snow. Still no word has come from Rab. The groom I sent to Tomintoul found no evidence of his arrival. Surely, Rab had reached Tomintoul before the storm broke, unless an accident befell him on the way. I begin to fear the worst.

Benvulin, 5 December

Having been told that a shopkeeper reported seeing Rab pass through Tomintoul, I began to wonder if he had ridden to Carnmore to see Livvy Urquhart. Yesterday, I myself drove to Carnmore in the gig, which I was forced to abandon in Chapeltown. The track leading to the distillery was mired in mud and slush, barely passable on foot. I do think the Braes of Glenlivet are the most godforsaken place I have ever encountered.

Livvy Urquhart professed not to have seen Rab, although she appeared much distressed by the news of his disappearance. When I confronted her with her father's tale of the monies given to my brother, she told me her father had been mistaken, that she had withdrawn her inheritance in order to make much-needed improvements to Carnmore. Her son, Will, who was present throughout the conversation, said nothing at all.

In the end, I had no choice but to take my leave and return to Benvulin. As I traveled, I could only imagine that my brother, set out upon an ill-advised visit to the Braes, had wandered from the road in the storm, and that the spring thaws will reveal his poor remains, now buried beneath the snow.

Until that time, is it cruel, or kind, to keep hope alive in the children?

Kincaid took the train from Gatwick Airport to Victoria Station. He stopped at one of the gourmet coffee stalls in the Victoria concourse, then walked the few blocks to the Yard. The blue skies he had left behind the previous morning had disappeared, leaving the city air feeling dull and sulfurous.

They had put Tim Cavendish in one of the better interview rooms. Hazel's husband looked as if he hadn't slept, or bathed, since Kincaid had seen him on Sunday evening. The growth of dark stubble on his face made Kincaid think of him as he'd known him when Gemma had first moved into the Cavendishes' garage flat.

"Hullo, Tim," he said, removing two coffees from the small carrier bag. Tim had always been particular about his coffee. "I thought you could use a decent cup."

Nodding, Tim accepted the container. "I wasn't sure you'd come, after the way I spoke to you the other night. You've always been a good friend to me, Duncan; you didn't deserve that. I thought that if I just carried on denying everything, it would go away. But it didn't."

"Do you want to tell me what happened, now?" Kincaid asked, taking a seat on the opposite side of the table. "I know you drove to Scotland, to Aviemore."

"I haven't much future as a criminal, obviously. It was bloody stupid leaving that receipt in the car. But then, I wasn't thinking very clearly. I hadn't been thinking very clearly for a long time." Tim turned the pasteboard coffee cup in his hands but didn't lift it.

"Maybe you should start at the beginning," Kincaid suggested.

"The beginning?" Tim's abrupt laugh held no humor.

"Can you believe that I was bored with my life? Every day, I saw the same self-absorbed patients, every evening I went home to the same comfortable routine, and I saw my dreams of doing big things, memorable things, vanishing year by year.

"I never said anything, but I was a bit less patient, a bit more quick to crush Hazel's enthusiasms. It all seemed petty to me—a new rose for the garden, a new recipe for dinner, what book Holly liked best that day. I even had the temerity once to accuse Hazel of not living in the real world. She looked at me with such astonishment, such disappointment.

"And then, even when I saw her with him, it didn't occur to me that I'd brought it upon myself."

"You saw Hazel with Donald? In London?"

"It was quite by chance—but then most life-changing events happen purely by chance, don't they? I was walking down the Liverpool road at lunchtime one day when I saw Hazel go into a café. When I glanced in the window, she was sitting down at a table with him, and the expression on her face . . . I realized I hadn't seen that look in years . . . if ever." Tim shook his head, as if it still amazed him. "My world turned upside down. From that day forward it was all I could think about. I followed her. I watched her. I dug her mail from the rubbish bin."

"Did you find anything?" Kincaid asked when Tim didn't continue.

"No. It wasn't until she told me she wanted to go to Scotland that I realized who he must be. Donald Brodie, her first love, the man she almost married. It wasn't until the day she left that I found the confirmation—she'd been careless enough to leave an old photo, and his business card, under her blotter."

"That's when you decided to go after her?"

Tim turned the coffee cup in his hands again, then at last lifted it to his mouth, wincing as if the liquid pained him. "I had to see for myself. That's all I could think as I drove. It was late on Friday evening by the time I found the B&B. I slept for a few hours in a lay-by, then I found a place to hide the car and walked to the house through the woods. It was daylight by then. I saw them together, in the meadow . . . after that I don't remember much."

"This was Saturday?"

Tim nodded. "I know I watched the house all that day, and as it began to get dark, I saw the gun cabinet through the open scullery door." Tim met Kincaid's gaze, his eyes red-rimmed. "I don't know what possessed me. I could see them moving about, and when the kitchen was empty, I walked into the house. The gun cabinet was unlocked, and I took the first one to hand."

Kincaid felt cold in the pit of his stomach. He found that no amount of forewarning had really prepared him for this. Dear God, how could he charge his friend with murder?

"I went back to my hiding place," Tim went on, "and I watched her come out with him after dinner. I heard them arguing, and later . . ." He swallowed. "I thought I would shoot him. I thought perhaps I would shoot them both.

"But when they came out of the wood, I found I was paralyzed. I'd never shot a gun. I didn't know how to do it, or how far it would shoot. I think it was then that I began to realize the absurdity of it—that I was actually contemplating harming another human being. Then he—Donald—went into the house, and I had missed my chance.

"Hazel stood there in the moonlight, looking after him . . . and then suddenly she dropped her face into her hands and began to sob as if her heart would break." Tim fell silent, and it took all Kincaid's patience not to prompt him.

"I almost went to her," Tim said at last. "But then how would I have explained myself? What she had done was human, and forgivable. What I had done . . . what I had contemplated doing . . . was truly terrible . . . inexcusable by any standard I had ever held. Can you understand that?"

Kincaid nodded. Hardly daring to hope, he said quietly, "Tim, what did you do then?"

Tim had sunk back in his chair, as if he had come to the end of the part of the story that mattered to him. "She went inside. I stood there with this *thing* in my hands, this gun, trying to figure out what to do with it. It didn't seem right to just set it down on the ground and walk away. After a bit, I tried the scullery door. It was locked, so there was no way I could put the gun back.

"Then I noticed the garden shed. I went inside, and put the gun on the potting bench. Even then I remember seeing the irony in it. Life and death."

"And then?"

"I walked to my car and drove back to London. I stopped and slept in a lay-by for a few hours near dawn; I'm not sure where. That day was a blur. I didn't want to go home on Sunday—I didn't see how I was going to face Hazel the next day. There's no going back from something like that.

"And then, when I heard Donald Brodie had been shot, I wondered if I'd done something I couldn't remember, if I had completely lost my reason. I went over and over things, trying to find a gap. I've never been so terrified. You can see why I didn't want to talk to anyone else; it all sounds utterly mad."

"Tim, are you telling me that you *didn't* shoot Donald Brodie?"

"I'm only guilty of intent, and that, in my book, is bad enough."

"Not in the eyes of the law." Kincaid's mind raced. If Tim had left the gun in the garden shed, what had happened to it? Louise was the gardener, but if she'd found it, why hadn't she said so? Unless . . . Shock fizzed in Kincaid's veins. Unless it was Louise Innes who had shot Donald.

Gemma drove south on the A9, pushing the posted speed limit. She'd left a message for Chief Inspector Ross, asking him to meet her at Benvulin. It was time for a conference, even though it meant confessing to trespassing on Ross's turf as far as Callum MacGillivray was concerned.

Callum had told her he'd seen Louise from a distance on Sunday morning, walking across the river meadow with a shotgun. He hadn't thought she'd seen him, but he had begun to wonder when she'd come calling on Sunday afternoon.

Gemma remembered Louise making an excuse to go out, shortly after the police had finished their interviews that day. And then yesterday, when Louise had been out gathering boughs, had she slipped into Callum's cottage with Pascal's tablets? It was Louise who did the rooms in the B&B, Louise who would naturally have seen the bottle of painkillers, Louise who could have pocketed it so easily.

Drops of rain began to spatter against the windscreen, and Gemma slowed, swearing. Rain after a dry spell always made driving conditions particularly hazardous, and she couldn't afford an accident. Moving over into the center lane, she resumed her musing.

Louise, then, had had the means and the opportunity, but *why* would she have shot Donald Brodie? And where did Tim Cavendish come into it? Reaching for her phone, she speed dialed Kincaid, but the call went directly to voice mail. He was probably still in the air, she thought, glancing at the dashboard clock, but he should be landing soon. She hung up without leaving a message; she would talk to Ross first.

But if Louise had used the shotgun, why had residue not shown up in the swab results? It took more than scrubbing with soap and water to remove nitrate traces. An image came back to her—Louise arranging the boughs she had cut, her hands scratched and dirty, a nail broken. She'd guessed Louise normally wore gloves when she gardened, but what if Louise had been wearing her gloves when she fired the gun, and they had protected her hands? She could have found some way to dispose of the gloves, but then she wouldn't have wanted to call attention to their absence by getting a new pair.

Was there any physical evidence to support Callum's statement? Callum could be easily discredited in court, given his demonstrated grudge against Donald over Alison Grant. Without motive or forensics evidence, the case would be difficult to prove. Nor did it help to go into an interrogation blind, without some idea of the reason behind the crime.

If anyone might understand Louise's motives, Gemma realized as she exited the motorway, it was Hazel.

The rain stopped, then started again, drumming against the windscreen in volleys. As Gemma turned into Benvulin's drive, she saw a figure sprint from the house to the distillery office. The woman was recognizable even at a distance, in the rain, by the fall of long, dark hair.

Gemma parked the car, grabbed her anorak from the backseat, and held it over her head as she ran for the office herself. The temperature had plunged in the half hour since she'd left Inverness, and a biting wind plucked at her clothes.

She found Heather already at her desk, the phone to her ear. When Heather looked up at her entrance and covered the mouthpiece, Gemma said softly, "Hazel? Is she still in the house?"

Heather shook her head, frowning. "No. She left a few minutes ago."

"Left?" Gemma repeated blankly. What could have possessed Hazel to leave without news of Tim?

"She borrowed my car. She said she wanted to go to Carnmore. I think it was—" Heather's attention shifted back to the phone. "Yes, I'm still holding," she said into the mouthpiece, then covered it again as she looked back up at Gemma. "I'm sorry, Gemma. I've got to take this call. It's the chairman of the board."

Gemma was debating whether to wait for her to finish her call or to go on to the Inneses', when Heather added, "Oh, by the way, Louise rang a few minutes ago. She was looking for Hazel as well."

20

❧

Fair the fall of songs
When the singer sings them.
Still they are caroled and said—
On wings they are carried—
After the singer is dead
And the maker buried.
    —ROBERT LOUIS STEVENSON,
      "Bright Is the Ring of Words"

From the Diary of Helen Brodie, Benvulin, 25 March 1900

TODAY, BENVULIN SHIPPED *the first of many casks of our best aged whisky to the Aberdeen grocers. I have labored over the winter to keep the distillery running until this contract could be brought to fruition, and now we can only hope that this sale stimulates interest from other blenders.*

None of this, however, would have been possible without the mysterious infusion of funds into our bank account. Livvy Urquhart has never admitted to the gift, and her father, when I called upon him in Grantown, avowed he must have been mistaken. So I have incurred an unacknowledged debt that I cannot repay, and if Rab's children have an inheritance, they will owe it to the Urquharts.

Margaret has not returned from London, even to visit the children. I will keep them here and raise them with the care I would give my own.

The thaws came early this spring, with much rain. No amount of searching, however, among the moors and tracks, has turned up any sign of my brother. I would have been content with even a button from his coat, so that I could set my mind to rest.

Benvulin, 15 May 1900

As the months pass without word or sign of my dear brother's body, the doubt has grown in my heart like a cancer. What if, I ask myself, Rab did visit Carnmore on that fateful day, and some misadventure befell him there?

I called on Olivia Grant once again, and spoke to her like a sister. Still she denied me most forcefully, saying that Rab never came to Carnmore. But there is a change in her since the autumn, a new grimness in her countenance, a hardness to her manner. I took my leave as firmly, saying I meant to pursue the matter.

But what, in truth, can I do? I have the word of a shopkeeper in Tomintoul who thought he glimpsed my brother, cloaked and hatted, riding through the village—nothing more. What authority would give credence to such a tale told by a grieving sister?

Do I owe the survival of everything my brother

*held most dear to a woman responsible for his
death? Such a terrible irony seems more than I can
bear. For if our life here at Benvulin has gone on as
before, the light has gone from mine.*

*I will not forget what we owe the Urquharts, nor
will I allow those who come after me to do so.*

As Hazel drove, the last entries in Helen Brodie's journal kept repeating in her head. As the road snaked over
the tops of the moors, she glimpsed the snow markers
and shuddered. Rab Brodie could very easily have been
lost as a blizzard swept over the hills, and if so, it was
highly unlikely his remains would have been found in
this vast, trackless expanse of heather and bracken. His
sister's affection for him had made her imagine things,
and Hazel understood the need to lay blame for the
death of someone so loved.

And yet . . . the images from her dreams clung, insinu-
ating themselves into Helen's story like wraiths. Blood
and whisky . . . a violent death at Carnmore. Will
Urquhart had been her grandfather, Olivia Urquhart her
great-grandmother. Was it possible that her dreams were
somehow a reflection of Livvy's experience, a translated
snippet of consciousness?

She shook her head. That was nonsense, even more
daft than Helen Brodie's suspicions. And yet . . . the
Brodies had taken Rab's death at Carnmore for fact—that
much was obvious. Helen had passed the story, and her
diaries, to Rab's children, and so it had come down the
generations.

Donald had known it, that much was clear—perhaps
not when he had first fallen in love with her, but later,
after his father's death. Was that why he had left the interest in Benvulin to her? To settle a debt? As a mark of

forgiveness for the sins her family had committed? Or both? Had he meant to tell her? She would never know.

But what she did know was that she couldn't let it rest. She had to go back to Carnmore, where it had all begun.

Carnmore, November 1899

"Rab, you mustn't stay!" Having seen him ride into the yard and dismount, Livvy had flown out of the house and clutched at the sleeve of his coat.

"Livvy, I got your note. Tell me what's happened."

Livvy looked round wildly; the yard was empty, but it wouldn't remain so for long. "You must go, please, before someone tells Will—"

"Will? Livvy, I've ridden all the way from Benvulin in a lather. I am not leaving until you tell me what's wrong. If this is about your father, surely we can work something out—"

"No, it's more than that." Realizing that Rab wasn't going to budge, Livvy took the horse's bridle and began urging the beast towards the back of the warehouse. The wind that had blown from the east throughout the day had died, and the peat smoke from the kilns rose to meet the bank of cloud hovering over the hilltops. "Come this way, then. We can talk in the warehouse." Will was overseeing a distillation run and should be occupied in the still-house for a while longer.

Livvy tethered the horse to a stunted rowan and led Rab into the warehouse through the back door. The angels' share hung heavily in the still, cold air. She turned to him, breathing hard, her back against a rank of casks. "Father told Will, and Will—I'd no idea he would mind so much. He's furious with me, and with you. It's as if he's held back everything since his father's death, and now—"

"Livvy, I can pay back the money, with interest, in the spring. Surely, I can make him see reason."

"No, Rab, I don't want you to try." The truth was that her sweet and biddable child had become a man, a stranger, and she had seen something in his eyes that frightened her. "Just give me time, I'll talk to him, and my father. This was my idea; I won't have them blame you."

Rab grasped her shoulders, as he had the night of the harvest-home, and she felt a shuddering ache run through her body. "Dear God, Livvy, I've never seen you like this. You are so beautiful I can hardly bear it." He plunged a hand into her hair, and she felt it tumble loose, cascading down her back. "Have you any idea how much I want you? There must be a way—"

"Rab, no." She twisted in his grip, panic warring with desire. "We can't— You're married, and I—if Will—"

"You're a grown woman, Livvy. You can choose what you want."

"But I can't, Rab," she whispered. "I've seen that." Yet she had stopped struggling, and when his lips came down on hers, she returned the kiss fiercely. She was lost, and she knew it. Her body had no defense against him.

"You bastard." Will's voice cut through the haze of her need like ice.

Rab let her go, and stepped away.

Will stood in the doorway, his eyes lit with a cold fury. "First you cheat my mother out of her money, then you try to seduce her. Or have you already?" He came towards them, fists clenched.

"Will, be sensible," Rab said easily, but Livvy felt him tense. "You don't want to insult your mother—"

"Me? Insult my mother?" Will's voice rose and cracked. "How dare you suggest it, when you've made a mockery of her, and of me, and of my father's memory—"

"Will, your father has nothing to do with this. Your father wouldn't have wanted to see another distillery fail—"

"You think my father would have wanted to see another man with his wife? You think my father wouldn't have wanted me to defend his honor?" Will was within striking distance now, his fists raised.

"I think your father wouldn't have wanted you to get hurt, Will." Rab rocked forward on his toes. "I outweigh you by a good three stone. You're going to regret it if I hit you."

"Stop it, both of you," shouted Livvy, but it was too late. Will's right hand had flashed out in a blur of motion. Blood streamed from Rab's nose, and then they were grappling and shoving, grunting with effort.

Livvy tried to pull Will away, but he flung her off into the dirt. Rab got in a punch that grazed Will's head, but not even his weight and experience seemed a match for Will's anger. They came together again, in a parody of an embrace, and for a moment Rab had Will pinned against the casks. Then Will twisted free, quick as a cat, and Rab spun with him. Will staggered back, then catapulted himself forward, stiff-armed, and gave Rab a shove that had all his weight behind it.

Rab fell, hard, into the casks, and Livvy heard the crack of bone against wood. Will was still on him, pummeling wildly with his fists as Rab slumped to the floor.

"Will, stop!" screamed Livvy, clawing at him. "He's hurt, Will." At last she got her arms round her son's waist and pulled him away. Only then did Will seem to realize that the other man wasn't hitting back.

The smell of whisky filled the air, burning Livvy's throat. The bung of the cask where Rab had hit his head had come loose, and whisky dripped to the floor.

She looked down at Rab Brodie's crumpled form with

growing horror. Livvy's mother had died in her arms, as had her baby daughter, and her husband. She knew the face of death when she saw it. Still, she knelt beside him, shaking him, sobbing as she stroked his cheek. There was no response.

"Dear God, Will, you've killed him," she whispered, her voice cracking.

Will sank to his knees, as if his legs had suddenly refused to support him. "No. He can't be. I'll get help. The men are gone—I sent them home early, with the weather closing in, but I can go to the village—"

"Will, no." Livvy felt an icy calm envelop her. She had lost everything that mattered to her, except her son. She would not lose him, too.

"There's no help for him now," she said. "We've no proof that this was an accident. Helen Brodie has powerful friends. I won't have you go to prison."

"Prison? But I never meant—"

"What you meant doesn't matter now. If I hadn't—" *She shook her head hopelessly. "Will, this is going to be between you and me, our secret. I won't have you suffer for what I've done."*

"But we can't—"

"We can. We'll bury him here, beneath the casks. No one will ever know."

But she would. She would carry Rab's death with her like a mark, and for her, there would be no forgiveness on either side of the grave.

The confines of the old warehouse were dim, and several degrees colder than the outside air. Although it was not quite noon, the sky had darkened ominously.

Hazel stood, letting her eyes adjust to the light, looking round the cavernous empty space. The ranks of casks that had filled it in her childhood were long gone, but for an instant, she thought she caught the faint scent of whisky. Had the angels' share leached into the stone itself, a permanent reminder of the past?

No, she told herself, it was just her imagination, as were these dreams. But here the images seemed stronger, and if she closed her eyes she could almost hear their voices. Olivia and Will Urquhart, Rab Brodie. She could put names to them now, if not faces.

Suddenly, she remembered a recurring childhood terror. There had been a spot in the warehouse, halfway down the left-hand side, that had always inexplicably frightened her. Had there been a reason for her fear?

With a swift decision, she left the warehouse and walked across the nettle-studded yard to the old barn. She dug around in a jumble of rusty tools, brushing cobwebs from her face, until she found an ancient spade. The wood of the handle was cracked, the head slightly loose, but it would have to do.

Going back to the warehouse, she stood in the doorway, closing her eyes again, deliberately placing herself within the dream perspective. Sweat broke out under her arms, on her forehead, as she felt again the panic of her dream.

She walked forward, slowly, twenty paces, then stepped to the left. The casks had stood here; the earth was packed as hard as concrete. When she jabbed the tip of the spade into the ground, the shock reverberated up her arms. But she swung again, and again, her face set in determination, until her hair was damp with sweat and her hands were numb.

She knew this ground; she knew there was only a shallow layer of topsoil over rock. If they had buried Rab Brodie here, they had not buried him deep. She dug on, beginning to wonder if she was mad.

Hazel had almost given up when her spade struck something more yielding. Dropping to her knees, she scrabbled in the dirt with her bare hands. There—she brushed away another layer of soil, more gently this time, except that it didn't feel like soil. It crumbled in her fingers . . . was it peat? Beneath that, she felt something pliable, a leaf—no, it was cloth, a heavy cloth . . . wool . . . a man's coat, perhaps? The fragile scrap seemed to disintegrate even as she touched it, revealing the dark knob of a stick—no, it was bone, bone stained with the rich, deep brown of peat.

Hazel snatched her hand back and clapped it to her mouth, stifling a moan. She hadn't believed it, even as she dug, not really, but now the grief in the dream came back to her as if it were her own.

Her eyes swam with tears and she began to weep, short, hiccoughing sobs that grew stronger until they wrenched at her chest. Was she crying for Livvy Urquhart and Rab Brodie, or for her grandfather, Will . . . or for Donald . . . and Tim . . . and herself?

The spasms began to ease and she sat back, sniffing. She would have to tell someone—it was past time Rab Brodie's death came to light.

The light voice came from behind her, making her heart jolt in surprise. "Hazel? What on earth are you doing?"

Hazel stood and squinted at the small form silhouetted in the doorway. "Louise? What are *you* doing here?"

"I came to see you." Louise came forward until Hazel could see her more clearly. "You know, we really haven't had any time alone together for a chat since you've come."

"Has something happened? Is it Tim? Or John? Have they arrested John?"

"No. I don't think they will arrest John," said Louise, and there was a note in her voice Hazel couldn't identify. "What *are* you doing?" she added, coming close enough to peer down into Hazel's small trench. "You've been digging."

"I—I'm not sure." Hazel felt suddenly reluctant to say. "I thought . . . there was someone buried here, a long time ago."

Louise knelt and poked a finger into the hole. "Bones?" She looked up, her eyes wide. "You've found another body? Well, hasn't this been a week for revelations?" Standing, she picked up the spade Hazel had abandoned and raked the tip over the soil.

Hazel put out a hand. "Louise, don't—"

"Possessive about this one, too, are you?" Louise stopped, leaning on the spade.

"What— I don't understand." Hazel's heart began to thud.

"Not everything belongs to you, Hazel. Did you know that? Did it ever occur to you that other people deserve a share? That other people have feelings?"

"Louise, what are you talking about?" Hazel whispered.

"Did you never think, all those years ago, how I might have felt?" she hissed, her voice full of venom. "*Louise, the invisible. Louise, the third wheel.* I watched you together, and you never noticed. I *loved* him, and you never saw it. And then you threw him away, as if he were so much rubbish, and left me to patch up his wounds."

"Louise, it wasn't like that at all—"

"You discarded him and moved on to the next one, as if you were changing shoes. But I kept on. I loved him, and I waited. I married John, because he was available, and I waited a little longer. I chose the property here, the

closest to Donald I could find. I thought he would see . . .
if I gave him enough time . . . if I could show him what
he was missing.

"And then, you came back, picking up where you left
off, and he was so blind he didn't see you would do the
same thing again."

"But, Louise, I didn't—"

"But you did. I told him that morning, told him that
you had packed and gone, without even telling him good-
bye. He didn't believe me."

"You . . . saw Donald?"

"I was out walking. Someone had left John's little gun
in my potting shed, and the rabbits had been into my garden, so I took the shotgun with me. I wanted to think; I
was so happy when I saw you drive away, but I knew I
couldn't show it, not yet. I didn't know Donald was out,
as well, until I saw him coming across the meadow.

"He met me with a smile. He wanted to share it all with
me, your joyous reunion, his plans for the future. I had to
tell him, then, that you were gone.

"He didn't believe me, at first." Louise shook her head,
as though his stubbornness still surprised her. "When it
began to dawn on him that I was telling the truth, he
wanted to go after you. That was too much, after everything you'd done to him. I couldn't bear it.

"I told him he was a fool. I told him that you would
never really care for him, not the way I did." She fell
silent, and Hazel waited, too sick with horror to speak.

When Louise did go on, her eyes seemed to have lost
their focus. "He laughed at me. I told him I loved him,
and he laughed at me. He thought I was joking, at first.
And then, when he realized I meant it, he looked at me as
if I were something nasty, an insect found under a log.

" 'I wouldn't have you if you were the last woman on

earth, Louise,' he said. 'You're a wee cold spider, always watching, always waiting, always looking for your advantage. You should watch yourself—you'll be lucky I don't tell your husband what you're up to. Now, let me go.' He shook my hand off his arm."

"What— What did you do then?" Hazel asked hoarsely, in spite of herself.

"I didn't think," answered Louise, with an air of wonder. "I just raised the gun and pulled the trigger. He looked so surprised."

Hazel took an involuntary step back, stifling a sob. "Louise, why are you telling me this?"

"Because Callum MacGillivray didn't die, and I have no doubt he'll be telling Chief Inspector Ross that he saw me that morning."

"You— You poisoned that poor man?"

Louise didn't seem to have heard. Her gaze had focused on Hazel again, fully intent. "You're afraid of me, aren't you?" she asked, as if the possibility had not occurred to her. "I told you, I only came here to talk . . . but then, it all comes down to you, doesn't it . . . And I have nothing to lose." Louise smiled, tightening her grip on the spade, and Hazel's blood ran cold.

Leaving Tim in the interview room, Kincaid went out into the corridor and rang Gemma from his mobile phone.

"Gemma!" he said with undisguised relief when she answered. "Listen, I've just talked to Tim. He *was* there over the weekend, all right, and he did take the gun from the cabinet. But he says he didn't shoot Donald Brodie. He left the gun in the potting shed. In which case—"

"Louise took it."

"You knew?"

"I talked to Callum. He saw her, walking through the meadow with the gun. That's why she poisoned him."

"Have you told Ross?"

"I left him a mess—" The phone signal broke up.

"Gemma, you don't mean to talk to Louise yourself?" he asked, with dawning dread. "You realize that if this woman shot Donald, and poisoned Callum, she's capable of anything."

A garble of static came back to him, interspersed with a few intelligible words. ". . . no choice . . . Hazel . . . gone after her . . ."

"Gemma, where are you?" he said, only realizing he was shouting when a passerby in the corridor looked at him oddly.

". . . pole in . . ." he thought he heard her say, and then very clearly, ". . . the Braes of Glenlivet." Then the phone connection went dead.

The rain had turned to snow as Gemma passed through Tomintoul. Fat, white flakes splattered the windscreen like stars, then vanished beneath the wipers. As visibility diminished, she regretted the time she'd taken to drive to Innesfree, but she had hoped against hope that Louise had not followed Hazel to Carnmore.

But when she arrived at the B&B, she found not Louise, but Pascal, fuming. Ross had had him driven to Aviemore to make a formal statement, and when he'd returned he'd found both Louise and his car gone. "I left her the keys," he explained, "in case she needed to move it. I had not parked this morning with the intent to stay."

"We'll have to hope courtesy is its own reward," Gemma told him, patting his arm. "What about John and Martin?"

"Still at the Aviemore Police Station. I think they were waiting for the return of John's car."

"Come on, then. I have to drive back past Benvulin. I'll drop you." She had explained the situation briefly on the way; then, after leaving Pascal at Benvulin's gate, she called Ross again and this time left a detailed message.

Perhaps Kincaid would try to reach him, she thought as she made the turning at the Pole Inn. She'd pulled over for a moment in the pub's car park and tried to ring Kincaid back, but she'd lost her mobile phone signal, and she didn't want to take the time to use the call box.

The snow grew heavier as she crawled along the track that led into the Braes, her sense of urgency mounting. By the time she reached Chapeltown, she could see only a few feet in front of the car, but she kept going along the farm track that led up towards Carnmore. If she got stuck, she would worry about it later.

But her luck held, and when she could make out the more solidly white shapes of the distillery buildings, she stopped the car. She slipped out, careful to make no sound. A few feet on, when she recognized both Heather's Audi and Pascal's BMW, she hesitated. As Kincaid had said, Louise had shown herself to be capable of anything, killing, or attempting to kill, both with forethought and without.

She went back to the car and, quietly popping the boot, took out the tire tool. It was the best she could do.

The snow cloaked her and muffled her footfalls as she neared the distillery. She could see that the door of the old warehouse stood open, so she approached it obliquely, then stood just at its edge, listening with increasing dismay as Louise matter-of-factly related murdering Donald.

Hesitating, torn between the desire to let Louise talk and the fear that she might act, Gemma almost left it too late.

Hearing an odd note of excitement in Louise's voice, Gemma charged in, tire tool raised, shouting, "Put it down! Put the spade down!" just as Louise swung hard at Hazel's head.

Hazel ducked, her reflexes saving her all but a clip across the top of the scalp, and then Gemma was on Louise with a fury she hadn't known she possessed, screaming at her as she pushed her to the ground, pinning her across the chest with the tire tool.

Louise went still as Gemma sat astride her, panting. "Two against one," Louise said. "That's not fair. But then life's always bloody unfair, isn't it?"

21

❧

Peaceful bounty flowing
Past like the dust blowing,
That harmony of folks and land is shattered.
Peat fire and music, candle-light and kindness . . .
Now they are gone
And desolate these lovely lonely places.
—DOUGLAS YOUNG

GEMMA HAD MANAGED to bind Louise's hands with a frayed bit of rope Hazel had found in the barn when they saw a pulse of blue light through the snow. The Northern Constabulary had arrived.

"I wasn't sure you'd come," Gemma said a half hour later, as she and the chief inspector watched Louise being shepherded into the marked car. Ross and Munro had driven behind it at a furious pace all the way from Aviemore, he'd told her, afraid the snow might shut down the road altogether.

"I've been in this job long enough to know the truth when I hear it, lass, though I'll not easily forgive ye for stealing a march on me with Callum MacGillivray. I was on my way to hospital when I got your message."

"He might not have told *you*," Gemma said, feeling comfortable enough now to tease him a bit.

"Oh, aye, there is that. I suppose there is a place for the feminine touch. But that one . . ." Shaking his head, he watched the car holding Louise pull away. Gemma had related to him Louise's revelations, as well as describing her murderous attack on Hazel. Hazel, still bleeding freely from a scalp wound, was being ministered to by a very competent Sergeant Munro. "With that one," Ross continued, "it's a fine thing ye had your wits about ye."

"I only hope you'll find some physical evidence to back up what she told us."

"Don't ye worry, lass. We'll find it, now that we know what we're looking for," Ross had assured her.

The next day the police search team had turned up Louise's gardening gloves, buried in the carrot patch in the garden. The gloves tested positive for gunpowder residue and, under forensic examination, revealed minute traces of human blood and tissue—Donald's.

The snowstorm had ended almost as quickly as it had begun, and by Thursday, the day of Donald's funeral, even the slush had vanished. The May sun shone out of a clear, blue sky, and the birds sang blithely as Donald Brodie was laid to rest in the Grantown churchyard. Standing between Hazel and Heather, Gemma found that she was glad she had known him, however briefly. A complicated man, neither saint nor sinner, but a man whose passion for life, for the whisky he made, and for one woman made him well worth mourning.

As for the bones in the warehouse at Carnmore, Ross had authorized a forensics team to remove them from the site. A DNA sample had been taken from Donald's body;

if the remains were found to match, Rab Brodie would be buried beside his great-great-grandson.

On Friday morning, Hazel took Gemma to the railway station in Aviemore. The little wooden building looked more than ever like a gingerbread house, and the still-snowcapped peaks of the distant mountains were as crisply white against the blue of the sky as those in Toby's drawing. It was a beautiful country, thought Gemma, the sort of country that got into your blood and stayed.

They sat together on the platform bench, waiting for the London train in companionable silence, until Hazel said, "I've been thinking about John. He suspected, didn't he, that it was Louise? He knew she took the gun out occasionally, and he knew she'd been behaving oddly. No wonder he seemed terrified."

"What will he do now, do you know?" asked Gemma.

"He told me he meant to sell the farmhouse. Legally, Louise owns a half interest in the property, and he told me he couldn't bear to share anything with her, even if only on a piece of paper."

"But he's worked so hard. It was what he'd always wanted."

"I know. I've been thinking about that, too."

Gemma glanced at her friend, recognizing an earnestness in her tone of voice. "You have an idea."

Hazel smiled. "It would depend on Heather's agreement, of course. But you've seen Benvulin House. It's a drain on the business as it is, and there's no one wants to live in a place that size—why not turn it into an elegant small hotel? There are other distilleries that have done the same thing successfully."

"And you're thinking the hotel would need a manager?"

"Something like that. There might even be a place for Martin."

Gemma patted her arm. "It's a kind thought. Some good should come of this." She still couldn't think of Louise Innes without a shudder. "But what about you, Hazel? What are you going to do? That's the real question." She knew that Hazel had at last talked to Tim but not what had passed between them.

"I don't know," Hazel said slowly. "For now, I'll stay on a few more days, as much as I miss Holly. I've arranged it with Tim so that I can ring her every day."

"Will she be all right with Tim?"

"I think so, yes. For the time being."

"Hazel—"

"There's your train." Hazel stood as the diesel locomotive came into view, braking for the station. "Don't worry, Gemma. I'll ring you. You go home, look after Toby, and Kit. And, Gemma"—Hazel hugged her quickly, then kissed her cheek—"thank you. You've been a good friend."

"Mummy, are you still angry with Callum?" Chrissy had pulled a stool up to the kitchen doorway and perched where she could watch her mother cooking. It was her favorite position, Alison realized, when she had something she wanted to discuss.

Alison turned the sausage in the pan and checked the potatoes before she answered, giving herself time to think. "No, baby," she said slowly. "I don't suppose I am."

She'd heard from Mrs. Witherspoon—who'd heard it from Janet MacGillivray—that Callum had been released from hospital, but he hadn't rung her.

"And it wasn't Callum's fault that Donald was killed?" asked Chrissy, her small face intent.

"No." Alison answered this one more easily. "It didn't have anything to do with Callum at all."

Chrissy nodded once, as if settling something in her mind. She watched Alison in silence for a few minutes, but Alison knew her daughter well enough to guess she had more to say.

"Does that mean I can take riding lessons, after all?"

"Christine Grant, do ye never think of anything but the horses?" Alison said, half laughing, half exasperated.

"Sometimes." The corners of Chrissy's mouth turned up. "Especially when I'm hungry. So can I, Mummy, please? Callum said we wouldn't have to pay."

"We'll not be accepting charity from Callum MacGillivray," snapped Alison, singeing her finger on the pan. "And ye know we can't afford—" The sight of her daughter's face brought her to a halt—the disappointment quickly marshaled, the round, gray eyes suddenly expressionless. Was her pride worth that high a price? Alison wondered. "Well," she said slowly, "maybe we could accept a wee discount, from a friend."

"Are you and Callum friends, then?" asked Chrissy, with a hopeful note.

"Aye. I suppose we might be. But, mind you, baby, don't be expecting anything more. Callum and me, we're . . . well, we're as different as chalk and cheese."

"It's okay, Mummy." Chrissy's serene smile held an unnerving hint of satisfaction.

The long, flat miles between Cambridge and London slipped away, as they had so often in the past, Kincaid thought as he watched the landscape recede in his rearview mirror. He had brought Tess with him when he'd picked Kit up at Nathan's, and now, after an ecstatic reunion, both boy and dog were quiet.

Glancing into the backseat, he saw Tess stretched out full length, breathing the short, whuffly breaths of doggy dreams. In the front, Kit sat back with his eyes closed, but Kincaid didn't think he was sleeping. They hadn't yet had a chance to talk, although Nathan had rung Kincaid from his office and related his own discussion with Kit.

Opening his eyes, Kit said suddenly, "Are Tim and Hazel going to get a divorce?"

Kincaid had given Kit and Nathan a sketchy version of the events in Scotland, but Kit had obviously read between the lines. "I don't know, Kit. I suspect things are going to be difficult for them, and sometimes . . . sometimes things don't work out even when people want them to."

"What about Holly? Will she stay with Hazel?"

"I think that's most likely, yes," Kincaid said uneasily. He hadn't really thought about how Hazel's situation would affect Kit, but he saw now that it was another prop gone in the structure of Kit's existence. "Kit, we won't lose Hazel and Holly, no matter how things work out."

Kit looked at him, accusation in his blue eyes. "You can't promise it."

"No." What Kit wanted, Kincaid realized, was a guarantee against fate, and he couldn't give it. Kit had been buffeted by life, thrown like a football from one family to another, from one possible future to another, with no power to choose anything for himself.

Kincaid thought back to his conversation with Nathan. Nathan had tactfully suggested that Kit be allowed to decide whether or not to have the DNA testing, and although Kincaid had disagreed at the time, now he began to wonder if Nathan had had a point.

No promise in the world could give Kit the sense of security he so desperately needed . . . but what if Kit felt he had a say in his own destiny?

Nathan was right. Kit was old enough to make his

wishes clear, with or without a DNA test. They didn't need proof to be a family, and it occurred to Kincaid that perhaps *he* was the one who had required a stamp of approval. Did he honestly think he would love Kit any more if he knew their genetic codes were a match? Or was it that he thought Kit would love *him* more? Was he still trying to prove something to Ian McClellan, with Kit as the means?

The idea made him grimace. If that was the case, perhaps it was not Kit who needed to grow up and be sensible. He looked at his son and saw all the things that made him who he was, and he knew that there was nothing a bit of saliva could change. "Kit," he said, "we need to talk."

At Tomintoul, Hazel went into the village shop and bought the best two flower bunches on offer. They were a bit past their prime, but they would suit her purpose.

She drove on, up into the Braes, then down into the hollow of Chapeltown, beside the Crombie burn. The small churchyard of Our Lady of Perpetual Succor was deserted, but Hazel found the markers easily enough. Will Urquhart lay beside his mother, in the shade of a rowan. After laying a bouquet beneath each headstone, she sat on a stone bench in the sun, her eyes closed, until she felt as if she were bleached down to her bones.

Then she left the car in the car park beyond the church and, taking only her bag from the boot, began to climb the track. The sun rose higher, stripping away the shadows, melting the last lingering patches of snow. By the time she reached Carnmore, she was sweating.

Taking the keys Heather had given her from her pocket, she unlocked the door to the house. Slowly, she walked through the place, assessing the damage and the assets. The structure seemed sound, other than a few warped floorboards beneath the broken windows. Her parents had left some of the old furniture—pieces she now realized might have belonged to Livvy Urquhart. She found that the memories of her childhood in the house had become entwined with her dreams of Livvy, and that she didn't really mind.

Eventually, she came back out into the sun and sat on a boulder by the distillery gate, weighing her choices. Curlews called in the distance, and once, as she looked up, she thought she saw the outline of a falcon skimming high above.

Donald would have wanted her to keep Benvulin as it was; he had seen her as an anchor against the tide of the future. But Donald was gone, and she could no more bring him back than she could resurrect the woman she had pretended to be in the years of her marriage. Who was she now, and where did she belong?

It seemed almost certain her marriage was damaged beyond repair, and she—how could she go back to counseling others, when she had been unable to help herself?

She looked around her, at the house and the weathered but still-solid buildings of the distillery. It was a hard life in the Braes, an isolated life, one that left its mark for good or ill. But it was her heritage, and her daughter's. Could she bring Holly here? Could she subject them both to the unknown?

There *was* a way, if she had the courage. She could sell her shares in Benvulin to Pascal's company. She could let Benvulin go, let Donald go, and by doing so she could give her cousin Heather the control of Benvulin that she had earned. It might not be what Donald would have chosen, but it was the living that mattered now.

And then, it was just possible that with the money from the sale, she could bring life back to Carnmore. It would mean starting the distillery on a shoestring, but she reminded herself, many Highland distilleries had begun as single stills run by farmers' wives. She was resourceful, and what she didn't know, Heather could teach her.

She saw the kitchen painted red, filled with the aroma of baking. She saw the copper stills gleaming in the still-house, and the casks stacked in the warehouse, stamped once again with Carnmore's name.

Opening her bag, she took out the bottle of Carnmore whisky, her gift from Donald, and a tooth glass she had brought from Innesfree. The whisky felt warm from the heat of the sun, like a living thing, and when she pulled the cork the smell tickled her nose, sweet and sharp.

Carefully, she poured half an inch in the glass and sipped it, holding the buttery liquid in her mouth until it melted away. Then she raised the bottle and let a few golden drops trickle out onto the bare earth, a libation for the past, and for the future.

Superintendent Duncan Kincaid is called to investigate the shocking death of a woman found burned beyond recognition in a Victorian warehouse in south London. When his lover and partner, Gemma James, is asked to trace a friend's missing roommate, she and Duncan discover that their cases have several disturbing links.

Set against a backdrop of Dickensian Southwark, repository of old secrets, the case plunges Duncan and Gemma into the dark recesses of human relationship. Two women are missing, a little girl is abducted, and no one is really what they seem. The detectives must discover the truth as innocent lives hang in the balance.

Turn the page to preview

In A Dark House

The next new mystery novel from award-winning author Deborah Crombie

Rose Kearny liked night shifts best, when the station was quiet except for the muted murmur of voices in the staff room as everyone went about their assigned tasks. There was something comforting about the camaraderie inside held against the dark outside, and in the easing of the adrenaline rush after a call out. And she considered herself lucky to have ended up at Southwark, the station where she had trained, and the most historic in the London Fire Service.

She and her partner, Bryan Simms, were checking their breathing apparatus after the first bell of the night—a little old lady in a council flat, having decided to make herself a bedtime snack, had dozed off with the chip pan on the burner. Fortunately, a neighbor had seen the first sign of smoke, the blaze had been easily contained, and the woman had escaped serious injury.

But every fire call, no matter how minor, required a careful examination of any equipment they had used. Tonight she and Bryan had been assigned BA crew and their lives depended on the efficiency of their breathing apparatus—and on one another. Simms was a good partner, as steady and reliable as his square, blunt face implied, and not inclined to panic.

He looked up at her, as if sensing her regard, and frowned in concentration. "What's in a name?" he asked, as if continuing a conversation. "That which we call a rose by any other name would smell as sweet."

For a moment, Rose was too startled to respond. Not that she wasn't used to being teased about her name, or her fair looks, but this was the first time one of her fellow firefighters had resorted to Shakespeare.

Taking her silence as encouragement, Bryan went on, grinning. "But earthlier happy is the rose distilled, than that which withering on the virgin thorn grows, lives, and dies in single blessedness—"

"Piss off, Simms," Rose interrupted, smothering a laugh. She had to admit she was impressed he'd gone to the trouble of memorizing the line. "I'd never have taken you for a Shakespeare buff."

"I like the second one. It's from *A Midsummer Night's Dream*," said Simms, and she wondered if she had imagined a blush in his dark skin as he bent again over his task.

"You don't say," Rose retorted with a smile. "And *Romeo and Juliet* as well. Aren't you the clever one." Her father, a high school English teacher, had begun quoting Shakespeare to her before she could talk. "Look sharp there," she added, glancing at his neglected equipment. "You don't want to miss a crack in that hose."

She'd started with the Southwark Fire Brigade six months before Bryan, and she never missed an opportunity to remind him of her seniority. It was hard enough, being female in what was still basically a man's profession, and she certainly couldn't afford a partner with some half-baked romantic idea about their relationship.

Rose meant to go far, perhaps even brigade chief one day, and she wasn't about to let an entanglement stand in her way. Not that she was averse to a night out and a bit of a recreational cuddle, but not with someone on her own ground. And the job left no time for a real relationship. If you wanted to be good, you had to eat it, sleep it, breathe it. She worked two day shifts, then two night shifts, then had three days off, but those days she devoted to keeping fit and to studying forensics. She wanted more than the ability to put a fire out, she wanted to understand the why and how, and fire investigation was a way to move up in the ranks.

It was now after midnight, and she intended to use her down time to study if things remained quiet. She'd just stowed the BA set and pulled out her books when the bells went for the second time that night.

Rose felt the familiar jolt of adrenaline, and then she and Bryan and the rest of the Watch were running for the pole-house. Descending to the appliance bay, they began rigging in fire gear as the Duty Officer called out "Pair," over the Tannoy, meaning that both the Pump and the Pump Ladder were needed. As if of their own volition, Rose's hands performed the familiar rituals; fastening her tunic, tightening the throat buckle, pushing back her hair before slipping on her helmet and adjusting the chin strap, clasping her belt so that the weight of the small axe rested against her hip.

The Station Officer, Charlie Wilcox, ripped the call slip off the teleprinter. "It's just round the corner—warehouse in Union Street," he told them. "Sounds like it's well away—we'll need sets on this one."

Within seconds they were aboard the appliance and rolling into Southwark Bridge Road, sirens wailing and blue lights flashing. A fine drizzle blurred the September night, slicking the tarmac and haloing the street lamps. As they swung round into Southwark Street, Wilcox called out from the front, "It's showing."

As the pump came to a stop, Rose saw a bank of smoke hanging heavily over the street, and in the lower windows of a brick Victorian warehouse, the telltale red-orange flicker of light. Acrid smoke stung her nostrils as she leaped from the back step of the appliance and pulled on her mask. She caught a glimpse of huddled bystanders as Wilcox said, "Rose, Bryan. It looks as though the worst of it is still confined to the first floor. Take in a guideline and check for occupants." He turned to his Sub Officer, Seamus MacCauley. "Check round the back, will you, Seamus? See what we've got."

The other BA team from the pump ladder was already laying hose line as Rose and Bryan tallied in their BA sets, checked their radios. "Door's open," she heard Wilcox shout as she pulled her visor down, and she registered a faint surprise before focusing again on her task.

They went in low, Rose leading, peering through the smoke, feeling their way into the dense blackness. The heat seared, even through their coats, and she could hear the groaning and cracking of a well-established fire. She fell against something soft and bulky, went down on her knees. Through a momentary thinning of the smoke she saw shapes piled above her like a giant child's tower of blocks. The disjointed images suddenly coalesced.

"It's furniture," she said. "Someone's piled up bloody furniture." The polyurethane foam used in furniture cushions and mattresses was highly flammable—the thought of the devastating fire that had started in the furniture department of the Manchester Woolworth's crossed her mind, but she banished it, concentrating on the job at hand.

Still on her knees, she moved forward, feeling her way round the obstacles, trying to find a suitable place to tie off the line. Suddenly, there was a loud crack, then a series of pops, and the heat bloomed as debris rained down on them.

"Flashover," shouted Bryan. She felt him grab her waist belt. "We've got to get out of here. Forget the line, Rose."

Even with Bryan's weight dragging at her, her momentum carried her another foot, her hand still outstretched with the line.

"I said, forget the fucking line, Rose. Evacuate! Evacuate!"

Even though her stubbornness, her refusal to let the fire get the better of her, was one of the things that made her good at her job, she knew he was right. Going on would be suicidal, and nothing could have survived this blaze without protection.

Hemmed in on one side by a sofa, on the other by what seemed to be stacks of lumber, Rose tried to turn back the other way. As she maneuvered her body round, her gloved hand came down on something that yielded beneath her fingers. It felt malleable, like flesh, with the brittleness of bone beneath.

Rose looked down, blinking eyes burning and swollen from the heat, and felt the bile rise in her throat. "Jesus Christ," she said. "We've got a body."

"Want some coffee, guv?" asked Doug Cullen, popping his head into Detective Superintendent Duncan Kincaid's office. "I mean real coffee, not that slop," Cullen added, nodding at the mug on Kincaid's desk.

Kincaid grimaced at his sergeant and laid down his pen, stretching the stiffness out of his shoulders. "You just want an excuse to get out, and we've not been here an hour." They'd come in early the past few days, catching up on accumulated paperwork, and the warren of cubicles that made up Scotland Yard's CID had begun to seem more like a prison than an office.

"Guilty." With his thatch of straight blond hair and wire-framed spectacles, Cullen looked more like a schoolboy than a detective sergeant. But in the year since Kincaid's former partner, Gemma James, had been promoted to detective inspector and posted to the Metropolitan Police, he had learned to work well with Cullen, respecting the younger officer's intelligence and dogged persistence when faced with a problem.

Not that Cullen or anyone else could truly replace Gemma as a partner. Although he and Gemma had been living together since the previous Christmas, he found he still missed working with her.

Glancing out his window, he was tempted to play truant along with Cullen, but the pile of paper on his desk argued against it. Besides, the day had gone perceptibly grayer since he'd come in, and he wasn't in the mood to get drenched. "Okay," he said, stifling a sigh. "A coffee. But just coffee, mind you, no poncey lattes."

Cullen grinned and gave him a mock salute. "Right, boss. Back in a tick."

It was a bad sign, Kincaid thought, when going out on such a dreary morning seemed preferable to work, but administrative reports had never been his strong suit. Not that he didn't have the aptitude for it, he just lacked the patience. He hadn't joined the force to become a bloody bureaucrat, yet that seemed more and more the case. And he had reached the point in his career where he felt increasingly pressured to seek promotion, but such a move would mean still less work in the field.

Could he stay where he was, watching the university fast-trackers like Cullen pass him by, without becoming bitter? It was not a prospect he wanted to consider, so with a scowl he turned his attention back to the performance survey on his desk. But when his phone rang a moment later, he leapt on it like a drowning man.

It was his guv'nor's secretary, summoning him to a meeting with the chief superintendent. Kincaid straightened his tie, grabbed his jacket from the coat rack, and was out the door with only a twinge of regret for his missed coffee.

Chief Superintendent Denis Childs had moved office recently, now commanding a view of the parks and the river, but in spite of his elevated status the man remained as Buddha-like as ever. His round, heavy face betrayed little emotion, but Kincaid had learned to read the slightest flicker in the deep brown eyes half hidden by folds of skin. Today, he detected apology, annoyance, and what might have been a trace of worry.

"I'm sorry to put this on you, Duncan," said Childs, his voice surprisingly soft for a man his size.

Not a promising start, Kincaid thought, settling himself in a chair. Perhaps he should have stayed with the paperwork, after all. "But?"

"But as you have nothing pressing on at the moment, and as you have a knack for soothing ruffled feelings . . ." Childs's lips turned up in the smallest of smiles. "You seemed the best man for the job."

"I'm not going to like this, am I?"

"You can look on it as a diplomatic challenge. It will mean liaising with the Fire Investigation Team and Southwark CID. A fire broke out in the early hours of this morning, in a warehouse on Southwark Street. Do you know it?"

"Southwark Street? That's near London Bridge Station, isn't it, not far from Borough Market? But why send me?"

"Patience, boyo, patience. I'm getting there." Childs leaned back in his chair and steepled his fingers together, a familiar gesture. "This particular building is Victorian, and was in the process of being made over into luxury flats. The fire apparently started on the ground floor, but by the time the brigade got there it had done considerable damage to the upper floors and had begun to threaten the building next door."

"The warehouse was empty, then, if it was undergoing renovation?"

"Not quite. When the brigade got inside, they found a body among the debris. Quite badly burned, I'm afraid. And no identification."

"A tramp, smoking—"

"Possibly, although tramps aren't usually found naked with no effects. And it gets a bit more complicated. This particular building happens to be owned by one of our more illustrious MPs, Michael Yarwood."

"Yarwood?" Kincaid sat up a bit straighter in surprise. "I didn't know Yarwood was developing property." The vocal and abrasive Yarwood leaned far to the left of Government's moderate Labor, and was often heard publicly castigating anyone capitalist enough to make a profit. "This could be awkward for him, I take it? And the press will be on it like flies."

"An understatement. A public relations nightmare in the making, to be more accurate, especially with an important by-election coming up. Not to mention that the loss adjustors are already sniffing round and muttering about possible insurance fraud. It seems Yarwood hasn't had the early interest in his leases that he expected."

"Ouch." Kincaid winced. "So he might have a very costly boat anchor on his hands—or he did until last night."

"Not that he'd admit it. But he's worried enough to have rung the assistant commissioner and called in a favor."

"And that's where I come into it?" Kincaid said, enlightenment dawning.

"Yarwood says he only wants to be sure the investigation is given high priority—"

"Meaning he wants to be sure his interests are well-represented." Kincaid weighed the prospect of taking on such a politically sensitive case against going back to his performance reviews. It could prove messy, both literally and figuratively. He hated self-important politicians, and fire scenes had always given him a bit of the creeps.

"You can refuse, of course," said Childs, with a deceptive gentleness Kincaid recognized. Not only did Childs want him on the investigation, he knew that Kincaid could use the good mark in the AC's book.

"Is the body still in situ?" Kincaid asked.

Childs permitted himself another small smile. "I told them to wait for you."